Praise for these other

romance by *USA Today* bestselling author

"Kieran K[...]
with heart.'[...]

"Kramer dishes up another delight[...] m[...]ce that is deftly seasoned with [...] s[...]appy dialogue, and plenty of smoldering sexual chem-[...]try. Readers who fell in love with Susan Elizabeth Phil-[...]ps's *Dream a Little Dream* (1998) or *Ain't She Sweet?* [...]04) will definitely want to add Kramer's latest sexy, sp[...]rkling, spot-on love story to their reading lists."

—*Booklist*

"[F]illed with smart, believable characters and fresh, witty st[...]rytelling. A sexy, poignant romance wrapped in South-e[...]n charm and lightly accented with Hollywood glamour."

—*Kirkus Reviews*

[A] superbly written, powerful, and touching book."

—*Fresh Fiction*

## SWEET TALK ME

"The perfect combination of good-natured sass, sultry sex-ual tension, and hint of Southern crazy. I loved this book."

—Tracy Brogan, author of *Crazy Little Thing*

"A sweetly sexy love story that is everything a romance should be . . . a knockout!" —*Booklist* (starred review)

## ALSO BY KIERAN KRAMER

*You're So Fine*
*Sweet Talk Me*

### THE HOUSE OF BRADY SERIES

*Loving Lady Marcia*
*The Earl Is Mine*
*Say Yes to the Duke*

### THE IMPOSSIBLE BACHELOR SERIES

*When Harry Met Molly*
*Dukes to the Left of Me, Princes to the Right*
*Cloudy with a Chance of Marriage*
*If You Give a Girl a Viscount*

# *Trouble*
# WHEN YOU
# WALKED IN

## KIERAN KRAMER

St. Martin's Paperbacks

.i 11690222x

TROUBLE WHEN YOU WALKED IN

Copyright © 2015 by Kieran Kramer.

All rights reserved.

For information address St. Martin's Press, 175 Fifth Avenue, New York, NY 10010.

ISBN: 978-1-250-00993-7

Printed in the United States of America

St. Martin's Paperbacks edition / August 2015

St. Martin's Paperbacks are published by St. Martin's Press, 175 Fifth Avenue, New York, NY 10010.

10  9  8  7  6  5  4  3  2  1

To my North Carolina family . . . you've enriched my
life so much, and I love you all!

I'm proud to call myself an honorary Tar Heel.

"Come up into the hills, O my young love. Return!"
—Thomas Wolfe, *Look Homeward, Angel*

# ACKNOWLEDGMENTS

As always, I can't say enough good things about Jennifer Enderlin and the extended family that is St. Martin's Press. You've been so good to me—all of you—and I'll always be grateful for your support, your good humor, your patience, and your friendship.

I must also give a huge shout-out to my readers, both old and new. My books aren't complete until they get into your hands and you work your own sort of magic on them. You bring good will, vivid imaginations, and your hearts to the pages of my stories. You make them so much more than what they were when they existed as mere words on my laptop. Thank you for your kindness and generosity— you give me so much more than I can possibly give you.

I'd also like to thank my family and friends, who've stuck with me through ten novels! I should have bought stock in DiGiorno pizza back in 2010, when I started this incredible journey. You've all been wonderful, loving, my biggest cheerleaders, especially Chuck, Steven, Margaret, and Jack.

Here's to the next ten novels, and here's to you—every single person who's ever wished this author well.

Thank you.

# CHAPTER ONE

If a ridiculously handsome man talks too loudly in a library and no one's there to hear but a repressed librarian, an old lady with a hearing aid, and a plastic pageant queen, does he still make a sound?

Cissie Rogers—who bristled at all stereotypes, even if they might ring true—decided then and there that a librarian doesn't entertain such questions. A librarian shushes people, no matter how hot they are. It's her job, even if the man is Boone Braddock, local mayor, football coach, and town stud.

She was back in large-print fiction with Mrs. Hattlebury when the front door of the Kettle Knob library opened and a woman's laughter filled the air—a woman's *fake* laughter, which trailed off with an artificial sigh.

Cissie's skin prickled. There was only one person in western North Carolina who laughed like that: Janelle Montgomery.

"Boone Braddock," Cissie heard Janelle say, "stop it. Stop it right this instant."

What did Janelle want Boone to stop? Kissing her? Being too sexy for his own good?

"Where's the librarian?" he asked in his whiskey-and-gravel voice.

Boone Braddock had never been in the library. Ever. And he was looking for Cissie.

She stopped breathing. Her palms instantly dampened. And her lower belly—contrary to her wishes—began a slow tingling burn of awareness.

She prepared to round the corner with her finger to her lips, but Mrs. Hattlebury grabbed her arm. "Rumor has it those two were caught doing it like rabbits up near Frazier Lake in broad daylight last week," the old woman whispered loudly in Cissie's ear. "But Chief Scotty let 'em off the hook. He has to, don't you know."

"I hate mayors," Cissie whispered back. Sexual frustration made her ornery. "They think the rules don't apply to them."

She wished *she* could have sex by Frazier Lake—but not with Boone, not if he couldn't even remember her name. With Mr. Darcy. Too bad he wasn't real. Maybe if she dressed up Boone like Darcy—

No. They were nothing alike.

"All politicians are that way," Mrs. Hattlebury reminded her in her strong Smoky Mountains drawl.

"Especially mayors." Cissie's words were soaked in Southern inflections, too, like warm bourbon cake. But Mother was from Vermont, so Cissie sounded a little less local than her Kettle Knob neighbors.

As for her declaration, she knew she was making no sense, but she didn't care. When it came to Boone and Janelle, she was a mass of petty insecurities, and she indulged them freely, the way she couldn't stop herself from eating freshly popped popcorn, no matter how full she was.

"You don't really hate all mayors, do you, dear?" Mrs. Hattlebury asked too politely, which meant she thought Cissie might be a tad touched, as they said around here—like Cissie's grandmother Nana Rogers, who actually wasn't touched at all. She managed the local community theater, but you know theater people . . . they're crazy, in the best way.

"No." Cissie made a comic face and tried to chuckle. "Of course not. I didn't hate his grandfather. He threw good candy at the Christmas parade. No wonder we elected Boone. He brought the tradition back."

"Yes, the Christmas-candy angle," Mrs. Hattlebury said faintly. "That must be the reason a Braddock has been mayor of Kettle Knob for almost sixty years— except for that brief era we had a no-name mayor who threw stale, cracked peppermints at the holiday parade." She paused. "Are you sure you're okay, dear?"

"I-I need caffeine. The library coffeepot broke."

She needed a man, too, but surely her bitterness was all about temporary chemical withdrawal.

"Maybe it's just Janelle who gets on your nerves," Mrs. Hattlebury said thoughtfully. "She's a bit full of herself these days. But not Boone. We're glad he's mayor, aren't we?"

Cissie turned red. "He's an, um, adequate public servant." But she was thinking of him in those jeans of his and that indescribable place where his faded zipper flap rode like a rollercoaster over some pretty impressive terrain. He was more than adequate in that department. She was evil for having noticed, but she'd had sunglasses on at the time, so it was okay.

"Adequate?" Mrs. Hattlebury drew in her chin. "Why, Boone's smile lights up every room he enters! And don't forget what his great-great-great-great-great granddaddy—"

"I *know*," Cissie interrupted rudely, but how many times in her lifetime was she going to hear about Silas Braddock leading a ragtag unit from Kettle Knob down to King's Mountain during the Revolutionary War and springing a surprise attack on an isolated British outpost and soundly defeating them?

The Revolutionary War–era Rogers clan had been reading books, writing letters, and analyzing poetry at the time of the raid in the privacy of their home in Kettle Knob. No one had knocked on *their* door to ask for help at King's Mountain. But avid scholars that they were, they made sure to record the event after interviewing every man who'd gone. And they'd dutifully archived the account, which was given by future Rogerses to the library for safekeeping.

Mrs. Hattlebury pressed on. "Becky Lee and Frank, God love 'em, bought Kettle Knob Academy brand-new band instruments last week."

Boone's father, Frank, and his mother, Becky Lee, were the Tasmanian devils of western North Carolina. Wherever they spun their influence, dirt clods went flying— usually at the groundbreaking of one of their mountain golf resorts—and they made lots of money.

"They've never contributed a dime to the Friends of the Library fund." Cissie couldn't believe she'd said that out loud. You weren't supposed to talk bad about that family.

"But honey." Mrs. Hattlebury eyes softened in pity. "They're Braddocks. You're a Rogers. And ne'er the twain shall meet. Surely, you understand. We've all learned to appreciate the distinction. You each bring your own special gifts to Kettle Knob and live in harmony." She paused. "Don't you?"

If totally ignoring each other was harmony, then yes.

Mrs. Hattlebury kissed her good-bye, and Cissie sighed. She was tired all of a sudden—tired from staying up late with Nana last night stapling show pamphlets and tired of the way everyone in this town was slapped with a label from the time they left the womb like a bunch of canning jars lined up on a shelf. She didn't know why she'd ever come back—except of course she knew why.

She loved the smell of pinesap in the morning. The call of a mama bear to its cubs from far off. The way the mountains rolled like giant waves toward the Rogers home, humble as it was. And she loved the people here. There were only a few phonies. They looked out for one another, yet they were also fiercely independent.

Mountain stock.

There was nothing like it.

"Well, hello, Miss Librarian," gushed Janelle in her tight pink sweater, fluffy silk scarf, white jeans, and heels better suited to Manhattan than the mountains. A big wad of pink bubblegum flashed in her mouth.

Nowadays, Cissie was great with comeback lines—but mainly with older people. She still felt like a dork around cute single guys and some women her age, the rare few who hadn't lost their youthful mean-girl competitiveness.

Janelle was one who maybe hadn't. Cissie wasn't sure. As a kid, Janelle had been just as smart as she was pretty, but starting in sixth grade, she'd given up trying to win the spelling bee and the science fair. Pageants became her thing, that and wrapping boys around her little finger. Now, as the mayor of Campbell, she had that whole town enthralled.

And then there was Boone in those inappropriate jeans of his and brown boots. A serious mayor didn't wear Levi's and Carhartts—and then have the temerity to look like an Abercrombie & Fitch model! Nor did he have dimples when he grinned. And he most certainly didn't spend half his time on a football field exhorting boys with perfectly good brains to smash into one another and risk getting concussions.

Inside, Cissie's heart thumped madly. Unlike Janelle, she wasn't much into beauty tricks. Or fashion. But she *was* into books. She could go on *Jeopardy!* and win the Daily Double if it was about books. She could beat anyone in a book takedown. She didn't know what that was—yet—but it sounded kind of fun. Something involving a boxing ring, a roped boundary she could bounce off, and an opponent to shout down in the middle of the ring when the ref asked questions about the top ten hardcovers on the *New York Times* bestseller list.

"How can I help you?" she asked.

If Boone hadn't been so lucky all his life, his gaze these days would have turned slightly stupid, even cross-eyed, considering all the tackles he'd endured in high school.

But no.

When she looked into his eyes, she was brought back all the way to fourth grade, when he'd given her an apple from his lunchbox with a tiny heart carved into it with his thumbnail. He'd liked her for about five minutes. And then he'd moved on to some other girl—literally, by the time she'd finished eating that apple.

Maybe she shouldn't have eaten it. Maybe he'd wanted her to save it until the skin grew wrinkled and the tiny heart yellowed.

What did she know about romance?

Nothing!

"We've got some interesting news," he informed her.

His lethal levels of testosterone, combined with his clear-eyed confidence and scarily ambiguous use of the word *interesting*, made Cissie's temples thrum.

*Do you know my name?* she wondered. *How could you have forgotten that apple? And why are you here with news of any sort when you don't even have a library card?*

"It's good news," said Janelle, her glossy pink mouth bowed up.

Uh oh. If Janelle thought it was good, Cissie would probably hate it. And the fact that they were here at all . . .

Something wasn't right.

But Boone was here. Boone, in her library!

"And what news is this, may I ask?" She might sound like a prissy schoolmarm or a spinster librarian, but she wasn't a fossil. She refused to be a fossil. That happened when you had no lusty thoughts left. She had lusty thoughts. She had them all the time.

And they were about this guy, who was currently skewering her with the most compelling look she'd ever seen in her life: powerful, calm, yet somehow penetrating to her very soul—

As if he got her.

Something inside her flew open, like a paperback novel on a picnic table, its pages rattling in a brisk wind.

There was no way he got her, but it sure felt like it, probably because she was desperate and imagining things.

"For budget reasons," he said, "the county wants Kettle Knob and Campbell to merge libraries. They'll share a new space off the interstate."

Cissie's heart froze. It felt like something very basic was being ripped out from under her, and she was falling through clear space. Did Alice feel like this when she fell down the rabbit hole?

"Sit down." Boone yanked a chair out from a table.

She sat. Her knees knocked together. She was wearing black Mary Janes. All she needed was a blue skirt, a white apron, and long yellow hair. . . .

"It's not a bad thing," Boone said.

But this library was a huge part of North Carolina state history. It had stood for so much over the years: equality when people weren't treated equally, opportunity when no opportunity could be found. It was a treasure. A gem.

It couldn't merge . . . and disappear.

Why couldn't she say that out loud?

"This place will always have the historic marker on the outside," said Janelle in a bored voice, "in case you're worried we're forgetting the building's significance. We're not."

That was exactly what Cissie was thinking! And she was ashamed to admit it, but another thought galloped through her head, too, like Paul Revere on his horse, a totally self-serving one: *The legend of the library will end with me. The legend of the library will end with me!*

No more librarians would find their true loves here.

Including her.

"Do you need water?" Boone asked.

She couldn't deny what was going on in her body—somewhere deep inside lived not only a principled, scholarly Rogers but a hopeful, naïve youngish woman who'd just let *Brides* magazine slip out of her hands.

"Cissie," Janelle said. "Take a Fruit Stripe." She held out a pack of gum, one tin foil rectangle extended.

Cissie shook her head.

Janelle gave a gusty sigh. "It's a good arrangement. Honest, it is."

Cissie knew she shouldn't be thinking of herself right now. She should be kicking Boone and Janelle out of the library onto the sidewalk.

Wait until Sally Morgan came in with her special needs teenager, Hank Davis, later to shelve books. Sally thought the legend applied to volunteers, too. She might even drop to the ground, she'd be so devastated when she heard the news. She did that a lot, the dropping thing. She was big on emotion. And how would she and Hank Davis get to the other place? They'd need a car.

Cissie's jaw locked like an anaconda's.

"We'd use the storefront next to Harris Teeter," Boone went on, "halfway between the two towns, so everyone can stop by when they pick up their groceries." His dimples came out—as if *that* show of charm would make his statements less shocking and egregious.

Cissie's face heated up like a hot plate. The legend didn't matter. It was only a silly story, built on a fluke of fate. She'd explain to Sally that it wasn't worth losing sleep over. What mattered was the preservation of Kettle Knob's historic library.

Yes, that was what mattered!

"But that place used to be a tattoo parlor," she croaked, "and before that, a bar."

There. She'd spoken. Her ancestors would roll over in their graves if their precious historical documents were housed in a place that lacked dignity and decorum.

"Think how many more book customers you'll get," Boone said. "Plus, your inventory will increase when you team up with Campbell. The budget for new books will go down thirty percent, I'm sorry to say, but that's okay. Because if we stay here, we'll lose fifty percent of it. The rest would have to go to the upkeep of this old house, and the county thinks that's not an efficient use of funds."

*Blah blah blah.* Too much information, way too fast. But Cissie was a Rogers. She could think on her feet. . . .

Too bad she still couldn't think. It was that wretched legend her heart was hammering about. Sally would lose hope of finding the right man to be both father to Hank

Davis and a red-hot lover for herself. Nana would go to her grave without dancing at Cissie's wedding. And Cissie would never meet her soul mate.

Not that the legend was *real*.

But what was?

*Think, Cissie, think!*

Books were real. Books and historical documents. Same with Sally's lack of car and Cissie's almost-virgin status, which she wished she could pretend wasn't true, but it was.

"I-I can get the Friends of the Library to help with the upkeep," she insisted. "They already do help a lot"—bless their six elderly, gossip-loving hearts, they'd raised three hundred dollars last year—"but we can raise more money. If everyone chips in, we should be fine."

She looked pointedly at Boone, whose family could save the library by writing a single check, but his handsome brown-eyed gaze merely flickered with mayoral impatience and sex static, which was always humming within him, like an old transistor radio left on by accident.

"We're looking into moving the county waste management office here." Janelle tossed off the library's long history with the same insouciance with which she flung her shiny, hair-sprayed curls over her shoulder. "They're so cramped where they are."

*"What?"* Cissie heard her, but she didn't believe her.

"Uh-huh," said Janelle. "We're getting creative. As for the new library location, it's time we have a place where the communities of Campbell and Kettle Knob can interact and share resources." She sounded so phony. *Like that's a big surprise*, thought Cissie. "We'll have the opportunity to read, research"—Janelle cast a smoldering look at Boone—"and enjoy our archival documents. Together."

Only Janelle could make going to the library sound like a sex act.

Cissie was about to sneeze. She turned away, held her breath, and by some miracle got the sneeze under control. But the tiny break was enough to remind herself that a Rogers always sounded reasonable. They won things with their heads.

"Those were Rogers papers," she reminded Janelle, "bequeathed to the town of Kettle Knob. Campbell didn't send anyone to King's Mountain, nor are they represented in any of our archival documents, except in passing reference as a neighboring town."

Campbell thought it was hot stuff because a superfamous female pop star with current hits used to go to grade school there.

And a lot of rich people lived in Campbell, too, in Boone's parents' original fancy golf resort, which was now old enough that it was described in the newspaper's crime column as an "established high-end neighborhood" every time someone got their leaf blower stolen or their Mercedes keyed. Most Campbell residents commuted to their doctor and attorney jobs in Asheville and only came to places like Kettle Knob to feel like they'd gone backward a hundred years for a few minutes.

And now Campbell had attracted a high-tech research facility with international connections.

But apart from that, Campbell was boring.

"Campbell doesn't even have a good scenic overlook for couples to make out at," Sally said every Valentine's Day, which was when the Campbell Country Club held its annual two-hundred-fifty-bucks-a-ticket black-tie gala to benefit heart research. "Every mountain town should have at least one."

"That King's Mountain raid was definitely a Kettle Knob thing," Boone agreed with Cissie now. "But . . ."

*But?*

*His* family had led the local charge in the historic battle. Cissie's family had documented it.

There were no *but*s!

She told him all that with her eyes. But he didn't appear to be able to read her anymore, if he ever had. Probably because Janelle crossed her arms so that her breasts nearly spilled out of the top of her sweater. Boone didn't exactly look at them, but they were like the elephant in the room—two DD-sized elephants.

"Campbell never bothered to save local accounts from the Civil War, either," Cissie went on doggedly. "We have nine leather-bound Civil War–era journals in our collection."

All donated by the Rogers family.

Janelle's mouth soured. "Campbell was too busy to record anything."

*It was too busy being high on itself, like you*, Cissie wanted to say. But she was a coward. And maybe she was wrong about Janelle being a narcissist. After all, everyone had been wrong about Cissie in high school. She wasn't nerdy. Much.

"Listen." Janelle dropped her arms. With her boobs back into place, tension eased a tad. "It's time to put old rivalries behind us. Think of it this way: the *county* sent a regiment to King's Mountain. We're not going to get nitpicky about where those citizens lived, are we?"

Okay, so Cissie was on the right track about Janelle, and surely, Boone wasn't okay with this plan.

"You gotta admit, it's hard to find this place," he said.

He'd never found it, that was for sure. "It hasn't changed location in over a hundred years," Cissie reminded him.

He shrugged his manly shoulders. "You're tucked away behind Main Street. But if we move right off the interstate? The library will be hopping. Kettle Knob's history will be more accessible than ever to more people. It's a win all around."

Cissie's ears burned. Something was happening to her fingernails, too. She'd never felt them before, but now they were all tingly and buzzy, and the sensation was going up her arms.

"I know what this is about," she said.

Getting into Janelle's pants. Spreading the Braddock glory. That was Boone's win-win.

"Better resources for Kettle Knob and Campbell," he replied like it was a no-brainer. "Progress despite trying times."

Cissie turned to Janelle, hoping she'd have better luck addressing her. *Don't think sleeping with our mayor means you're going to get your hands on our precious Kettle Knob documents*, she wanted to say. *Don't think that Campbell can boss us around. And don't you dare think you can ruin our stupid legend.*

But she couldn't get the words out.

The truth was, some part of her must have really believed all the hoopla. Deep inside, Cissie thought she'd find true love *here* . . . with a stranger who walked across the threshold and swept her off her feet.

She was such a schmuck.

But who could blame her? Daddy had been the librarian, working on his British lit PhD part-time, when Mother came to a writers' retreat at nearby Appalachian State and ventured to Kettle Knob to check out the historic town, only to be smitten with Daddy instead.

They might be in Cambridge, England, now, researching esoteric subjects and lecturing for three years, but they wanted grandchildren. She knew this because last week Mother had called and said, "I'm writing a thesis on A. A. Milne's *Winnie-the-Pooh*. Did you know Milne went to Cambridge?" which surely was a broad hint.

And if Cissie had to sleep alone the rest of her life because karma boomeranged on her for not keeping the legend going, she'd be unhappy, to put it mildly. She imagined she'd start muttering under her breath and yelling at children. She might even die behind her desk at the beer joint turned tattoo parlor turned library.

*Old maid librarian.* Such a cliché. And from a different century. Modern librarians were hip and together. . . .

"Start preparing," said Janelle. "It's gonna happen."

Waste managers were going to take over this beloved space!

"That's a bit premature to suggest," Cissie eked out, but just barely. In her head she said, *Over my dead body*, the way a scary, possessed person would have, in a voice that came from the depths of hell.

But no. She couldn't manage that. A Rogers stayed calm and logical. Except for Nana. She was a throwback to some earlier rabble-rousing generation, probably from medieval times.

"Suzie—" Boone said.

*"Cissie."*

"I meant Cissie—"

Too late. He was the mayor. And he'd given her that apple. He should be ashamed of himself. How many were in their high school graduating class? Seventy-five? And they'd been together for twelve years, many of them?

On shaking legs she stalked past him and Janelle to

her desk, where she sat down with a *plonk* and stared stonily at the front door. She felt very alone.

If ever her soul mate were to show up, now would be a really good time. Especially as time was about to run out.

## CHAPTER TWO

Cissie Rogers's back was straighter than a goal post. The way she stared down Boone, with those high-beam blues, reminded him of the blinding field lights surrounding the Kettle Knob football field at night during a big game. If you looked at them too long, you just might throw the football out of bounds straight to your overly adoring mother and her gushing friends in the stands, every cool jock's worst nightmare.

Janelle paused at the front door of the library. "Cissie's a real librarian. I mean, old school." She said it like it was something to be pitied, then winked and left, throwing him one last glance over her shoulder.

Bubblegum and cattiness aside, Janelle was hot. When she walked in those precarious high heels of hers, she didn't wobble. Her movements were sinuous, coordinated—the sign of a true athlete, something Boone could appreciate. She had a good head on her shoulders, too. But contrary to the rumors—and he'd heard a few doozies lately—he wasn't even remotely interested in sleeping with her.

He could think of a lot of reasons, but he'd start and

end with one: when she laughed, it was never because something was funny.

Cissie still sat at her desk, but now she was pretending to be busy as hell.

No wonder. He'd been to school with her. He was the mayor of a small town. He should know everyone, and he thought he did, but once in a blue moon, he'd come up against a local he'd never held a real conversation with.

Cissie Rogers was one of them. All the Rogerses kept to themselves, except Nana.

He walked toward her, stopped. "Cissie—"

She looked up from her perch, her face as serious as an owl's behind those rimless frames. An ancient memory flooded back—him giving her an apple in grade school. He'd been fascinated by her glasses, which back then had had black, rectangular rims. He'd wondered if they were like magnifying lenses and wanted to hold them over his report card, angle them to the sun, and focus a sunbeam to light that report card on fire. But then he'd decided that he wasn't sure he was ready to have Cissie as his girlfriend, as exciting and necessary as the glasses experiment sounded. She was smart. He was afraid she'd laugh at him if she ever saw his grades.

They always sucked.

"The library's closed," she said now, firmly, the way a librarian should.

"It can't be." He looked at the clock above her head.

She stood and moved to a two-drawer wooden filing cabinet behind her chair. "I'm taking special inventory. There's a sign on the door."

"There's no sign. And it's only two o'clock."

"It—it must have fallen."

"Cissie—"

"It's time for you to go." Her shoulders looked so small. But her chin was up. She was the perfect librarian, he suddenly realized. She guarded these books the way a trained Doberman guarded a junkyard.

"You're not happy about this move," he said. "I know it's a huge change. But we have to face certain economic realities."

He was in mayor mode now. He'd learned at his grandfather's feet. He knew how to handle conflict among the town council. "Talk to me. I went about this the wrong way. Obviously."

She said nothing for a few seconds. "Is this a done deal? Janelle said it was."

Voters usually loved him, but he was sure she didn't. "I signed off on it this morning. We're going to move out of here six weeks from today."

They locked gazes.

Her pupils were large and black, her lashes long. The outer tips of her eyes curved up the slightest bit, or maybe that was the lens refracting their shape. He didn't know.

"I don't have any choice here." He wondered why he was still trying to explain when she might as well be holding her index fingers in her ears. "The county's in charge. If I'd put up any fuss, we were going to lose out even worse than we have it now. Besides which—this library building, cool as it is, is too small"—*and too decrepit*—"to handle the growth that's coming to western North Carolina. Kettle Knob's last to see it, I know. But we need to be prepared. To be proactive."

Boone had always been able to see the big picture, to strategize, to win despite long odds, whether it was as a student, as a football player, or as a football coach— but especially as mayor. Kettle Knob might be quaint, but the town was investing its revenue, mainly tourism dollars, in a thoroughly modern way, seeking ways to increase its tax base without losing much of its authentic charm.

But sometimes, authentic charm had to go.

Like now.

It wasn't nice, nor was it pretty.

It was the economy.

It was politics.

Someone else walked in then, a woman with two young kids. Maybe she was from the new apartment complex. He didn't recognize her.

"I'm so sorry," Cissie told her. "We're closing unexpectedly for admin reasons. I can give you five minutes."

"But I planned to be here half an hour." The harried visitor looked at her oldest, a boy about five, who was holding hands with an angel of a toddler girl. "He has a dentist's appointment. I'd rather wait here than there."

Boone could see Cissie give in—the way her eyes softened right before she smiled at all of them. "We have some new books in the children's section. I put them on the table."

The woman smiled back. "Great," she said, and took off with her kids in tow.

Cissie got busy pulling a piece of paper out of the printer and writing on it with a marker.

Boone stood and watched. This was an act. He knew it. "Hey, you can't shut the library down because you don't like what I just told you."

She wouldn't look up. Her grip was firm on that marker, and she wrote doggedly: "Library closed for inventory. Will reopen tomorrow morning at 9 a.m."

She ignored him.

"Come on, Cissie. Say something." He was a good mayor, not a dictator.

She tore off a piece of tape from a tape dispenser and

put it on the upper left corner of the back of the sign. Then she tore another piece of tape and stuck it on the other upper corner. "I want to work *here*," she said, her words flowing plain and clear, like water. "Not there. *This* is our library."

She'd never spoken so confidently before. He would have remembered. The Cissie in high school had clung to the shadows, and this grown-up Cissie . . . He'd never noticed her before. She didn't hang out at The Log Cabin. He never saw her at the Campbell Country Club or high school football games. Maybe every once in a while, he caught a glimpse of her at the grocery store, or the drugstore, but she'd never made eye contact. Neither had he. It was easy not to. He was on his cell phone constantly. She was shy.

Maybe he should have looked up. Said hello. If he had, would her mouth be trembling the way it was now, so slightly that he might be imagining it?

A mad part of his brain was tempted to kiss that little quiver away, infuse her with a bit of gumption. "We need some energy here in Kettle Knob if we want to stay viable as a town," he said. "I love tradition, too, but we also have to move forward."

"The town documents have to stay *here*." The little quiver now moved to her voice.

Huh. Maybe it came from anger and determination. Sheer stubbornness.

*Dislike.*

Might as well get it over with. She was going to hate him even more in just a second. "Janelle had it right," he admitted. "The papers are part of the merger. The agreement is that specific."

Cissie's eyes flared. "You know the Rogers family never expected *that* to happen when they donated them to the town. They trusted—"

"And their trust hasn't been misplaced," he said, getting a little angry himself. "The papers will be archived, protected, the same way they are here—for the whole county to admire."

"In a tattoo parlor." Cissie's eyes filled with censure.

He hadn't been this disapproved of since he was eleven and his mom caught him stealing a whole blackberry pie off the counter to share with his friends in their tree fort.

A tattoo parlor was a huge step down from this fine old building, and Boone didn't like it, either. "I swear"—he wished he knew Cissie well enough to put his arm around her shoulder and give it a squeeze—"I'll make sure you're comfortable at the new place. No one will boss you around. You'll have your own desk. Your own space. It will turn out to be a place you can be proud of. You've got nothing to worry about."

She brushed by him and marched to the front door, if a body could call her quiet gait a march. There did seem to be something very forceful in it, though. Something intimidating.

It was her upset librarian's walk, he realized.

He watched her tape the sign on the door window and turn back to him. She said nothing, her cheeks bright red circles. And then it dawned on him. Times were tough, and she wasn't paid particularly well.

"Are you worried about the gas money?" he asked, and then wondered if she even had a car. "Maybe we could work you up a small raise to cover it."

"That's not it at all." Her expression was pained. "And how would that fly when the county is cutting so much money from the budget anyway?"

It wouldn't, of course. He'd have paid it out of his own pocket. But he wouldn't tell *her* that. Let her think he was stupid. He was used to pity from academic types.

"Good-bye, Mr. Mayor. You can see your way to the

door." She brushed past him again, her dainty ears pink as she strode past her station to the potted palm and disappeared around the corner, presumably to visit with the family in the children's section.

The front desk sat untended. But disapproval hung in the air, left in her wake.

She didn't like him. She didn't like him at all.

The feeling was mutual, he told himself when he left. She was a stuffy librarian. A judgmental book snob who probably didn't know anything about football. Or trout fishing. Or four-wheeling.

But when he got in his truck to go to football practice, Cissie's snapping eyes stuck with him. And on the field, he yelled way more than he usually did.

"Something's up with Coach," one of the boys, the team captain, murmured by the water hose during a quick break.

"I heard that," Boone said. "Get back to practice."

He glared at the kid and his teammate hard. Which wasn't like him, either. He didn't use fear tactics to get the boys motivated. And he didn't take out his own personal or professional frustrations on them.

The picture of that forbidden blackberry pie, flaky, with syrupy juice oozing out of those three holes poked in the middle by one of his mother's silver forks, loomed in his mind's eye. He remembered grabbing it—a piece of crust coming off the edge and falling to the floor, to be eaten by his dog—and turning to see his mother standing in the kitchen doorway.

"Richard would never have stolen a pie," she'd said.

No doubt Richard wouldn't have been so hard-hearted, either, especially to young kids who played football.

"Hey," Boone called to the backs of his two players.

They turned around.

"Let's get pizza after practice, okay? The whole team. On me. Tell everyone to work their butts off first."

The team captain grinned. "Sounds good."

"And I don't want to hear any bad language out there," Boone said. "We're raising gentlemen in this town."

The two guys looked at each other. He knew what they were thinking: *Coach is old-fashioned.*

Yeah, he was. And getting older by the minute.

"Coach," the team captain said with a twinkle in his young eye, "we heard a story about you. . . ."

"Oh, yeah?" This was why the kid was team captain. He was ballsy.

"About you and Mayor Montgomery," said the other boy, his Adam's apple bobbing.

Whoa. He was ballsy, too.

"It's not true," Boone said blandly, "and you'd better be glad you're standing a good twenty feet away from me, or I'd be knocking your two heads together. Do I look dumb enough to involve myself in illegal, illicit activities anywhere, much less Frazier Lake, where half the retired population of Buncombe County spends their afternoons fishing—or involve a woman in such a scenario? That would be pretty rude of me."

"No," the boys said together, almost happily.

"Right answer, fellas." It was rough being a good example all the time, but someone had to do it. Some of the boys didn't have father figures, so Boone stepped in when the situation called for it.

"We mean it as a compliment, sir." The team captain's cheeks flushed. "You've dated all the hotties of Buncombe County."

"*Date,*" Boone said. "That's the operative word. And the number-one rule of dating is you never, ever mislead a woman for any reason whatsoever. You treat her like a piece of your mama's best fine china, too. It's why those hotties still speak to me."

"You go, Coach," said the team captain.

The two boys fist-bumped.

"Stop kissing my butt and get out on that field," Boone said sternly. "It's time for some hitting drills."

"Yes, sir!" they both cried, and took off.

But in the thirty seconds it took Boone to meet up with his players, he wasn't thinking about practice at all. He was thinking that he'd never once made out with a woman who wore glasses, especially a librarian.

# CHAPTER THREE

"I heard," said Laurie Huffman, Cissie's best friend, at her front door. She lived in a two-bedroom 1940s cottage on a side street off the town square. A fake stone well perched on her front lawn, the wooden bucket dangling inside it filled with purple pansies. "The library might be moving, and you and Boone and Janelle had a showdown."

Cissie stopped on the front step. "How did you hear already?"

"Through the Kettle Knob grapevine, which is alive and well. Mom's pretty much one of the hubs."

"Wow." Cissie stepped over the threshold into a tiny foyer with a toy fire engine parked at the stair steps.

"Come see the new couch," Laurie said. "I mean, the old couch from Mom's attic reupholstered by *moi* with an ancient staple gun. And then we'll head out."

The couch was soft pink with little yellow flowers all over it, very *Little House on the Prairie*. Laurie had a yen to make her own cheese, churn butter, and live off the land, although she'd done none of those things.

"It's so you," Cissie said.

Laurie pulled her down on it. "I also heard about

Boone and Janelle at the lake. I don't think it's true, though. Janelle just wants him bad enough to invent stories. Believe me, Boone is not that type. He'd never be seen with his naked butt in public."

"Maybe he's changed since high school."

"People don't change," Laurie said. "Look at your parents. When was the last time they called you?"

"I call *them*. That's our arrangement."

"They're selfish academics who've never paid attention to you, and you're *still* trying to win them over."

"Laurie, they love me. And I love them." Sure, they were in their own little brainy world all the time. Always had been. But when they remembered to come out of their offices, they were very sweet. And she had Nana to make up for all the hugs she might have gotten otherwise.

"I know," Laurie said, "but somehow things should have worked out differently for you. And I blame them."

"What's wrong with me the way I am? I love being a librarian."

"Nothing. But part of me imagines you as the stripper librarian. I can just see you on that pole, holding a book. You know what I mean?"

They both chuckled.

"You have this weird idea that I'm some wild woman waiting to be unleashed." Cissie took her glasses off and polished them on her sleeve. "But I'm happy. And as for Boone, I don't know why you'd think I care about his love life."

She'd always been too embarrassed to admit she had a crush on the hottest guy in town. She was supposed to go for intellectual types who played chess rather than football.

"Come on," Laurie said. "Until he marries and settles

down, Boone's going to be every woman in Kettle Knob's fantasy."

"But you're married and settled down. Perry's *your* fantasy."

Laurie made a face at her. "You've clearly never been married."

"Is everything . . . good? I mean, you love Perry, right?"

"Of course." Laurie hopped up, held out her hand, and pulled Cissie to her feet. "You'll understand once it happens to you."

If it ever did. "If the library moves, the legend is over."

Laurie's mouth dropped open. "I forgot about that. So now we have to fight for you to stay where you are, no matter what."

"But I don't believe in the legend," Cissie assured her.

"Who cares? It still might be true! And I, for one, am not going to see your chance to meet your soul mate go down the tubes."

A few minutes later, Laurie followed Cissie up the mountain to her house. They parked their cars out front, beneath the massive oak tree that had stood there for probably six hundred years, according to the tree experts.

Sam and Stephen, Laurie's little boys, ran straight to the front porch, sat backward in two rockers, and started rocking for all they were worth.

"You're the slowest driver ever," Laurie told Cissie as they walked up the front steps.

"That's our secret, right?"

"Okay. But when are you going to get used to living on a mountain?"

"Driving ten miles below the speed limit helps me believe I won't go over the edge," Cissie explained.

"There are *guardrails*."

"I know. You've told me a hundred times. And I'm still going to drive how I drive."

Laurie grabbed the backs of both rockers and stopped her sons' madcap ride. *"Down."*

Cissie threw open the front door, which was always unlocked. "Nana, I've brought you your favorite boys!" she called from the kitchen, never dreaming she'd be living back home at age thirty-two. She'd figured she'd be married by now, maybe with a child or two of her own. She'd make love every night on a four-poster Shaker-style cedar bed with a crocheted canopy topper in front of a roaring fire with her version of Boone Braddock—

No. With Mr. Darcy, of course. Boone was now officially off her fantasy list, no matter what Laurie said.

"Nana!" the boys cried in unison. "Where are you?"

Laurie set a pie dish and two identical catalogs on the kitchen counter. "Are you sure she won't mind buying more? What if she has a whole attic full?"

"I know she doesn't," said Cissie. "She loves that gift wrap. Don't feel guilty."

Laurie bit her lip. "Well, I do make the best chicken pie in town. I hope that'll help lessen the pain when she writes out the checks."

"And y'all need to stay for dinner."

Laurie shook her head. "We would, but Perry might come home early tonight from his trip."

"I hope so." Cissie was glad for the distraction of her BFF and sons, but how would she tell Nana that the library was going to be no more? Their family history was tied up in that place.

"Where is she?" Sam asked.

Usually when Cissie came home she heard her grandmother singing or whistling. But the house was strangely quiet. She refused to panic. Nana was fit as a fiddle.

"I hope she's all right," Laurie whispered.

Which only made Cissie panic more. She handed off the boys to their mother. "Let me check. Y'all wait here a minute."

"Okay." Laurie made the boys wash their hands at the sink.

Cissie slung her purse over a chair and walked nonchalantly through the kitchen into the great room, where every wall was lined with books. Dexter, their sixteen-year-old Siamese cat, lay curled in a patch of sun on the faded olive plaid armchair, his usual place in the afternoon.

"Nana?"

She wasn't there.

Cissie paused for a moment, listened. But all she heard was the distant whine of a chainsaw somewhere on the mountain and from upstairs, the staccato sound a brand-new playing card makes in your bicycle spokes as you're riding downhill.

She turned. Marveled at the precision and vibrant colors of a long line of small wooden blocks spiraling around the plank floor and ascending up the staircase to the second floor.

*Oh, Nana.*

Cissie pressed her palm to her cheek. "Laurie! Get out here with the boys. Fast."

They ran in. Waited.

Watched.

When the rippling waterfall of toppled rectangles knocked down the final one—the red one at her feet—Cissie clapped, then chuckled when she saw what the back of that domino said:

*Time to hug some boys.*

"Hurray!" Sam and Stephen yelled.

Cissie put on the kettle.

Life with Nana was never dull.

When the kettle began to huff and cough, the family matriarch appeared in the kitchen, her hazel eyes sparkling. "I don't want tea, do I, boys?"

"No!" they cried in unison. "You want a toddy!"

"Exactly." Nana looked at Cissie and Laurie. "What eighty-five-year-old person wants tea?"

"What's a toddy?" asked Stephen.

"An older person's vitamin drink," said Laurie.

"You're only eighty-two," Cissie told her grandmother.

"I know, but I feel eighty-five today."

Laurie laughed. "There's an actual difference between feeling eighty-two and eighty-five?"

"Hell, yes, shug." Short for *sugar.* "You try setting up all those dominoes. But I did it for these rascals." The boys hugged her around the waist. "And maybe myself, too."

"You're the bionic woman," Cissie said. "And brave. Dexter could have brought the whole thing down."

"I worked around his napping schedule," Nana said. "And here's a confession. I got Mr. Reader to help."

Cissie drew in her chin. "The bug man?"

"He didn't have any other appointments after ours. Rule number fifty-five, boys: your bug man is not just your bug man. Take advantage of that fact."

The two boys high-fived each other.

*"Nana,"* said Cissie.

"Rule number fourteen." Nana was on a roll. "A girl's gotta have some adventures, whatever it takes, especially when she could kick off at any moment."

"Don't say that," said Cissie.

"Kick off?" asked Sam.

"She plays football!" said Stephen.

"I knew it!" Sam crowed.

They bumped chests in a Neanderthal display of approval.

Laurie laughed and kissed Nana's cheek. "Ready to be shaken down?"

"Where's my catalogs?" Nana asked the boys. "I'm itching to buy gift wrap. A ton of it."

Sam and Stephen stared at each other in delight and ran to get the catalogs. Twenty minutes later, they were gone and the chicken pie was in the oven.

"I'll get the Jameson," Nana told Cissie. "Meet me on the front porch for a cigar. It's time you learned to smoke one. Give you some hair on your chest."

"I don't smoke cigars. They stink. And I don't want hair on my chest."

But she'd go. She'd sit upwind of her grandmother while she smoked her cigar and drank her whiskey and water, no ice, and talked about the world as if it were her oyster, which it had always been.

It was five thirty in Kettle Knob, definitely happy hour, Cissie supposed. And after what she'd heard today, she'd have a glass of wine, although she wasn't big on drinking wine, except on Saturday steak nights with Nana.

She'd have a glass of merlot.

Make that two.

She leaned on the counter, shocked at herself for guzzling that first glass, and wondered what the world was coming to. She'd talked to Boone Braddock. The library was shutting down and becoming a county office for waste management. She'd have to work in a strip mall, far enough away from Nana that she'd be worried about her. And definitely too far for Sally and Hank Davis to continue volunteering.

"Whatcha so down about?" Nana asked her on the porch.

Dexter strolled out to keep them company. He sat on his haunches and took in the view. A steady wind blew from the northwest, across the mountaintops, maybe all the way from the Dakotas. Why not? It seemed as if they could see that far.

It was hard to be down about anything when you were looking at a vista so majestic and peaceful that it literally took your breath away. The Smokies were like a cluster of worn old women with rounded shoulders, millions of years of wear and tear softening their lines but not breaking them. No storm or wind, not even time, could move these mountains. They'd be here long after Nana and Cissie were gone.

Cissie sighed, sat in a rocker. "I've got some bad news about the library."

"Spit it out."

"It's shutting down. We're merging with Campbell. At the Harris Teeter strip mall."

Nana paused a moment, took a sip of whiskey. "It was a good run. Over a hundred years. Not much in mountain time, but in human time—in USA time, especially— it's pretty damned good."

"But we can't just give up."

Nana took a puff of her cigar, and a strong, sudden gust lifted her hem up over her knees. She smoothed it back down. "We're getting that old northwest wind, the one we get once a decade or so. Last time it was here, it blew off Billy Shoemaker's hairpiece and knocked half the letters off the theater marquee. They found an *M* two miles away in Leena Douglas's garden."

"Nana. Let's get back to the subject."

"The wind *is* the subject, honey. Sometimes things happen you have no control over."

"You're the spitfire of the family," Cissie insisted. "You can't be telling me to sit there and take it."

"It depends. Sometimes weathering the storm is better than fighting back, and sometimes it's not. What can you do about this problem, anyway?"

"I don't know. I really don't. They've already signed the papers." Cissie thought a second. "I could write a letter to the editor."

"You could." Nana leaned down and picked up Dexter one-handed. He circled a couple times in her lap and settled down.

"You don't seem very riled up," Cissie said. "I thought you would be."

"At my age, nothing is big enough to rile me. I've seen it all."

"But this means . . ."

"What does it mean?" Nana tapped her cigar on an old porcelain bowl on a wrought-iron table to her left.

"It means—" Cissie thought about everything she'd always counted on, including true love. These mountains. Chocolate cake to drive away the blues.

"Out with the old, in with the new, as they say." Nana's eyes twinkled.

*"No."*

"Why not?"

"Because old matters." Cissie leaned over and pet Dexter's smoky ears, and he let out a rusty meow. Cissie took Nana's hand and squeezed.

Nana squeezed back. "You mean Dexter, not me, right? I'm not old. *Yet.*"

Cissie laughed and kissed her grandmother's bony knuckles. "Of course, I mean Dexter. But old Rogers family papers matter, too. And—and folklore."

"Kettle Knob library folklore, especially." Nana chuckled. "My, oh, my. You don't really believe in that old story, do you?"

"What harm is there? You still throw salt over your shoulder when you spill it."

"Habits. They're easy to fall into."

"Tell me about it." Cissie sighed. "Nana—"

She couldn't bear to say it out loud.

"Honey." Nana's voice wasn't pitying. But somehow, Cissie's eyes and throat stung. "You don't have to say it. I know what you're thinking—that you're in a rut."

Cissie nodded. She started rocking, too, and kept her eyes on the farthest peak. "But the fact that you guessed I'd say that . . . You must have been thinking I was in one, too."

"Not at all." Nana blew a big smoke ring, which lengthened and twisted into a figure eight and was carried away by that pesky wind. "It's not like you don't get out. You go to work. The store. The occasional birthday party, show, or church thing. Stop being so hard on yourself."

They rocked in silence a minute or two, Dexter perfectly content with the motion of Nana's chair.

"I want more." Cissie stopped rocking.

"That's my girl." Nana smiled.

"Hey, you said I was *fine*—"

"And you are. If you're satisfied. But I suspected you weren't, and if you're not"—Nana shrugged—"you have to do something about it. Or become as petrified as that old stump." She angled her chin at a tree stump a hundred yards off that had been used over several generations for splitting wood.

Cissie sighed. "It's hard when your best friend is married and has two little boys. And the single people in Kettle Knob my age are either busy working parents or into extreme sports ranging from skiing to hang-gliding to bar-hopping marathons on a Saturday night. I'm just so . . . boring."

"Honey, we live in a small town. You have to make do. Get creative."

Cissie finished off her merlot. Her head was buzzing a little.

"And you're not boring," Nana said. "Lord, child. You're the opposite. Just remember this isn't a practice run. Sometimes I think I'm in one long dress rehearsal and I'll get to live all over again and do things right the *next* time."

But there was no next time, was there?

There was only now.

Cissie stood. "I'm going to do something about the library. I just don't know what yet." But she wasn't going to budge on her belief that the library should stay. She was going to be like those mountains.

"In my day," Nana said, "people did splashy things."

"Says the woman who was at Woodstock."

"Letters to the editor are a start. But you never know if a paper will publish it or when. And if they do, they can edit the fire right out of it. I suspect Edwina will sit on yours. She's a big fan of anything Boone Braddock does. So is the whole town, for that matter. And that includes me, you know."

"You can't approve of this."

"My gut tells me no. But I can't discount Boone. He's no dummy. He might have his reasons. You sure you listened?"

"Of course I did." Cissie's blood started to boil. "I can't win against him. He's too popular."

Nana didn't deny it.

"I need to do something besides a letter. I need to *make* news. Not react to it."

"Bingo," said Nana. "That might go against the grain. Rogers folks tend to sit back and record events—and then file them away. Not me, though. I never had patience for that."

"You're a bad influence." Cissie grabbed her cigar and took a puff. "And I love it." She coughed.

A brown leaf scuttled across the porch, and old Dexter jumped off Nana's lap to chase it.

"What are you going to do?" Nana arched a thin gray brow.

Cissie stared at her, and an idea bloomed. "Something I think you'll like."

# CHAPTER FOUR

Cissie was busy rearranging the pencils in her ceramic cup to angle out like flower stems on the old maple desk that faced the entrance of the library. And for the millionth time since fourth grade, she swore she'd stop daydreaming about Boone Braddock bringing her real flowers—pink Gerbera daisies—and leaning over the desk and kissing her in the bargain.

Especially since he was now Evil Incarnate, the man about to ruin the library and her own romantic future if this legend were to be taken seriously.

Of course, she didn't. But still, she hated to be the one who ended the streak. It had lasted a century, apparently, although who was keeping track?

"No one," she said out loud. "None, nada, zip."

It was just a silly story that had gathered momentum over the years.

Silver-haired Mrs. Hattlebury, who—let's face it—was one of Cissie's dearest friends even though she was forty years older, walked in on a whoosh of cool mountain air and a flurry of orange and red autumn leaves, which she beat back with her shopping bag. "Has he come over the threshold yet, dear?" Her sharp eyes sparkled. "Your soul mate?"

So much for *none, nada, zip.*

Cissie made one last tweak to her pencil arrangement and forced herself to smile. "No," she said lightly, "Prince Charming hasn't arrived today, but if he did, he'd be after a vixen like *you*." Mrs. Hattlebury loved to be teased about her past as a bad-girl extra in several Elvis Presley movies.

But the older woman was not to be deterred. "I got your flyer. What terrible news. You might not have much time left for your intrepid lover to show. I'm so distressed on your behalf."

"I'm *fine*." Cissie put her hand to the side of her tightly wrapped bun—it was hair colored, the forgettable hue that never made it onto color wheels at the beauty supply store—and vamped for an invisible camera from behind her glasses. "Maybe I'll face the door and do this all day, like you in *Jailhouse Rock*. To heck with my librarian duties. I've got a man to catch."

Mrs. Hattlebury chuckled. "I didn't meet my perfect man until later, either. I was all of twenty-four. An old maid in those days. But I had to compare everyone to Elvis. So what was a girl to do?"

"You hit the jackpot with Colonel Hattlebury."

Mrs. Hattlebury smiled dreamily. "The colonel's a younger man, too. By three years." She patted Cissie's hand. "So don't limit yourself, dear. Writers' conferences abound in this area. Surely we'll get some luscious male scholars visiting Kettle Knob in the next six weeks. And you can count on me to help tonight. I'm bringing a tuna casserole."

"You are?" Cissie began. "Food's not really necessary—"

"I'm bringing my favorite pickled beets." Laurie's

mother, Ginger Donovan, came around the corner. Her new hobby was spending time in the archives room researching local family history. "Just to be nice, really."

"That, um, *is* nice." Cissie couldn't stand pickled beets.

"But the truth is," Mrs. Donovan went on, "I like the idea of picking up milk and eggs and my books all at once. A library next door to Harris Teeter sounds mighty fine to me."

Cissie placed a hand over her heart. "But this building— it's been our library forever."

The lights flickered on and off, as they were wont to do. Even Cissie didn't believe it was a sign from the library gods that they were displeased. No, ancient wiring was the cause.

Mrs. Donovan smiled pityingly at her. "You always were a sentimental thing. I remember you changed the name of your favorite Barbie doll after Laurie cried and said she wanted it for hers. What was it again?"

"Kathryn MacKenzie." Cissie had always wanted to be a Kathryn MacKenzie, a woman with a beautiful, breezy name and perky smile. Instead, she'd named her Barbie Polly—Polly Seymour, which now that she thought about it, was a prescient choice. It sounded like the name of a girl who said *underpants* instead of *panties* and didn't have many boyfriends.

A girl very much like Cissie.

"I hate to tell you, but we need a much bigger movie section, darlin'." Mrs. Donovan shook her head. "I can't figure out how to rent a movie from my TV. That's just too much for this overstressed brain." Before Cissie could answer, Mrs. Donovan pointed at Cissie's flat, un-Barbie-like chest. "Back to you and this legend. The dean at Tech is mighty cute if you don't look at his profile. And he's available. I'll call him right now and see if he'll come in. And then the magic"—she winked—"will happen."

Mrs. Hattlebury tut-tutted. "Cissie doesn't want to marry a man with three chins who's twice her age." She looked expectantly at her. "Do you, dear? Would you consider it?"

"No," she said firmly. "Besides, doesn't the legend says this romantic hero has to be from out of town? So ladies, that's enough matchmaking for today. You had your Elvis Presley fixation, Mrs. Hattlebury, and I have my own for Mr. Darcy." *And an aging high school football star turned mayor who until yesterday had never entered the library in his life—anathema to any woman with half a brain.* "I'll just have to hold out for someone who really suits me. Okay?"

"Oh, that's fine, that's fine," Mrs. Donovan said, and laid a book and two DVDs on the desktop. "Who needs sex anyway?" She lowered her glasses. "Jay-kay. That means just kidding, according to my grandsons."

Sam and Stephen, Laurie's two handfuls.

Mrs. Hattlebury chuckled. "I need a new Dick Francis for the colonel. And could you find me one of those sexy Katharine Ashe historical romances? She's my favorite."

"Her latest is divine," Cissie said, and finished checking out Mrs. Donovan's items.

When she handed them over—one DVD was *An American in Paris*—she had a scary yearning to be in Paris herself, eyeing guy candy from her seat at a sidewalk café instead of moldering away in Kettle Knob, swallowed up by a big old desk, lots of expectations, and her share of disillusionment.

But then the dream disappeared in a flash when she caught a glimpse of her perfectly stacked library cards to be stamped, and she was glad for her old desk. It was sturdy, and she knew who she was behind it.

*Here lies Cecilia Rogers, the best librarian who ever lived. She knew her books and her other media, although she balked at being called a media specialist. No, she was a librarian, the best who ever lived.*

That was what her tombstone would say, minus the second "best whoever lived," although driving the point across was not a bad thing, particularly when you were dead and couldn't defend yourself against the onslaught of other librarians wanting to take your Best Librarian title.

Mrs. Donovan hugged her newly borrowed treasures to her chest and leaned in. "Woman to woman, Cissie"— she looked around at the empty space and crooked a finger at Mrs. Hattlebury, who leaned in, too—"Don't give it away. That could be the problem."

Mrs. Hattlebury nodded sagely. "It's bad enough when it only *appears* to be your problem. I was a pariah in my hometown after *Easy Come, Easy Go*, but luckily the colonel was from New York City and found my staged licentious behavior on Elvis's set fascinating."

"That's why the legend of the library will be good for you, sugar." Mrs. Donovan winked at Cissie. "Some brainy stranger will walk in here and not know a thing about your history and sweep you off your feet. Before it shuts down. I feel it in my bones."

Mountain people always felt things in their bones. Cissie knew just what she meant. But nothing was happening in *her* bones.

She stamped the date on a bunch of small manila

cards with fine blue horizontal lines—this was an old-fashioned library of limited means, so technology was slow to come by—and smiled with her mouth closed. She stamped so hard, she was about to lose it—just a little. "I promise you," she said to both ladies, "licentious behavior is not my problem." *Stamp. Stamp.* "I wish it *were.*" *Stamp.*

She wished she could go for casual affairs . . . whenever she flicked through magazines and saw gorgeous male models or watched her favorite Hollywood male celebs on TV or in the movies. But something in her was too much like Elizabeth Bennet. She wanted the real deal: a man to work hard, to think hard, to win her. She wanted the chase, the wooing, the drama, the *romance.*

And then Boone Braddock walked into the library again—for the second time in his life.

# CHAPTER FIVE

"You gotta be kidding me," Boone said to Cissie as soon as he stepped over the library threshold. "You're holding a *sit-in*?"

"Ssshh!" She put her finger to her lips—a trembling finger, he might add—and her ears turned scarlet.

Damn. He was being told to shut up. In the library. Like it was 1942 or something.

"I'll see you later," Mrs. Hattlebury told Cissie, then walked around him with Mrs. Donovan in tow.

They were holding books, but what else were they doing hovering over Cissie like that? Scheming, no doubt.

"Hello, Boone," Mrs. Donovan said in a saucy sort of way.

Mrs. Hattlebury gave him a flirtatious once-over.

"It's a fine day, ladies," he muttered, his eyes still on the person in charge.

"He's hotter 'n doughnut grease," Mrs. Hattlebury whispered behind his back. Mrs. Donovan giggled, and they shut the door behind them.

Older women had such dirty minds.

Librarians were—well, they were difficult. Prickly and stubborn. And they didn't know how to dress. Cissie was wearing a drab green sweater and a high ivory collar, like a schoolmarm from the 1800s. If that was fashionable, he'd eat his Tom Landry–style fedora the football players all made fun of.

"Is there anyone else here?" He strode to her desk and stood in front of it, his arms crossed over his chest.

Cissie puffed up like a dandelion gone to seed. "No one else has come in yet. But any minute we'll get someone."

Sure, she would. "How many people on average visit each day?"

"It depends." Her mouth thinned, and she looked down and away at some papers on her desk.

He bent his head to stay in her line of sight. "Just give me an eyeball figure."

She threw him a scornful look. "At least a dozen, sometimes twice that." Then looked away again.

"Huh." He wasn't impressed.

Now she crossed her arms over her delicate little chest and looked right at him. "Why are you here?"

He had a stupid urge to pull those perky glasses off, yank her up from her chair, and kiss her senseless. "It's a public library," he said. "I have every right to be. And I'm here to warn you that if you go through with your plans for tonight, you'll face arrest."

Her cheeks paled. "If you'd actually get Chief Scotty to arrest me for holding a peaceful protest about keeping a sweet old library open, then expect some publicity, which in turn may bring a lot of embarrassment to this town. Is that what you want?"

Shoot. Who ever knew a librarian could be so conniving? They were supposed to be kind and helpful. "No," he said, "but I'm sure that's what *you* want."

"Maybe I do. It's for a good cause." Her eyes behind those lenses glinted with something fierce. She reminded him of her grandmother for a flash of a second, the one everyone in Kettle Knob called Nana.

His pulse was its usual slow, stable rhythm. But his chest tightened with annoyance. "Be careful what you ask for. You just might get it. Think about what it would feel like to have an arrest on your record. And how it would feel to have all of Kettle Knob aggravated at you for bringing the Asheville news trucks to our quiet little town. I can't promise you that you'll be able to keep your job."

"I've already thought about it." Her starched collar stood in stark contrast to the cool column of her neck. "Good-bye, Mr. Mayor."

He turned on his heel. "Have a nice day, Miss Rogers," he called back without looking at her. "Yours here will end promptly at five o'clock, when the library shuts its doors for the evening."

At the door he ran into wiry Sally Morgan and her handsome fifteen-year-old son Hank Davis, who loomed over his tiny mother. He wore a Steelers jersey, jeans, and extra-large sneakers. Sally had on a black sweatshirt that said "BATMAN IS MY BOYFRIEND," gray sweatpants, white socks, and black rubber shower shoes.

"Excuse *me*," she said in a big huff, and pushed by Boone, her hand gripping her son's. A neat row of pink curlers lined her thin brown hair.

The Morgans were one of the oldest families in the nearby holler. Sally's clan didn't favor dentists, and usually quit school after third grade and took up homeschooling, which for their family was more a survival course: learning to shoot squirrels out of trees like nobody's business, traipsing through the woods and gathering flora and fauna for selling to pharmaceutical companies to make into medicine, and figuring out how to keep fires going in their ramshackle homes through long winters.

She was also a helluva mom to her special-needs boy.

Sally made sure Hank Davis got what he needed from the school system, the family custom of shunning traditional education be damned.

"Poop," said Hank Davis, loud, like a foghorn in the night, to no one in particular, and grinned broadly.

"Hey, Hank Davis." Boone was glad to get outside, where the stronger-than-usual wind was blowing everything clean, including his head. The library was stuffy—he felt all weird in there, especially because of that fascinating owl-like creature behind the desk who disapproved of him.

Sally held the door open and stared out at him. "Don't you talk to me, Boone Braddock. Don't you say a *word*." She pointed at him with her stubby little finger capped with a neon yellow nail. "You got the devil in you bad."

Boone stuck his hands in his front pockets, thumbs out. "If you'd like to hold a reasonable discussion about the library—"

"Poooooooop," said Hank Davis.

"Is that so, Hank Davis?" Sally said. "Are you saying Boone is a piece of poop? He don't listen real good. Maybe you better say it again."

"I heard him," Boone said.

"Humph," said Sally. And slammed the library door in his face.

Boone sighed. Being mayor of Kettle Knob was manageable most of the time. But suddenly, it wasn't.

He headed to Starla's diner. A sign that said "Boone Braddock for Mayor" hung in the front window.

When he walked in, the whole place went silent for a minute. And then he saw the flyer that had arrived at his inbox at school and on his desk at town hall on every booth and table and a few on the counter. Across the top of the paper were big, bold, black capital letters, like the world was about to come to an end or something.

He picked one up, stared at it, his jaw clenched, and tossed it back onto the counter.

Cissie Rogers had a lot of nerve.

"A sit-in at the library tonight?" Starla said when she brought over his usual: a bacon pimiento cheese sandwich with a pickle and a cup of fruit. "Really?"

"I got it under control," he said. "Did you have to let her leave these here?"

"I believe in free speech," Starla said, "especially when it's someone as shy as Cissie Rogers doing the talking. This might be interesting."

Boone dumped three creamers into his coffee mug and swirled it around with a spoon too hard. "We don't need interesting, Starla. You know that. We like it simple around here."

The diner owner put her hand on her hip. "I'll withhold judgment till I learn more about it."

"You're not going?" He speared a strawberry with a dented fork.

"Nope." She waved a hand at a passing pedestrian. "But I'm bringing them some pies. It's an event. A town event."

"Not a town event. It's a protest, that's what it is."

"They'll need food." Starla was adamant.

But before she moved on with her coffeepot, she winked. Only three guys in town got the wink, and Boone was one of them. The other two were Hank Davis and Chief Scotty.

He needed that damned wink. Something was about to go down. But hell if he was gonna yell timber.

# CHAPTER SIX

Two hours to go to the sit-in. Cissie wasn't sure who would show, but all afternoon, food had been coming in from her regulars and some not-so-frequent patrons. So that was promising, wasn't it? None of them had given her a solid answer about whether or not they were attending the actual event, but she was hopeful—and pleasantly full. A too-tempting slice of Starla's famous rhubarb-raspberry pie had seen to that.

"A sit-in is a form of civil disobedience, which is when you stand up to your government," Cissie explained to a pair of sweet, soft-spoken teenage girls who'd brought in a dozen Krispy Kreme doughnuts and a plate of chicken salad sandwiches from their mamas. The girls loved the library's dystopian near-future young-adult fiction collection (Cissie still couldn't say that in one breath).

"Oh. My. God," said one of the teens. "Civil disobedience is what happens in *Fracture the Universe*. So this sit-in should be cool!"

"Maybe sabers will be involved," said the second one.

"Or hoes." The first one's eyes gleamed. "I just wish we had viscous radiometric gel to help out. Too bad it hasn't been invented yet. An ounce of it can take out whole armies."

Cissie turned her wince into a helpful smile. "No, tonight's gathering is a peaceful protest. We stay here after hours and say we don't like the library being moved."

"Oh," they replied in unison, their shoulders drooping.

Cissie felt like a failure of a rebel at that moment, but she was quickly distracted when Frank and Becky Lee Braddock walked in.

She immediately noted that Boone's face was the perfect blend of his parents'. He had his father's square jaw, dark brown hair color, and brown eyes, along with his mother's prominent cheekbones, thick lashes, and straight nose. If he got his mouth from either one of them, Cissie couldn't tell. Becky Lee's was thinned out. Frank's was scrunched up.

Boone's lips were wide and sculpted. Sensitive. Maybe even soft. But that was just Cissie's guess. She'd hardly been near him for years. Yesterday, she'd noticed how expressive his mouth was as he'd listened to her. If she hadn't been so angry and upset, she might have been flattered that everything she'd said he'd reacted to without even having to use words.

Kind of like when she poked Dexter's belly, and the cat turned to grab her finger. There was something charming about two separate beings who really had no place together joining up for a moment.

Yes, she hadn't cared for Boone's opinions about the library, but at least she didn't feel invisible around him. She felt connected. She wasn't sure what it was, exactly, but it came from the same space as that sharp-clawed paw with its soft pads, curled possessively around her finger. Maybe that was why she craved him coming back. . . .

Would he tonight?

Or would he stay away?

Out of the corner of her eye, she watched Frank's burly chest visibly expand beneath his navy blue golf shirt with fancy gold embroidery on the chest pocket. He was a tall man, even taller than Boone—maybe six-four, and he wore his tan slacks well. No gut hanging over his fine leather belt, and his arms were well muscled.

Becky Lee's dainty chin came up a fraction of an inch, and her hands grasped her chic ivory handbag even closer. She was dressed for the country club in her silk emerald blouse, pearls, straight skirt, buttery pale ivory boots, and the fluffy ivory wool shawl draped around her shoulders.

Uh oh.

They weren't here to browse the bookshelves. And they certainly hadn't brought food.

"So will I see you tonight?" Cissie asked the two girls. Her heart pounded, but she managed a warm smile.

One of the teenagers shook her head. "*Project Runway*'s holding a marathon, and I have algebra." She inhaled a gulp of air. "But about *Fracture the Universe*, Miss Rogers, didn't you love when Penday stabs World Leader Number Four through the heart with a poisoned barb she pulls out of her metal corset?"

"Oh, yes," said Cissie, nodding. "That . . . that was splendid." She did love reading the books her teen readers read.

The girl beamed. "I can't wait for the next one in the series."

"I know, right?" said the other one shyly, then looked at Cissie. "If my mother will let me, I'll try to come. How long will this sit-in run?"

"I don't know," said Cissie. "Maybe all night."

"I wish tomorrow weren't a school day," the second girl said, her braces glinting.

"Yes, my timing wasn't great." But Cissie didn't know when timing would be good. You couldn't hold a sit-in during business hours, or it wasn't a sit-in. Friday nights were football nights. Saturday night was date night, not that she had a clue about that. But the bowling alley, movie theater, and the few restaurants were buzzing. And a lot of Kettle Knobbers went to church the next morning.

She said her good-byes to the girls and mentally shook herself out. This was her space. She knew who she was at the library. She had to approach the Braddocks and find out why they were here, not run and hide behind the shelves.

Becky Lee, whose auburn hair was straight and cut in a long, shiny bob, approached. "Miz Rogers?"

Her twang was a little like a banjo string strung too tight, but Cissie focused on not letting herself be scared. She had no reason to be.

"Mrs. Braddock. Welcome to the library."

"Thank you." Becky Lee flashed a polite smile.

*"I'm Frank Braddock."* Boone's father's introduced himself in a booming voice.

Cissie curled her left shushing finger into her palm. "Hello. Cecilia Rogers. Please call me Cissie."

He pumped her hand once, his rings digging painfully into her flesh, but she refused to flinch.

"How can I help you?" She really wanted to help the two of them out the door, if she was being perfectly honest. "Are you looking for a specific book?"

"No, sirree." Frank's voice dipped so low, Cissie felt her rib cage vibrate. "We're here to talk about this proposed sit-in."

Becky Lee gave a slow shake of her head. "That's not the way we do things around here." Her words and deceptively soft tone could have come from *The Godfather.*

"There's a first time for everything, right?" Cissie didn't sound very convincing, much to her chagrin.

The couple exchanged a meaningful look.

"I'm just trying to make a point," said Cissie, wishing she could channel the dystopian female heroes her teen friends loved. "We don't need to move the library. We shouldn't. It's not a good idea for a lot of reasons. I'd love to sit with you and talk about them. Or you could join us this evening at the sit-in for an in-depth conversation."

Then Becky Lee adjusted her purse. "Miz Rogers—"

"Please call me Cissie."

Becky Lee hesitated. "Cissie," she finally said, "our son Boone is mayor here." *Well, duh!* "And when he makes a decision, it's in the town's best interests."

Was Cissie supposed to nod happily and agree to everything they said? What kind of world did they live in?

And why was she nodding happily at everything they said?

What was *her* problem?

She stopped nodding. "Maybe Boone thinks it's right to move the library," she ventured, "but I don't."

There. Finally.

She hadn't been exactly forceful. But it was better than nothing.

The Braddocks merely stared at her.

"Now let me tell you about mine and Frank's dedication to this area," Becky Lee started up again.

She went on and on about how beautifully and carefully they'd developed different mountain properties. Two more patrons came in while Becky Lee spoke. Cissie was dying to get to her customers, but Becky Lee kept going. Frank grunted his approval every now and then when his wife used phrases like *quality of life* and *impeccable taste* and or words like *family, resources,* and *dedication*.

Finally, Becky Lee was quiet.

"Thank you for coming in." Cissie had no idea what that speech had to do with the library, but she refrained from saying so.

"It was our pleasure." Becky Lee didn't look pleased.

Frank outright glowered at Cissie. "Let's keep Kettle Knob a happy place where nothing goes wrong. Have you ever noticed that about this town?"

"Yes, it *is* a happy place," said Becky Lee with a fake smile.

"I, um . . . I'm sorry." Cissie stuck out her thumb in the direction of the front desk. "I have to go. Someone wants to check out a book."

She couldn't wait to get busy helping that person, to get back to the safety of her big desk and those manila cards with the blue lines. When she looked up again, Frank and Becky Lee were gone.

# CHAPTER SEVEN

Cissie waved good-bye to her last library patron at 4:55 p.m., and then she remembered: She wasn't going to lock up. She was staying there. In protest. To express her outrage.

Too bad it was so quiet.

But then Sally and Hank Davis showed up with a little boy in tow, three sleeping bags, and three pillows.

"Oh, I'm so glad you're here!" She took their stuff and stashed it behind the desk. Then they had a four-way hug.

"Boom," Hank Davis shouted. "Boom!"

"Exactly," said Cissie, knowing in her heart that per capita she had the loudest library on the East Coast.

"Dow Jones industrial average," Hank Davis added to show off.

"He's gonna watch *Frozen* with Charles," said Sally. "Remember him? My sister's kid."

"Of course I do," said Cissie. "Welcome, Charles."

Charles stuck his thumb in his mouth and glared at her. He was the most surly five-year-old she'd ever met. He even had a five o'clock shadow, unless that was a bunch of Oreo cookie crumbs.

Yes, she saw a pack of them sticking out of his pocket.

"Maybe the legend will work and somebody sexy will come over the threshold tonight." Sally wiggled her eyebrows. "If so, I'm ready for him." She leaned over and whispered in Cissie's ear, "I got me a special nightie in my purse."

"It can't be very big if it's in your purse." Cissie tried to peek.

Sally pulled it back. "It's not. It's teeny-tiny. Actually"— she was in whispering mode again—"it's a thong."

"You can't seduce someone in the *library*," Cissie murmured, "and in a thong. Especially with Hank Davis and Charles here. You're going to have to sleep in your regular clothes. And who are you expecting anyway?"

"Who knows," said Sally happily. "This is the best night of my life." She twirled. "We're in the library when it's *closed*. It's not like the Greyhound station, which is open twenty-four hours a day. This place has standards. This place is off-limits at night." She paused. "Maybe for good reason. Maybe it's haunted."

"Boom boom," said Hank Davis.

Charles grabbed his hand. "Let's go." He dragged Hank Davis over to the children's section.

Sally's gaze grew wary. "I hope it's not haunted. So many years have gone by. What if someone a long time ago forgot to return his library book, and now since you're here when he walks at night, he's gonna come give it back?"

"I'll say no," said Cissie. "He can keep it."

"Why do ghosts wear clothes?" Sally asked. "Shouldn't they be naked after they die?"

"I have no idea. But look!" All at once, Mrs. Donovan, Mrs. Hattlebury, and an entire Amish-looking homeschooling family with five kids from the new apartment complex came in the front door. "Welcome!" Cissie said.

Everyone was carrying food, too.

Cissie was prepared. She'd cleaned off both old card tables from the storage room and put them out. "Please, leave everything there." But the tables were already covered in casserole dishes, cake plates, and pie pans. There was even a cooler of bottled water and Cheerwine someone had dropped off.

"Let's pull out some chairs," Mrs. Donovan said.

So they did and put all the food on them, Sally making comments about every new dish: "Now that's one I'm gonna try!" "What the—?" she said about another one.

"Marinated tofu chunks," said the Amish woman, "mixed with the ancient grain freekeh."

"I'll say it's freekeh." Sally chuckled.

One of the toddler Amish children starting sticking her fingers in some banana pudding.

"She's so smart." Mrs. Hattlebury gently pulled her fingers out and handed her over to her mother. "That's my banana pudding. Made with a secret ingredient." She winked.

"We don't do refined sugar," said the Amish woman. "And we're not Amish, in case you're wondering. We're part of the homestead movement. We brought a tent." She indicated the large green nylon bag on her male partner's back.

"That's so interesting," Cissie said weakly. "I'm touched that you came to the sit-in. Thank you. Please feel free to . . . sit. Or stand. Or read books. Or pitch your tent. Somewhere by the magazines, I should think. I suppose we'll eat in another hour or so."

The family shuffled off to make themselves at home.

"You use Chessmen cookies from Pepperidge Farm, don't you, in that banana pudding?" Mrs. Donovan asked Mrs. Hattlebury sweetly.

Mrs. Hattlebury glared at her. "I'll never tell." She put

her hands on her hips. "How is the newspaper reporter going to be able to tell we're sitting in? This looks like a party."

"Well, it's not," said Cissie. "It's a protest. Big difference."

"I'm not really against the library moving," Mrs. Donovan reminded her. "I'm here for Laurie. She couldn't come. The boys both have earaches from all the Play-Doh they stuck in them today. I'm her placeholder."

"Wasn't that nice of you," Cissie murmured, and tried to be thankful she had a placeholder for Laurie rather than be annoyed at Mrs. Donovan for disagreeing with her about the library. "Laurie called and told me." And Cissie was glad she had. Laurie had sounded sorry she couldn't be there and promised they'd get together soon. She'd also apologized for her mother in advance.

Nana came in a few minutes later with her sleeping bag and pillow and stopped flat at the door. "Wow! This looks like a party!" She was wearing her red-and-white-striped footie pajamas.

"It's *not*," said Cissie. "But we sure have a lot of food."

Nana held up a canvas bag. "And Jameson and cigars." She chuckled in her naughtiest fashion.

"Oh, no," said Cissie. "This is an alcohol-free, cigar-free sit-in."

"I thought I'd try," Nana said. "I did bring the paper plates and plastic forks you asked for."

Mrs. Donovan and Mrs. Hattlebury had settled in at the front desk and were playing cards.

An hour went by. Everyone kept well occupied. The homesteading kids got to watch *Frozen*. Their parents quietly read the *Whole Earth Catalog*. The gin rummy tournament, which now included Nana, was in full swing.

Cissie didn't feel she could really participate in all the

happy activities. She had to maintain the sit-in presence and act serious and troubled—because she was.

But no else came in. Not even a reporter from the *Bugler.*

"You need to call Edwina," Nana said.

"I shouldn't have to call the newspaper editor to get someone down here." Cissie acted nonchalant, but her feathers were definitely ruffled. "This is a legitimate story. Not much happens in Kettle Knob."

"That's right. We're such a happy place," said Nana, just like Boone's parents had said.

Cissie eyed her suspiciously. "Do you really believe that? I heard someone else say the same thing today. Or are you spouting propaganda?"

"We *are* happy. Aren't we?" Nana laid down three aces on the desktop.

"Yes." Cissie sighed. "We're happy."

What was wrong with her? Why did she not feel happy deep down? Was she really going to be one of those women who needed a soul mate to be truly fulfilled? She loved her job. She loved her friends. She loved where she lived. She was *fine.*

Another half hour went by. Still no one else came to sit-in. And the newspaper didn't show. She'd even left a flyer with the local radio station.

"Let it go!" Hank Davis shouted. "Let it go! Let it go!"

Sally came out from the back. "Hank Davis and Charles are hungry. It's time to eat."

So everyone ate, and with each passing minute, instead of being happy that her good friends and family had shown up, Cissie fretted.

Nothing was being accomplished.

Nothing.

"But it is," Nana reassured her when she hovered

by the card game and expressed her frustration. "The wheels of justice turn slowly, imperceptibly. Nothing we do is wasted. Every vote counts at every election. Every protest matters."

"Speaking of elections, we've got one in a little over three weeks," said Mrs. Donovan. "Governor, US congressmen, Kettle Knob mayor, and some school board members."

"Well, Boone's got it locked up again," said Nana.

"I don't remember the last time anyone ran against him." Mrs. Hattlebury laid down her cards. "Gin!"

Mrs. Donovan blew out a breath and tossed down her cards. "I brought Scrabble if anyone wants to play that."

The homesteading family came out, their tent folded up and returned to its bag. "We're going home," said the father. "Thanks for dinner."

"Nothing really happened," said the mother with a friendly shrug.

Cissie threw Nana an "I told you so" look. "Thanks for coming anyway."

"Maybe write a letter to the editor next time," the father suggested.

"But there isn't going to be a next time," Cissie said. "This is it. Now or never. The library will move if we don't stop it."

She handed the family an entire lasagna, waved them off, and swallowed a lump in her throat when they shut the door, which wasn't easy. The wind was gusting pretty hard. How many more times would that library door open and shut before closing forever?

And then it opened again.

Boone stood there with Chief Scotty.

"You sure are here a lot lately," Cissie complained to the mayor, but inside her heart leapt, mainly because he was the handsomest man she'd ever seen. She had another reason to be excited to see him, too, a political reason.

If his stubborn jaw was anything to go by, this sit-in was about to get good.

# CHAPTER EIGHT

The library meant the world to Cissie Rogers, obviously, and Boone wasn't going to patronize her. He intended to follow correct procedure. While he was at it, he'd try not to be seriously turned on by how fierce she apparently was beneath that strait-laced librarian outfit. He'd bet a million bucks she'd picked it up at Party City on the stereotyped professions costume aisle and used it to disguise her true supergirl nature.

Scotty stepped forward. "Miss Rogers, I'm sorry, but you're on property under the jurisdiction of the county, and the sheriff has authorized me to ask you to move. The library is closed for the evening."

Boone was secretly touched at how she stood straighter and said, "I'm sorry, Chief Scotty, but I'm not going anywhere." Everyone had gathered behind her. She looked back at them, smiled hopefully—they smiled back—then looked at Scotty again. "And neither are my friends."

Mrs. Donovan raised her hand. "I actually want the library to move, but I'm a placeholder for my daughter."

"Don't make excuses, Ginger," Nana told her. "You're here, so you count."

Scotty scowled. But Boone wasn't worried. He'd already gone over with him what he expected him to do.

"If you refuse to leave," the good chief said, "then I'll be writing each one of you warnings"—not fines; Boone had already talked to the county commissioner about that—"for trespassing."

Cissie's face was red. "Well, all right, then."

"Don't you dare go to the newspaper and tell them we've messed with your plans, Mr. Mayor," Sally said to Boone. "You've messed with *ours*. I don't get my milk at the Harris Teeter. I get mine at the gas station. I'm not gonna switch just so I can pick up a book at the library. I don't like Harris Teeter milk. That carton is ugly. No book is worth that purple carton."

"Excuse me?" he asked.

"You told us we'll be able to pick up our milk and books at the same time," Cissie reminded him, "at the strip mall. You said it would be convenient."

A little boy sucked his thumb hard and glared at him.

Boone stifled a laugh. "I'm sorry, Sally, but I might just have to do that. Contact the media."

"Oh, no!" said Mrs. Hattlebury with mock dismay. "Now you've really caused us problems."

Did she honestly used to be in Elvis movies? Because an actress she wasn't.

Boone shrugged. "A mayor's gotta do what a mayor's gotta do." He pulled out his cell and dialed Edwina.

She picked up instantly. "Oh, Lord, Boone, are you down at the library?"

"Yes'm."

"Don't make me come down there. I'm watching a good show on TV. I'm tired. Everyone knows we need a bigger library and that the waste management people need that building."

"I think it's important you record this event, Edwina," he said calmly.

"Poop," said Hank Davis.

The little kid broke into guffaws.

"You tell Edwina that Nana's going to play the trumpet outside her window tonight if she doesn't come," Nana said, "and it won't be pretty. I've never played a trumpet in my life. Someone donated one to the theater today."

"Did you hear that?" Boone asked the editor.

"Yes." Edwina sighed. "I don't know why everyone calls her Nana. She's a tough old bird. I'll be down in half an hour."

He put away his phone. "The *Bugler* is on the way," he told the little ragtag group. "And if you don't like the publicity, well, it's your own fault. Chief Scotty gave you a chance to leave."

Scotty was busy writing out warnings at the front desk.

"That's going to take you a while, Chief," Cissie said primly. "Would you care for a cookie while you work? Or some chicken casserole? We have a lot of food."

Damn. Boone was hungry.

"No, thank you." The chief had a deep ridge on his brow. He was concentrating hard on scribbling those notices. "My wife's got a pot roast waiting for me at home."

Cissie cast a quick glance at Boone. "You probably have to rush off, too, Mr. Mayor."

Well. Now that she'd gotten what she wanted from him—publicity—she was done with him. And hey, he'd had a long-ass day. Just finished up with the football players. An extra-tough practice. He couldn't wait to get home.

But leave? Why should he give her the satisfaction?

"I'll wait for the chief." He tried to look more official than he ever had.

"You need to eat, Boone." Mrs. Hattlebury looked him up and down.

"Since you're a bachelor"—Mrs. Donovan gave him the same brazen stare—"your cupboards are probably empty."

"Or them cupboards is filled with potato chips and Scotch. Like my ex-boyfriend's," offered Sally.

Boone pulled an ear. "Maybe I'll take a cookie."

Cissie's eyes widened. She wanted him gone. *Bad.*

"Make that some casserole, too, please," he said. "Why not?"

Cissie's lips thinned.

Scotty finished up his last warning just as Mrs. Hattlebury came over to Boone with a plate full of all kinds of delicious: cheesy tater-tot casserole, three-bean salad, chicken casserole with mushrooms and artichoke hearts, a tossed salad, and a slice of home-baked bread.

"It's a shame for this all to go to waste." She gave him an approving smile.

And then Boone had an idea. The football parents assigned to provide a Thursday night meal for his first-string team this week had to cancel for tomorrow night. And it was a much-valued tradition. It kept the unit cohesive, like family. And here was a feast.

"Hey," he said to the small gathering, "I have a way to get a bunch of people down here before Edwina shows up. Some boys from the football team. They can help eat up all this food and maybe make your crowd a little bigger. You know, more impressive." He explained about the weekly dinner getting cancelled.

"This'll fill 'em up," said Mrs. Donovan.

"You must be on our side of this fight now," said Sally. "We could use a strong, handsome man."

"He's helping the team *and* helping Cissie," gushed Mrs. Hattlebury.

"He's just being pragmatic, ladies," said Nana. "Don't get all starry-eyed."

"But he's cute," said Sally. "And he didn't have to come to the sit-in. Talk about *nice*."

"You have to admit, he's a good sport, Nana," Mrs. Donovan said.

"He's charming, I'll grant him that," Nana conceded.

"He came with the *chief*," Cissie reminded everyone. "He didn't bring food to support us. He *doesn't* support us."

Boone bit into a huge cinnamon cookie. "This is delicious," he mumbled around the chewy morsel, and grinned.

*"No,"* said Cissie, her throat working. "No, Mayor Braddock isn't going to take over here. Sir, I'd like to speak with you, please. Outside?" She indicated the back door.

He swallowed the last of his cookie. "Fine."

But the back door was stuck.

"Oh, shoot. It always jams when it's about to rain," Cissie said. "How about here?" She indicated another door near the magazines.

"All right by me." He tried not to admire her pert rear as she strode purposefully toward their destination.

It was a broom closet.

"Whoa," he said when she had to squeeze in next to him to be able to shut the door.

It was pitch-dark until she pulled a string tickling his face. One measly overhead light bulb came on.

"This is the only place we can get any privacy," she whispered hoarsely, and moved her elbow out of his stomach. "I'm mad, and I don't want the others to see me this way. I-I'm supposed to be leading this movement, and it wouldn't be right for me to . . . flip out."

"Flip out?" He was getting turned on again. She was close. Very close. "Why would you flip out? What does that involve exactly?"

"Losing my temper," she hissed.

"Nothing wrong with that."

"There is if you're a librarian." She hesitated. "Besides, a Rogers thinks with her head when there's a problem."

"So what's the problem?"

"*You* are. You're not on our side in this fight, and yet you've convinced some people here that you are. And they've become complacent. We can't afford to be."

"If you want, I'll tell them I think the library should be moved."

"You do that," she said. "Because when I remind them what you think, no one seems to believe it."

He opened the broom closet door. "The library should be moved!" he yelled.

And shut the door again.

She sent him a droll look. "You're not funny."

"Come on. It was funny."

She refused to admit it.

"Is there anything else," he asked, "before we leave this meeting?"

"Yes." She looked down, her lashes fanning her cheeks. "You really need to stop being so . . ." She looked up and away. Bit her lip.

"So what?" He was honestly concerned.

"So"—she scrunched her eyes closed—"so *sexy*." She opened them again, and her lids fluttered madly for a second or two.

"Hmm." It was getting hotter in here. "I'll try."

"Don't think that's a compliment," she warned him.

"It's not?"

"No."

"Okay."

"As for the boys"—her manner was brisk again—"yes, we need to look like we have a crowd. So they can come. But if they don't actually want to participate in the sit-in, they'll have to go home right after Edwina leaves and they get a meal."

"Fine." She smelled good. Like cotton candy and spicy fallen leaves mixed up. "How would you feel about them calling the cheerleaders? You could feed a whole marching band out there. We could call them, too."

"But this is *not* a party," Cissie said. "You shouldn't even be here. Chief Scotty should have come on his own. I almost think you did it to torment me—because you have the upper hand, and you have to rub it in."

There. She'd finally gotten that off her chest. He could tell she'd been bursting with it.

"Your parents did the same thing," she added.

"My *parents*? What happened?"

"They showed up here this afternoon and tried to intimidate me."

*Surprise, surprise.* "I should have guessed they would. Sorry about that."

She looked small and vulnerable, and he felt sorry for her. And mad as hell at Becky Lee and Frank. "I'm not like them," he insisted. "I didn't come here to intimidate you."

"But why would you be here?" Cissie's tone had an edge to it. "It makes no sense."

"It makes sense to *me*." He put on his best wise-ruler face. "I'm mayor of this town. I want to be around when stuff happens." Especially when an interesting woman was in charge, a woman he'd never noticed before, a woman who intimidated *him*.

"But nothing's happened," she said. "I'm not stupid.

I know you and Chief Scotty are going easy on us. And I can guess that old Edwina doesn't want to come down and report on this. She's biased. She worshiped you in high school and probably still does."

"I don't know about that."

"Well, I do."

"You were looking at me in high school?" he asked out of genuine curiosity.

She blushed. "Who wasn't looking at you? You were the most popular boy. I couldn't help seeing you everywhere. You were in the spotlight."

"Well, now *you* are, so take advantage of it. Take advantage of *me*."

Oops. That was a dumb thing to say. There was a split second of utter silence. Her pupils widened. And all he could think was that he was in a closet with a hot librarian, every man's fantasy. Maybe she was wearing black lace panties and a plunging black bra beneath those frumpy clothes.

"I mean, of course, take advantage of my connections," he segued smoothly. "I'm willing to share since I'm earning brownie points with my students. Starla must have donated six pies out there. And there's banana pudding."

Cissie studied his face for a second. "Okay. If your boys are going to call the cheerleaders, could they please also call some other girls? You know, some of the ones who didn't make the squad? And they might as well call up the entire football team. I feel sorry for the second string. They should have a meal, too."

"Deal."

Fifteen minutes later, a bunch of cars and pickup trucks showed up. A *whole* bunch.

It was a party. No doubt about it. The noise level was

through the roof. The food was decimated within twenty minutes. Some smart kid had brought a box of big garbage bags—"I told him to," said Boone—and all the dirty plates and garbage went in there.

But there was no sign of Edwina.

"They can't go yet," Cissie yelled to Boone over the sound of teen voices. Every once in a while, she heard, "Boom!" from the children's section. Sally, Hank Davis, and Charles were surrounded by cheerleaders watching the end of *Frozen* with them.

"Don't worry," Boone said. "They're teenagers. They don't want to go home."

"Don't they have homework? It's a school night."

"The football players and cheerleaders all have study hall before practice. A whole two hours to get schoolwork done."

"Oh, good." She felt better about that.

And then some music came from out back. Cissie peered through the window. Someone had parked a pickup in the dirt parking lot, opened all its doors, and turned up the radio to a hip-hop station.

"That's Nana's truck!" And there was Nana in her red-and-white-striped pajamas, outside chatting with some teens. Many more, both guys and girls, streamed out of the library through the door Cissie hadn't been able to budge earlier.

"Who got this door open?" she cried.

"Where there's a will, there's a way," Boone said.

"Outta my way, everyone. I gotta bust a move." Sally hustled Hank Davis and Charles out the door.

"Hey, ho . . . hey, ho," Hank Davis said over and over, louder and louder.

"Look at Nana and those kids dance." Mrs. Donovan put her arm around Cissie's waist. Together they basked in the refreshingly cold night air wafting into the room. "This is a sit-in?"

"It *was*," Cissie replied. "It's a party now."

And it looked like fun. She couldn't have fun, though. She had to protect the interests of the library.

"Don't you fret," said Mrs. Hattlebury. "It's a sit-in, all right, although I prefer to call it a dance-in now. They're on library property out there."

"Yep," said Boone. "And they're raising a ruckus. Someone in the neighborhood is gonna call Scotty and complain."

"Good," Cissie piped up from the depths of her despair, which was evaporating again. They needed trouble. They needed it badly. "As long as no students get arrested. I don't want them to ruin their futures. Scotty can arrest me, if he has to."

All she had to look forward to was being a librarian in a strip mall. And withering away like a prune since she probably was never going to have sex again. Think of all the youth-preserving hormones she'd be missing out on. Sex gave them to you. Nana told her that was why she looked sixty instead of eighty-two.

"Scotty's not going to arrest anyone." Boone's voice was warm and titillating.

For a second, if Cissie didn't listen to the words, she could imagine him talking dirty to her in bed.

"If I were you," he said, "I'd think about having some fun at your sit-in."

The words *fun* and *sex* each had three letters, so they were pretty closely related, right? What if he'd said, "I'd think about having some *sex* at your sit-in?"

Cissie almost giggled, but then she remembered she was acting absolutely deranged due to extreme sensual deprivation.

"No," she told him, standing firmly in her Hanes white

cotton bikini briefs. "This is serious business. As soon as Edwina shows—"

And then a country song came on, a slow one. Boone grabbed her hand. "Come with me," he said, and pulled her out the door. "We're gonna dance."

# CHAPTER NINE

A big gust of wind lifted Cissie's skirt. "I don't really know *how* to dance—" she began.

"Shush," said Boone.

Wait—*she* was the shusher!

He pulled her up against him. "Don't think. You just have to feel it. Like this northwest wind. It's been blowing across the mountain all day."

His warm drawl reminded Cissie of a scratchy wool blanket, the kind every Kettle Knob family kept in their car trunk in wintertime. You didn't want it . . . but you did. No other blanket would do when it came to saving your family if your car was stranded in a snowstorm. It had to be the old army blanket or nothing.

"But if Edwina sees me—" She couldn't get her foot action right.

"She'll think you're bold."

The wind tugged at his hair, and Cissie felt its wildness, *his* wildness. In another life, maybe he'd been a Celtic warrior and she'd been a princess he'd kidnapped and made the cook in his camp, and they'd fallen in love inside his crude tent made of elk skin.

"This is a helluva sit-in," he said. "Not some boring one. Anyone can have a boring one."

"True." Cissie felt herself being drawn in against her will. Her feet were moving in the right direction finally. And now . . . now she was swaying, and bumping up against Boone—against that zipper of his that she'd noticed behind her prescription sunglasses. His chest was broad, his arm around her back strong and possessive. He had rhythm—the type that made a girl think in directions she probably shouldn't. This was only one dance. But she couldn't help it. She was mere flesh and blood.

"Coach! Looking good!" The catcalls were endless.

"Ignore 'em," Boone said. "I'll get them back later."

"Fine," she mumbled. He was so cute and naturally good at everything. And she was awkward, just like she'd been in high school. She'd thought she'd outgrown it, but it always came out, this insecurity of hers, at inopportune times.

"I've got a question for you," Boone said, probably to break the weird silence.

"Yes?" She was glad to say *something*, especially because the song, which up until now, she'd found completely harmless, was romantic enough to be embarrassing.

"You know what you said earlier, about how I need to stop being so sexy?"

She nodded, and her heart beat painfully fast.

"Normally, that'd be a come-on if a girl said that to a guy."

"Oh, no, no, no," she said. "Please. Don't think that."

"I don't. You made it painfully clear it wasn't."

"Right." She desperately wanted to adjust her glasses on her nose, but she restrained herself.

"Why is that, though?" he asked. "Why should I stop being so . . . sexy? Your words, remember. Not mine."

He grinned, and the warmth in her belly blossomed to a flame that traveled to her nether regions. Had Elizabeth Bennet ever had that happen when Darcy looked at her? *Nether regions* sounded nice and Austen-esque.

Cissie looked quickly down. "Because it gives you an unfair advantage. Look how all the women behaved when you were inside." She forced herself to look up again. "You charmed them," she said lightly.

"But not you?"

They danced another few seconds.

"No," she said. "You're a rogue even to ask."

He threw back his head and laughed. "Rogue. How many people say that these days?"

"I read a lot," she said with a genuine smile. "I get caught back in other centuries quite easily."

She looked over his shoulder. By God, maybe she'd just participated in some flirtation. And she hadn't been half-bad. But she was flirting with the man who was going to wreak havoc with her future, one way or the other, if she didn't get her act together.

Nana, Sally, and Hank Davis were holding hands, swinging them high, and singing along with the chorus, which was all about kissing, while Charles stood in the middle of their circle, sucking his thumb and swaying back and forth.

Cissie pulled away. "I need to get back inside." She really didn't because Mrs. Hattlebury and Mrs. Donovan were keeping an eye on things around the shelves. "But thank you for the dance."

She sounded brittle again.

So be it.

Light from the rear windows of the library made it look cozy inside. She strode toward the back door feeling Boone's eyes on her. Had he been able to feel her worn, rubbery bra strap through her blouse? Had he seen the desperation in her eyes?

"Hey!" Boone called after her.

She turned. "What?"

"The library needs to move." He shrugged. But his expression was friendly.

She almost smiled at him but caught herself just in time. "No, it doesn't."

God, he was dangerous.

Inside, she started picking up some of the chairs by the card tables and putting them back where they belonged, beneath the low wooden reading tables.

"So." A sharp voice hailed her from the door just as she'd finished tucking her last chair under a table. "You're upset about the mayor's news."

Edwina wore a beautiful saffron sweater over black tights and boots. Her eyes were sharp and assessing. She'd always been that way. In high school, she'd roamed the halls like a shark, looking for gossip, anything she could report on in her underground newspaper.

She'd been insatiable.

"Hello." Cissie wouldn't thank her for coming. This was news she was making, although to all appearances, it seemed to be a party.

Mrs. Hattlebury cackled with glee about something a teenager said in the adult fiction section around the corner. Near the magazines, several other students chattered loudly with Mrs. Donovan about the football game next week.

Outside, music pounded.

Edwina took a peek into the dirt parking lot and turned back around. "This was a cute attempt at a protest, and I'll write it up. But the library's going to move, sweetie."

"Don't patronize me, Edwina. We're not sixteen

anymore." Cissie was surprised she said that. It came out so easily, too.

"Whoa." Edwina shut her notebook, tilted her head, and stared at Cissie as if she were a stranger.

"This was more than a cute protest," Cissie went on doggedly. "It's a real one. And if *cute*'s all you can come up with, please don't bother writing an article."

A new song blared from Nana's pickup truck. Another hip-hop one. Two girls raced out of the fiction section and headed out the back door, laughing.

"Hmm." Edwina tapped her foot. "You might have yourself a backbone, Cissie. I never knew. Or maybe this is a fluke."

Cissie had no answer for that. Maybe it was.

"There's only one way you can keep the library here," Edwina said. "Become mayor. Convince your town council not to cooperate with Buncombe County and Campbell. Even if the council still wants to go through with it, you're more than a figurehead. You get final say. You know about the weak-mayor, strong-mayor systems of town government?"

"No. Can we save that particular civics lesson for later? I'm applying a different one right now. It's called a sit-in."

"We've got the strong-mayor type," Edwina went on with efficient ease. She really ought to be working in a bigger market where that kind of brass was valued. "It's unusual in a small town, but it's good when you want to control a situation. Do you know what it takes to run for mayor?"

"No. And I don't—"

"It's all laid out in the town charter," Edwina said, "and that's online. Let me give you a hint: you'll need to collect signatures. If you come up with the right amount, you can actually get on the ballot. You have seven days left to get your shit together."

Cissie threw up her arms. "I can't run for mayor, even if I wanted to—which I don't. I'm a librarian. I like my job."

"The mayor's seat is a part-time position, and you already keep shorter hours than you did five years ago. You could do it. Quite frankly, what else do you have to do?"

*Ouch.* "You haven't changed, Edwina."

"Neither have you."

*Double ouch.*

They exchanged wary glances.

Cissie wanted to be a tad different from the girl she was in high school. She really did. And from the oh-so-tiny spark of regret she saw in Edwina's eyes, Cissie suspected that she might, too.

Was it impossible to change when you stayed in your hometown? Where expectations were already set in stone?

Cissie heaved a big sigh. "Look, I'm just really confused. You practically worship Boone. You *want* him to be mayor. So why would you tell me to run against him?"

Edwina's mouth quirked up on one side. "Because you Rogerses and Braddocks have a long history of ignoring each other. It would make a great story, quite frankly, and I love a great story even more than I love Boone Braddock, which I freely admit I do. What straight woman or gay man in this town doesn't?"

Cissie sighed. "I'm not interested in becoming your pawn so you can sell papers."

"Come *on.*" Edwina tried to smile naturally, as if she were advising a friend, but she couldn't carry it off. She was all about the job. "It'll be cool. Everyone will talk about the person brave enough to take him on."

"Nor do I succumb to peer pressure." Cissie paused a beat. "Not that I ever did. Which is why I was a nerd in school, but hey, I'm glad I was. Sort of."

"Good for you," Edwina said dryly, and looked at her cell phone. "I have to go." She strode briskly to the front door.

"Wait!" Cissie beat her there and blocked the entrance. "You got at least one picture, right?"

"No." Edwina made an exasperated face. "Eff your little sit-in. I think I might have a real story to cover."

"Hey! That's not fair. This is news!"

"News, my ass." Edwina pushed her way around Cissie and left.

Cissie followed her out onto the sidewalk and watched her get in her little orange sports car. In the distance, a siren wailed. Someone must be complaining about the noise in the back parking lot. She knocked on Edwina's window. "I wouldn't leave yet," she yelled. "The police are coming."

Edwina made a face and took off.

"Meanie!" Cissie called after her.

Now the siren sounded farther away instead of closer, which sadly meant that Chief Scotty was going elsewhere.

Cissie inhaled a deep breath of cold mountain air. Tonight hadn't been a success. She was glad everyone was having fun, but it was all for naught. She wanted to go home. In fact, she needed to send everyone home right now.

She dragged herself back inside and was just about to shut the front door when Chief Scotty drove up after all, his sirens turned off. He got out of the town's only decent police cruiser and walked purposefully up the sidewalk toward her.

Boone, emanating his own kind of authority, which

had something to do with raw sex appeal, appeared right behind her.

Cissie found herself wedged between the law and the mayor. Literally.

"The chief and I need to talk," Boone said. "But don't leave. Stay right here." He lifted his arm over her head and held the door wide open.

"Don't tell me what to do," Cissie said.

The music in the back parking lot had stopped.

"Go under." Boone indicated his raised arm. "Please."

Something serious in his voice made her comply. She ducked under his arm, which meant her breasts brushed against the side of his torso, like sideways limbo. Hopefully, he hadn't noticed, although she sure had.

"You got the message?" Scotty asked him.

"Yes." Boone had his scary-mayor face on. Or maybe that was his scary-coach face. "I'll get Nana."

"Wait," said Cissie. "*I'll* get her."

"Hurry, then," Boone said. "She wandered back inside a few minutes ago. See if Mrs. Hattlebury and Mrs. Donovan can send home whoever's left. I've already dismissed the parking lot crowd."

"*Hey.*" How many times was Cissie going to have to assert herself? It was exhausting for an introvert like her. "I'm in charge of this sit-in. I'll dismantle it when I'm ready, which happens to be now. But that has nothing to do with what you two want."

"That's not why I'm here." Scotty looked at Boone, his expression grave.

Cissie's heart skipped a beat. That look wasn't good.

"I was going to tell you and Nana both at the same time, Cissie." Boone's voice was soft. Worried. "A huge tree just fell on your house. It set off a security alarm. The porch and the kitchen—maybe more—are pretty much demolished."

# CHAPTER TEN

Boone's protective instincts jumped into high gear at the distraught look on Cissie's face. Her brow furrowed, and her mouth opened as if she wanted to speak.

He squeezed her forearm gently through her cottony-prim blouse. "Is someone watching the house for you and Nana? It doesn't appear anyone's there. But we need to make sure."

"No," she whispered. "But there's Dexter, our Siamese cat." Her voice broke. "He's really old. I hope—I hope he's okay." Her eyes flooded behind her glasses, but she quickly brushed the tears away with her sleeve.

"Let *me* get Nana," said the chief, "and I'll ask Mrs. Hattlebury and Mrs. Donovan to clear everyone out." He strode off, his keys jingling from his belt, where a gun was firmly holstered.

Boone kept his hand wrapped around Cissie's arm. "We'll take you and your grandmother up there to see what's going on."

"I don't believe it." She shook her head. "It had to have been our wonderful oak. It's six hundred years old. Imagine all the winds it's lived through."

"I guess every tree has its life-span. It's a terrible shame."

"It's like losing a friend. Our house has been there almost two centuries. And Dexter"—Cissie sucked in a breath—"I don't want him afraid. Or suffering." She looked up at Boone with such worry in her eyes. But the fierceness was still there, too, he was glad to see.

"I don't know what to tell you." Misery settled deep in Boone's gut, the old, familiar kind having to do with seeing hurt that he couldn't fix. "Let's stay hopeful until we see what's going on."

Fifteen minutes later, he was relieved to learn that the volunteer fire department had responded and found the cat. He was yowling fiercely but contained in a box when Cissie and Nana arrived. They both cried over him.

And then they cried over the house.

It wasn't a total loss. About 25 percent of it was un-inhabitable. But those were crucial parts. No roof, a crushed kitchen. Stairs that had buckled. Jutting beams at crazy angles. That giant tree, its branches like a gnarled hand holding the broken pieces together.

For the first time since Boone had known her, Nana looked old. He could tell Cissie saw it, too, by the way she hugged Nana's shoulder and wouldn't let go.

Edwina approached them carefully. "What a terrible irony, Cissie. I had no idea the news was at your house."

"Don't even come near us until tomorrow," Cissie said.

"And we're not going to tell you anything or let you take pictures unless you put the sit-in on the front page," Nana added.

"All right." Edwina wasn't one to be meek, but she turned right back around, got into her orange sports car, and drove away.

"We'll find out more about the extent of the damage in the morning," Scotty said. "You'll need to find another place to stay in the meantime, ladies. Let me know if I should get the Red Cross involved."

"No, thank you." Cissie's tone was firm, for Nana's sake, Boone was sure. "We'll figure out something for tonight and come up with a bigger plan tomorrow."

"I'll leave you with the mayor, then," Scotty said. "Any questions, call me. I'll be in touch." He took off, back to the circle of firemen preparing their truck to depart the scene.

"Dexter will have to come with us." Nana's voice was a little wobbly.

"Of course," Cissie said. "I'll call Laurie."

"Oh, no." Nana sighed. "She's got her hands full already with those boys."

She took the words right out of Boone's mouth. They'd never get a moment's peace at Laurie's.

"And Ginger's in a one-bedroom condo," Nana went on. "Her living room's always filled with Pampered Chef products. So she's out, too. How about Olivia?"

"Colonel Hattlebury's allergic to cats," Cissie said quietly.

Nana put her fingers to her forehead. "I'll call someone from the theater. But I don't know who yet. I-I can't think right now. Can you, Cissie? Who do we know? Can you look on your phone?"

"You'll stay with me," Boone said before Cissie could drag out her cell. "I've got plenty of room."

He lived even farther up the mountain than they did. The night was dark and moonless, and the curved road took them right to the edge of the slope. When he pulled up on his circular drive, gratitude welled up in him for the sprawling old homestead.

Faber had skipped right over his own son Frank and left the house to Boone. Thanks to his grandfather's largesse, he could offer these people hospitality.

The sit-in seemed long ago.

He held Dexter in his box, and they all climbed up the wide flagstone steps. Cissie took the cat while Boone unlocked the door. Then he took the box back and they walked through the vast entryway, straight to the kitchen in the rear of the house.

He put Dexter in his little shelter on the floor. They'd decided in the car not to let him loose until he was in Cissie's room with the door shut. A fireman had given them some cat food, a litter box, and a bag of kitty litter they kept in the back of one of the station vehicles for emergencies like this, when a family was unexpectedly displaced.

"What can I get you?" Boone asked his guests. "Water? Tea? I can also make you a sandwich. I've got cookies and milk, too. You name it."

"Water for me, please," said Cissie.

Nana seemed understandably distracted. "Nothing, thank you."

"You sure?" He tilted his head at the space on the other side of a half wall fronted by a counter and bar stools. "We can sit in front of the fire and unwind if you'd like with a little sherry. Or a cocktail. I make a mean Manhattan."

Their forlorn faces broke his heart. He wanted to fix things real bad.

"You're such a sweet fellow," Nana said when he brought Cissie her water. "But no. No, thank you. I think I just want to lay my head down on a pillow and fall asleep."

She looked at Cissie as if for guidance.

"That sounds good to me, too." Cissie pulled Nana close again and kissed her cheek.

She was a damned good granddaughter.

The guest rooms were on the second floor. Boone was worried about Nana making it up the stairs and offered her his room on the first floor, but she flatly refused.

"The stairs at home are what keep me fit," she said, but then her face fell.

Those stairs at home were gone, weren't they?

There was a palpable sadness in the air as he picked up Dexter's box again and they ascended the steps to the second floor. He guessed he wasn't very good at making people feel better. But he'd keep trying. He showed the ladies to their rooms, which were connected by a luxurious bathroom.

"There are plenty of towels under the sinks," he said, "and extra toothbrushes and toothpaste. Soap, shampoo, and terry robes, too. If you look in the bureaus, you'll see a bunch of old large T-shirts. I hope those will do as sleep shirts tonight."

He didn't have a stash of girl clothes. This place wasn't any old bachelor pad. It was dear to him. No woman friend had ever met his requirements for sleepover status.

"T-shirts will be grand," Nana said with a little quiver in her voice. "Thank you, darlin'."

Dexter meowed in his box. Cissie hugged her grandmother good night—Boone did, too—and they shut her door.

It was just the two of them now. An awkward silence descended. But then Dexter scratched at his cardboard trap.

"Patience, cat," Cissie whispered.

"We need to get him situated," Boone said. "Your room is down here."

It was only twenty feet down the hall, but it felt like a lifetime getting there. Years and years of knowing each other but never interacting hung between them like brittle porcelain shelf objects never moved, dusted, or noticed anymore. It was embarrassing.

"Thanks again for having us over," Cissie said. "It's the last thing either of us expected."

"It's not a problem." Guilt assuaged him. He had a house to come home to, unlike Cissie at the moment.

"I love the rag rugs up here," she said, "and the plank floors everywhere."

He liked that she liked the place. "My great-grandfather designed the house. The decorating up here was my grandmother's doing."

He opened her bedroom door and gestured for her to go first, then came in behind her with Dexter's box. He leaned back against the door to shut it before putting the box on the floor. Nana sang a little ditty in the bathroom.

"Bless her heart," Cissie said softly, "after the night she's had?"

"Yeah," he agreed. "I'll bring up the rest of your cat's equipment. You can let him loose meanwhile and have him get used to the place."

"Okay."

He opened the box, and Dexter sprang out. The expression on the cat's face would have been comical if it also hadn't been sad. Dexter had lost his home. At least for a while.

Cissie smiled wanly. "He's fine. Look, he's already found a chair." And he had. He'd leapt into the sole armchair in the room and was in the process of curling up. "I wonder if I'm that predictable?"

Boone assumed it was a rhetorical question.

"On the one hand, it's good to know what comes next." Her voice was soft and sexy, and she didn't even know it. "But on the other, when things shift beyond your control, you're not always flexible enough to go with it." She stared at the wall. "I've been sitting behind that desk in the library a long, long time." Then she looked at him. "Sitting's bad for you. It's the new smoking."

"I guess it is," Boone said, feeling bemused. "Hey, you're tired. You'll be plenty ready to tackle the world in the morning. Why don't you get settled? I'll come back up in five minutes."

But when he returned with Dexter's water bowl, food, and kitty litter, Cissie hadn't moved. He dropped everything off and paused at the door. "I have to tell you something," he began. But he didn't know how to say it.

She sat on the edge of the bed. "Yes?"

He couldn't help marveling that a librarian, of all people, was about to sleep over in his private abode. "I'm really glad you weren't at home tonight."

She looked at the carpet. A delicate furrow appeared on her brow before she looked up at him with those large, luminous eyes, which her glasses couldn't disguise. "Maybe I have you to thank for that. You want to move the library. I staged the sit-in. And so . . ."

He hadn't thought of that. "Life's weird sometimes."

She nodded.

"Anything else you need?"

Now she gave a tiny shake of her head.

"Cissie," he said carefully, still ashamed that he'd called her Suzie, "I want to help." He didn't care if she wanted him to lasso the moon. He'd do it, just like George Bailey in *It's a Wonderful Life*. "Are you sure there's nothing else?"

She paused. "I can't sleep," she finally whispered. "I know I won't. I'll be up all night thinking about stuff."

Of course she would. The wind had died down a lot, shifted directions even, but it was still making its presence known, as it did most nights on the mountain. Every little sweep and moan of it would remind her of what had happened to that grand tree and her family home.

Boone knew a way to get her through the night. He was a dog thinking along those lines, but she was driving him crazy with her closed-off librarian expressions and her total disregard of him as a man. He couldn't help imagining her with no clothes on. They were in a bedroom. He took a swift glance at her hand. Neither one of them was married or engaged, and they were closing in on midnight.

What guy's thoughts wouldn't turn to sex?

"I get that," he said. "Tonight's been really rough."

She looked at him with a slightly wistful expression, her toes turned in, her hands gripping the side of the bed. Was she thinking about how much she wanted to sleep? How much she wished she hadn't lost part of her house? Or how much she wanted him to leave?

"Hey," he said, "if you'd like to come downstairs and watch a movie and have a drink or two to unwind, we can." He had a lot to do in the morning, but of course, he'd do that. It was the very least he could do.

"I'd love to watch TV," she said, "maybe. But . . ."

"But what?"

She bit her lip. "I'd rather—"

"I'll help out with anything. You name it."

She looked toward the bathroom door. All was quiet there, although Nana had left on the fan.

Something in him kicked up a notch. His sixth sense. His sixth *sex* sense. That look on her face when she was checking to see if Nana could hear . . .

She was being kind of furtive—he could swear that was guilt warring with something else on her face. Her mouth was pouty, and her color was high—

He saw desire. Plain as day.

Cissie Rogers wanted him.

He had an immediate physical response, which was why he made a casual quarter turn, put his hand on the doorknob, and prepared himself to be propositioned.

Or not.

She was probably too shy.

"I'd like to—" Cissie took a deep breath.

"Maybe you should just go to bed." He'd never been with a girl like Cissie.

"I don't want to."

"You should anyway."

"But I never got to tell you what I'd like to—"

"I've got to go downstairs." He looked at his wrist, which had no watch on it.

"But I want to sleep with you," she blurted out.

*Shit.*

"Boone? You said"—she swallowed hard—"to ask for anything."

"Yeah, um . . ." He scratched his temple, thinking he could calm the tribal beat of his primitive heart, which wanted nothing more than to lay her down and have his way with her right there. "That's a *big* request." Her eyes widened. "Not that I have a problem with you asking or anything."

The hot librarian wanted to sleep with him, even though she didn't especially like him. And she had the guts to say so. It blew his mind.

"Is that a yes?" Her eyes were beautiful, the same smoky blue as the haze that clung to the mountains. "I thought we had fun dancing. . . ." She trailed off.

They both watched her foot trace a little pattern on the floor.

"We did have fun," he said. "It's just that—"

"Never mind. Really." Her face was bright red. "I stepped on your feet in that parking lot, didn't I?"

"No, you didn't," he lied, and tried to smile. "Don't misunderstand me. I'm a guy, and I'm flattered. But I'm also seriously worried about you regretting this in the morning. You've had a helluva night. So my gut is telling me no way. I need to walk away right now. And you'll be glad I did."

*"Don't."* She stood up, her fingers splaying, then curling. "I'm thirty-two years old. A huge tree I always thought would be standing long after I'm gone fell on my house tonight. I could have lost my cat. I'm worried about how Nana will handle the interruption to our lives, and whether this was a big shock to her system. I'm losing my library, and heck—what else have I got to lose? Things could go up in smoke like that." She snapped her fingers. "Any day."

She inhaled a sharp breath and wrapped her arms around herself.

He went to her, put his hands in his front pockets, thumbs out, his favorite "I'm at ease" pose. He sometimes assumed it even when he wasn't relaxed. It reminded him to be.

"Nana will be okay," he said. "And if she's different after this for a while—maybe a little slower or more cautious—it's only natural that it happens. That's her adapting. And so will you. You're strong. In your prime. You act like thirty-two is ancient."

She lowered her lashes. "In sex years it is."

That was funny. But probably not to her.

"I've seen you at that library," he said. "Don't forget, you carry that person around with you. The woman who shushes people who dare to break her rules. She's a force to be reckoned with."

"You think so?"

"I know so."

"Thanks." A sliver of a smile made her lips all the more luscious. "Sometimes it's hard to remember. And—sometimes I want to forget. I want to let go. Let someone else be strong." She looked right into his eyes. "You can make that happen."

She wasn't giving up.

"Please?" She bit her lower lip. "As a one-time favor? No strings attached?"

He exhaled. "I don't know."

"It'll be the perfect cure for insomnia," she assured him. "Because that's what I'm going to have tonight, and not just from the tree and the sit-in. Part of it will be because"—she did that sneaky looking-around thing again—"you're downstairs."

"You're doing your damnedest to seduce me, aren't you?" He tried to speak low, for Nana's sake—God forbid she hear any of this—but it came out sounding like he was seriously charmed and turned on.

Which he was.

His unlikely seductress nodded, her eyes wide.

He let a beat go by. "All right, Cissie Rogers, I'd love to sleep with you." And it was true. He couldn't wait to get started. Maybe he'd burn in hell for it, but right now the little devil on his shoulder was wide awake and in charge.

"Oh!" Her face brightened. "Do you . . . do you have protection?"

"Of course."

"Then I guess we can"—she looked away shyly—"proceed."

"As long as we understand each other. This is a one-time thing."

"And Nana and I are finding another place to stay tomorrow."

"That's probably a good idea. But what about next time I see you? You're sure you're up for the, ah, potential awkwardness?"

"Yes," she said plainly. "But are you?"

"I'll be okay." She was kind of cute being worried about him.

"I'm sure you've done this before, and you probably walk through town and see lots of women you've—" She paused.

"That's probably a good place to stop talking." He wanted to smile, but she was too pretty right then behind her glasses. All he could think about was kissing her. Right then and there. Kissing away the worry he saw in her eyes.

He leaned forward to do just that, but she laid her hand on his chest.

"I didn't finish explaining," she said. "And I really need to. But . . . I'm not sure what else to say. *Yet.* I think it'll come to me as we go along."

"Maybe it will." She was a little complicated. But he could handle that.

# CHAPTER ELEVEN

Cissie might not know exactly what her long-range plan was, but when Boone took her hand, she knew she was leaving behind her rut for good. The library, the house, her soul mate . . . she had a lot of grabbing and a-gettin' to do, not much control of any of it, and time was rushing by. She was going to be like Nana and seize life by the horns and ride it hard.

She gulped at the metaphor. It was very easy to make it entirely sexual. But tonight with Boone was only a start.

They went down the stairs at a trot, feet in syncopated rhythm. The awkwardness she'd felt earlier was gone. They had a shared purpose, at least temporarily.

"You can change your mind," he said as they passed the media room she hadn't noticed earlier.

"I don't want to." She was still clinging to his hand.

He stopped and leaned her up against a wall. She was terrified. Excited.

She wanted him.

He pushed her glasses up, pulled some hair back from her face. "Cissie Rogers," he murmured, his palms on the wall on either side of her face. "Who knew?"

His mouth was a mere fraction of an inch away from hers.

*Kiss me now. Now.* She jutted her chin up.

He gave a little laugh. "Still waters sure run deep."

He slanted his mouth over hers, and she melted into him. *Perfect* is what she thought, and when his tongue claimed her mouth as his territory to explore, she changed her mind. *This. This is even more perfect.*

No, it wasn't possible to improve on perfection, but the rules didn't apply to her anymore. Starting tonight. She was kissing her fantasy man, and he exceeded her every expectation.

"You're a very sexy woman." He caressed her hip.

She felt adored. Desirable.

"You're like candy," she whispered. And she was having fun. So much fun.

"Really?" he murmured against her mouth. "You and me together are a lot like a Hail Mary pass. You don't expect it to work. But when it does. . . ." He paused. "You know what a Hail Mary pass is?"

"I do now."

He grinned. "You're a good sport." Then he put both hands around her back and yanked her playfully close, his eyes full of all kinds of promise.

Oh, boy. She tried to focus on his gorgeous face, but the zippered-up part of him drew most of her attention. Her heart rate ratcheted up. He was ready for her in a major way. She couldn't help blushing and didn't remember being nervous the last time she'd gotten this far—she'd been pretty annoyed, actually, because it had been with a pushy guy she'd met at a college reunion weekend a few years back—but now she was nervous all over.

"Boone?" She simply had to go for it. This part wouldn't be nearly as bad as the actual asking had been. She could get through it.

"Yeah?" He nuzzled her ear with his lips.

It tickled. But she loved it. "Remember I told you I might have other stuff to tell you as we went along?"

"I do."

She let a small sigh escape. "I'm almost a virgin. I've had sex once. Ten years ago."

He immediately pulled back. "Really?"

It was embarrassing to admit. Part of her felt like crying. All that suppressed stress she'd tried to ignore, the years of worrying, wondering, waiting . . .

She nodded, heat rushing to her face. "So I'm not sure that I'm doing it right."

He smiled. "There's honest-to-God"—he put up his palm—"no wrong way."

She was glad his tone wasn't pitying. He was treating this like a practical matter. Her nerves retreated a half step. "You're sure?"

"Positive." He swung her up into his arms before she even knew what he was doing. "Sex is like heaven. Or Disney World. Fun all the time. Leave your cares behind."

He started whistling "When You Wish upon a Star."

Happiness surged through her like . . . like the chocolate river in Willy Wonka's factory. Why not? She'd always wanted to jump in that river. Now she allowed herself the simple joy of watching her legs bounce as her soon-to-be-lover carried her past the kitchen and kicked open a partially closed door.

They entered a vast space, the master bedroom. It was all guy. She focused on the quilt on the bed that some gifted mountain artisan had labored over. It was abstract: wobbly circles, rings of deep color—reds, blues, yellows. So much energy!

Like Boone. He probably had a lot of energy on that bed.

She was getting more scared and excited than ever. She tried hard to disguise it by breathing long, slow breaths through her nose and not letting her chest rise and fall too much.

"That's actually an antique pattern," he said. "I commissioned someone to copy it."

"It looks like it could go in MoMA." The Museum of Modern Art in New York City. Maybe he didn't know what that was . . . had he ever left Kettle Knob? She didn't feel she could ask. And she certainly didn't want to come across as a snob and start explaining—

"I fly to a MoMA gala once a year," he said with a chuckle.

That must mean he was a big contributor. "I wasn't wondering—"

He had the grace to kiss her then, long and deep.

She'd made the best decision of her life tonight.

On the opposing wall, across the stretch of floor where he stood cradling her, was a plump divan, a cool modern reading lamp, a small table to hold books (she saw *To Kill a Mockingbird* on top), and a massive flagstone fireplace flanked on either side by floor-to-ceiling windows which marched down the length of the room.

No curtains.

"Wow, what a view. All stars. And that moon." Her heart hurt just looking at it.

"Incredible, isn't it?" His tone was husky. Reverent.

She felt the crush consume her. It was like coming over the top of a Ferris wheel, the dip in your stomach, the rush—but she couldn't do that. She couldn't fall for this guy.

*Why not?* an inner voice taunted her.

He was too popular with the ladies. She could never take him seriously. And then there was the library—her territory—which was in danger. As was her family's legacy. Her friends' happiness. And the deliverance of her soul mate.

No, scratch that last thing. No soul mate was going to show up like a UPS package at the library.

"Do you have electronic hidden shades or something?" She needed to get back to ordinary topics.

"I do, but I never use them," he said. "I love nighttime on the mountain. And I'm a natural early bird. I'm up before sunrise most days. But when I'm here for it, I take it in. Nature's Prozac. I got these windows put in a couple years ago."

Her room at home had a beautiful view, too, but the windows were small. She'd always loved it, but this place brought nature's magnificence inside.

Boone was definitely one of nature's finer examples of man.

He set her down on a fluffy sheepskin rug. "Any time you want to stop what we're doing, just say *Pluto*. Or *Daffy*. Okay?"

"Are you kidding? I'm not going to want to stop. Although if I did, I'd say *Ariel*."

"Okay." He grinned, but then his face grew serious. "Do you want to talk about it? Your big dry spell?"

He tugged her onto the bed like they'd been lovers for years, kissed her once—a deep, erotic kiss that made her nearly moan out loud—then pulled back to give her space. Leaning on his elbow like that, he looked like a mythological god.

She could barely breathe from the nearness of all that sexy. "I had a fiancé in grad school." God, she hadn't thought about him in years. "He kept saying he wanted to wait. I thought that was his way of respecting me. So the one time we got together—well, it wasn't like Disney World or heaven. Okay?"

Boone fell back on his spine, a beautiful sight, and looked up at the beams on the ceiling. "There's always an exception to every rule. Too bad you discovered that the hard way."

She noticed his zipper again. "Well, since it wasn't anything to write home about, it worried me. I pressed a little harder and found out that he was actually in love with another girl and didn't know how to tell me."

"That sucks."

She sighed. "Pretty much. Although I've seen him on Facebook." He looked over at her, his eyebrows raised. "I'm not stalking him, I promise! He and his wife— yes, they got married—show up on pages of mutual friends—and I'm really glad, obviously, that it didn't work out between us. We weren't . . . soul mates."

"You believe in soul mates?"

"That's like asking someone if they believe in Santa Claus. You might say he's not real. But I won't say that. Ever."

He leaned close. "There's no fat man in a red suit and a white beard flying around the sky on Christmas Eve."

"I didn't hear that," she said with a grin. "I was singing 'Rudolph the Red-Nosed Reindeer' in my head."

He smiled back, and she felt that connection again, as if he really got her. She couldn't help a small shiver.

"You cold?" he asked.

His tone undid her. He actually sounded like he *cared*. "Nah." She shrugged. "Just a little freaked out by this whole night."

"That's understandable." He scooted up a little closer, his warmth a bank of coals against her body. "What happened after the breakup? Were you scared off from other guys?"

"For a little while. I came back here, licking my wounds. Mother and Daddy and Nana seemed to appreciate having me around. I got the job at the library. Hung out with Laurie. But no guy that I wanted to be with ever showed up. And time just went on. Life happened. Next thing I know, I'm thirty-two and asking a near stranger to sleep with me."

"Funny that I was here the whole time." He wrapped a tendril of her hair around his finger. "And we're not near strangers. We go back to grade school."

"Yes, but—"

"But what?"

"I was invisible to you until yesterday."

His expression was grim. "I'm not going to deny it and make you more mad."

"I'm not mad." She closed her eyes, then opened them. "Yes, I am."

"I'm sorry." He sounded sincere enough. "But it's a two-way street. You made no effort to talk to me, either, all these years."

"That's because you're on this huge pedestal. I'd have to cup my hands around my mouth and shout up to you. Clash some cymbals together."

"I don't buy into that kind of excuse making. You could have propositioned me ten years ago, and you decided for some reason not to. That's your style. So own it."

"I don't have a style."

"Oh, yes, you do."

"Me? A style?"

"Uh-huh." His eyes gleamed.

"I'm not some easily predictable person. Okay, I am, somewhat. But I'm fighting against that. As I've told you."

"Let's talk about now." He pulled her up off the bed. "We're going to sit in the hot tub on the back deck under a canopy of stars. Get you warmed up a little. Help you forget that last guy."

"You must take all the girls back there."

"Actually, no. Never have."

"Why not?"

"That's too long a story to tell to a near stranger." He turned her around to face a door, presumably to a bathroom. "Now go get naked. There's a bathrobe in there if you're so inclined."

He was a real smart aleck.

She wished she could dwell on that, but now she had to get ready. The whole crazy scenario began to seem real when she saw her very boring undergarments (sigh!) hung over the bathroom towel rack. And when she wrapped her naked body in a heavy white cotton robe—man-sized—she felt very girly. It helped that when she looked in the mirror, her cheeks were bright red, and so were her lips.

Kissing a hot guy was a better beauty trick than any makeup or lotion.

"Keep this going," she whispered to herself. "You can do it, you vixen, you."

She could be an Elvis girl.

But deep in her heart, she was still afraid. Perhaps there was a reason it had been so long since the last time she'd been intimate with a man. She looked over her always-too-curious eyes, her broad, brainy forehead, her nose—which was her finest asset, princesslike, elegant—and her chin, which even she could see was distinctly stubborn.

When she came out, Boone was already in boxer briefs. She wondered if he'd done any Calvin Klein ads in New York when he was there. He should have, and his image should have gone in Times Square on one of those massive billboards.

"Ready?" he said, as if their arrangement was no big deal.

"Sure." She gave a little laugh and wished she didn't feel like she was going to the guillotine when he escorted her outside to the back deck. Thank goodness the big wind was gone, but the cold, crisp air hit her hard. She was glad to breathe fresh oxygen, but she could never get naked in this. Ever.

"Don't worry," he said. "You'll sit on the edge, warm your feet and calves while we sip some champagne, then slip off the robe when you're ready and get in."

"But it's so cold, steam is rising from the water." She tried to sound equally casual. "I don't want to compromise my immune system. I-I can't afford to get sick. Not when I have to fight you on the library and deal with the insurance company over the house."

"You won't get sick. Hot tubs and sex are good for you."

"I thought that was Guinness's slogan."

He laughed. "I'm borrowing it tonight."

Only the lamps from his bedroom illuminated the deck when he helped her up on the side of the hot tub. She wiggled onto a sturdy portion of the edge, glad the water was dark.

Suddenly, the water lit up at the same time the house lights disappeared. The stars became clear bits of crystal in the inky night sky.

"Oh, my gosh," she said.

He handed her a glass of champagne, and she didn't even say thank you. She was too wrapped up in the spectacle above their heads.

"Ah," he said. "This feels good."

Her heart jumped. She looked down, and he was in the tub. *Naked*. The boxer briefs were flung over the side. But she couldn't see anything. There were too many bubbles. And he had a glass of champagne in his hand.

She wished she could see. But it was good that she

couldn't. She was already trembling from nerves. She swallowed down the rest of her champagne to assuage them.

"Wanna join me yet?" he asked above the soothing whir of the hot tub.

But she drew her legs up. "I'm still getting used to it."

"Take your time. How about I top off your champagne?"

"Yes, please."

He'd never get there without standing up and really stretching, which might involve a show of some kind.

"No!" she said too loud. "No, thanks. I'm fine. I, uh, think it's too late for drinking. You know, more than one glass. We have work in the morning. I forgot."

He shot her a skeptical look. "All right."

They sat in silence for at least three seconds, but she couldn't bear it. What if he was thinking about her? He probably was. She was the only other person there. What kind of thoughts was he thinking? Sexy ones? Scornful ones? Pitying ones?

"Are you thinking . . . anything right now?" she asked him.

He took a healthy sip of champagne. "Yep."

"Like what? What's on your mind?"

"You dropping your robe and getting in the water while I close my eyes. You telling me when I can open them again."

"Oh." She could do that. She set her glass down. The champagne fizz was going to her head already. She pushed back her robe, felt the icy air on her breasts, tummy, and back, and slid down into the welcoming heat of the water.

Utter bliss. Cold versus hot. Square of light in bowl of dark. Bubbles dancing beneath her arms, between her legs, her fingers . . .

And then her toe touched his, and she pulled her leg

back. *Scary, naked man. Sexy and strong.* The words filled her head. She was dying to touch him. She stole a glance back at his room. Remembered *To Kill a Mockingbird.*

"Have you ever read Dick Francis?" she asked him, which was her form of foreplay.

"No," said Boone.

"You're in for a treat." And then she remembered that she was sharing her deeply personal book love with her enemy. Her stack of library cards loomed before her, and her neatly catalogued books.

Boone was the mayor. Boone was why those books and cards were going to be moved to a strip mall.

"You're thinking about something," he said.

She was a librarian first, the instigator of a secret sexual liaison second. She couldn't forget it. "Why do you suppose that?"

"When you got in the water"—his voice took on a husky quality—"you forgot to tell me to close my eyes."

# CHAPTER TWELVE

When Boone wrapped his foot around her calf in the hot tub and used it as leverage to float himself over next to her, Cissie was no longer thinking about her love of Dick Francis and *To Kill a Mockingbird*. She wasn't thinking about books at all. Or the library.

All her good intentions flew right out of her head.

"So," Boone said when they were practically hip-to-hip. Bubbles popped and churned between them.

"So," she replied, feeling wary but also hypnotized by the timbre of his voice. It was a crackling fire, merry and bright and warm, with an undercurrent of white-hot embers that sparked off and landed right where her naughtiest thoughts were, illuminating them, searing her through from top to bottom.

She was a shameless hussy to sit in a hot tub naked with Boone Braddock. Why, she barely knew him!

And here he was putting his arm around her. His fingers were this close to her breast. He pulled gently on her and drew her close enough that their hips actually did touch. The whole side of her naked body touched his. The shock of it—the thrill of it—made her ask for more champagne.

"Please," she said, as if she was going to die.

"No prob," he responded like a man used to having sex all the time. She wondered if he and Janelle were still hot and heavy.

"We're going a little fast here." She gulped down her second glass and put it on the side of the tub. "Usually, people have first dates in clothes."

"They do."

"I know I'm the one who suggested this, but—"

He didn't say a word. Not a damned word. She was hoping he'd help her out of this situation. A gentleman would, but he just kept looking at the sky. And then he poured himself another glass of champagne.

"Boone?"

"Yes?"

She shrugged. Tears stung at her eyes, but he couldn't see them, she was sure, with all the steam whirling around them.

He put his glass down and turned her right shoulder so she was facing him. "If you want out, I'll pass you a towel. But if you stay, I'm not going to ignore you next time I see you. I'm not going to talk to anyone at all about what transpires here tonight. But I'll remember it. Because it's going to be good. Trust me on that."

She just kept leaning and leaning toward him, her eyes on his, and her mouth parted, and then she had her arm wrapped around his slippery neck and she had to cling harder because she was kissing him, a champagne-flavored kiss for the ages that went on and on, even as he pulled her onto his lap, on top of some very hard evidence that he found her an agreeable sex partner.

Finally, she broke off for air. "Mmm," she managed before he grabbed her bottom with both hands and they started up again.

It got very, very sexy because she was straddling him now, and there was no place for him to go but inside her.

She pulled her rear up to give him some space, even though she didn't want to—she wanted to sit on him while he thrust inside her, but he was acting as if he didn't even notice they could do that.

"Do people do it in hot tubs?" She was trying to give him a hint. Hopefully, it was subtle. But she was feeling really desperate, so maybe it didn't come across that way.

"All the time." His hand cupped her right breast, his thumb making swirling motions around her nipple. His other hand was on her waist, but then it was between her legs stroking her, steam and bubbles and water be damned.

She went rigid at the sensation. It felt good—so good.

"You're gorgeous," he said.

She relaxed into him, and he put two fingers inside her. His mouth flirted with her breast, then took full possession of her nipple.

No more thinking. Instead, she clenched hard, arched her back. Her hair dangled so low, it touched her butt. His thumb pulsed provocatively over the hard nubbin which had seen no action with a man in over a decade.

She came so swiftly, she almost got whiplash.

"Whoa," Boone said when her hair flew forward again, her back curving toward him.

The hot tub was oblivious. It just kept churning away. The stars didn't seem to notice anything was different, either.

Cissie rested her forehead on his. "I don't know what to say. Except . . . I loved it."

He grinned. "That's only the beginning."

The pulsing radiance continued to flow through her.

She shivered, and not from the cold air on her shoulders. She felt powerful. Ready—

Ready for more sex.

Ready for other things, too.

It was like the world had only just now blossomed inside her.

"Let's take it inside," Boone suggested.

The night air grew chillier. A hoot owl called from the trees below. Far away, a train whistled past. It was lonely out here. But inside was warm. That was where Cissie wanted to be. In Boone's bed.

Oh, how she wanted to be!

But it wasn't going to happen. It couldn't. Not now.

She sucked in a breath, feeling extremely wistful, her forehead still resting on his. Reluctantly, she pulled back. "I said there was something else I needed to tell you, but I didn't know what it was. Now I know."

"I thought it was about your sexual experience. Or lack thereof."

"I thought so, too. But that's not all."

"Spill."

She looked straight into his eyes. She could barely believe what she was about to say. "I'm going to run for mayor."

He chuckled. "Very funny. I can just see it, you and me in the middle of a debate, and I have a sudden recollection of your beautiful naked breasts right as I try to talk about the town budget." He pulled her close, his mouth headed straight for one of her nipples, which were standing at full attention, aching for his touch. The V between her legs wasn't done with him, either.

But they had to stop. It wouldn't be right.

She pushed off him, stood up, and waded to the opposite side. "I really mean it." She grabbed a towel and put it over her breasts. "If I can get the signatures, I still have time to get my name on the ballot. I didn't think I could do it. But I don't have anything to lose."

"Cissie, this is crazy."

"It's not *crazy*. But you're probably wondering how this came to me."

"I kinda sorta am."

"Fooling around with you. Taking that chance, and having fun, and right after I—after you—after I, um—"

"Experienced extreme satisfaction?" he supplied for her.

"Yes." She nodded brightly. "It just unfolded in my head like a big banner: 'Cissie Rogers for Mayor.' "

"That's a great story," he said. What did it say about his sexual prowess? She wanted to stop fooling around. She wanted to run for *mayor*. "Maybe someday it'll go in your autobiography, the one that sells like hotcakes after you win the governor's office. Or heck, the presidency."

"I don't need your sarcasm."

"How about some facts, then? The election's in less than a month! And you decide in the middle of sex in a hot tub that you're running for mayor?"

"Yes."

He slapped a hand to his forehead. "I'm definitely losing my touch."

"Stop taking this so personally."

"It's hard not to, considering you're running against *me*, the guy who was being rather friendly with you in that hot tub."

"I know it sounds odd—"

"What about your job at the library?"

"I'll call in my sub, a retired librarian in Weston. I use her for a week every summer and whenever I get sick or have to take Nana to an appointment. She'll be glad of the work."

"But what about your house? It's going to need some attention."

"Insurance will cover the repairs, I'm sure. That's what it's for. I'm not going to panic and run scared about a lot of paperwork and some phone calls."

"Rebuilding is pretty involved."

"Well, I can't bother my parents. I'll insist they leave it to me."

"Oh, yeah? How about finding a temporary place to live, too? You can really afford to take on a mayor's race in the midst of all that?"

"Nana and I will stay with friends, even if we have to move every couple of days."

"That's rough. If not for you, then for her."

Her shoulders slumped a little. "I didn't think about that. You're right. Maybe I can find her a permanent place, and Dexter and I can move around. Whatever," she said blithely. "We can do it."

She tried to get out without getting naked, but it was too much hassle. She leapt out, grabbed another towel, and wrapped it around herself, but not before he'd enjoyed the view.

"Get used to seeing me dressed again," she said. "I'm your political opponent. As soon as I read up on it more. Maybe I'll call that nonprofit group that's all about electing women. . . ."

"I'm about to get out naked, too, Miss Political Opponent. Better look away."

She looked away.

"I'm decent now," he said.

When she looked back, he had a towel slung low across his hips. Her teeth started to chatter.

"Go on inside," he said. "Rinse off in the shower. I'll meet you in the kitchen."

Gone was the lover. He knew he sounded like a mayor again. A stranger.

"Okay." At the door, she turned around. "Edwina mentioned that running against you was the only way I could stop the library from moving, but I wasn't at all interested earlier tonight. It seemed an impossible thing. But then there was the tree. And the—the—"

"Masterful way your opponent goaded you into running."

She sure liked recalling that moment, didn't she?

"I'm sorry you're mad." She opened the door. "Thank you, by the way—"

"Please don't thank me."

"And I'm really sorry about"—she actually looked at the towel over his crotch—"about *you*."

"Don't worry about me. I'll survive."

"That's a relief," she said, her voice thin.

And then she rushed inside.

# CHAPTER THIRTEEN

The next morning, Boone woke up at 6:00 a.m. feeling two things: hungry and sex starved. He decided that the best way to approach the situation was to run on the treadmill—his daily morning ritual—then go all out and make waffles. They were his specialty. He didn't like Belgian ones, only the skinny, square ones he could cook in his mother's old waffle iron. With the skill of a master chef—which he called himself on a regular basis because who else was there to brag on his cooking?—he whipped up some cream, rinsed off fresh wild blueberries, warmed a leaf-shaped bottle of genuine Vermont maple syrup, and mixed the batter.

He had the coffee going and the bacon sizzling on the griddle when Cissie made an appearance in the kitchen at seven. Last night popped into his head like a movie into a DVD player, and that was fine by him. He saw himself kissing her pert, naked breasts, the graceful way she arched her back at his touch, and that little moan she gave deep in her throat before she curled back into him like a jungle cat.

If he ignored the part about her running for mayor, the memory put him in a great mood, although he knew sooner rather than later he'd run into a wall of sexual frustration that would make him a difficult man to be around. To avoid that—he had several meetings that day, one of them with a bunch of older ladies who made quilts for vets—he had to keep busy. Stay hospitable. Cissie would be leaving soon. That was his aim, to charm her right out of his house.

She looked warily at the walls, the floor—classic morning-after slinking-around behavior. He knew that tune, although he had no reason to slink. He'd only done what he was asked. And she'd loved every second of it.

He made it easy for her by lifting a mug off the hook below the cupboards and filling it with fresh, hot coffee.

"Thank you so much." She wrapped slender fingers around the mug. "It smells delicious in here. You didn't have to go to all this trouble."

Polite chitchat worked for him, too. "I wanted to send you off with a good breakfast. You've got a big day ahead of you." He kept himself busy at the griddle. "Is Nana up yet?"

"Yes," she said, "and she's going to phone some people about possible places to stay after breakfast."

"That's great." He mentally crossed his fingers. "Paper's on the table."

"Thanks." She wandered over and glanced at the headlines.

He preferred TV news himself. But he took a look at the front page every day. "How's Dexter?"

"He's doing well. Still curled up on the chair." Her voice sounded a little thin.

Still embarrassed about her abrupt departure last night, maybe? He wouldn't be surprised.

No doubt she also had a lot to do to get her house back in shape. And on top of that, if she wanted to run for mayor—he still couldn't believe it—she really had a full plate. He almost felt sorry for her.

"Boone," she began, her fingers rubbing her right temple.

Here it came. The big apology or the backpedaling. She'd probably woken up feeling stupid that she'd told him she was running for mayor as a result of getting off in a hot tub.

"Yes?" He'd be totally gracious about it. That was his thing. Mayors rose above pesky distractions and problems to see the big picture, and in this case, it was that this woman craved more excitement in her life. Plain and simple. It was practically stamped on her forehead: *I need more sex, more fun.* She should put aside the books now and then and stop dressing like a nun.

"I'm tiptoeing around," Cissie said in a confessional tone, "because I have a little headache from the champagne. And maybe my sinuses are acting up." Sure, they were. Good cover. "Do you have any pain relievers?"

"Right here," he said gallantly, and handed her a bottle from the cupboard.

"Thanks." She downed two brown pills with her coffee. "And about last night?"

"What about it?"

She looked right into his eyes. "I'm not at all sorry it happened."

He laid his bacon fork down. "Is that so?" She sounded the opposite of discomfited. In fact, she was her prim, bossy librarian self again.

"And I'm still running for mayor," she added, taking a big, calm sip from her coffee with those luscious lips of hers that had been all over him not eight hours before.

The waffles. He'd focus on *those*.

But he was having no luck. You could only stare at steam coming out of a waffle iron for so long before you surrendered to an overwhelming compulsion to look at the woman who was driving you slightly nuts. "It's best that we just forget it ever happened," he said. "We both have a lot going on."

Her cheeks flushed pink. "I'm not going to forget it. I liked it. A lot."

So this was a librarian's way of handling sex talk! It turned him on like nobody's business. Of course she'd liked last night a lot. He had, too. They were hot together. Searing.

But didn't she know the rules? If you call something off, you don't keep talking about it, especially if the other person never—

Not that he'd whine. Women had their reasons. And he was a gentleman, always, unless specifically asked by a lady to be otherwise.

He trained his eye on the bacon, turned over a few pieces that didn't need to be turned over. "I'm not sure we should be talking about it." He flipped open the waffle iron and jabbed the brown squares with a fork, tossing them onto a plate. "Seeing as we're political opponents and all. We should keep things completely professional."

"I have every intention of doing that when I leave here," she said earnestly. "But I felt I should talk to you now so you don't feel guilty. *I* seduced *you*. And I'm fine."

"Uh-huh." He wished he had this on tape to watch later. He could laugh at this situation he found himself in. Yes, he could.

"Furthermore"—there was that librarian voice again— "if I have to dip my toe in politics, I'm starting in a great place, right? A small town, against someone I sort of know, a man who's obviously wrong about the library but who also housed me and my grandmother when you didn't have to and—and you also—"

Finally, she didn't know what to say.

"Serviced you?" He threw her a serious look. "That's what I am: a man dedicated to service—usually of a different kind, of course."

She didn't laugh. She didn't even wince. "I guess you could put it that way."

"Come on, that was funny," he said.

"Oh, all right." She chuckled. Finally. "I'm not used to joking with a man about sex."

Now it was his turn to wince. Awkward silences were so, well, *awkward*.

"Plus," she went on with renewed enthusiasm, which she might have gotten from all that caffeine (he made strong coffee), "I'm from a local family with lots of ancestors who were politically active in their own way. So this is a fine place for me to start."

"I guess so." He opened the cupboard with the plates and threw her a casual glance over his shoulder. "Sure you don't want to run for town council? That might be an easier way to get acclimated."

Because there was no way she was going to win the mayor's race against him. Should he come out and tell her that? All night he wondered if he should. If he did, he'd sound arrogant. If he didn't, then he'd watch her juggle the race with all the other stuff she had going on, knowing full well she was fighting a losing battle against him. If she had good friends around here, maybe they'd get her to see that. He wondered if Nana knew of her plans.

His third option was to caution her—in a nice, subtle way—in campaign speeches that she didn't stand a chance. Speaking of which, he was going to have to make some speeches since he now had an opponent.

Part of him was seriously annoyed. He'd gotten spoiled by the lack of competition. Another part of him said, *Bring it on*. A spirited race might be fun.

Yet there was nothing worse than two unequal teams playing and the weaker one getting routed. Especially a nice woman with a grandma who needed her. A woman he was sorely attracted to, against his better judgment. Braddocks and Rogerses didn't mix. One was all about action, the other was all about thinking.

*Warn her she needs to stay in her library, surrounded by all those books, after all.*

"The council members don't have the influence you do," she said, which was true. "I Googled the way it works here. You're more than a figurehead mayor. You hold real power. So I couldn't accomplish what I want to on town council." She sighed. "No, I've got to run for mayor."

"You're ready for everything else the mayor's office entails?"

"I'll have to be. And I look forward to the challenge."

"I see," he said. "Do you think you can convince Kettle Knobbers that you're ready?"

"The Rogerses have been here since the beginning. I'll have no problem explaining that I have a vested interest in what goes on here. *And* the intelligence and fortitude to make decisions on behalf of the town."

"What about the library?" he asked. "Won't you miss being around all those words? You might have to cut back your hours."

"I won't like it, but I'll do what I have to do." He heard a stubborn streak in her voice. "Sure you won't change your mind about moving it?"

"I'm sure."

"I have a proposition for you." She got closer, and he could see her thinking hard.

Dear God, she'd best not be offering him what he thought she might. A sexy romp on his bed in exchange for him quitting on his plan for the library? He'd have a hard time resisting.

Heat rose in his groin.

*Get a handle on yourself, Mr. Mayor.* He pulled out the whipped cream and thought bad thoughts about where he could put it on her. Somehow she looked incredibly alluring with that lock of pillow-flattened hair stuck out at a funny angle. The sprinkle of freckles across her nose was awfully cute, too.

"What if I told you about more authors you'd like besides Dick Francis? I'd find out about your special interests. I could come up with a customized list"—she widened her eyes—"that would blow you away!"

Her excitement disarmed him. "Maybe you should offer this service on the web." No woman had had him so off-center since he had first kissed a girl in third grade.

"Maybe I *will*," she replied. "Although Amazon kind of does that when they show you books you might like based on previous books you've read. But my site would be even more specialized." She put her coffee mug down and leaned forward, as if to share with him Warren Buffett's greatest investment secrets or the pope's personal cell phone number: "Reading a great book can change your life."

He wouldn't know. Actually, he did know. He did. And it pained him to the core, that knowledge.

He hardened his jaw. "A librarian offering custom booklist bribes . . . that's pretty cool. But no thanks."

The waffles were done. He pulled out a chair for her and fed her good. She had quite an appetite, he was happy to see. She hardly said a word, except for the occasional "delicious" or "mmm, this is good." She was too busy scarfing down three waffles, six pieces of bacon, two dollops of whipped cream, half a cup of blueberries, and two more cups of coffee.

Funny. He'd always thought she was shy and retiring.

She'd seemed that way all through school. And she'd kind of disappeared into the woodwork since moving back home after college, so he had to admit that this new Cissie, the impassioned book lover, ardent sex partner, and consumer of big breakfasts, shocked and intrigued him.

Flat out—the librarian, the hot tub hottie, and the waffle fan were all adorable. And he wanted her.

Bad.

Nana's singing in the hallway thankfully called him back to reality.

"Where's the coffee?" She posed at the door looking like a police interrogator, her mouth a hard line.

"We're known for having some scary bears around Kettle Knob," Boone said back, "especially in the morning. I'd say most of them are two legged and inside their kitchens about right now."

His remark was corny, but it got a chuckle out of Nana. She made a beeline for the pot. He'd laid out creamer and crystal sugar rock stirrers he'd picked up at a local flea market, along with some fake sweetener he kept for his mother. "Sorry," she said while doctoring her mug. "I should've said good morning first."

"Hey, we can't all be chirpy at daybreak," he assured her, glad to get off the sex train barreling through his mind. It was heading straight to that brick wall that would turn him into a brat the rest of the day if he wasn't careful.

"Nana, no worries about today," Cissie said. "Insurance calls, places to stay, Edwina's questions—we'll handle this thing together."

"I know we will, honey." Nana patted Cissie's shoulder.

Boone got Nana's breakfast ready, and his, while Cissie stayed at the table with her coffee. They kept the conversation nice and simple—no more references to the tree through the roof or finding a place to stay. But he couldn't help thinking of Hot Tub Cissie every time he looked at her. So he focused on Nana. Asked her about her latest show. What kind of music she liked. If she had a favorite place to travel.

The minutes passed, and much as he enjoyed their company, he needed them to go. Cissie's presence was too much to handle.

He was just about to pick up the last waffle—because his guests said they were done—when the front door rattled and someone knocked. Loudly.

"Who's that?" Nana said right away, her fork and knife paused over her plate.

Boone's heart sank. Whoever was at the door—one or both of his parents, he was sure—would slow down the whole process of getting Cissie gone. He stood to gear up. "I'm almost sure it's my parents." He took the time to make eye contact with both of them. "I'm sorry. The fun's over, ladies."

# CHAPTER FOURTEEN

Old bones might creak and ache, but they also knew things. Nana was no fool. She took her time with her waffles, sipped a second cup of coffee. She'd seen the way Boone had danced with Cissie at the library the night before. How he'd invited them to his home and practically bent over backward to make them comfortable. He respected his elders, but that special treatment hadn't been for Nana, much as the diva in her might wish it was.

It had been for Cissie.

"Booooone!" Becky Lee Braddock, prissy woman that she was, had a lovely trill to her voice that Nana envied.

"Hey, Mom. Hey, Dad," Boone said from the front door.

Three sets of feet came down the hall, two pairs clumping in boots and the other click-clacking. And then the Braddock family—minus Boone's sister Debbie and her brood—came back to the kitchen, Boone leading the way.

Lord save women everywhere. He looked magnificent when he stood in front of the stove and put his fists on his hips, rather like the king in *The King and I*—but in well-worn jeans and with masses of delicious brown hair tickling his neck and stubble that made a girl, no matter her age, want to grab that jaw and kiss him senseless.

And it wasn't impatience with his mother that had put that steely look in his eye, either, Nana knew. It had been there all morning, long before Boone's mother had arrived, and it had to do with Cissie. The crackle between these two was almost palpable. Not to mention that Nana had gotten up last night and peeked in Cissie's room and seen an empty bed.

She'd been a good grandma. She hadn't asked that morning what had happened. They could have been downstairs watching TV for all she knew.

But as soon as she walked into that kitchen this morning, she'd felt it. Sex. Attraction. Two people who were drawn to each other like magnets, even though from outward appearances it didn't make sense.

Yes, something had definitely gone on the night before.

Cissie had her hand on her abdomen, as if all those waffles she'd eaten now sat heavy in her stomach. But Nana would guess she wasn't worried about Boone's parents—she was worried about leaving Boone's house. And it would be a cold day in hell before Cissie would admit it to herself. Nana knew her granddaughter. Cissie was as stubborn as she was.

Cissie froze a fake smile on her face. Nana's was real. This was all going to be very interesting.

Becky Lee Braddock didn't know the meaning of subtle, that was for sure. Surrounded by cloying perfume and an aureole of blown-out hair, she swept into the kitchen in her trunk show clothes and froze inside the door. A disguised Paul Bunyan—otherwise known as her husband Frank, dressed in predictable plaid pants and a preppy pink polo for a day on the links—was right behind her, his silver hair combed and shellacked to the side like Bob Barker's used to be on *The Price Is Right*.

"Well, who do we have here?" Becky Lee looked back and forth between Cissie and Nana.

Not very original of her. Nana tried not to feel superior, but she couldn't help herself.

"We know who, wife," Frank boomed, "Nana and Cissie Rogers." The man was so literal, it hurt Nana's soul. Thank God *he'd* never been mayor. But that style had helped him plow over all the real estate development competition, too. "We heard about the tree falling through your roof, ladies."

"That's a sorry thing to happen." Becky Lee shook her head.

She seemed nicer for it, so Nana settled back in her chair. "Thank you for your concern. We'll get through it."

"I reckon you will." Frank doing empathy in his baritone nearly knocked the kitchen windows out.

"Mom, Dad," Boone said, "what are you doing here? It's early. If I'd known you were coming"—he paused significantly there—"I'd have made you breakfast. We're all out now."

"Son"—Frank clapped Boone's shoulder—"it's all right. Your mother doesn't eat in the morning. I had Bojangles' chicken biscuits."

"They don't need to know you had Bojangles'." Becky Lee sucked in her cheeks.

"Why not?" asked Cissie. "I love their biscuits."

"Because biscuits are so—" Becky Lee shuddered.

"Low class, is what she wants to say," Frank interjected. "That's her favorite word these days."

"Great, Mom and Dad," said Boone. "I assume you know you just insulted my house guest. Me, too. I'm a biscuit fan. And probably so is all of Kettle Knob."

"I'll have you know I turn my nose up at biscuits," lied Nana.

"Do you?" Becky Lee said with interest. "We can do better in this day and age than shortening and white flour baked together into something that resembles a hockey puck. But my husband can't seem to agree with me."

"Take a girl out of a shack and put her in a mansion, and she starts thinking she's too good for the food that stuck to her ribs as a child," said Frank.

Nana started to like him, just a little.

But Becky Lee turned away from him like he was a bad germ. Sadly, she latched on to Cissie. "So you stayed here last night, obviously."

"Yes, they did, Mom," said Boone, before Cissie could answer.

Oh, Boone had it bad. Nana took another sip of coffee to hide her smile.

"And you're on your way to another place to stay after breakfast?" Becky Lee was too smart to ask Nana this. She was still locked on to Cissie.

"Yes, ma'am," said Cissie, her lips a bit white around the edges.

"Mom—" Boone's brow lowered.

"I'm just asking, son." Becky Lee's eyes were wide.

"In fact"—Cissie stood—"We're heading out right now."

Nana wasn't looking forward to roaming around Kettle Knob looking for a place to stay, especially when she hadn't made her phone calls yet. But from the look in Cissie's eye, she wouldn't fuss.

"I just have to get Dexter," Cissie added.

"Dexter?" Frank asked.

"Our cat," Cissie explained. "He's upstairs."

"Your allergies . . ." said Becky Lee to her husband.

He wrinkled his nose. "I thought I wanted to sneeze. . . ."

"Right." These two were driving Nana crazy. "We're off." She rose from the table, too.

"I'm sure you're anxious to go," said Becky Lee.

She was starting to get on Nana's nerves in a big way. But what could she say? *No, I'm not at all anxious to go. It's comfortable here.* Because then Boone would feel bad, and he didn't deserve to. He'd already been a prince inviting them to stay the night.

Nor could she say, *I'd love to see Cupid shoot a few arrows at these stubborn young people, so I want to stay to see that happen.*

Nope. If Cupid were to do his work, he was going to have to find another way.

"It's time to get started," was all Nana said. She meant time for Cissie to get started on living life to the max, of course. Maybe her little tryst with Boone was a beginning.

"Good luck," said Frank.

Cissie still looked as if she'd eaten too many waffles. It was her mad-sad face. She'd put it on since she was a baby, when someone tried to feed her peas or left her alone in her crib.

"No, Dad," said Boone. "The Rogers ladies aren't leaving."

Glory be! A jolt of pure happiness lifted Nana's shoulders a fraction of an inch higher.

"They're staying here—with their cat," Boone went on in an unyielding tone, "until their house is finished. My place is convenient, and I have tons of room."

Nana could tell he wasn't sure deep down it was a good idea for him. No doubt he was reluctant to spar with Cissie and even more reluctant to fall in love. It was a messy collision of souls, and it was never very convenient.

As Cissie proved the next second: "No, thank you. We have to leave." Her jaw was set, just as if that spoon of baby peas was right in front of her mouth.

"That's right, they're going," said Becky Lee, then looked at her husband. "Surely, you can help them find a more suitable place. Boone's a bachelor. He doesn't know a thing about hosting anyone."

"Well, I—" Frank looked helplessly around the room.

"Dad, you don't need to help them or me," said Boone. "I got this."

"What about the cat? How will your father visit?" Becky Lee wrung her hands—thank God she'd never auditioned at the community theater—then turned to Cissie. "You don't want gossip."

"Gossip?" Cissie had never cottoned to it, which was why when it happened, she usually remained blissfully ignorant of it—by choice.

Becky Lee sent her a *duh* look. "You're single, and Boone's the most eligible bachelor in Buncombe County. Girls around here can get catty. Watch your back at Walgreens. That's a hive of intrigue, especially by the cards section."

"In that case, Boone had better beware," Nana said, "because there's no one in this entire town, state, and country more eligible than Cissie. He just might find himself in front of some crosshairs himself. Metaphorical ones, I would hope, maybe at the Ace Hardware."

"Everyone, please stop worrying," Cissie said. "We can't stay." She looked at Nana. "I haven't told you yet, but I'm running for mayor."

*My, oh, my, exactly what had happened last night?* "Fabulous idea." Nana knew full well that a little loving did wonders for a person's outlook. As did sit-ins, of course. And near misses with trees through house roofs. But loving, especially.

Cissie smiled like the Mona Lisa, further proof that the girl had been up to no good.

*Hurray!*

"You're running for *mayor*?" Frank practically blew back Cissie's hair. "Against Boone?"

Becky Lee looked at her son in triumph. "You can't have her here *now*."

Boone shrugged and looked effortlessly sexy holding his coffee cup the wrong way. "I knew she was running. She told me last night."

Becky Lee gasped.

It was getting old, her melodrama.

"I did tell him," said Cissie. "And we can't stay here. We've made other plans."

Lord, she was a fool. But Nana had been there once, too.

"I agree," huffed Becky Lee. "There are a million other places y'all could live. This is . . . this is outrageous."

Boone was like a rock. "What are Cissie and I going to do, Mom? We're running against each other for political office. This isn't war. Or *Survivor*. Or *Jerry Springer*, for that matter."

"Humph," said Frank in Cissie's general direction. "I still want to know why you think Boone's not doing a good enough job that you have to run for mayor, young lady. Except for a miserable eight years, the Braddocks have been mayors of this town for nigh on five decades. What kind of political experience do you have?"

"Why, none," she said, then turned to Nana. "We really can't stay."

"Let's talk in private," Nana replied.

"Mom and Dad, you should probably leave now," said Boone.

"But I want to *know*—" Becky Lee nearly stomped her foot.

"It's not a good idea for Nana and me to stay," Cissie said, her mad-sad face firmly in place, giving her away to anyone who knew her well.

Cissie wanted to stay.

Nana smiled at Boone. "I'd love to live here for a short while, dear."

Cissie opened her mouth to speak, but Frank cut her off. "Pardon my French, but you don't have a chance in hell of winning the mayor's office, so you might as well quit before you begin."

"Dad," said Boone, "you weren't speaking French. But you *were* being rude." He put down his coffee cup. "When we get this thing settled," he said directly to Cissie, which was brave of him, "we'll go to the post office and get your mail temporarily redirected here."

"That's a drastic step," said Becky Lee. "I'm sure the ladies will understand if this is too much for you."

"You do have your coaching duties," his father added. "You're in the middle of football season."

"And you have the election coming up," Becky Lee reminded him. "Let's hold the victory party here this time. You never entertain, and you should." She smiled at Nana. "That's the Braddock way."

"So we've heard." Nana didn't give a hoot that she'd never been invited to a Braddock party. "And apparently, so is presuming that a Braddock will win before the election is even held."

"You deserved that, Mom," said Boone.

Becky Lee glowered at him.

Frank had the grace to clear his throat. "Funny, isn't it? We're the two oldest families in town, and we never socialize."

"And now we're going to have Braddocks and Rogerses living in the same house," said Boone.

"I never agreed to that." Cissie's neck was getting pinker by the second.

"I can find you girls a place," said Frank hastily.

"No, Dad," said Boone. "They're *staying*. As soon as Cissie and Nana get things straightened out."

"Don't presume, please." Cissie got all prim and proper, which meant she was overwhelmed. "I haven't made up my mind yet."

"*She's* making up *her* mind about whether to stay with the man she wants to defeat in the mayor's race?" Becky Lee clung to her pearls. "It doesn't seem right somehow."

"Excuse me for a moment, everyone." Nana didn't wait to hear any polite assents before she moved to the far corner of the kitchen. "Cissie, dear, come over here."

Cissie followed like a little lamb. The crazy conversation had messed with her head.

"I want to stay," Nana told her in a low voice. Over Cissie's shoulder she saw the family of three huddled in their own conversation, apparently intense, as Boone's mouth was a thin line, Becky Lee's arms were crossed tightly over her silken tunic, and Frank was tugging on his ear.

Cissie's face registered panic. "I-I can't."

"Sure you can. I know you and Boone have some kind of thing going on." Cissie's eyes widened slightly. "But you can handle it."

"Why should I?" At least she didn't deny it.

"Because we'll never find accommodations this good, I promise. We may very well sleep on a pullout couch, or blow-up mattresses, with dogs sniffing our faces, cigarette smoke, and TVs going all night. Either that, or a pristine room with two twin four-poster beds, and we'll be required to dress for dinner and know the difference between eight spoons and forks and be on our best behavior all the time. Not to mention we've got Dexter. This place is as close to feeling like home as we'll get. And you need home. So do I."

Cissie's face fell. "I don't know. . . ."

"Use whatever energy you have going with Boone to fuel you. I don't care if it's positive, negative, or both. You haven't looked this good in years."

Her granddaughter rolled her eyes like a teenager, another good sign. "That's the altitude, probably. We're higher up here."

"Bull. It's sex. This is your nana speaking. Don't lie to me."

Cissie pressed a palm over her eyes. "Oh, God."

"Child?" Nana took her hand. "Give me an answer."

She dropped her hand. "Okay. We'll stay. But we need to keep it top secret. We'll have to get Mrs. Hattlebury to pretend we're living with her. And if things go downhill . . ."

"We'll deal with it, I promise." Nana hugged her.

They walked back to the group.

"We'll stay," Cissie said. "As long as we can pretend we're living with the Hattleburys. So just don't tell anyone."

"I predict fun times," Nana added.

"Great." Boone had quite the gleam in his eye. "Why don't you stick around a while, Mom and Dad? While we get everyone settled in?"

"No, I don't think so." Becky Lee looked at her pretty gold watch.

"We have things to do," Frank said, and made Nana's sternum rattle.

"That's a shame." Boone did his best to sound sincere.

Everyone started walking out of the kitchen toward the front door.

Nana almost chuckled. The master of the house probably thought keeping his parents at bay was the only reason he wanted Cissie and her to stay. Nana would play along, let him feel like a genius. Soon enough, Boone would get whacked between the eyeballs by the deeper motivation walking right next to him: Cissie, on her high horse, but prettier than a mess of fried catfish, as smart as the day is long, and plenty fun once she made up her mind to have some.

*Help her with that, Boone*, Nana said silently to his back. She and Dexter would stay well out of the way.

"How about coming back for supper?" Boone asked his parents.

Oh, he was diabolical.

"No," his mother said faintly. "Thank you very much for asking."

"We're busy." His dad was too irked to be polite.

"Don't let this stop you from dropping in almost every day." Boone tested his newfound luck even more. "I sure would miss that."

"I'm afraid we're booked for the next couple weeks," said his mother.

"Yes, sirree." Frank was mighty fond of that word.

"What a shame." Boone held the front door open for them.

"Well, it was nice talking to you both," Cissie called to them.

"Bye bye," said Nana, to get one last dig in at Becky Lee.

Talking about a victory party already—that was too smug by half!

When Boone shut the door behind them, he came back

into the kitchen. "Well." He grinned. "Welcome to my abode."

He might as well have been a lion making sure his lioness knew he was coming after her, come hell or high water.

As proof, Cissie's mad-sad face was gone. Her eyes were a brilliant deep blue. She was excited, despite herself, although she did her best to appear serious. "Thank you for your hospitality," she said solemnly to Boone, supposedly because Nana was making her be nice.

But what she really meant was, *I'll be waiting. Don't take me for granted. And you'd better be good.*

Nana nearly giggled aloud. *Oh, to be young again!*

"We sure do appreciate your offer," Nana said in her best helpless-old-lady voice. "We'll try to stay out of your way. Especially Cissie, being your opponent in the election and all."

"No need to." Boone grinned.

Nana tried to pretend she didn't see him looking down Cissie's shirt.

"But Nana's right." Cissie, oblivious to the perusal, made a valiant effort to stave him off. "Maybe we'll see each other in the kitchen because we have to, but other than that . . ."

"We don't even need to do that," Nana said. "We have the kitchenette upstairs, and a TV, too."

"None of that's necessary," Boone said. "We can rise above the fray and leave politics at the office."

The man was desperate for her granddaughter, that much was clear to Nana. "Cissie?"

"Yes?" She cast a half-lidded sideways glance at Boone.

Hell, they were like two thirteen-year-olds with their first crush.

"Promise to trust me on this one, okay? Out of respect for your elders." Nana rarely pulled that card out. But sometimes you did what you had to do. "We'll stay out of Boone's way."

"Of course, we will." Cissie had a bit of pique in her voice.

Good. She was as committed to keeping her promise as a bride with three grooms.

Nana laid her wrinkled hand on Boone's arm. "Give us at least the first week when she's collecting signatures. She doesn't need her enthusiasm watered down by feelings of guilt. If you spoil us too much, that's exactly what'll happen. She'll ring a doorbell with her clipboard, think about your waffles and coffee"—and probably his superior lovemaking skills—"and walk away before anyone even gets a chance to answer."

"Her?" Boone angled his jaw at Cissie. "I can't see that happening. When she makes up her mind—"

"She's stubborn, I know," said Nana. "But I'm older and wiser than you both. You don't need any distractions, either. Your parents had a good point. If we run into each other, fine. But no special treatment. This is a fine house, room enough for all of us to keep to ourselves. Isn't that lovely?"

Bless their hearts, they both went silent.

# CHAPTER FIFTEEN

An entire long, busy week passed for Cissie. She'd made numerous calls to the insurance people. A massive tree cleanup had begun. Boone assured her that his architectural contact was working on a new, improved design for the front of the house, and pending Cissie's approval, the building contractor had been hired to implement it.

A tree man in a cherry picker dumped all of Nana's and Cissie's clothes from their bedrooms into garbage bags and brought them up the road to Boone's house.

And Cissie had collected almost all the signatures she needed to get on the mayor's ballot. Nana told her to pretend she was in a play and act the part of the successful candidate. Stepping outside herself like that would take some of the edge off her nerves.

Funnily enough, that strategy worked. It didn't come naturally to Cissie to go up to strangers—and even people she knew—and start up a conversation. But when she gave herself lines, so to speak, she could do it. Her real self, the shy one, was tucked away safely inside.

She focused on the newer part of town, which included the recently built apartment complex. Surprisingly, she was a big hit there. She felt like a *real* candidate when they told her about how their water bills were too high and that there wasn't a park nearby. They also wanted to know why the elementary school didn't have a mascot and a statue of a colonial North Carolina patriot out front. All sorts of issues came up, which Cissie doggedly recorded on her cell phone's note-taking app.

Being mayor was a big job. And somehow Boone did it part-time. She admired him for being able to, although there were many items that needed addressing that he either hadn't heard about yet—or hadn't gotten around to.

But if he hadn't gotten around to them, no wonder. He'd barely been home the past week. Football practice had ramped up. And she'd read in the *Bugler* that the mayor's office had to entertain a visiting delegation from Germany, a group who'd come to see whether they should open a tire plant ten miles outside of Kettle Knob. It would employ nearly two hundred people, so that was a very big deal.

She'd only seen him three times the past seven days— once when she'd walked into his study to get a book around midnight and caught a glimpse of him there, poring over a bunch of papers.

"School stuff," he'd told her before she'd backed out.

He'd looked so handsome and tired, all at once, that her heart had nearly beaten out of her chest. She wished she could have gone in there and sat on his lap and kissed his cares away.

The second time had been in the downstairs kitchen to borrow some milk, but Nana had been with her. Cissie had been in her ancient striped flannel jammies, and she'd blushed.

The third time had been when she was going up the stairs as he was coming in the front door. She'd stopped on the tread and said hello and wished she could find an excuse to walk downstairs, but she couldn't come up with one.

Nana was right. She needed to stay away. *He* was the one making her highly anxious about the library! Why would she reward him with her attention?

He was just so damned attractive. And smart. And accomplished—in hot tubs and out of them. If only he'd been any other man in town.

But he wasn't. He was Boone. She'd even asked Nana one more time if they could move out of his wonderful house, and Nana said she didn't have time for such nonsense—she had a play to put on, and Cissie had more important things to think about, too.

Now it was time to walk into Starla's diner, where most Kettle Knobbers who had lived there for any length of time liked to gather. Cissie needed only four more signatures, and she was bound and determined to get them from tried-and-true locals. Walking down Main Street the past forty minutes, she'd picked up twelve signatures. She was a pro.

Outside the restaurant, in the shadow of the big elm tree, she gathered herself. Yes, Boone's mayor sign was plastered to the window, and Braddocks had dominated Kettle Knob politics the past sixty years. But that was no reason to slow her down.

She took a breath and opened the diner door. The usual hum of chatter died down to a brief silence. Some customers at the tables and counter stared openly at Cissie. She didn't frequent the diner very often. And in a small town, anything out of the ordinary was cause for speculation. But this time, she was sure everyone knew why she was there.

The chatter started up again when she walked to the counter.

Starla was busy making milk shakes. Cissie waited

until she was done. "I hope you got my note about the pies you made for the sit-in. They were delicious. Thank you."

Starla wiped her hands on her apron. "It was my pleasure. And I did receive your note. I must say I enjoyed getting a piece of mail in my mailbox that wasn't a bill."

Cissie smiled. "Well, you've probably heard the news. I'm running for mayor."

"I had heard that, and I think it's very cool."

"I heard the same thing," said an older gentleman on a stool next to Cissie. "It's interesting that a Braddock and a Rogers will be running against each other."

This was her chance to explain her platform.

"What really matters," she said carefully, "is that we have different opinions about how to carry Kettle Knob into the future. I think we need to preserve our town as best as we can, and that includes keeping the library where it is."

Starla moved a pair of salt-and-pepper shakers over by the menus. "It's a worthy debate that needs to be addressed. So hand over that clipboard. I'll be happy to sign it."

Cissie grinned and pushed it across the counter. "I promise next time I'll stay for lunch."

"You should." Starla scribbled her name on the form and pushed the clipboard back to Cissie. "We take the pulse of Kettle Knob right here every day."

"Would you like to sign it, too?" Cissie asked the old man.

He shrugged. "Sure. Why not see this old family rivalry played out?"

"There's really no rivalry." Cissie wished people would move on past that and stick to the issues. "We've just always had different interests. And now they overlap."

"Sounds intriguing," said a woman behind her.

Cissie turned around. It was someone from the theater, one of Nana's best character actors.

"No one has challenged Boone for mayor since he's been elected, and I'd love to see him really work to get voted back in." The actress held out her hand. "So I'll sign."

"Thanks." Cissie handed over her clipboard. This wasn't going to be so bad, after all.

"I don't think you'll win," the woman said as she wrote her name, "and I don't agree with you about the library. But good for you for trying anyway. Things have gotten dull around here. We need some drama."

"I don't want drama." Cissie clung to patience. "I'm running for a substantial reason. And I wouldn't do it if I didn't think I stood a chance. I know as much about Kettle Knob and what we need here as Mayor Braddock. It's good to get a change occasionally. We don't want anyone running this town on autopilot."

"Are you saying Mayor Braddock is?"

That voice!

Cissie resigned herself to a confrontation of some sort. When she turned, Janelle stood in front of a table of four diners, chic and confident as always. "Hi, Janelle. I'm simply saying that we need a fresh perspective."

Janelle put one hand on her hip. "As mayor of the neighboring town of Campbell, I disagree. Boone's an excellent mayor, and he's a fine high school football coach. He succeeds in both places, and it's because he knows what makes a winning team."

Cissie was no longer "in a play" in her mind. She was Cissie. Bungling, shy Cissie. She wondered yet again if she should be wearing something more exciting than her librarian clothes: skirts, blouses, simple dresses. And she also wished she had the chutzpah Janelle did.

"I'm saying," she began slowly, her heart pounding,

"Mayor Braddock's been unchallenged so long that it's time to shake things up at Town Hall. What he does with the Kettle Knob Academy football team is an entirely separate matter."

"I beg to differ." Janelle pulled out a stick of gum and folded it into her mouth.

"That's your prerogative," Cissie said.

"What do you propose to do to get town council on your side?" Janelle worked that gum like there was no tomorrow. "Why should they be? You have no experience in government at all."

Cissie girded her loins. "I'm a public librarian with eight years' experience managing our library under my belt."

The old man clapped, which gave Cissie a little boost of courage.

"Before I ran for mayor," Janelle countered, "I was president of the Junior Service League and Miss Buncombe County. *Twice*."

Well, la-di-da!

"We're both capable women," Cissie insisted. "It might behoove you to throw your political support behind the same girl who pulled you through Algebra Two in high school *and* taught you the difference between an atom and a molecule in seventh grade. I also recall selling all of your Girl Scout cookies for you outside the drugstore in fourth grade when you were too shy to do so because there was a German shepherd down the street who jumped his fence all the time."

So there.

Janelle had red flags on her cheeks. Cissie couldn't believe it, but she felt she was holding her own.

"Hi, Cissie." Boone appeared from behind Janelle and smiled at her in the courteous way a mayor should. "How's it going?"

"Fine," she said quietly back. But she was remembering his outright grin when he'd danced with her at the library. And she'd seen it again in the hot tub.

Oh, that hot tub. She'd been desperate to forget that night, but it was impossible when her body wanted it to happen again.

"Excuse us." Janelle doggedly chewed her gum, her eyes narrowed at Cissie. "We're meeting someone." She pushed rudely past, her large breasts swiping Cissie's tiny ones.

"See you later," Boone said.

*At home*, is what he meant.

He brushed by her, too, in a polite, professional way. Their hands accidentally touched, and a shock went up Cissie's arm as she remembered clutching that hand in the hot tub. She hadn't realized how much she craved seeing and touching him until this moment—when she had to pretend they didn't live in the same house.

Of course, they were mayoral opponents, too. On opposite sides. Their jobs were to defeat each other. He'd gotten the message, obviously, and now it was her turn. She should walk away.

But she didn't. She followed them.

And was shocked at herself. Maybe Nana was rubbing off on her. Or maybe it was the fact that she'd spent a whole week being brave.

Boone talked to people all the way to his seat. He slid into one side of the booth, Janelle in the other.

Cissie stood in front of them. "Who are you meeting?" she asked with a smile.

Janelle's heavily made-up eyes widened. "Why do *you* care? It's official business."

"County business?" Cissie had every right to know if it was. She was a citizen.

If it wasn't, then she was just a nosy person butting

into the private affairs of two very good-looking people. But it was a chance she was willing to take.

"As a matter of fact, it *is* county business," Boone said. "We're going to be talking to the county administrator about budgets again."

"Shouldn't all of Kettle Knob have input into those kinds of talks?" Cissie asked. "I didn't hear a word about the library until it was too late."

"That's why you vote your town council and mayor in," Janelle said smugly, "to see to these matters for you. Your newspaper should have covered the meeting, and if you had any objections, you should have voiced them then or petitioned the council to appear before it at the next meeting."

Cissie refused to be cowed now, even as Janelle unbuttoned her cardigan to reveal a sexy pink-and-white-striped silk blouse which put Cissie's camel turtleneck to shame.

She turned to Boone. "Did Edwina cover the issue of the library? I never saw it in the paper."

He didn't seem impressed by Janelle's décolletage, thank goodness. "She usually does." He pulled out a cell phone. "Let's ask her right now. Take a seat." He indicated the space across from him.

Cissie slid in next to Janelle, who stared at her as if she were a toadstool.

Cissie smiled back. It was mildly entertaining getting under Janelle's skin. "Here we are," she said. "Old friends."

Janelle scowled. "What is *up* with you?"

"Don't you remember Girl Scouts?"

Janelle finally looked a bit disconcerted. "That was a long time ago. People change."

"I didn't change. I still love Thin Mints. Do you?"

"*No.*" Janelle shifted uneasily. "I've moved on to dark chocolate, if you must know. It's actually good for you."

*Not as good for you as hot tubs and sex*, Cissie wanted to say.

And that was when she saw a bug stuck in the back of Janelle's hair, its spindly legs waving frantically.

Luckily, Cissie liked bugs. She felt sorry for this one. It was one of the ugliest bugs she'd ever seen. Janelle had hated learning about bugs and snakes in Girl Scouts.

Cissie tucked a napkin in her fist and put her arm on the back of the booth behind Janelle's shoulders.

"What are you *doing*?" Campbell's mayor asked.

"Stretching." Cissie smiled. "Remember the Girl Scout hug, though?"

*"No."*

Janelle was such a liar. She remembered. Cissie could tell by how vehemently she denied it.

Boone said something dreary to Edwina about meetings and recorded minutes. Everything he said sounded sexy, so while Janelle's attention was diverted by his husky drawl, in one swift motion Cissie pulled the bug off Janelle's hair with the napkin.

"Ow!" Janelle said, and scooted closer to the wall, away from Cissie.

"Sorry, my ring got caught in your hair." Cissie tucked the fisted napkin in her lap. She had no idea if the bug was alive or if she'd accidentally killed it. And she wasn't wearing a ring. Hopefully, Janelle wouldn't notice.

"Uh-huh," Boone was saying into his phone. He clicked off and put it away.

"What did Edwina say?" Cissie had been too busy with Janelle to eavesdrop properly.

A look of chagrin passed over the mayor of Kettle Knob's handsome face. "Edwina didn't cover that meeting. She was at a baby shower. She sent her fledgling reporter, who's since been fired for his crummy reporting skills. He's back working at the video store."

"So?" Cissie ignored Janelle's annoyed sigh. "Did *he* cover it?"

Boone shook his head. "He never mentioned the library issue in his article. It was an oversight. And we should have caught it at the mayor's office."

"You should have." Cissie couldn't let him off the hook, as much as she was totally into falling asleep every night remembering their hot tub encounter and those kisses in the hall at his house. "Edwina should have been more careful, too."

"*Our* paper in Campbell covered it." Janelle pulled out her lipstick and reapplied it in the reflection from her spoon.

"But your paper only comes out every two weeks, and it's for Campbell, not Kettle Knob. I have no reason to read it," Cissie said.

"Well"—Janelle dropped her lipstick in her purse and snapped it shut—"it was in there. It's a county issue."

"I think you should tell the county to slow things down," Cissie told Boone. "Get the people's input on the library merger before you follow through."

He had his thinking face on. "If the county guy ever shows up for lunch, I'll certainly bring it up." He called the waitress over.

Her name was Zoe. "Hey." She smiled at the table occupants. "I'm new in town. Nice to meet all of you."

Introductions and greetings were exchanged, followed by orders.

Zoe came back a minute later with Boone's pie and coffee, along with Janelle's tea.

"My brother's the news anchor at the ABC station in Asheville," Zoe said. "I should tell him about you two, Mayor Braddock and Miss Rogers. Your race should make for a good regional story—a Braddock versus a Rogers. I hear there's an old rivalry there."

"Not really," said Cissie faintly. "We're trying to stick to the issues."

"She's right." Boone's khaki-clad knees bumped up against Cissie's, and he didn't move them.

She didn't move hers, either.

She looked down at the napkin in her lap.

*Move your knees*, she told herself.

But she wouldn't. No, she wouldn't. Some deep inner hussy in her didn't want to.

Why wasn't he moving his knees? Was he even aware they were touching hers? He had to be.

She couldn't look at him. A horrible longing came back to her. Went straight to the breathless part of her and then to the warm center of her, which he'd so expertly trifled with, like the cotton candy man does at the circus when he waves spun sugar in your face and you get a whiff of utter deliciousness.

Zoe laughed. "Political issues don't bring up ratings as much as juicy human interest stories do."

"There's nothing juicy about this." Cissie's heart pounded hard from the knee situation. She knew very well she and Boone were juicy, but she had to think about the library.

She felt something stir in the napkin.

"Excuse me, I need to go." She stood and cast a hasty glance at her tablemates. "I enjoyed talking to you."

And touching knees . . .

"Likewise," said Boone politely.

But she saw a glint in his eye. He was remembering her naked, she was sure of it.

"Wish you could stay, Cissie," Janelle lied, and tossed off a fake smile for Boone's sake.

Cissie was all steam, heat, and misplaced passion— it belonged on the issues, not on Boone's body!—when she attempted to wriggle past Zoe and instead bumped hard into a man in a suit—the guy from the county. The napkin fell.

Where?

Cissie couldn't tell.

But there was a pageant-queen kind of scream. And there was the bug on the tabletop, scurrying toward Janelle, who screamed again and drew her knees up so hard she jostled the table and knocked Boone's coffee and blackberry pie into his lap onto those khaki pants.

"Dang." Boone stood and stared at his crotch, which was covered in pie and coffee.

"Where's the bug? Where's that damned bug?" Janelle shrieked.

"I'm so sorry," Cissie babbled, and grabbed another napkin off the table. She shoved it at Boone. "I was only trying to help. I'll wash those for you tonight—"

Zoe, who was also busy trying to calm Janelle, froze and looked at Cissie.

Janelle instantly stopped screaming. "*What* did you say?"

The man from the county said, "Sorry I'm late. Can I order now?"

"In a minute." Zoe looked between Cissie and Boone then reached into her apron pocket.

"I'll bet you're not supposed to make calls during work hours," said Cissie.

"Yeah." Boone threw the waitress his best mayoral look. "Take this man's order, please."

"I plan to," said Zoe, clutching her phone, "just as soon as I finish texting my brother that the two people running for mayor of Kettle Knob are living together."

"I never said that," said Cissie.

"Nor did I," added Boone.

"But she's doing your laundry," Zoe said.

"That's ridiculous." Janelle chewed her gum faster. "Why is she doing that, Boone?"

"It's only temporary," said Cissie.

"You *are* doing his laundry?" Janelle's eyes widened. She looked at Boone. "She is?"

"No," he bit off. "I do my own." He took a breath and looked around. "But she and Nana are living at my house right now until their own gets repaired."

"What about the Hattleburys?" Janelle's gaze was indignant.

"Nana and I don't know proper table etiquette," said Cissie lamely. "I can't tell a soup spoon from a teaspoon."

Janelle's perfectly sculpted chin jutted forward. "So you're telling me that out of everyone in Kettle Knob, Boone's the only one you could move in with when a tree falls through your roof?"

"No," said Cissie. "But it's convenient. He's just up the mountain." On a crag, one that was actually quite hard to get to. "Nana's older now, and we did what was easiest for her. And it's also none of anyone's business." She pretended she was in the library and looked down her nose at Janelle and then at Zoe.

Zoe grinned. "It's a good story."

"Then what are you doing working here?" Boone asked the waitress. "You should be writing for Edwina at the paper. She needs a reporter."

"Maybe I will." Zoe's eyes gleamed with new ambition.

No one even noticed that the bug was sitting right in Boone's empty saucer.

Cissie swiped it off the table into another napkin before Janelle could see. "I'm leaving." She picked up her precious clipboard, then remembered the county guy. "And you shouldn't move our library," she said firmly. "It's a *very* bad idea."

# CHAPTER SIXTEEN

Boone had gone a whole week without interacting with Cissie, thanks to Nana and her house rules. He'd had glimpses of the contrary librarian—two without her knowing. She liked to walk outside, and he'd watched her out his bedroom window, like a sick stalker except he wasn't one. He was the owner of the property, and he had a right to know where everyone was, especially a single, available woman who dressed in boring schoolmarm skirts and blouses that covered everything up and got his blood hotter than if she'd been in short shorts and a halter top.

So when she showed up at the diner, he'd been a little discombobulated by actually being in the same room as her, and then he was seriously impressed that she'd had the balls to follow him and Janelle to their table and ask them what they were talking about.

Things started to get weird when she'd been so awkwardly friendly with Janelle while he was on the phone. But he put two and two together when he saw the bug on the table and the squashed napkin in Cissie's fist.

The girl had to get herself into everything.

The best part had been sitting directly across from her

in the booth. He was taken right back to the hot tub, especially when their knees had knocked together—and neither one of them backed off.

It was a highly erotic experience.

Either that, or it was a silly game of Who's the Most Stubborn and Weird About Not Moving Their Knees, and he dug that, too.

He felt the absence of her when she left the table. It made him realize he'd been bored for a very long time. But after he exited the diner—gossip flying right and left about him and Cissie—and headed to his parents' house, he forced himself to think about other things that stressed him.

As he walked past the life-sized portrait of Richard in his parents' entryway, which he'd only done a million times before, he didn't need to look at the painting to recall that his late brother's thirteen-year-old gaze was compassionate, brave, outright heroic.

And Boone had never known him.

He wasn't one to fall into self-pity telling his family's tragic tale about Richard's cancer, or get psychologically wrapped around the axle, especially as his parents were straight out of psych textbooks themselves: for as long as Boone could remember, they'd tried to make Richard live on in him.

But Boone was used to it. Carried the weight lightly. He loved his parents. The more mellow he stayed about the situation, the less weird they were. It was only when he didn't call them on it and let them play out the fantasy too long that they ran into trouble.

So far his method had worked pretty well.

Except for one thing.

And there was really no way out of it now. It was embedded so deeply in their family story, Boone forgot that the lie was wrong to hide—except on a certain day in the autumn, when the weight of it was too heavy. It was a day he hated to go through every year, and that day was coming up.

He refused to think about it now. He had something else he had to do, something almost as painful. He wouldn't do it if it weren't necessary, but it was. He knew when he was in over his head.

"In here!" his mother called to him from the kitchen.

"Where's Dad?" he asked when he crossed the threshold.

"In his study." Mom leaned her cheek up for a kiss. "How's everything at your house with those two guests of yours?"

"Just fine," he said, "but the cat's out of the bag. Everyone knows. It was bound to happen sooner or later."

Becky Lee sighed. "What will people think about you living with your opponent? It's all very strange. What's the world coming to?"

"Don't worry, Mom. None of this is a big deal."

She pressed her lips together. "I think you're wrong. It *is* a big deal." She put down her paring knife. "I hear you were invited to the country club for lunch with some VIPs, including that lovely young singer back here for a visit—"

"Who's had a string of loser Hollywood boyfriends—"

"And the lieutenant governor. My goodness. Yet you turned them down."

"Yep." She didn't have to know he turned them down because he was overwhelmed at work. "Hey, I need to get a book from my room."

"Be my guest." Her tone was terse.

`Everything was fine. Boone was Richard's brother, but he was his own man, first and foremost, and his parents didn't have the power to sway his choices anymore.

He knew full well Frank and Becky Lee's flaws. He could scorn their sometimes selfish, boorish ways and love them and forgive them, all at once. They were only human.

Boone was an ambitious, bright thirty-two-year-old male.

He also read at a fourth-grade level.

He had dyslexia, and he hid it well from the world. It used to be his parents' choice.

Now it was his.

He wasn't ashamed of having serious reading challenges. But his parents were. And rather than risk getting rejected by anyone else—not in that mushy emotional way his parents had held him at arm's length, but on the job, on the team, at school, or in town—he kept it to himself.

He was a practical man who'd learned to work with his strengths and minimize his weaknesses.

He went to his old bedroom. Found the faded Hallmark card in his desk drawer. Sat on the edge of his bed and reread it twice. Three times.

Then he took out his cell phone and dialed. "Hey, Ella. It's Boone."

"Boone! How are you?" Ella was a potter, a few years younger than Boone. She had her own little business from home.

"Good. It's been a long time."

"Yes, it has."

He paused and looked at the card. "Your mom once told me that if I ever got painted into a corner to talk to you. She said she'd let you know I might take advantage of that offer someday."

"Mama got me to promise, and I did. I'm happy to help, Boone. Hearing you talk about her really brings her back."

"Yep. I miss her."

"Me, too."

He released a breath. "Well, I was hoping I'd never have to call. I thought I had this thing licked."

"Tell me what I can do," Ella said immediately.

"I can only ask my assistant at Town Hall to do so much reading for me without her wondering why I'm not doing it myself. It's for that reason that I don't ask her to check over the *Bugler*'s reports on town council meetings. That's an easy task I can do at my desk. But I missed an edition because I was swamped at school. There was a big oversight the mayor's office should have caught. I'm pissed no one on the town council noticed, actually. But the buck stops with me."

"I get that."

"I would love for you to read the *Bugler* for me and call me afterward and tell me any stuff you think I should know. I'd like to hear from you how they report on our council meetings, especially. Meanwhile, every day I try to keep up with all the other paperwork a mayor has to deal with, plus I grade papers at the high school and read all the emails there from the principal and the office. Sometimes I'm up all night trying to catch up."

"Boone, I wish this didn't have to happen."

"I'm okay with it. Honestly. I've always had everything under control. But these days . . ."

He told her about having to spend more time campaigning the next couple weeks now that he had an opponent—and about all the hours he'd be spending on the football field in addition.

"I'm going to be overrun with reading," he said, "so I'm going to need this additional help. I'd love to offer you a part-time job as my personal assistant."

"I'm interested."

"I'm glad. I understand you already have your own

career, your own priorities. But I'll pay you well, and I'll do all my own work. I just need someone to read things to me faster than I can do it myself."

"How many hours a week are you thinking?"

"Ten to fifteen, whenever you can fit it in. We can do some of this over the phone. I'll give you my direct number so you don't talk to my assistant. Sometimes we'll have to be together in the same room, though. I'll have stacks of papers to go through with you. I'd like to do that in private at your house, if you don't mind, the same way I used to do with your mom."

"That sounds fine."

"I'll park in your backyard, okay? I want to keep this on the down low as much as possible."

"That'll be easy. I have a lot of privacy here at the end of the block. In fact, you coming over here helps a lot. I don't have the most reliable car. Let's get started. Tomorrow sound good?"

"Perfect." His whole body relaxed a little. "Thanks. I'll swing by after breakfast."

"Great. The kids will be at school."

It was hard for him to speak about Mrs. Kerrison without his throat tightening up. "I can't say enough good things about your mother. Without her, I wouldn't be where I am today."

"Don't make me cry, Coach," Ella said on a low chuckle. "Or should I say 'Mr. Mayor'? I'm honored to work with you. And the cash will help. Always does. Making a living as a potter ain't for sissies."

"I hear you."

They chatted a little more about Ella's kids and how she was doing since her husband had left her, moved out of state, and wasn't paying any child support. Boone wished he'd thought about hiring her for something way earlier than now, just to help her pay her bills. When he hung up the phone, he was glad their business relation-ship would benefit them both.

But he'd not tell anyone. Especially his parents. They never talked about his "little problem," as they referred to his dyslexia, as if his six years being tutored in secret by his former sixth-grade teacher had never happened.

Richard hadn't had any trouble reading, according to his mother. Nor had Debbie, who was a professor at Duke.

Boone had been the only one.

# CHAPTER SEVENTEEN

"You don't look like no mayor," Sally told Cissie at the library the next afternoon. "And you need to. The television people are coming."

"How do you know?" Cissie's goal was to keep things normal at the library for as long as possible. She and Sally were working together on a new reading poster to hang behind the front desk—a scholarly worm sticking out of an apple, a book in its hand.

In a cartoon bubble, the worm said, "Reading Is Good for You!" Sally had painted the whole thing herself with poster paints on a roll of white paper donated by the meat department at the Harris Teeter. It was a funky worm, like something out of a psychedelic movie, and the words above his head were equally eye-catching, all zigzaggy and crazy, like Sally herself.

Cissie loved this poster. She could stare at it all day. Yes, a bookworm was a predictable theme in a library, but Sally's worm was special. The older people who saw it would talk to her about the good old days when they were students and brought their teachers apples. Toddlers would wave to the worm. Hank Davis already loved it.

He and Sally had done what they called the Worm Dance in front of it.

Speaking of her two favorite volunteers, it pained Cissie's heart to know they wouldn't be with her anymore at the new library if Boone's plan went through.

So maybe it was a long shot, her winning the election. But until the outcome was made clear—and even afterward—she was going to run that theme into the ground: keep the library in Kettle Knob, in part because she needed to keep Sally and Hank Davis with her.

They made the library special. They made her *life* special.

Sally finished painting a strangely cool top hat on the worm. "The redheaded reporter lady called while you was in the children's section with the Amish mama and her kids."

"That waitress at Starla's moved fast." Cissie picked up an empty jar of blue paint, wondered if she should bother ordering another for the craft closet, and decided that yes, she would.

"Oh, it wasn't Zoe who got in touch with them." Sally's chest puffed up. "I did."

*"Sally."*

"Well, of course I was gonna call! 'Cause no one did nothin' after the sit-in was over."

"You're right," said Cissie, her shoulders sagging.

"You was so busy getting signatures, and I was here with your replacement, and she didn't care nothin' about the library moving. She got on my last nerve with the way she hums all the time. Hank Davis hated her real bad. We're glad she's gone."

"Iron Man," said Hank Davis, and brought Cissie a *Where's Waldo?* book, his favorite.

Of course she would look at it with him. She took it and sat at a table. "Sit here," she told him, and patted the seat next to her.

"She cain't, Hank Davis." Sally ripped the book out of Cissie's hands. "The TV people's coming tomorrow. And Cissie ain't ready."

"Sure, I am. I know exactly what to say!"

"No one will care 'cause you ain't got style. You gotta get some style, like me and Hank Davis. The redheaded reporter lady say you cain't wear stripes or polka dots. They're interviewing Boone, too."

"That family isn't Amish."

"Don't change the subject. Nothin' matters but the TV people. And you. Go get your hair done. Get you something else to wear."

Cissie looked at her perfectly serviceable gray sheath dress and dusky pink cardigan. "I like this outfit. Gray and pink go well together."

"On your mama," said Sally. "Not you. Right, Hank Davis? Shouldn't Cissie wear bright red? Or orange? Somethin' like what I wear?"

Hank Davis picked up all the pencils in Cissie's pencil cup and put them back in, sharpened points up.

"That means yes," said Sally.

Cissie let the pencils be. "Okay. I'll try to look nicer for the interview. Although why I should—"

The library door opened, and in came Laurie. "She ready, Sally?"

"Just about."

"What are you talking about?" Cissie had a bad feeling.

"I'm taking you shopping," said Laurie, "at the new outlet outside Asheville. They have a free personal shopper if you spend over five hundred dollars."

"I can't do that!"

"Sure you can." Laurie flashed a shiny gold credit card.

"And then you're going to the beauty parlor," said Sally.

"I can't do that, either." Cissie balked. "I have a library to run."

"And I had an entire high school front office to run." Laurie folded one arm over the other. "Am I there right now?"

Cissie was touched and annoyed, all at the same time. "You didn't take off because of me. . . . Did you?"

"Hell, yes, she did," said Sally. "We got it covered. Me and Hank Davis is gonna run the library while Laurie gets you all sexed up."

"Sexed up?" Cissie was petrified at the thought. "That would be entirely inappropriate."

"I know." Laurie grinned. "And I love it. You and Boone are going to be interviewed at the same time."

"I can't wait." Sally did her Worm Dance. Hank Davis joined in.

"You never told me you danced with Boone at the sit-in," Laurie chided Cissie.

"It wasn't as if I wanted to," Cissie said. "He grabbed me by the hand and pulled me out the door."

Sally kept dancing, but she and Laurie exchanged knowing looks.

"Iron Man," said Hank Davis in the middle of a gyration.

"Don't you turn on me, too, Hank Davis." Cissie felt her face turn scarlet.

"She likes Boone," said Sally to Laurie.

"Who wouldn't?" Laurie put her hand on her hip and looked Cissie up and down. "And now you're living with him. And *doing his laundry*."

Sally finally stopped dancing. She clapped her hands,

bent over at the waist, and laughed so loud, it hurt Cissie's ears. Laurie giggled, too. Hank Davis leaned down and looked at his mother's face.

"I know." Sally waved a hand at him and kept laughing. "I'm gonna stop."

Cissie was about to complain when Sally finally stood up straight. "Hank Davis, put your hands over your ears."

He did as he was told.

"If you can't say it in front of him, don't say it at all," said Cissie.

"Okay, then." Sally pulled Hank Davis's hands down. "I won't say it."

But then she and Laurie sent Cissie very knowing looks.

She turned redder than ever. "I only kept it secret so people wouldn't look at me the way you are now."

"Honey," said Laurie, "as soon as you left Starla's, it spread around Kettle Knob like wildfire that you and Boone are living in the same house. Everyone thought you were staying with the Hattleburys. They swore up and down you were."

"Because Nana and I asked them to." Cissie refrained from rolling her eyes.

"I heard it from Hank Davis," said Sally.

Hank Davis stood tall and silent, like a totem pole.

"I left school before Boone got back for football practice," Laurie said. "But I heard he was acting like it was no big deal."

"Because it *is* no big deal." Cissie collapsed in the chair again. "Our tree fell through our roof."

"You could have stayed with me," Laurie said.

"You've got the boys."

"That's true. You'd be on Xanax by now if you stayed with us."

"How about me and Hank Davis?" Sally asked.

"I love y'all, too, but—"

"But we live in a garden shed," said Sally. "The pretti-est one you ever did see. I'm into the small house move-ment. You ever heard of that? Only cool people do it."

"Yes, but it would have been me, and Nana, and Dexter—"

"It's okay, sweet Cissie." Sally came over and ran her palm over Cissie's hair. "This is a good thing, you and Boone doing the hokey pokey."

"We are *not* doing the hokey pokey," Cissie whispered. Luckily, Hank Davis didn't appear to get what they were saying. "Boone's my political opponent."

Laurie crouched down by Cissie. "You're not yourself. Something is going on. Am I right?"

"You're right." Sally kept stroking Cissie's hair. "Hank Davis, go get me my purse. It's got a peppermint in it. I left it in the car. You eat that peppermint. And if anyone tries to come in the library, you shout, 'Boo!' I'll tell you when you can come back."

"No," said Cissie. "We can't do that to our library patrons."

"You do as I say, Hank Davis!" Sally was firm. "You say, 'Boo!' and scare them away."

Hank Davis walked out the front door of the library.

Sally looked at Cissie. " 'Boo!' ain't gonna hurt no-body. We all like 'Boo!' It adds excitement to our day."

Laurie took Cissie's hand. "Come on, darlin'. What's up?"

"Okay." Cissie inhaled, then exhaled. "I'll tell you. But you have to keep it a secret. Because it doesn't mean any-thing."

She told them both about her first night at Boone's house, about how forward she'd been and how amaz-ing he'd been in response, and as she did, she realized it *did* mean something: her crush on him was stronger than it had ever been.

It was so *stupid*.

But he was such a great kisser.

And more.

It was that *and more* part that she kept lingering on, although she could spend all night daydreaming about how he kissed.

"Even his knees are special," Cissie confessed.

"His knees?" asked Sally.

"Oh, yeah." Laurie nodded knowingly. "I remember those knees from high school."

She did?

"You are one lucky woman," Laurie added.

"*He's* the lucky one." Sally kept stroking Cissie's hair. "When's it gonna happen next?"

"Never." After this library situation was over, if Cissie lost the race, she really needed to move—someplace where she didn't cling to schoolgirl fantasies about hooking up with the quarterback. She needed a life. Somewhere out there was a perfectly average-looking guy with a big brain who would be crazy about her. She just knew it.

But she wasn't excited about it.

Laurie stood up. "Let's get going. We have no time to waste. Your eyebrows are in sore need of trimming. Boone doesn't like bushy eyebrows."

"I don't care *what* he likes," said Cissie.

"It's time to be the honey. Boone's the bee." Sally tugged on Cissie's hand.

"No," Cissie said. "*I'm* the bee, and I'm going to sting him for trying to move the library. I'll go get made up for the TV show if that will win me some votes, but I won't do it for Boone. Everybody, out of my way."

She grabbed her purse from the front desk. Laurie

came trotting after her. Cissie didn't even bother to look back to see what Sally was doing.

On the sidewalk, Hank Davis yelled, "Boo!" as she walked by.

But she didn't even flinch.

# CHAPTER EIGHTEEN

When Boone got home, he could feel Cissie in the house. He wished he couldn't because he needed to focus. He went straight to his study, shut the door, and called Ella. An hour later, they'd accomplished what they'd set out to do—to get through a big document from the county they hadn't had time to cover that morning when he'd gone to her house.

When he hung up, he tried to think of an excuse to go upstairs, but he'd made that floor so self-sufficient, there was nothing his guests really needed.

Besides, he still had tons of schoolwork to do. He needed to eat something easy and catch up on entering some student test grades in the online system the school used. He zapped a quick frozen dinner in the microwave, ate it quickly, and was on his way to his study again when Cissie and Nana came downstairs and caught him in the hallway.

At least, he thought it was Cissie.

Her hair was different.

Way different. It had golden-brown highlights that shone in the glow from the amber wall sconce like silken threads in a tapestry. And she looked like she'd just had a satisfying roll in the hay. He could see that the effect came from someone chopping her hair into different lengths around her face—it was wispy and kind of messy. But it was also curled on the ends, as if she'd decided she was also a demure lady.

She wore jeans and an old mustard yellow barn coat, and she'd never looked prettier.

"How are you two ladies?" he asked.

"Stupendous," Nana said.

"Pretty good." Cissie didn't look quite at him.

He wondered if she was embarrassed about her hair. Or maybe it was the scene she'd caused in the diner with that bug. Or their knees touching . . .

"Your hair looks nice." He thought it looked fantastic. But he didn't want to overdo it.

"Thanks." She sent him a tiny smile, and shoved up her glasses.

*Her glasses!*

They no longer had invisible frames. They were narrow tortoiseshell, geek-chic modern, straight out of a women's high-end fashion magazine. He wouldn't compliment her on them, though. If he overdid it, she'd think she looked bad before, and she never had. Even at her most buttoned up, she was someone he should have noticed long ago.

"I'll buy you a new pair of khakis if the cleaners can't get the stains out," Cissie insisted, those blue eyes earnest with regret.

"No need." He'd refused to let her launder his pants, and there was no way he could get them clean. "I have a lot of pants in my closet. Besides, you're not the one who screamed and knocked over the coffee and pie."

"Goodness, all over a silly bug," said Nana.

None of them had had a chance to discuss the situation the night before, maybe because Cissie had clearly hidden herself away upstairs and Nana had been at re-hearsal.

"It came from outside and got stuck on her hair," Cissie explained, "but it was in the restaurant, which is reason enough to be . . . squeamish."

He knew she really meant hysterical and out of control. It was nice of her to let the mayor of Campbell off the hook. "I wondered why you were being so friendly to Janelle. You two aren't exactly pals."

"Well, she should be Cissie's pal now," Nana said. "I would have let the bug stay."

Cissie's purse was slung over her shoulder, so the two women were obviously headed out. Boone felt a little be-reft at the idea of being alone in the house, although he knew he should get back to work. "Where are you off to?" he asked anyway.

"We have to take more pictures of the house for the insurance people before the sun goes down," said Nana. "They just texted Cissie. They want to see more before they give final approval to the contractor tomorrow morning."

Boone had been superbusy the last couple days, but he'd checked on the site on his own the morning after the tree fell, when the roofers had covered the house with tarps and the tree cutter had started working. The insurance company had hired the most reputable guys right away.

"Today I had to show them documentation that we got the tree pruned regularly," Cissie said, "and that no ar-borist had ever suggested it would fall."

The insurance company had better not give these ladies grief.

"Can I come with you?" Boone's school chores would have to wait, but he consoled himself that he was giving moral support to two people who might need it.

"I'd love it if you took my place," Nana said, looking suddenly older and weary. She was a good actress, but Boone was no dummy. "Tonight's my only night off from the theater until the weekend."

"You don't have to go with me," Cissie told him. "I can manage."

"It'll go quicker with two people taking pictures," he said. "We're running out of time. We can take my fun truck."

His '65 Chevy, cobalt blue with shiny chrome bumpers.

Cissie had no choice but to say yes, unless she wanted to be extremely rude, which he knew she would never be. She hugged Nana, and they were off.

They weren't going on a date, but when they walked down the front steps of his house together, Boone felt a different vibe between them.

"I've seen you in this truck around town," she said at the shed. "I've always wanted a ride in it."

"Oh, yeah?" When he opened the door for her, he couldn't believe she'd been living below him on the mountain for years and they'd never connected, not even to wave to each other when he was driving.

The truck rode smoothly down the steep road. He kept his gaze ahead—you really had to when one little mistake meant you'd go off the edge of a cliff—but he was very aware of her. She smelled like honeysuckle and warm cotton.

There was some tension in the air, definitely, and for a lot of reasons. But he'd do his best to put her at ease. "So are your parents really leaving it up to you and Nana to take care of everything?"

He turned into the Rogerses' property. It was fronted by nothing more than a beat-up black mailbox. The truck swayed and bounced down their dirt driveway.

"They're very laid back," Cissie said.

He stole a glance at her now that it was safe to do so. "They must be. They sound a lot different from my parents."

The house came into view—it pained him to see the remnants of that beautiful old tree cut up into pieces and stacked for hauling away. The front porch and kitchen were nothing but matchsticks and broken windows.

"It's so sad," she said.

Her profile was beautiful, he thought, as he put the truck into park. They looked at the scene for a good ten seconds without speaking.

"All the stories told on that porch," Cissie whispered. "All the living done in that kitchen."

"You'll rebuild. And you'll be happy with it." He got out, walked around the truck, and opened her door.

"Thanks." She slid out.

"I wish I could fix this for you right now."

Her smile was a little wobbly. "Wouldn't that be nice?"

"Why don't we each take pictures, and then we'll compare them when we get home?"

"Sounds good."

Home. He liked thinking of her going back there with him.

What was wrong with him? He was getting soft. He really didn't want someone to share his life with up close and personal—he was a public servant with some private issues, and he'd like to keep it that way.

But for now, he enjoyed seeing this woman blossom right before his very eyes. She looked sexy and cute walking around with that camera in her hand.

"Stop!" he called to her.

She looked back, caught him poised with his camera, and grinned despite herself.

He snapped the picture.

"Not fair!" She laughed. "Stand still."

So he did. He was used to getting pictures taken for the paper with constituents—at the recent spate of church autumn festivals, he'd been besieged—and the *Bugler* often took photos of him on the sidelines of Kettle Knob Academy football games.

Cissie snapped the picture and lowered her phone. "You should have been a menswear model. For Levi's."

"Someone must have paid you to say that."

"Nope." She sounded a little flirty, but then she turned away from him to take another picture of the house.

He wanted to race up to her, grab her by the waist, turn her around, and kiss her. But of course, he couldn't do that. He walked thoughtfully past the freshly cut wood and took pictures of the house instead. They only crossed paths once, and when they did, Cissie sighed and said, "This is torture, seeing everything up close."

"Yeah, it is," he agreed.

But he meant her. It was torture not pulling her close and kissing her.

He took a bunch more pictures to dull the sexual ache. It didn't work, especially when she came up to him and he could smell her shampoo or perfume or whatever it was that reminded him of lace and flowers and dainty girl stuff.

"I think I'm ready to go," she said.

"Already?"

"Sure. Didn't you take a lot?" She got elbow to elbow with him to scroll through her pictures. "Mine are pretty good."

"Mine, too. But let's go look at the sunset." He didn't dare grab her hand. He angled his head toward the front of her property, where the lawn disappeared into nothing but rock, a sparse couple of bushes, and empty space, below which were rolling mountains and a scarlet red sun dipping behind them and casting beams of light across the magical landscape.

They walked to the promontory together.

"Why," she said, "would anyone live anywhere else but here?"

"I don't know." He was quiet. "If something took me away, I'd always have to come back."

"Me, too." She inhaled a deep breath and smiled up at him.

There was no agenda there, just a connection between two small beings admiring a big, beautiful world.

"Thanks for letting me join you." It felt right and natural to reach for her hand.

She grasped his fingers back. Squeezed. Let go a half second later. "We should get back. I have to watch *Jeopardy!* with Nana." She shot him a shy-as-a-rabbit smile and walked away.

Scurried, more like it.

That made him smile, but still he lingered for another second or two. A magnificent tree and part of a homestead might be gone, but there was so much left here on Rogers land to cherish and protect—a view, a family history, two incredible women. No insurance company in the world could assess or cover their value.

Boone's legs were longer, so he beat Cissie back to the truck and had the door open and waiting.

"You're such a gentleman," she teased him.

"I am." Something in him, near his heart, stirred. He was fifteen again, on a first date.

But it wasn't a date.

And they were both in their thirties. Real love—the passionate, soul-wrecking kind—was for people with boundless futures. For dreamers and doers who weren't tied down by facts, like families who needed them, jobs that were fulfilling but weren't perfect, and towns that had grabbed hold of them long ago and demanded they never change.

She looked down at her lap, and he shut the door. He wanted to know more about her. He could ask Nana, but he didn't want to give her the satisfaction. He got that Nana didn't come tonight for obvious matchmaking reasons. Older people couldn't stand seeing two younger single people together but *not* together.

He just knew that Cissie's grandmother was back home chortling right now, and he didn't begrudge her that—in fact, he was crazy about Nana. But he was going to go about this his own way.

"What was it like for you, growing up in that house?" he asked Cissie on the way back up the mountain.

"I always assumed everyone had parents like mine. There were no rules. They almost treated me like a peer."

"That must have been weird."

"I amused them—they asked me questions and laughed at all my answers. When I was a teen, they liked to engage me in big intellectual debates. They were very affectionate but only up to a certain point. Inevitably, they went back to their research and left Nana in charge of the household. And of me."

"Wow." His parents were all over him, all the time. Still were.

"Can you imagine having Nana in charge of you?" She chuckled.

"No. I'll bet you two got up to all kinds of mischief."

"Nana did. Not me. Both my parents and Nana encouraged me to be an independent thinker—but their way was through academia. Hers was all over the place . . . in the store, on a stage, at school. I didn't cooperate, however."

"You were shy at school. You seemed to love the rules. Forgive me for saying."

"It's okay. You're right." She smiled, but he saw some wistfulness there. "The last thing I wanted was to be Miss Independent. It was too scary. I wanted parameters that I never got. I wanted to be fenced in with all the other kids. I didn't know how to, so I made rules and stuck to them. At least it was something."

He was quiet a minute. "You like being a librarian?"

"Yes." She sighed. "I admit that part of it is because it's an orderly profession. There's cataloguing. Stacks of books. Alphabetical everything."

"Are you OCD at all?"

"Nope. Just neat and organized. I can walk away from a mess if there's something better to do."

"Like what?"

"Something exciting . . . like a great movie. Or a good book."

"Or a cute guy?"

"No," she said. "Stop teasing me."

"I'm not teasing. You told me about the boyfriend in college. But surely, since then . . ."

"I've been out on the rare date. Not locally. It's always been when I visit my college girlfriends, who sometimes set me up with their guy friends. It's happened at a couple weddings, baptisms, and thirtieth birthday parties, too."

"Ever gone on one of those dating sites?"

"*No.*"

"Me, either."

"I have nothing against them. I know sometimes they work. But I'm not good at meeting strangers. It stresses me out."

"That makes sense."

"I know why you haven't used those sites."

"Why?"

"You don't need to."

He pulled up into the shed and switched off the key. Turning to her, he placed his arm across the back of the seat. "That's not why."

There was a beat of silence.

"Will you tell me why?" she asked quietly.

He reached out, grabbed a lock of her freshly cut hair. "No."

She kept her eyes on his. They were deep smoky blue pools of understanding behind those fashionable frames. But how did she know that was what he needed? Someone who understood that he just couldn't speak about it?

Most people would have pressed.

She didn't.

The shed was warm and quiet around them. Dust motes kicked up in the beam of red-orange sunlight between two buckled wall boards behind her head. Night would fall very soon.

He wanted to kiss her. Badly. In the light, on meadow grass, with a blue sky overhead. And in the dark, too, beneath cool sheets, their two bodies hot and melded.

She was ripe, ready. He saw it in the way her lips were slightly parted.

"We should go," he said. And wanted to kick himself.

"Yes."

He didn't want to go. He only said that because he was afraid. He had no idea why. He'd never been afraid before when it came to women. But something in him said, *Forget this. Stop lingering. Move on before it's too late.*

Still, they sat.

He pulled a little on that lock of hair framing her face and drew her closer to him until they were a nose apart. "I want to kiss you."

"But you'd better not," she said softly, and pulled back an inch. "We're political opponents."

He took off her glasses and put them on the dashboard. "Someday, we won't be."

"True." She looked away. "But by then, one of us will have lost. There might be hard feelings."

"I didn't think of that. So we might as well go for it now."

She looked back at him, a delicious wrinkle on her brow. "A kiss. Anything more and we can't be effective candidates. I'll stay on my side and you stay on yours."

"Good plan."

She leaned forward. He met her halfway.

The kiss was long, slow, and deep. He immediately hardened, but he forced himself to stay on his side of the seat. She tasted of sweet mint. Her mouth was a pillow—soft, warm, and inviting. He wanted to caress it with his own mouth and tongue forever.

She whimpered. Put her hand on his neck, right above his open collar.

"I want you," he murmured against her mouth. "I can't forget seeing all of you, holding you. Touching you."

"I can't forget, either." She sighed. "But we have to."

"I refuse to forget." He reached out with one hand and caressed her breast. She leaned into his hand. Sighed. The kiss went on, pure erotic torture—

She gave a little cry and wrenched away. "I can't. If we keep going like this . . ." She grabbed her glasses from the dashboard and put them back on.

He looked down. There was only maybe half a foot of space between them. "Time to go, huh?"

"Nana will be looking for me. And I have to get these pictures emailed." She quickly rolled up her window.

He did the same.

"We're being stupid," she said sheepishly.

"Stupid is good sometimes."

She laughed, and he loved it.

"I guess you're forbidden fruit," she said, "my opponent in the election. It's all very understandable from a psychological standpoint."

"It's very understandable from a guy standpoint, too," he said. "You're pretty. Outright sexy, actually. Of course I want to kiss you."

"Really?"

"If you'd even looked at me once in high school the way you looked at me five minutes ago, I would have been knocking down your door. It's not the new hair and the glasses. It's *you*."

She dimpled. "Thank you." She looked away, then back. "I'm shy except with my family and friends, like Laurie and Mrs. Hattlebury and Sally."

"They sure are an interesting group of friends."

"I know." She gave a short laugh, opened her door, and slid out of the truck before he could get to her door and open it himself.

"It's all right," she said, when he came around a second too late. "Sometimes a girl has to open her own door. Just to remember how nice it is when a man does it for her."

He shut it behind her. Pressed her up against it.

"Damn this election." He took off her glasses again and kissed her for all he was worth.

One more time.

# CHAPTER NINETEEN

Cissie couldn't help hoping that the whole world would notice how professional she looked and how confident she felt the day of the television interview. She arrived at the library in brand-new slim black cigarette pants, black flats, and a short zebra-striped trench coat carelessly tied over her jewel-toned turtleneck. She also carried a tote bag filled with changes of clothes.

But when the redheaded reporter walked into the library with a posse of a cameraman, a lighting guy, and someone with a black backpack—presumably a makeup person—Cissie did a double take. This person wasn't the redheaded reporter she'd been expecting.

"Anne Silver?" She worked at *Morning Coffee*, a Sunday morning news program seen across the country. "What are you doing here?"

Anne smiled a smile Cissie had seen hundreds of times and introduced herself. "Please call me Anne. May I call you Cissie?"

"Sure." Cissie couldn't cover up her shock. "But—but you're from a national network show."

Anne took her jitters in stride. "I thought they told you we were coming."

Cissie tried not to feel nervous, but who wouldn't? "I assumed it was the affiliate in Asheville."

Anne smiled, her peach-tinted lips shining under the library's old electric chandelier. "The Asheville station contacted us, and we thought it would make a great story for *Morning Coffee*." She gazed around the room. "Your story will fit in perfectly. It's a slice of Americana: two people running for mayor who also live in the same house."

Cissie didn't want to be on national TV. She didn't want the entire country to hear about her staying at Boone's house. It was bad enough that their region was going to speculate about what was going on between them.

"The real issue is so much bigger," she said, glad she'd found her voice again. "It's about protecting good things, like this old library, in the face of pressure to modernize all the character right out of a place."

"This building *is* charming." Anne sounded sincere and her eyes registered genuine concern. It was how she'd gotten to be so famous. "But let's be blunt: that fight is going on everywhere, and it will always go on. Things get old, Cissie, and we have to decide every day: should we save them—or move on? Your situation is different— quirky—because of the two players involved."

Cissie felt the edge of panic. "I could call someone else right now to find a new place to stay. And then your story would be meaningless."

"Go ahead." Anne sounded perfectly friendly. She folded her hands, the epitome of calm. "I'll wait." She gave a little chuckle. "Honestly, if the story is that flimsy, we'll fly back to New York, and we'll tell our Asheville affiliate to be more careful screening potential stories before they call us."

Cissie pulled out her phone, paused, then put it away. She felt so stupid in the face of Anne's poise. "But my grandmother likes him," she said softly. "She has a nice, soft bed, and basically her own apartment. I'm not going to uproot her. I just don't want to."

Anne's large eyes were luminous with sympathy. "It sounds like she should stay there. But what about you? Couldn't you move?"

Damn these TV people. They certainly knew how to prod.

"Of course I could," Cissie admitted. "But families stick together." She really meant it, too. No way was she going to leave Nana and Dexter alone in that big house, then go find a couch to sleep on somewhere else. "And— and it would be stupidly obvious why I moved, which might set even more tongues wagging."

Yes, it was a bonus that she was staying with an incredibly good-looking guy with amazing skills in the sex department.

But Boone wasn't the main thing.

*Yes, he is*, an unrelenting voice in her head said. *You care about Nana's comfort, but don't lie, don't lie, don't lie. . . .*

"I know how small towns work." Anne shook her head slowly. "I'm from one. So I understand your plight."

Cissie's hand rested on the big maple desk, the one that had been used by librarians in this building for over a hundred years. "I want to focus on the reasons I'm running for mayor," she said. "Not my living situation. If you can't do that, I'm sorry, but I can't participate."

Anne finally looked a little worried. "Okay." A few seconds went by as she appeared to be considering the situation. "Here's what I propose: I promise we'll be evenhanded. We'll concentrate on the issues with an in-depth look at both candidates' views. We'll mention that you're living together, but we'll explain *why*. Please. Let's go forward with this. You'll be able to tell all of America why your library should be saved. They can't vote in your election, but they can take your message back to their own communities."

That was a really convincing argument. "Okay," Cissie reluctantly agreed. "I'll do it. But I mean it, Anne. I'm counting on your promise."

"I assure you, I didn't get to the network by being a shoddy reporter."

Cissie did feel better.

"I want you to get excited now," Anne said. "This'll be fun."

"It will?" Cissie felt that panic again when she saw the cameraman lifting his camera to his shoulder. The lighting guy had been busy working all along, and now he was ready.

"We'll need to do a little touch-up first," Anne said, and the makeup lady stepped up to do just that. "And after we capture you in your work environment, we'll meet up with the other crew and Mayor Braddock. That's when the interviewing will begin."

Cissie had this, even when Sally and Hank Davis came in five minutes later and Sally fell to the ground when she saw Anne, and Hank Davis yelled, "NASDAQ," over and over, as loud as he could.

Two other patrons came in a few minutes after that, the teenage girls who loved dystopian near-future young-adult fiction, Cissie explained to Anne in one, long breath. The cameraman got a great shot of Cissie stamping old-fashioned cards the girls had signed and tucking the cards into old-fashioned pockets in the backs of their books.

The camera guy also took tons of shots of the library, both inside and out.

Cissie felt so proud when he lingered in the archive room, where one particular letter—the one her ancestors had written about Kettle Knob's role in the battle of King's Mountain during the Revolutionary War—was framed on the wall.

"So Boone's family fought in that battle?" Anne sounded impressed.

Cissie nodded. "And our family *wrote* about it and made sure we saved the account. This is it. The original."

"Cool." Anne didn't sound as impressed by the Rogers family's feat as she did by the Braddocks'.

Cissie was used to that. Quiet academic types were used to being overshadowed by the big, messy marauders whose accomplishments they documented. But then she had to wonder . . .

"Have you met Boone yet?" she asked Anne.

The reporter's eyes lit up. "Oh, yes. What a fine example of a modern mountain man."

Cissie wanted to laugh. If Boone heard that description of himself, he would, too.

Even so, a spark of unwanted jealousy flamed and she shoved it aside, but not before checking to see if Anne wore a wedding ring.

She didn't. *Damn.*

Maybe it wasn't too late to back out. "Anne?"

"Yes?"

The cameraman was still shooting the library—now he was focusing on the beautiful old molding on the ceiling.

"Never mind," Cissie said. This was her chance to show off her library, to celebrate Kettle Knob. On national TV.

She was lucky.

Really.

Boone wondered if he ever should have agreed to this interview. His first instinct had been to say no. But his parents had convinced him that it would be great for Kettle Knob.

And he'd caved.

"For corn's sake, you're the *mayor*," his dad had said when he and his mother barged into the house at breakfast time. Every minute or two, Frank held a handkerchief to his nose to ward off the hideous possibility of cat dander. "Turn this opportunity down, and you'll look like you're not proud of your town."

Cissie was already out of the house—she'd fled before Boone could see her, but he'd heard her little crap car coughing its way down his elegant driveway. Nana was upstairs watching the *Today* show with Dexter.

"If they try to make this about you and Cissie Rogers," his mother said, "that's your own fault. And you'll just have to put a stop to it." She inclined her head. "That TV upstairs sure is loud."

"We like *Good Morning America*," his dad said.

Of course, Braddocks and Rogerses would like different morning programs.

But now they'd both be on the same one.

"We want *real* North Carolina," Anne said to Cissie and Boone a little later. They'd met at the town gazebo, a perfectly nice place to conduct an interview. "Which is why we thought we'd chat about your mayor's race here on the town square and then cut away to you four-wheeling, white-water rafting, and maybe even listening to bluegrass."

"You're pulling our leg," Boone told the cameraman. "Right?"

The guy shrugged.

"No," said Anne. "There's a bar in town—"

"It's called The Log Cabin." Cissie's face had gone white.

Some people just didn't like white-water rafting, and Boone figured she must be one of them. Or maybe it was four-wheeling she hated. No one could hate blue-grass. He was tempted to throw an arm over his oppo-nent's shoulder and pull her in for a hug, but that wouldn't do, not with the hawk-like Anne waiting for any sign of romance between them.

Anne stood a little taller. "You both look surprised. But our program prides itself on getting to the heart of a setting. Don't you remember the time we interviewed the modern-day gold prospector near the rattlesnake nest in Nevada? And how about that wonderful woman in Ohio who built her own hot air balloon? We inter-viewed her at one thousand feet."

As a matter of fact, Boone did remember. "That was years ago."

Anne smiled. "We're trying to bring back some of the adventure aspect. We've gotten lame, according to focus groups. So we did our research." She looked at her camera-man. "What else does the typical resident do around here, José?"

"Trout fishing, kayaking, hunting, making granola, crafting, quilting, zip-lining . . ."

Were these people for real?

Boone cleared his throat. "I fish. I kayak. I've hunted quail a couple times, and I go four-wheeling regularly. I've even done my share of zip-lining. Heck, I support quilt artisans and crafters, and I regularly go to local places with really excellent live bluegrass. But I have *never* made granola. I don't know about Ms. Rogers." He looked at Cissie.

"Of course I do." She tossed him a cool glance. "I thought everyone made their own granola around here."

Wow. She was being flippant and standoffish, and

he liked it. He wanted to pick her up, sling her over his shoulder, and take her back to his cave.

"Cool," said Anne. "How about the other activities, Cissie?"

"Absolutely. Except for the hunting, I do them all." She was lying through her teeth, but she shot him a brazen look of challenge.

He didn't blink.

Oh, it was on.

"Great." Anne clapped her hands. "You two are *so* North Carolina!"

"I've got to be honest." Cissie had her best prim-librarian face on when she nudged up her glasses. "I have serious doubts about this rafting idea. I don't see why we need to go that far, or do all those other things. It smacks of a ratings grab. And it feels condescending."

She was brave to talk back to the big New York reporter. Boone had to admire her for that. And here he was sitting like a country bumpkin waiting for directions, mainly because Cissie distracted him. She was sitting too close.

Anne Silver was like her name—elegant and polished as a silver tray in his mother's dining room. Cissie was more your morning mug of coffee. Beneath that stylish outfit and hair, she was still someone who felt necessary and comforting. Someone who jolted you out of your rut.

And it pissed him off. He barely knew this girl. How could she be making such a big impression on him already?

*You do, too, know her. You liked her in fourth grade . . . not just her shiny spectacles but her lack of interest in being anything other than herself.*

Anne's reply was immediate. "I assure you, we're not

trying to be condescending, Cissie, although I appreciate your candor. Isn't that what mayors have to do every day, handle multiple tasks, sometimes at once, often thrown at them unexpectedly?" She looked between them both, an assessing gleam in her eye.

"I have no doubt." Cissie's tone was firm. "But it's an odd way to test our political mettle."

"Ditto what Cissie said," Boone said. They were rivals, but they kept landing on the same page. "I'll be frank, too. I agreed to do *Morning Coffee* to give the country a solid look at Kettle Knob. Your producer told me the segment won't be all about the mayor's race."

"We're doing an excellent overview of your town," Anne said. "We'll talk a little bit about its history, and we've already got some shots of the diner, the town square—with a super shot of the gazebo—a residential street with some charming cottages on it, and of course Town Hall and the library. We're also sending a crew up to get outside shots of your houses while you're on your adventures. Boone, I hear you live in a spectacular home."

"Heard?" he asked skeptically.

"Okay, we looked it up on Google Maps," Anne admitted. "As for Cissie, the story of the big tree that's fallen through your roof will provide a lot of drama."

"That tree is the only reason Nana and I are at Boone's," Cissie said.

Oh, nice. He felt real special now.

"Of course, we appreciate his hospitality," Cissie added.

Too late.

He moved a few inches away from her just to make her feel bad.

But she didn't. She was smiling. He looked where she was looking. At the foot of the gazebo steps, Sally and Hank Davis held a big sign that said "Cissie for Mayor."

The letters were painted like stained glass and in a strange, almost primitive font that was actually quite cool. Hot-pink ribbons hung through holes reinforced with Hello Kitty duct tape at all four corners.

"What's that about?" Anne asked Cissie.

"We don't have a budget for signage." Cissie sounded happy as could be. "So Sally is making mine out of butcher paper and cardboard and hanging them wherever she can."

Which was strictly against code, but Boone would whisper in Scotty's ear not to bother enforcing it.

"What will happen to your signs if it rains?" Anne asked.

"My team and I will try to rescue them," Cissie said, "but if we can't get to them fast enough, I guess they'll get mushy and fall apart."

She was running a crude grassroots campaign. There was something very appealing about that. She was smart and capable, yet how would that hold up against a guy who had all the experience and very few complaints from his constituents about his time in office?

Anne turned to him. "What about you? I saw one sign for you in the window at the diner. That's a rather measly amount of publicity. Do you advertise another way?"

"No." He felt a twinge of embarrassment, which was a new thing for him. "I've done very little up till now"— he looked at Cissie, who arched a brow at him—"but I'm ramping up."

Now *he* was fibbing. He hadn't made a single plan.

"You have a little over two weeks to the election," Anne reminded them both.

Sally got busy hanging Cissie's sign on the back of a bench. If Scotty complained, Boone would insist that hot-pink bows were much better fasteners than tape.

"Do you wish you had longer to campaign?" Anne asked Cissie.

"Not really." Cissie pulled a strand of that newly golden-brown hair behind her ear. "I can get everything I need to say out in a little over two weeks."

No way would her house be ready to move into in by Election Day. In fact, by Boone's estimate, it would be at least four weeks. So when she lost the election, she'd be looking for a new place to stay, he had no doubt.

He wasn't looking forward to that. In fact, in light of the short time frame he had left to hang out with her, he'd tell Nana tonight—politely, respectfully—that it was time to relax her over-the-top, crazy rules about where they all stayed in the house, which she'd extended just this morning. He was on to her. Nana obviously wanted him to crave what he couldn't have, and it was working. He couldn't take another minute of knowing Cissie was there walking around above his bedroom ceiling, and he couldn't get to her. At least to *talk*.

He wasn't a sex pervert. She was cute as a button, and entertaining as hell, and she didn't put up with anything she didn't like from him, which he found refreshing.

Plus, yeah, he kinda sorta did want to make out with her and then get her naked—in the worst way, actually—somewhere preferably soft and cushiony, like his bed.

"How about you, Boone?" Anne asked him. "Your opponent didn't surface until now. So is the election coming up too soon for your taste?"

"It actually is," he said. "I wish I had longer. A lot longer."

Anne's phone rang. "Excuse me a minute." She took the call and walked down the gazebo steps to a nearby tree. The cameraman trailed after her and lit up a cigarette.

"Why would you want longer to campaign?" Cissie's glasses glinted in the sun.

He couldn't tell her the truth: he wanted longer with her in the house. Longer with her talking back to him, and just being there.

"A politician never reveals his campaign strategies," he said instead. "Especially to his rival."

They were foes, all right. He loved their more intimate battles. She slayed him with her sexiness, set fire to his blood. He wished he could lay her down on the gazebo floor and have his way with her.

She blushed, and he knew beyond a shadow of a doubt she wasn't thinking about the mayor's race. She was either reading his mind or remembering their kissing session in his pickup truck. Her mouth was set just so. . . .

He now recognized that as her hot-and-ready expression. But he had to steel himself against her charm. It wouldn't pay to embarrass himself with a public display of how much he wanted her, especially with a film crew and a nosy reporter hoping for any sign of attraction between them.

But the devil was sitting on his shoulder again. "Maybe Nana has the right of it, after all." He could never be like Richard. He liked blackberry pie too much.

And other things.

Cissie's pupils darkened. "What are you talking about? What did Nana say?"

"You know. About us staying apart. Look what happens when we get together."

"We can handle it." She sounded like she didn't believe it herself.

The devil in him kept talking. "You look incredibly beautiful in those new clothes."

"How do you know they're new?"

"Well, they're different from what you usually wear. I wonder why the change in your look? Your hair, too?"

"Maybe I did all this to impress the *Morning Coffee* people. And to look like a legitimate mayoral candidate."

"I like it."

"Thank you, but you had nothing to do with any of it."

"Are you sure about that?" he said low.

"Yeah."

"You're a bad liar."

"And you're just plain bad."

"I guess I am. Right now, I'm not thinking of impressing any national TV audience or even of winning the election."

"You should be." She sounded flustered. "Because I am."

"Are you?" He moved an inch closer.

"No," she said. "But what I'm thinking is none of your business."

"Does it have to do with me?"

She hesitated. "Yes. But that's all I'll say."

"Can we play Twenty Questions?" No one could resist Twenty Questions.

"Okay, three questions, and I quit."

"Am I clothed in this thought of yours?"

She bit her thumb, then released it. "No."

He chuckled. "Am I with you?"

"Yes." She crossed her arms and frowned.

"Are you naked, too?"

"Yes," she said, then glared at him. "Now step off, Boone Braddock."

"Just give me three more questions."

"No."

"Come on. This is fun."

"Why does this remind me of being back in grade school?" She tapped her foot. "Get on with it."

"Are Anne and her cameraman still by the tree?"

She looked over his shoulder. "Yes."

"Looking our way?"

"No."

"Anyone in the shop windows? Any pedestrians nearby?"

She shook her head. "That's way over three questions."

"All I want to do is tell you something. I have to, as a matter of fact."

"Have to?"

"Yes. Have to."

"Okay. It had better be important, and—and decent."

"Oh, it's important, all right."

"Is it decent?"

"Hush," he said.

She bit the edge of her lower lip, and he whispered something in her ear.

# CHAPTER TWENTY

All day Cissie had been thinking about what Boone had suggested to her in the gazebo *sotto voce*, and it was driving her crazy. It was a good thing she'd had tons of opportunity to distract herself. She'd kept them from smashing their raft into a boulder while white-water rafting. And she'd run an ATV pell-mell through a grassy field filled with boggy places and probably snakes.

Not only that, she'd told a national TV reporter that Kettle Knob needed an indoor swimming pool facility, not another shooting range, and if the town council didn't get the message from Boone that the health of all its citizens mattered, she'd be sure to tell them herself as mayor when she got in office.

She was on a roll.

No doubt she could tell a man she'd already fooled around with once that she wanted to do it again.

She stole a glance at his profile. They were in his boring truck (not the pretty blue one), going home to clean up before they had to meet the TV crew at The Log Cabin that night. Boone looked straight ahead, but the corner of his mouth quirked up. He'd seen her looking.

"What's so funny?" she asked, playing dumb.

"You're staring at me."

"I'm only checking to see how muddy you are."

"Uh-huh." His grin broadened.

"You are so conceited. I'm not checking you out like that."

"Like what?"

She crossed her arms and sighed. How was she ever going to get around to propositioning him—preferably in a subtle, come-hither way—when she kept pretending she wasn't interested?

It was embarrassing, that was why.

What if he didn't want her back? What if the hot tub and the make-out session in the shed had only been flukes? He might have already made the decision that they didn't suit.

But then she remembered what he'd said in the gazebo.

"Hmmph," she said.

"What?" He shifted to low gear to go up the steep incline leading to his house.

"What you said in the gazebo. That was so wrong—right when I was trying to be dignified and act like a possible mayor. I think your comment proves you're not taking your job seriously."

There she went again, shooting herself in the foot! But she was right. How could she be right and still want to sleep with him?

"What I told you has nothing to do with my job as mayor. Should public servants not be allowed to have personal lives?"

He sounded so serious, which made her feel weird. It wasn't like she wanted to get into a *relationship* with him. The man was a football coach who didn't like libraries. How could she ever discuss books with him?

But he rocked at kissing. And other things. "Sure, you

can have a personal life," she said, "but not when you're technically representing our town."

"Okay," he said, "so no *sex*"—did he have to put such emphasis on the word?—"when I'm on duty."

"Right."

"Guess what? I'm mayor twenty-four seven, three hundred sixty-five days a year. I think as long as I choose a time where I'm not using the taxpayers' money—and I'm discreet—I can have sex any damned time I want."

She just looked out the window. He was getting riled up, and inside she was, too, in a very bad-girl way. How many people had she ever had such a conversation with?

None. Zip. Nada.

"Do you think the constituents really need me at three in the morning?" he went on, his voice getting lower, silkier.

"No. But you shouldn't tease your opponent like that."

"Wait a minute. You started it in the gazebo. You said you were thinking about me with no clothes on."

"You forced it out of me." What was wrong with her? She wanted to have sex with him at three o'clock in the morning in the gazebo! That's what he'd whispered in her ear, but in a much more interesting way, with luscious details that had made her whole body strain toward him in her zebra-striped jacket.

She should be all over him now, kissing his neck while he was driving. Why was she acting so defensive and uninterested? "And here's the other thing," she said.

"Yes?"

"It's cold at three in the morning. And the gazebo floor looks *hard*." Sabotaging herself once again. She really did have some sort of hang-up.

He laughed. "I promise you, you won't feel the cold. Or the floor."

She rested her jaw on her fist, leaned against the window, and stared outside at the passing woods, catching glimpses of faraway mountains between the branches and leaves. Sand formed behind her eyes.

She needed to stop this.

"The truth is"—it was like speaking with a bunch of rocks in her throat—"I'd love to make love with you inside the gazebo. Even if it's cold. And the floor's hard. That's why I brought it up again. I-I just don't know how to say things right."

Shoot. She sounded so *stupid*. And formal. Her heart was beating so hard, she thought she might run out of breath and die.

He was silent. She dropped her fist and looked straight ahead.

The truck's engine whined as the steep incline got steeper.

"I'd love it, too," he said quietly. "And I always know exactly what you're trying to say. Even when you don't say it that way."

"You do?"

"Uh-huh. Since our very first conversation in the library. I even know what you want to say when you don't speak. It's why I let you have the shiny red ATV today and I took the ugly brown one."

"Really? I never said—"

"Exactly. But you wanted it. You were gonna die if you didn't get it."

"That's true." She couldn't help but laugh.

Feeling a shock of warmth, she looked down to see his hand laid over hers on her lap. It was the most amazing feeling. Her fingers unfolded of their own volition and grasped his.

But there was no time to wonder what was happening because the entrance leading to his house was in front of them, and Boone needed his hand back to hold the wheel while he unrolled the window with the other and pressed a button to open the wrought-iron gate.

Whew. Good thing that little moment of intimacy was over. She wasn't quite sure she was ready for that. She'd been on her own so long. A neophyte was what she was— at relationships with guys. At her advanced age, too.

Maybe she'd buried her nose in a book more often than she'd realized.

Real life was here.

And she was scared.


Boone knew he shouldn't have grabbed Cissie's hand like that. It wasn't that he wasn't a gentleman. He paid attention to the women he slept with. He was thoughtful. He'd held many a woman's hand before.

But never like that.

Never so protectively.

Never so tenderly.

There was an awkward silence between them while he navigated the driveway. And then he shut down the engine in front of the house instead of pulling into the side garage. "Here we are. We've got a couple hours. Hungry?"

He'd reverted to proper host.

"Yes. Very." A patch of red crept up her neck. She opened her door and paused. "I'm going to run up and shower first. Then maybe we can meet in the kitchen."

"Sounds good." He was rattled by that hand thing. Best to slow things down. They still had a TV crew to face tonight anyway.

He watched her butt while she went up the front steps, locked into wanting her despite his best intentions. Keys in hand, he caught up with her to open the door. But the massive oak slab swung open when she turned the knob.

The television was on. Savory aromas came from the kitchen. A slow-burning anger tightened his jaw. "Mom? Dad?"

"In here, son!" called his mother from the media room.

He exchanged a look with Cissie. Her eyes were guarded.

"Sorry," he muttered.

"No, no. It's fine." She tried to smile. "I'll say a quick hello and go on up."

"Great."

It sucked to have parents who didn't respect boundaries, who basically thought they *owned* you.

It was his fault. He'd felt sorry for them. He'd enabled them. Up until now, he'd been able to work around the problem, but not anymore.

He'd tell them right now.

*Go. Go home.*

He rounded the corner with Cissie. She could say hi, and then when she left, he'd kick them out.

"Oh. *My*." Janelle stood next to his dad. "Look at you two!"

She looked the part of wealthy, cosmopolitan girlfriend off to watch a polo match or something equally highbrow. His mother and father were smiling their fake country club smiles.

Boone threw his keys on a low cocktail table. "Hello," he said abruptly, disgusted by the whole dynamic and mad at himself for not coming right out and saying so.

But the old-fashioned boy in him would not allow his parents to be humiliated in front of outsiders. When he talked to them in private, yes, he'd be blunt. But he'd also try to inflict as little pain on them as possible.

How he'd accomplish both things—putting them in their proper place, and not hurting them deeply—he had no idea. But it was something he could no longer avoid acting upon.

"We wanted to have a nice supper ready for you." His mother had retreated to her cool tone, which she employed with him when she was hurt or disappointed. "Janelle's going to tell us about her upcoming golfing trip to Bermuda, and we want to hear about your adventure with *Morning Coffee*."

"It's not over yet." He sent a steely look his father's way. "Hi, Dad."

"Son." His chin was set at a stubborn angle.

Oh, yes, Frank was definitely glad Janelle was there as a buffer. He knew damned well Boone didn't want them around.

"Janelle." Boone greeted her with a neutral expression.

He refused to say he was glad to see them. In Southern talk, that was tantamount to being seriously rebuffed, but did any of them actually hear him?

No.

"You've had quite a day, it appears." His dad rocked back on his tasseled Italian loafers.

"We've been on pins and needles waiting for some deets," Janelle chimed in as if she were a member of the family. Her pouty lips parted in a pearly white smile.

"It was long, and it's not over," he said. "We need to shower and get to The Log Cabin. They want us to hear some bluegrass." He wouldn't say they had a whole couple of hours before then.

Cissie stood slightly behind him, to his right. He wished she'd take a step forward.

"What time do you need to get back?" asked his shrewd mother. "The casserole will be ready in forty-five minutes."

He should lie, but they probably already knew. He

could see Janelle or his dad prying the information out of someone on the *Morning Coffee* crew left behind in town. "We need to leave here by eight. The band's not playing until ten. But it takes a while, apparently, to make the place, and probably us, camera ready."

"Sounds fun," said Janelle in a fake cheerful tone. She was obviously annoyed he was the mayor getting so much attention—not her. And he had no doubt she was jealous of Cissie. "Maybe I'll go," she added as if she'd just now thought of it.

"That's your prerogative," Boone said. Again, damning words for anyone truly interested in listening. But Janelle was not one of those people. She had her agenda, and she was going for it.

"I'm heading up for a shower." Cissie was the only quiet, sincere one in the room.

The rest of them—including him—were playing a big game.

"I'm heading to the shower, too," he said. "And it's going to be a long one."

"We'll be waiting." His mother was as unyielding as his father.

When Boone turned around to go, Cissie was already gone, slipped out like a shadow. Who could blame her?

He had a brief vision of her stripping down and washing all those mud flecks off her body. And then he had a dastardly, brilliant idea. "Mom, why don't you all watch *Jeopardy!* with Janelle and compete against one another while I'm in the shower. You know that DVD you gave me for Christmas?"

"Great idea!" Becky Lee clasped her hands together.

A flicker of total horror crossed Janelle's face.

"You can answer," said his dad to Janelle, "but only if you put it in the form of a question. Or it won't count."

"I see." Janelle's smile had a tinge of sulk in it.

"I'll keep score," said Becky Lee.

Boone had to fight not to chuckle. Janelle deserved to be slightly tortured for being so presumptuous as to show up uninvited with his parents.

He checked off the first part of his idea.

Now on to the second.

# CHAPTER TWENTY-ONE

She didn't belong here, Cissie thought as she ascended the wide staircase at Boone's house, her thigh and butt muscles sore from the ATV, her back a little strained from the raft. She didn't belong with these people. They were all polished and perfect, and their interests were different from hers: country club parties, fancy shoes that probably cost a month's salary, and golfing trips to Bermuda.

And not one of them ever came to the library.

She had nothing in common with them.

She peeled off her muddy shirt and shimmied out of her jeans, which were soaked in ditch water and snug on her skin. She knew she didn't belong, so why was she so wrapped around the axle about Boone? Was it just because he was good-looking and sexy?

No. If that were all she cared about, she wouldn't be feeling so miserable now. Her heart actually ached.

She turned on the shower, stuck her palm under the needles of water, and waited for it to warm. The problem, as she saw it, was that she'd built him up in her mind all these years to be something like her romance-novel heroes.

That was it. She'd set herself up for a big fall. That was why her heart was sore.

The water heated almost immediately, and she stepped inside the vast space. At home she had to turn around in her shower with her elbows drawn in. Here, jets sprayed at her from everywhere. And there was a stone bench—not some measly little alcove in the wall, but an entire lounging area at one end where she put her shampoo, conditioner, razors, and loofah. She sat there every night to shave her legs.

Such luxury.

She could easily get used to it.

She soaped up her loofah and got busy. She wished she could scrub away all the vague insecurities she had around people like Janelle and Boone's parents. By the age of thirty-two, she should feel confident in her intelligence, her talent as a librarian. She should be proud that she was a loyal friend, daughter, and granddaughter.

Yet it didn't seem enough just a few minutes ago in Boone's media room.

She closed her eyes, let the spray hit her face hard.

Life was moving on. She had to stop second-guessing herself. She needed to grab it—

The door to the bathroom opened.

"It's just me," a male voice said softly.

She froze. A whisper of hope penetrated her gloomy thoughts.

Boone stood right outside the shower's glass enclosure. "Sorry about my parents and Janelle. Can I come in?"

Billows of steam rose around her. She blinked several times, kind of laughed and cried all at once, then swallowed it right back down.

He waited.

She cracked the glass door. It was funny that she didn't

feel insecure being naked around him, considering all her other issues. But she didn't. She wanted him to see her.

To touch her.

He kept his eyes on her face, which was the only part of her not shielded by the glass door. Instantly, their lips locked, and he kissed her as if she were his last hope. She kissed him back the same way, their tongues colliding, playing, exploring—

Things were already so hot between them, what would happen when she opened the glass door and let him in?

It was inevitable.

"Come on in," she whispered, and crooked her finger to make double sure that this vision of masculinity understood—

She wanted him.

He was already naked, a towel from his own bathroom wrapped around his waist. He let it drop, she held the door wide, and next thing their two bodies met inside the shower space, beneath the spray, and his hardened length thrust up against her belly. The water beat down like a million teasing fingers—*Hey, you two, don't think you won't be caught*—which was thrilling in its own way. Cissie's small breasts, crushed against Boone's slick chest, ached with pleasure. He held her tight between hard, muscular arms, and his mouth sought and found— ravished—hers over and over.

Finally, air must be had.

"How did you get up here?" The water might not totally drown out her voice, so she kept it low.

He looked amazing dripping wet. "Easy. The back stairs."

"Really?" She grinned. "I was hoping it would be harder to get to me than that."

"Well, considering that I had to go out on the back

porch, run around the side of the house, get into the garage, sneak into the kitchen, and open the door there to get up the stairs, it was hard."

"Oh, my!" She rewarded him with a lavish kiss.

He grabbed her butt, kneaded it while he kissed her back, and she tilted her lower belly into him, making him groan. But what was she going to do? Here she had the man she wanted to sleep with. They were both ready, but they were in the shower, and his parents—and Janelle— were downstairs.

It was hardly the ideal situation, yet somehow it couldn't be more perfect. She was already tingling all over, and the water made the sensation more exquisite, like sweet torture.

But the best part was his nakedness, the beauty of his form, combined with the surety and elegance of his movements. He knew what he was doing, in other words, and when his mouth plucked and nibbled the nipple of her left breast . . .

Something had to give.

She whimpered.

"We have to keep going with this," he said, and sucked hard, murmuring his delight.

"What if they hear?" She could barely speak, she was so blissed out.

He glanced up at her with an arched eyebrow. "Then that's their problem. They shouldn't have come to my house."

His annoyance was plain. Yet she knew she needed to mollify him. Now wasn't the time for him to confront his parents about anything. "But if you felt that way," she said carefully, while he kissed her neck, "you would have walked up the front stairs, right? You don't want to make your mother uncomfortable, and I don't blame you."

"I guess you're right." He ran a hand down her back

and over her rear, pulling her even closer up against him. "But they deserve to be uncomfortable."

"Maybe so. But today's not the day." She finally had the courage to reach low and cup him, then explore with tentative fingers.

The wonder of it!

He closed his eyes and released a slow breath. "You're killing me."

The water pelted them.

"Sorry." Reluctantly, she pulled her hand away.

He steered it back. "Don't be." This time he wrapped her fingers around him and squeezed.

"Oh." She smiled and continued her ministrations. His head fell back. It made her so happy to see him that way. She was disappointed when he grabbed her hand and made her stop.

"Later for me." He shot her a sweet grin, and she knew he was trying very hard not to scare her or make her feel inadequate, which made her feel cared for.

And that was the most lovely feeling in the world—

Almost.

His skin on hers was the loveliest.

Their mouths met again.

Hunger, need, surged through her. Now it was her turn to let her head fall back while he explored her collarbone, the tender part of her neck behind her ears, and once again, her breasts—which he seemed to think were treasures from heaven—with his mouth. Inch by inch, he nudged her back in the cavernous space until her calves were pressed against the stone bench. With a small tug on her hand, he got her to sit.

She looked up at him, her hand in his. What was next?

"This," he said out loud, and knelt before her, water pelting his back, running down his temples.

Heat shot from her belly, slowed in her chest, spread,

and flowed up to her face. She knew what was about to happen, and she was excited, but it was all so intimate.

*He's seen you in the hot tub.*

But not like this.

"It'll be all right," he said lightly, and kissed her, their mouths releasing, coming together. Tongues twirling. Sucking.

His fingers splayed on her upper thighs, he applied just enough light pressure to encourage her to spread them wide. They kissed as he caressed the tender flesh on her inner thighs. She found herself spreading farther apart, wanting him *there*.

Finally. She inhaled a sharp breath as his thumb traveled softly back and forth across her sheath, grazing the pearl where all her desire lay pent up, desperate for release. She lifted her bottom, wanting more.

The rough pad of his thumb stopped exactly where she wanted it to, and he used it to nudge, circle, pulse. She was about to lose it right there, but he stopped.

Wicked man!

"Please keep going," she whispered.

His pupils were small diamonds, possessive and sure in the way a tiger is of its prey. There was no turning back, his expression said. She was his at this moment.

*His.*

Yet she felt like a queen on her throne with her own adoring cicisbeo when he dropped his head to kiss her lower belly. She smoothed his wet hair back, basked in watching him lick, bite, and kiss lower and lower until his lips discovered her very center. She almost slid off the bench.

No one had ever done this to her before.

"Heaven," she said aloud, and had the strangest longing to let all her book heroines of old know that she was living a compelling story herself—compelling only to her, perhaps, but it was enough. More than enough. She was rich with sensation, glutted on glory, this godlike being showing her what her body was meant for, something so beyond what she knew and could reason out.

There was magic in this mingling.

He nuzzled between her legs at a leisurely pace. Still, she watched him, her hands kneading his shoulders, clasping his neck, raking into his hair. "I can't bear much more," she said, but she couldn't let him go.

He had to stay. He had to stay there and never move.

He laughed against her sweet spot, and that was enough to make her arch and emit a cry.

He looked up. "Do you really think you can be quiet?" His tone was teasing.

"No, you evil man," she whispered, and didn't bother to hide a silly grin. "But I'm going to try."

"I don't think you can." His expression—eyes lit with humor, his mouth open and curved upward—was so sexy and adorable in that moment, her crush deepened an almost painful degree. He was everything. She wouldn't be able to think of anything else. Ever. It was he. All the time. In her thoughts, in her soul . . .

"Let's bet," she said, wriggling on the bench. They needed to stop talking. And she needed to stop pining, spiraling deeper.

Pleasure would be the antidote. Simple brute pleasure. He'd brought her to that in the hot tub, and she wanted it again.

"What does the winner get?" His finger penetrated her—*Oh!*—her upper back curved inward—and then, miracle of miracles, two fingers, probing, circling.

"I don't know," she whispered, and squeezed reflexively against him. She wanted hard. She wanted thrust. She was getting impatient.

He chuckled again. "The winner gets whatever he

or she wants." There—one good thrust. "But whatever he or she wants"—he moved steadily in and out, and she hung with him, grabbing those fingers, clenching them back in—"has to take place in a certain gazebo in the middle of the night."

"Yes," she said breathlessly. "I can do it. I can stay silent. I want to win."

"Why?" His fingers kept up their work.

"Because I want you again. I-I do—"

"Sssh." He took advantage of her lack of attention, grabbed her bottom, lifted her high while she held to the edge of the bench, and thrust his tongue inside.

She let out a little cry. "How silent is silent? I have to win."

"Not a peep." His face was serious and loveable all at once, and then he got back to business, adoring her with a passion that she still couldn't believe was meant for her.

But it was. He could have had Janelle—Janelle had made that plain—but he was with her. "I don't care if I win anymore." Her voice was thin. She was gasping now. "Even if I lose, I win."

He laughed again. "I'm a lucky man." Fingers in, fingers out. Mouth sucking, nuzzling.

Water beating. Droplets sliding down the walls, his back, his hair. Steam everywhere, hiding him, revealing him.

"Do you trust me?" he said softly.

"Yes." She did, too.

"Then I want you to let go. Let it all go. I've got you."

"Okay." It was more than okay. It was her dream . . . to be able to let go. To know she could let go and still be safe.

He reached up and kissed her mouth.

It was their pact. She was his. He would take her where he wanted her to go. He'd be there with her.

And then in another blossom of steam, he disappeared. His mouth possessed her core with a new urgency. It was right. So right. The freedom that came from trusting another with her most primal self—it was a high unlike anything she'd ever experienced.

He put two fingers inside her again—such a welcome intrusion. She craved three. But she was small. He was being careful.

*Someday*, she dreamed. Someday they'd do it again, and she'd want that sweet stretch—she'd want *him* inside her.

She rode those fingers, claimed them, and then that thumb—the same wayward one—flirted like a feather with the pucker behind her core—such an unexpected, pleasurable shock!—and in an instant she came hard with his mouth still on her, her teeth biting the heel of her palm. She rode the crest over and over while he held tight to her.

Her head circled slowly as she returned to earth, and from her throat soft sounds of astonishment mingled with gratitude and an awareness that she was powerless before the roiling sweetness cradling them both in a cocoon of sexual energy.

He picked her up, pushed open the glass door. Set her gently down on her feet and lifted a towel off a hook on the wall. He patted her dry, then wrapped her tight. Still wet himself, he kissed her once, long and hard, then stepped back, grabbed his own towel, and slung it around his hips, where it didn't sit smoothly for obvious reasons.

"No," she said. "You're not getting away this time."

He didn't object when she unwrapped his towel and let it fall to the ground.

"Oh, my."

"Yours has to come off, too," he said.

She smiled. "But you just put it on."

"Mistake." He tugged it off, pulled her close. "You naked is something I can't get enough of."

He kissed her, and she kissed him back, pulling away to kiss his chest, his flat, taut belly, and then sinking to her knees on the fleecy bathroom rug to take him in her mouth.

"Damn," he whispered huskily.

In answer, she played with him with her tongue. Cradled the weight of him in the palms of her hands. He was glorious perfection, and it was such intense pleasure to feel his fingers curl in her hair, to hear him moan deep in his throat.

His butt flexed, hard as rock, and the length of him jutted, demanding release. She kept up with him, surprising him, she sensed, with her tenacity.

"*Cissie*," he uttered low.

She heard his desperate call for release and pulled away a few inches to look up at him. "This is a hot view."

His gaze was half-lidded. With water trickling down his temples and a faint shadow of stubble on his chin, he looked wild. Untamed.

"Is this some sort of payback?" he rasped.

"Uh-huh. For all the torture you put me through." She grinned.

But before he could say anything, she got back to business.

He was a force of nature. When he came, she was the sole witness to the mighty cataclysm.

She was speechless. And she had to admit—proud of herself, too.

He pulled her up beneath her arms.

Her knees trembled. "How was it?"

"Let's just say you've got skills." He lowered his chin, eyeing her in a way he never had, a way that made her toes curl deep into the rug. "I'm going to be thinking about that all night," he said. "I'm going to be thinking about *you*."

Her heart melted at that. "Good."

He sent her a crooked smile. "I've got to go." He took a step toward the door, then looked back. "You hungry?"

"Famished." She was so caught in his spell.

"We've got some campaigning to do." He paused. "Not just tonight, but for a couple more weeks."

"I know. I haven't forgotten."

He looked like he was thinking. "We're having fun."

"Yes. Fun."

He nodded. They stood silent another few seconds. What did it mean, this fun? At the moment, she didn't care. Because it was fun. Fun wasn't supposed to be dissected.

"I'll see you in the kitchen." He opened the door, winked at her, and left.

Slowly, she crouched on her haunches. Aw, shoot, she'd just sit her bum on the rug. Her knees still felt a little weak.

"Wow," she said out loud, and laid her head on her propped legs. She wrapped her arms around her shins and wondered about nothing, for the first time in a long time. Her chest, her head, all empty of nudges and angles and frissons of fear.

In that moment, she knew everything she needed to know: Guy gets girl. Girl gets guy. Girl is happy.

Period.

# CHAPTER TWENTY-TWO

Twenty minutes later, Boone was sitting at his desk and showing his dad his new laptop in his study—his mom and Janelle sat on the nearby couch—when Cissie came in, fresh as a daisy, prettier, actually, than he'd ever seen her.

He immediately hardened thinking of what had just transpired between them. How had he missed this woman right under his own nose all these years?

While his dad looked over his shoulder at the bells and whistles on the keyboard, Boone couldn't help thinking back to that fourth grade boy who'd thought he'd only wanted a shy girl's glasses. He could see now that he'd also wanted to be around the refreshing presence and steady comfort that was *Cissie*. When he got older and his hormones kicked in, he'd entirely lost track of noticing and admiring a girl simply for being who she was.

He'd forgotten about Cissie and been caught up in hookups instead . . . hookups that never went any deeper than casual friendships with a string of so-called girlfriends.

It was a bit revelatory for him to figure it out now: he'd always *liked* her. He'd simply never bothered to get to know her better, and now it felt like they were becoming friends, not just lovers, and it was weird.

Really weird.

It added a new dimension to the whole sex thing, that was for sure.

"Just in time for supper." Becky Lee addressed Cissie in a neutral tone. She knew better than to be rude in front of him, but she certainly wasn't going out of her way to be warm. "The casserole needs a minute or two to set, and then we can eat."

"I'm starved," said Janelle, as if it were Cissie's fault they hadn't sat down at the table yet.

"Me, too." Cissie smiled at all of them as if she hadn't a care in the world, and when her gaze swept over his, she didn't gift him with a secret special look.

Not that he expected her to.

Hell, he might as well admit it—he expected her to. He assumed he'd be able to tell that she was feeling the way he did, that there was something different from the usual going on between them.

Instead, she turned in a full circle to gaze at his books, oblivious to the fact that he was getting a surreptitious 360 of her sweet little figure. He felt a strong stab of lust.

She turned to look at him. "You *are* a reader. No wonder you never come into the library." She threw out her arms. "You have all this."

"Yep." He really wanted to move on.

Janelle crossed her legs so that her hem rode up to the top of her thighs. "He's a secret bookworm."

As if *she* were privy to any private information about him. Hah.

"Obviously." A big dimple appeared in Cissie's right cheek.

"These are all Grandpa Faber's," Boone said.

"I'm heading to the kitchen." Becky Lee stood up. She didn't make eye contact with him as she walked by the desk and out of the room.

"I'm following," said Frank.

Boone felt the old awkwardness. "Okay, then." He stood and walked to the door.

"I'll be along in thirty seconds." Cissie browsed with her hands folded behind her back, her neck straining to see titles on the top shelves. She was in her element. And she had no idea what effect she had on him.

Janelle stood and flipped her hair behind her shoulders in a pointedly sexy move. "Wait for me, Boone."

He paused long enough to let her catch up.

It amused him—and probably galled Janelle—that Cissie didn't even seem to notice how obviously possessive of him Janelle was.

"I do think I'm going tonight," Janelle said as they walked down the hall. "I want to see what Anne Silver is up to."

"Fine," he replied coolly.

"I can tell you're upset we showed up." She laid a hand on his arm.

If she wanted him to stop walking, he wasn't going to. "It's not easy coming home to unexpected guests when you've had a long day, but you brought dinner, and we'll do just fine." He refused to discuss his strong suspicion that she was trying to wrangle her way into the family. Best to let her think the idea had never occurred to him.

She sighed. "I'm sorry. Your parents asked me to come over. They think Cissie is after you. And seeing as I'm an old friend of the family and love your parents to death, I said, sure, I'll come and keep Boone safe." She laughed.

This time he did stop, right outside the kitchen. "Cissie doesn't deserve that. And I don't need a babysitter."

"Sorry." Janelle had the grace to look down, her long

lashes fanning her cheeks. "I know you don't need a babysitter." She sighed and looked up. "Maybe I'm a little jealous. She lives here, for God's sake."

"That's temporary, but it doesn't matter. You and I are friends. We work well together. Let's not mess that up."

She shot him a teasing grin. "I'll have you know I could have been getting a pedicure now. Instead I'm having your mother's beef stroganoff, and I don't eat beef."

"You're too kind."

She was smart, but he sensed she was too ambitious at that moment to pick up on his mild sarcasm, or if she did, to reprimand him for it.

Sure enough, she grabbed his hand and squeezed it. "I'm here for you," she said with a soulful expression he could tell she'd practiced in front of a mirror. "Always."

He was trying to extricate his hand when Cissie came around the corner and almost bumped into them. "Oh," she said, and added politely, "excuse me."

Janelle held his hand tighter, but he exerted some upper arm muscle to reclaim his fingers without looking like he'd strained to get away, the better not to embarrass the girl. "Let's eat," he said, like an idiot, and ignoring them both, strode into the kitchen, pulled out a chair, and sat at the table.

"Boone," his mother chastised him.

The tabletop was clear.

"We're eating in the dining room," Frank said.

Boone clenched his jaw, stood, and turned to face everyone. "I'm eating in my study." And before his mother could say a word, he went to the casserole on the counter and dug in. "I have a lot of work to do"—which wasn't a lie—"and this *Morning Coffee* business is getting in the way of it." He bent and kissed his mom's cheek. Her hands were still in oven mitts. "Looks delicious. Thanks."

And then he disappeared, but not before seeing the looks of shock and disappointment on his parents' and Janelle's faces, and maybe something like confusion on Cissie's.

Let them think he was an ass.

He really didn't care. He knew he would later, but right now, more than ever, he felt like an outsider in his own life.

Dinner was a misery. Cissie wished she could disappear the way Boone had, but she had something called manners. And she would never leave a friend in the lurch the way he had her, with grumpy parents who didn't like her and a woman who scorned her for no reason at all except that she wasn't as fashionable or cool when they were both thirty-two and should be past that sort of thing.

But even worse, she'd never get naked and cozy with a guy, then half an hour later be caught holding hands with another guy and talking in low voices.

She thanked Becky Lee for the delicious beef stroganoff, which she noticed Janelle pushed around her plate, and said her good-nights. "I haven't been to The Log Cabin in years," she added from the door of the dining room.

"You two be sure to make Kettle Knob look good," Frank said. "Boone's an excellent mayor, you know."

"I never said he wasn't." She felt a little sick to her stomach. These people weren't easy.

"But you're running *against* him," Janelle said. "That means you think you can do better."

"Heavens to Betsy," said Frank.

"I do declare," Becky Lee tacked on.

"I'll see you at The Log Cabin," said Janelle.

From the flatness of her tone, Cissie guessed it was meant to be some sort of challenge, but she'd ignore it.

"Okay, well. Bye." She waved her hand at them in a little arc, then backed out of the room. If only she had tossed her head, spun on her heel, and left without a word.

But who cared about them? She reminded herself she was a grown woman. No one could make her feel small without her permission. And that included Boone.

When she passed his study to go upstairs to freshen up, she knew what to do. His door was open a crack. She poked her head in without knocking and saw his forehead resting on his palm. He was staring at a stack of papers on his desk, his dinner untouched.

"I'm driving my own car." She tried her best to sound cool, but she couldn't help thinking of him in the shower.

He stood. "That's not—"

She shut the door in his face, quietly but firmly.

In her room, she picked Dexter up and hugged him close. He purred against her neck while she indulged the secret hope that Boone would show up in her bedroom to finish his sentence, the one she'd rudely cut off. But of course he didn't. Aside from the fact that his parents would probably see him, he wouldn't want to come up. Hadn't Janelle held his hand outside the kitchen? He hadn't seemed to enjoy it, but he'd let her do it all the same. Whether he was happy about it or not, something was going on between those two.

Frazier Lake, perhaps?

Cissie put Dexter down and grabbed her purse. She stood still, debated entering the bathroom to freshen her lipstick in the mirror, then decided against it. Seeing the shower would only remind her that their erotic encounter there had been a fluke, like the episode in the hot tub and that scorching kissing session in Boone's truck.

Things like that happened when young, healthy men and women lived in close proximity. She couldn't build a fantasy world around something that was merely a biological imperative.

She called Laurie and asked her to meet her at The Log Cabin. But Laurie was already going, and so was Sally. Hank Davis would stay at Laurie's with little Sam and Stephen. Perry wasn't home again, but Mrs. Donovan had volunteered to babysit. The boys would watch football with her while Mrs. Donovan graded papers.

So Cissie's plans were set, and they didn't include Boone.

When she tried to sneak out of the house, it was perfectly quiet, which meant his uninvited guests had left. But where was he?

A very girly part of her was disappointed. She'd always thought of him as a gentleman until tonight. A gentleman would have eaten dinner with everyone. He would also have said good-bye before leaving the house.

*But you're leaving without saying good-bye*, her conscience reminded her. *So does that mean you're not a lady?*

Yes. Yes, it did, and she'd fully enjoyed not being a lady with Boone in the shower. But she was a fool to expect anything more from him, especially when he was her opponent in the mayor's race, and she'd shut the door in his face, and Janelle was hanging on to him like a bad cloud.

"Get real, girlfriend," she said out loud to herself as she went down the front steps of Boone's beautiful home.

And there he was, over by the shed, standing next to the cobalt blue truck with shiny chrome, his arms crossed over his substantial chest.

"Were you really going to leave without me?" he asked her when she walked up.

Her face felt like a hot brick. "Yes, but I was hoping—"

"That I'd be a knight in shining armor and forgive your little rudeness in my study and be waiting here to

sweep you off your feet"—he picked her up in his arms—
"and kiss you and apologize for being such an ass in the
kitchen and abandoning you to my parents and Janelle?"

She wrapped her hands around his neck. "Well, are
you?"

"What? Going to apologize? Or kiss you? You can
only have one."

She girded herself. "Apology."

God, she was stupid. But she couldn't kiss him—not
now, not even after the election. This man was from a
different universe—one filled with bulldozers, golf
courses, and rich politicians—plus, he was involved, for
goodness' sake, with Janelle.

He dropped her to her feet. "I'm sorry I abandoned
you. And you chose the wrong thing. I could have kissed
your socks off."

"Did you and Janelle have sex by Frazier Lake?"

"What do you think?" He held open the passenger's
side door of the truck.

When she slid past him to get in, she was mad at herself for wishing she could reach up and kiss that stubble.
"I think you like women. And I'm all for that. I've bene-
fited from your expertise in that department. But I'm not
into sharing. Not that I plan to do anything else with you."

"No," he said with a straight face, "that would be terrible." He shut the door, walked around to the driver's
side, and got in. "Having fun is a no-no when you're
mayor or even running for mayor. Don't do it." There was
a tick of amusement in his jaw.

She refused to smile herself, although inside, she felt
better. There was something about him that made her
not want to be on opposite sides.

The truth was, she wished they could pull over and
make out right then and there.

Did he feel the same way?

Was it the forbidden-fruit angle they had going here?

She didn't know. All she did know was that she wanted him, no matter how mad he made her. Or exasperated. Or even sad.

Tonight she'd been sad when she saw him and Janelle in the corridor, so sad that when she'd sat to dinner with his parents, she'd had to focus very hard on her plate so as not to let a tear pearl up in her eye.

Neither of them said another word until they pulled out of the driveway onto the road.

"You still haven't said," she reminded him. Like they were best buds or something. She felt easy with him— even when she didn't.

That made no sense. But it was true.

"Oh, right." He scratched the side of his nose. "Janelle had sex with the lieutenant governor up by Frazier Lake. The married one. It was *his* butt sticking up in the air for the whole world to see. Scotty told me."

Cissie sucked in a breath. "How did the rumor come about that it was *you*?"

He shrugged. "She probably started it. Or maybe the lieutenant governor did, or one of his minions."

"Aren't you going to call either one of them on it?"

"Nope." He stared straight ahead. "I stay out of the fray. Let people think what they want. And that includes you."

"Hey."

"It's all right," he said. "I'm used to being that guy— the one who doesn't quite live up to expectations. Except as a football coach and in the mayor's office—till now, that is. Someone's running against me." His tone was deceptively casual.

"We didn't make any promises. And I didn't expect any."

"But you want confirmation that I'm a man who plays one girl off another."

"No. I was hoping for the opposite, okay? I wanted confirmation that you're a stand-up guy. But I don't know you that well, and I don't have a whole lot of experience with men. I can't just come out and trust you. Geez." She crossed one arm over the other.

"Wow. So you'll use me as a sex god. But that's it."

She buried her head in her hands. "You make me sound so shallow."

"I'm just stating the facts as I see them." He paused. "God, I feel used."

She lifted her head and narrowed her eyes at him.

Lucky for him, he didn't chuckle. But he looked too innocent by half.

"And this is your way of staying completely above the fray, right?" she said. "With stupid humor? Sue me for being a little wary when I saw you and Janelle. I wondered if I'd made a huge mistake."

Her throat was tight with emotions, waiting to be expressed in words she couldn't form because she didn't know what was going on.

"You're right, and I'm sorry," he said. "You should be watching out for yourself. We have an election coming up. And we both need to shore up and focus on it."

"You got that right," she whispered. Because she wanted to cry.

Why?

There was nothing to cry about! She'd seen a little action with this extremely virile man, and he was way better than her fantasies.

So what?

He was right. It was time to move on. A year from now she'd look back fondly upon this short sojourn as Boone's lover and pat herself on the back for being an adventuress. She'd even wax nostalgic with Laurie. *And then he lifted me up and put me in the truck. Like he was Richard*

*Gere. And he did it because he knew I wanted a hero like that. Just for a little while.*

"So what do you say to agreeing to move on past this awkward personal stuff?" he said. "Neither one of us needs it."

"No, we don't." Awkward personal stuff was painful. "Let's keep it professional."

"Good idea."

They pulled into the well-lit parking lot at The Log Cabin, where Anne Silver paced like a sleek leopard waiting for her quarry to show. Sally and Laurie were busy tying the hot-pink ribbons of one of Sally's "Vote for Cissie" signs onto the branches of a tree with a spotlight at its base, angling upward.

"Nana and I need to move out tomorrow," Cissie said.

Boone shook his head. "You don't."

"We do, and you know it. Too much . . . sex in the air."

He turned off the engine and turned to her. "Are you sure you're a librarian?"

"See?" She ripped off her seat belt. "You're doing your best to make me forget that I am."

"Damn. My secret political strategy is revealed."

She picked up her purse, opened the truck door, and landed on hard-packed gravel. "I'm going to fight harder than ever for the library, I'll have you know."

"You do that." Boone's eyes glittered. "Let the race begin. For real."

"For real." She shut the door with more force than was necessary.

And that was that.

# CHAPTER TWENTY-THREE

Women.

Boone watched Cissie stride off with her purse swinging over her shoulder and took pleasure in imagining himself telling a bunch of sympathetic guys at the bar at The Log Cabin that he desperately wished for his peaceful, boring existence back. No complex feelings. No misunderstandings or feminine glares. They'd all nod and clink beer mugs, and he'd bask in being right that women were a helluva lot of trouble.

It was a great daydream—especially awesome when you're pissed off—except that he didn't want that life back at all. He wanted *her*. Not just for the sex, either. He wanted her the same way he had to have his favorite boots or his day wouldn't go right—but somehow in a much more important way, the difference being the sun might hit the moon or something like that if he didn't have her. Whereas if he never saw his boots again, the world would still go on. He'd survive.

He had no idea why that was how he saw things, but he did, and he didn't like it one bit.

Maybe he was finally cracking under the pressure of being a well-loved, popular figure in Kettle Knob. Of having a beautiful home at his disposal, any woman he wanted in North Carolina (except Cissie), and two jobs that brought him a lot of fulfillment. Of having only one bad day a year.

Maybe he'd become soft. It happened in football all the time. Once you got complacent, you were done for, a sitting duck for a tackle, a fumble, or an interception.

It was good and dark, but two distant mountains were still rimmed in a fine line of orange-pink when Boone got out of the truck. Anne Silver's face lit up beneath one of the TV truck lights, and he knew right then and there he could ask her out, and she'd say yes. He'd take her out to dinner in Asheville and they'd have a great meal, laugh a lot, flirt. She might hint around about staying overnight in Asheville together. At the very least, she'd kiss him good-bye and ask him when he might come up to New York. He'd tell her he'd be up there soon for the annual MoMA gala, and he'd invite her to go with him.

Too bad nothing in that scenario appealed to him. But it was even worse that he knew how it would unfold. Was he that jaded? Smug? Old? What kind of track was he on that he could predict what was coming around every bend, the same way he knew every turn of the Nantahala River?

Cissie's crazy sign rattled in the light breeze that always blew over the mountain.

"So," Anne said, smiling at his approach, "it's been quite a day. You and Cissie did really well together. We got some terrific quotes from you guys about the mayor's race. Kettle Knob is gorgeous, and it's going to be a great segment."

He stopped a couple feet away, his hands in his back pockets. "So what's The Log Cabin about?"

"You're not in the mood for some good music?"

"Anne, let's cut through the small talk. Is there another

angle going on here, or is this just some more feel-good video to pad the story?"

She smiled. "I told you we're here to cover an entirely entertaining scenario about two people running for mayor of a small town, who also happen to coexist in the same house."

"Then where are the kitchen shots? Us drinking coffee and eating breakfast together? And how come Nana was never interviewed?"

A squiggle appeared on Anne's lovely pale brow. "We felt indoor shots would look too contrived. So we stuck with outside shots of the house. And we got the story of the tree without needing to speak to Cissie's grandmother."

"Who did you talk to, then?"

"A few locals. Let's see, the mayor of Campbell, a woman named Janelle Montgomery."

Boone's gut twisted.

"The owner of the diner, Starla, was a hoot to interview." Anne grinned. "And there were a few other people, all of whom spoke highly of you."

"Uh-huh."

"You're not having second thoughts about this, are you?"

"I'm hoping to attract a business or two to our area by cooperating." He caught a glimpse of a bunch of guys in their midtwenties entering the bar. "But no one had better be hurt in the process. Y'all are taking notes while you're here. But I'm keeping a few of my own. And I have a fondness for Twitter. It's short. It's sweet. It gets the job done."

"Wow." Beneath her new wariness—if he could call it that; maybe she thought a small-town guy like him wasn't anyone to take seriously—he could still see it, the invitation in her eyes. "You don't mince words, Mr. Mayor. Or should I say you do?"

"I'm the king of a hundred and forty characters or less when I need to be." He paused a beat. "This isn't a ratings game for me, Anne. It's folks. It's my town."

He walked away. Let her think he was a country bumpkin for talking like that.

"Mayor Braddock," she called after him sharply.

At the door, lit from above by a few lights beneath the roof, he stopped and made a quarter turn, only to see she'd followed him. "Yeah?"

"Don't forget to visit makeup." She was gorgeous, ambitious, and no doubt used to getting what she wanted. "They're inside by the bar."

"Sure thing." He pulled out his cell phone and snapped a picture of her. Then he tossed the phone in the air, watched it twirl back down, caught it in his palm again—just like the cowboys of old did with their revolvers—and put it away.

Let her wonder why. He didn't trust her. "See you inside." He slapped the doorframe with his hand and entered The Log Cabin.

The place was filling up quickly. He got his face patted down by the makeup people. Bought a drink for them when he bought one for himself. Hung out with the guys at the bar, the group of fellas in their midtwenties he'd seen earlier. Just about every one of them had been on the football team or in his PE class when he was still new at the high school.

"Hey, Coach!" they all begged him. "Let us buy you another beer!"

So he let them. Because Miss Cissie Rogers wasn't interested in even looking at him. She was miles away at the high-top tables, chatting away with Laurie, Sally, and various and sundry visitors—all harmless, except maybe one guy about his age who appeared to be ogling her.

"Another beer?" his young friends asked.

"Sure, why not," he said.

Anne came over and asked the boys how they felt about him running for mayor again, and every one said they'd vote for him and that he was an excellent leader of the town and the high school's football team. "What about moving the library?" she asked them. "Are you concerned about that?"

"No."

"Hell, no."

"I love that place, but the new place'll be bigger."

"Closer to Campbell. They got cute girls in Campbell."

Lots of laughter.

"What do you think of Boone's opponent?" Anne asked.

"Someone's running against him?"

"He doesn't stand a chance."

"It's a she, dummy. Cissie Rogers, The librarian."

"What does she know about running a town?"

"She's a smart woman," Boone finally interjected.

The boys—he still thought of them that way—stopped talking.

Anne turned the mike to him. "So you're taking up for your opponent."

"I'm just stating the facts," he said. "She *is* smart."

The boys—beer bottles poised beneath their mouths—watched closely.

"Do you think she'd make a great mayor, Coach?" Anne asked.

"Sure, she would," he said. "But I want to be mayor again." As one, the boys hooted and hollered, and he had to wait for them to pipe down. "I'm running on a winning record, and Kettle Knob operates in the black. We're growing. It's exciting. And I have lots of things left to do."

There the guys went, cheering for him again. It was awesome having his own fan club, but the truth was, Cissie was like a little car going the wrong way on a big interstate filled with a convoy of eighteen-wheelers, and he was the head truck.

The band walked onto a small stage with pink and blue lights aimed at the mikes, to much applause and whistling. Boone wondered how the musicians felt about *Morning Coffee* messing with their act—but one of his old students at the bar was the brother-in-law of the banjo player, and the kid said they were stoked. National exposure! You couldn't beat that.

So to celebrate, they all had another round.

The band started playing a tribute to Earl Scruggs— "Pike County Breakdown"—and were they ever good. Boone was mesmerized by the fiddle player's bow one second and the next by the banjo player's fingers, which were a blur as they plucked the strings. They followed that fast number by an Alison Krauss and Union Station hit.

Everyone whooped and clapped.

"You can forget all your troubles when you listen to bluegrass!" Laurie yelled in his ear and wrapped an arm around his waist. "Ah, Boone. It's good to see you having fun. I don't remember the last time, really. Yeah, you go to all the right parties, but you're never really into it, you know? You're too responsible. You're the mayor. And the coach."

She was right. He hadn't had legitimate fun just hanging out with people in a long time—honestly, since high school.

"We've missed your happy face," Laurie said. "The real one. Not the one you put on for your adoring fans at school or town hall."

What she said hit him in the gut.

*Your happy face. The real one.*

"It's in the yearbook," Laurie said. "That fabulous picture of you and the other football players after the game we won against Taylorville senior year. Remember?"

"Sure, I do. Taylorville was the team to beat." But he couldn't go back to that guy.

He got another beer.

Laurie declined his offer to buy her a drink. "You need to dance with Cissie tonight."

"I knew you had something on your mind besides just saying hello. Cissie and I are running a race against each other. Don't try to get us together."

"I just wanted to tell you how much she likes you," Laurie said.

"Sure, she does."

"No, she really does. But she's stubborn."

"I'd say she's cautious. With good reason."

"She doesn't have to be worried about *you*. You're one of the good guys."

"I appreciate the show of support, but that's enough matchmaking. Cissie and I are two adults. We can figure out our own love lives."

Laurie shot him a dubious look. "I don't know—I get the feeling you're both too stubborn for your own good." She kissed his cheek and walked away.

In the midst of the noisy crowd, Boone had a few seconds of alone time to reflect on what she'd said. It was a prudent choice, the not-dancing-with-Cissie decision. There'd be no relief from his wanting her, but on the other hand, no letdown, either.

Fantasies, he was discovering, came in handy when a man was trapped in a jail of his own making.

# CHAPTER TWENTY-FOUR

Cissie did her best to pretend to have fun when she first got into The Log Cabin, while the woman with the powder puff hovered around her. She was actually miserable and in a huff, all at once.

*That man*, she thought, after the makeup lady finished. She ordered a short plastic cup of white wine. When a nudge of pain pushed through, she drank it down, ordered another cup, and went right back to stewing about the fact that Boone had been cocky and amused at home and in his truck when he should have been penitent and sensitive.

She wanted a thoughtful, sympathetic man, one who was sorry when he acted like a child.

At least, she thought she did until she saw him at the other end of the room, looking so hot that her underpants practically melted off. She knew she'd take him any way she could get him. She looked around and caught a lot of other women looking, too, including Anne.

"Famous reporters should stick to their own kind up in New York City, not come south and try to poach the hottest guys from the local girls," Cissie told Mrs. Hattlebury a few minutes later at the high-top table they snagged by the stage between a speaker and a smaller bar with a huge crowd around it. It was way too hard for the camera crew to get to her there, which was a good thing. She needed a place of respite from them and the sight of Boone.

"You mean that Anne Silver woman?" Mrs. Hattlebury yelled.

The colonel stood next to his wife, bored, his eyes on the band, who were adjusting guitar and banjo straps, fixing mike heights, and twisting knobs on various black boxes on the floor.

"Yes, her," Cissie yelled back. "Famous reporters should also never get involved with the subjects of their stories."

"I agree," said Mrs. Hattlebury. "She looks at Boone like he's steak and she's got A.1. in her purse ready to pour all over him."

Cissie took a huge gulp of Mrs. Hattlebury's wine because hers was gone. "There's no way I'll get a fair shake on *Morning Coffee.*"

"I'm quite sure it'll be a Boone Braddock segment, and you'll be a paltry second-level participant," shouted Mrs. Hattlebury, who was the type of friend who confirmed your worst fears just when you secretly hoped she'd say you were crazy to be worried. "Honey, I saw all kinds of politics on those Elvis sets. A girl has to look out for herself. What will you do?"

Cissie sighed. "I don't know. Maybe I should say something to Anne."

"Which will backfire. No, you need to make sure you're not invisible here tonight."

"What do you mean?"

Mrs. Hattlebury's eyes glinted with mischief. "Why, darlin', you become the life of the party!"

"I'm no good at that," said Cissie.

Mrs. Hattlebury looked her up and down. "First, you have to get rid of that boring blouse."

"It's a fine blouse!"

"Stand still." Mrs. Hattlebury unbuttoned two more buttons at Cissie's neck, then looked over her shoulder at her husband. "I need your pocket knife, dear."

The colonel pulled one out of his jeans pocket without a word and handed it to his wife.

"What are you doing?" Cissie hissed when Mrs. Hattlebury opened the knife and poked at her shoulder.

"You'll see. Drink the rest of my wine. I saw you sneaking it."

"All right." Cissie did as she was told.

Mrs. Hattlebury tore off one of Cissie's sleeves.

"Good Lord," said Cissie, "this is crazy."

"Shush. Drink the colonel's beer."

"I hate beer."

The other sleeve came off with a loud ripping noise.

Cissie drank the beer. Air poured down the gaping V at the top of her blouse, and now her arms were uncovered. She had to admit, she felt better. The bar was getting hot and stuffy.

"Okay," said Mrs. Hattlebury, "now we need to add a little lipstick. Those makeup people didn't do their jobs. You need my Red Rumbler." She pulled a silver stick from her purse. "Lord, this hue was always Elvis's favorite."

"Did you ever kiss him?" Cissie asked.

Mrs. Hattlebury peered over her shoulder at the colonel's back, then turned to Cissie, her best bad-girl look on. "What do you think?"

Cissie stuck out her lips, and Mrs. Hattlebury did what she had to do. Which was followed by a massive hair teasing with the colonel's comb. When Mrs. Hattlebury was done, she gazed upward at Cissie's hair with something like early 1960s joy.

"Look at her, Edward," Mrs. Hattlebury said, a happy smile on her lips.

The colonel turned, and his eyes lit up. "Olivia, you're a genius."

"I know," said Mrs. Hattlebury serenely. "Honey, pull out your flask and pour Cissie a little libation, and then she's done for the night."

"Yes, dear." The colonel did as he was told.

Cissie thought she'd have to choke it down—it was straight Kentucky bourbon—but it went down quite easily.

"Are you sure about this?" she asked Mrs. Hattlebury, although she didn't care too much anymore about the answer because she was up for *anything* now that the band had started playing its first song.

The place exploded in whistles and claps, and Cissie wanted to get out of her corner.

Mrs. Hattlebury laid a hand on her arm. "You need to worm your way right to the front of that stage and dance your little heart out when the spirit moves you. And if you have down times, just look hot. Remember this face?" She did her standard Elvis-movie-extra look again. "Show it to the fiddle player. He's the cutest."

"Okay," said Cissie.

"But just once, to get his attention. After that, you do *this* face." Mrs. Hattlebury's expression was a slight variation of the other one with more intensity about the eyes. "That's the *smart* vamp look," she said, "and that's how I won the colonel. You"—she poked Cissie's chest—"want to win two things: the mayor's office and Boone. You have to take risks, child. No hiding behind words. You have to *feel*. Feel it so much that words won't do."

"All right."

"Now practice the smart vamp look, and you'd better mean it. Put all your love of books behind it, and everything you feel about that library moving, and then add in all that you feel about Boone. Or you'll come off looking like Janelle."

"God knows I can't let that happen." So Cissie practiced. And she put her whole heart into it. She did want the mayor's office, she cared about her family's documents being moved, and how would Sally and Hank Davis volunteer anymore? And why was Boone so deliciously handsome and charming, yet also totally exasperating and challenging and never going to do exactly what she wanted? Yet she wanted to jump into bed with him every time she saw his face? Or his back? Or his boots?

"Edward, take a look," Mrs. Hattlebury said.

Cissie practiced on him.

"Whoa." The colonel actually got a glint in his eye. "I like this Cissie."

"This is the real one." Mrs. Hattlebury dropped her lipstick into her purse and snapped it shut. "Next time she's not going to need beer, wine, and bourbon to get her out." She leaned close to Cissie. "Next time you're gonna use sex. Lots of good, mind-blowing sex."

"Really?" Cissie liked that idea.

"Yes, and after that, it's gonna stick, and you'll be this Cissie all the time. It's a perpetual cycle—great sex, fabulous Cissie, which means more great sex, and even more fabulous Cissie." She angled her head at the colonel, who still had his back to them. "That's *our* secret."

"Oh." Cissie gulped. "It's a . . . a good secret."

"Now don't get all prissy on me. Get out there." Mrs. Hattlebury grabbed Cissie's purse. "I'll watch this for you. And keep an eye out for Sally. She's passing out stickers that say 'Cissie for Mayor.'"

"Wonderful," Cissie said. Or maybe she said, "Fabulous." Or accidentally said a combination of both words because she was too excited—or tipsy?—to know what she was saying anymore.

But who cared? All she had to do was dance. And be the center of attention. That didn't require any words. Just feelings.

"Good to see you, Boone." Sally slapped him on the back. "Stop being so handsome all the time."

He put an arm around her. "And you stop being the best mother in the world because all the other mothers are gonna get jealous."

"They should be jealous. Hank Davis is the best child. Everyone wants Hank Davis in their family, but they can't have him." She crooked a finger at him, and he leaned down. "Janelle just got here," she whispered loudly in his ear, "and she's hot after you. But she's not good for you. Neither is that Anne woman. Only one woman is right for you. And she's running for mayor. But don't let that stop you from nothing."

And then she slipped into the crowd.

He immediately put his hand on the back of his shirt and pulled off a round sticker that read "Cissie for Mayor" and showed a pair of luscious red lips.

"Good lord," said a voice over his shoulder. "I can't believe that sticker. Talk about taking women's rights back a hundred years."

He turned. Janelle was jawing away on her gum and dressed to kill in a black leather miniskirt and a white lacy top. Her shoes were mile-high pointy red heels.

"They're just lips," he said, and stuck the sticker on his shirt pocket.

"*Boone.*" Janelle stuck her hands on her athletic hips. "How much have you had to drink? You're running for mayor. You can't wear *her* sticker."

"I'm in a bar. There's partying going on. This isn't the place for serious campaigning."

"Well, you have a TV crew here who thinks otherwise."

"I'm not their minion. Let them think what they want." He wanted to get rid of her, but he was a gentleman and couldn't walk off. And he was cranky, too, because he couldn't see Cissie.

He got an idea when he saw Colonel and Mrs. Hattlebury alone at a high-top table by the smaller bar. Janelle didn't like old people. "Gotta go talk to the Hattleburys. Want to come along?"

"No." Janelle shuddered and ran away.

Mission accomplished.

Now he could look for Cissie. Maybe the Hattleburys would know where she was.

"She's out having fun," said Mrs. Hattlebury. "See?"

There she was, at the front of the crowd, right below the stage. She was bouncing around in a shirt that was barely there—it gaped at the neck, and her slender arms were showing. Her newly golden-brown hair was all poufed up and sexy, and she was eyeing the fiddle player—

Who, dammit all, was eyeing her back.

Red hot jealousy took off like a race car in Boone's veins and spread from his groin to his feet and back up to his chest and then his temples, where it crossed a finish line with a banner above it that read "Crankier than ever."

And he'd thought he'd been at his limit. "What happened to her?"

The colonel chuckled. "I call it the Beach Blanket Bingo effect."

"She's being Cissie," said Mrs. Hattlebury cryptically.

Whatever she was being, Boone needed to be near her.

Even if just to tell her that the fiddler wasn't worth her time. Why, he was probably on the road most of the year hitting on girls at every stop.

"Looky there, the TV crew finally found a way to get to her," said the colonel.

Sure enough, Anne was barking at everyone in her path to get out of the way so the cameraman could get to a chair by the side of the stage. He stood on it and tracked that camera right on Cissie. The sound-boom guy managed to dangle a big fluffy black cloud of fiber above the crowd so it floated above Cissie's head, although how he'd be able to distinguish her voice from all the other sounds coming in from the band and the crowd, Boone had no idea.

Anne clearly wasn't after a heartwarming video clip at the moment. That *Morning Coffee* crowd wanted their drama, too.

"I'd better get over there," Boone said.

"You'd better," replied the colonel with unusual gusto. "Cissie might be your opponent, but she's Kettle Knob's girl, and those TV people are up to no good."

"You be careful, honey," warned Mrs. Hattlebury. "That fiddle player is casting a spell over her with that fiddle. A girl can get a little crazy when that happens."

You know who else could get a little crazy when the fiddle player flirted with Cissie Rogers? The man who had just kissed her all over her naked self in his shower.

Boone prided himself on being a civilized male. He appreciated good art. He could talk about politics, from international down to local. He was a great dancer. But he also loved brute contact sports like football. He liked crossing creeks in water up to his hips, a walking stick in his hand and a dagger on his belt, the better to cut open the trout he was going to catch later that day and fry in a hundred-year-old skillet tucked in his backpack.

He was a man's man who didn't ever have to show off his masculinity. A real man didn't have to. But there were times when the caveman in him came out.

The band started playing "Sitting on Top of the World," and a few couples started dancing. Everyone backed up to give them room and clapped and stomped, which complicated things, made it harder to get through the crowd. But he kept his eye on Cissie, clapping along by herself up front. She was looking up at that fiddle player and laughing—until the guy to her left—the ogler—turned and tapped her on the shoulder.

She looked toward him. He held out his hand. She took it.

They started dancing in the little cleared-out area.

The same way Boone walked deliberately, silently through the woods toward home when he was tired and hungry after a good camping trip, he headed toward Cissie. He was going to claim her. In front of the whole world. At least in front of his whole world.

She stopped dancing.

Everything got slow.

"I'm cutting in," he said to the other guy in a neutral voice. No need to be rude.

"I don't think so," said the other guy.

"Yeah, I am," replied Boone.

"Guys," Cissie said.

"I was with the lady," her dance partner said.

"She came with me," Boone answered. That reason should be enough for any man to back off.

"Boone." Cissie laid her hand on his arm.

He ignored it.

The other guy moved an inch toward him. "Well, I suppose either you abandoned her or she doesn't want to be with you. After all, she's been by herself this last half hour dancing up front. What's up with that?"

"I get you," said Boone, "but she's with me. All right? Let's just leave it at that."

"I don't think so," said the guy.

Boone looked down. Cissie was gone.

"You made her leave," the ogler said.

The music stopped. There was Cissie up front again. The fiddle player pulled her up onto the stage. She pulled a "Cissie for Mayor" sticker off her blouse, patted it onto his chest, and kissed his cheek.

Everyone hooted and hollered.

"Boone Braddock," she said into the mike, "and the guy who asked me to dance—I want you two to listen up. It's time for everyone to vote for Cissie Rogers for mayor. How many of you want the library to leave Kettle Knob? No one, right?"

Another raucous noise came up from the audience, but it didn't sound like *yay* or *nay*. More like *We're getting drunk in a bar.*

"You want the library to stay," Cissie informed her captive audience. "And I'm gonna fight tooth and nail to make that happen. How many of you want an indoor pool?"

The banjo player started playing to get her off the stage.

"You do, right?" she yelled. "Well, I'm going to get us that, too. But you'd better stop littering down by the creek. That's a disgrace."

The guitar player joined in with the banjo. The fiddle player whispered in her ear.

"But I'm not done—" she said slightly off-mike but loud enough for everyone to hear. She looked straight at Boone, her expression strained.

She was worried about him and the ogler, obviously. This speech was a ploy to get their attention off their brute male instincts.

Smart girl.

Smart even when she'd been drinking. Maybe she could wrack up a few votes at the same time.

A huge wave of lust and something else—something deep and true—swept through him. He smiled at her, even though he doubted she could see.

But then she smiled back, her face flush with drink and maybe a bit of lust herself.

"Everyone, clap for Cissie," said the lead singer. "She's been our best dancer all night. If you want a hot mayor who can party, this is the woman to vote for."

Anne and her crew were lapping this up. One camera was trained on Boone. He ignored it. The fiddler—who was actually a nice guy, it seemed—jumped down to the floor and held out his free hand. Cissie took it and gave a little leap herself.

And with her shoulders thrown back and her shirt unbuttoned to sexy level, she walked toward Boone, weaving through the crowd even when she didn't need to. She wasn't one for straight paths, he was coming to find out. She liked to stop and check everything out along the way. Her eyes, locked on his, were bright. She was excited. And maybe a little drunk.

"She's a handful," said Boone to the other guy. "No hard feelings."

"To hell with that," the other guy said, and threw a punch at him.

# CHAPTER TWENTY-FIVE

When that man threw a punch at Boone, all Cissie's Girl Scout instincts came to the fore.

She knew what to do without even thinking about it: she ran through the crowd, jumped on the stranger's back, and held on for dear life. She pretended he was a bucking bronco and that she was going to win the rodeo if she could stay on. It helped her cling harder when she screamed bloody murder in his ear.

Boone, meanwhile, was bleeding from his nose and yelling at her to get down.

"But if I do, he'll hit you again," she yelled back.

She was supposed to help people at all times. She'd promised the Girl Scouts. She was supposed to be courageous and strong, too. It was the Girl Scout law.

She wished she could tell everyone that she'd had a sudden, fond remembrance of her time in the Girl Scouts—ever since the bug episode with Janelle in Starla's diner—but she knew they'd laugh, especially Janelle in her spiked red heels.

She knew she might laugh, too, if she weren't so busy being sentimental, thanks to the alcohol, and busy hanging on to the crazy man's back.

"Get outta here!" Boone waved his hand, and his eyes were hard. "I mean it, Cissie. *Now.*"

And so, reluctantly, she half fell, half jumped off the man's back. Immediately, someone pulled her away by her armpits, and there came the sound of a whack— someone's fist hitting a jaw. Or a nose.

God, she hoped that wasn't Boone who got hurt again. Her eyes filled with tears. What was she going to do? She stumbled to her feet, turned to look, and was relieved— and horrified—to see it was the other guy this time. He put his hand up to his nose and winced.

Everyone shouted and backed away. The band stopped playing.

"Calm down, everyone," said the fiddler into the microphone.

Anne and her crew had the camera trained on Boone and the guy, who were circling each other.

"Walk away," Boone told him.

"Hell, no," the other guy said. "You pissed me off." And then he charged Boone, his head down like a moose.

Boone caught him in the gut, wrapped his arms around his back, and they wrestled their way down to the floor. The guy couldn't see but he punched Boone on his shoulder—twice in a row—and Boone shoved him away.

Boone sprang to his feet, his arms out wide. "Give up." He was breathing hard. "I'm holding back here. This is the wrong time and place to cause a scene."

The guy struggled to his feet. "I was with her. You come over like you're this big badass—"

"He is! He's mayor of this town!" yelled Cissie, and saw one of Anne's camera's trained on her. She'd forgotten all about that dumb *Morning Coffee* show. "He's also the football coach at the high school. He's a good man. And if *you* are, you'll stop right now."

But the guy went over to the stage, ripped a cord out

of the wall, picked up a black box about the size of a cooler, and lifted it over his head.

A collective gasp came up from the crowd.

"Don't be stupid," Boone said.

The crowd backed up even farther—everyone but the cameramen. Cissie saw Anne's eyes widen and her cheeks pale. This was Southern drama at its redneck finest.

"You break my amp, and you owe me five hundred bucks," the banjo player yelled.

"This is ridiculous," Cissie said. "You can't hurt his amp!"

She stalked over to her former dance partner, who was looking like a dazed, dumb giant at this point—like the Abominable Snowman on her favorite Christmas special—and pointed to the ground. "Put that amp down right now," she said in her best librarian's voice.

*"Cissie."* Boone's voice was cold. Scary. "Back away before I pick you up and carry you out of here."

"Do it," she told the man. "Or that TV camera will catch you committing a heinous crime on national television. You'll land in jail faster than a cat can chase its tail, but worse, you'll be on YouTube forever. People can be so cruel in the comments. Have you noticed?"

"Shit." The man put down the amp.

"That's better," she said.

*"Now,* little lady, I think you owe me a dance." He grabbed her arm.

"I don't think so." Cissie noticed his grip wasn't at all gentle. "Not after—"

Boone socked him in the jaw, and the guy went straight down.

There were screams, one of them from Cissie, then everyone was quiet.

Boone marched over to a table, grabbed a pitcher of beer, and poured it on the prone man's face.

He groaned. "What the—?"

"He's okay!" Cissie called out to Sally, who was moaning, "Lawd save us," from the floor, where she'd flung herself because of all the drama.

"Get the cameras out of here," Boone said to Anne Silver, then to the band: "Start playing."

They struck up an old Ralph Stanley tune.

"You okay?" Boone asked Cissie, his tone clipped.

She felt small and fragile all of a sudden. "I'm fine. What about you?"

"Fine."

She wanted to hold his hand and thank him. But embarrassment held her back. Plus, there was a tender feeling very deep that made her look away from him.

Chief Scotty approached, his expression wary. "Just what the hell is going on? I got a call that the mayor was involved in a fight."

"It was his fault—" Cissie pointed at the guy spread-eagled on the ground. He was wide-awake now, and she got the feeling he just didn't feel like moving. Maybe because a Florence Nightingale had appeared from behind the bar, a girl in Daisy Dukes with a rag filled with ice.

"I can explain," Boone told the chief.

"Who hit first?" Scotty asked.

"He did." Boone was so damned good-looking, even with a fleck of blood beneath his nose.

Cissie wished everyone would go away. This little feeling deep inside her needed protecting. . . . She wanted to be somewhere quiet, like lying on her bed, her cheek on the pillow, her gaze on something simple and sweet, like a flower in a Mason jar.

Scotty's mouth thinned inside his big jowls. "Did you hit him back?"

"Yes." Boone stuck his palms in his front pockets. Thumbs stayed out. "But I had to."

He was adorable. Cissie wanted to sigh. And jump his bones.

"Did you provoke him?" Scotty wouldn't let up.

Boone arched a brow. "He was dancing with Cissie, and when I tried to cut in—"

"Why'd you do that?" Scotty's jaw jutted out.

"The reason anyone cuts in," Boone replied patiently. "Because *I* wanted to dance with her."

OMG, he wanted to dance with her! She almost bit her thumb and twirled. Thank God she didn't. She would have twirled right into Janelle, who stood behind her with her arms crossed.

"That was outrageous," Janelle said.

"Yeah. It kinda was." A trembly smile formed on Cissie's mouth, but she shut it down fast.

"Don't get your hopes up." Janelle's glossy upper lip curled a fraction. "Chalk this one up to too much beer and testosterone on the dance floor." She stalked off in her red high heels before Cissie could say anything back.

She turned around to hear Scotty say, "You couldn't wait your turn? You had to be disruptive?"

"Come on." Boone frowned. "I wouldn't call cutting in disruptive."

"Aggressive, then." Scotty's gaze roamed over his face. "Have you been drinking, Mr. Mayor?"

"Yes." Boone's big, brown eyes glinted with challenge. "But not to excess."

"I don't know about that." Scotty slipped his little notebook in his pocket.

"It's not Boone's fault." Cissie felt compelled to defend him. "I was the one drinking to excess. I got onstage, and I got off. I danced alone, and then I danced with a stranger. I think Boone was a little worried about me. And when that man hit him, I had to jump on his back."

"You jumped on his back?" Scotty arched both eyebrows.

"Yes," said Cissie. "He was out of control."

"And jumping on his back isn't?" Scotty's tone was dry.

"I guess it is." Cissie bit her lip. "If you don't have a reason. But *I* did."

Scotty looked between them both. "Can you pass a sobriety test?"

"Just give me another half hour," Cissie said.

"Why?" Scotty put his hands on his hips.

"Because"—misery engulfed her, and she looked at the floor—"I-I drank too much."

She'd been so stupid.

"I'm ninety-nine percent sure I can pass," said Boone. "But I drank more than usual, I'll admit. I wasn't planning on driving for a couple hours yet."

Scotty let out a gusty sigh. "How do you think Kettle Knob will look on national TV now?"

Speaking of the TV crew, they were still there, getting drinks at the bar.

"I hope they'll minimize what happened here." Cissie felt guilty. "Maybe Boone can talk to Anne. She likes him way better than she does me."

"I'm not talking to Anne," said Boone. "We have nothing to apologize for. Let America see what they see. Kettle Knob can hold its own."

Scotty's expression was severe. "You're both coming with me in the squad car under protective custody for disorderly conduct while under the influence. Normally, I'm required to drive you home, but you've pissed me off, calling me away from town when you should know better. You'll have to contact someone to come get you at the station."

"You're not serious, are you?" Cissie couldn't believe it.

"Let this go, Scotty. The other guy started it." Boone's tone was calm, cool. Even so, *cranky* was the word Cissie would use to describe him at that moment. *Seriously cranky.*

"And he got his punishment." Scotty wasn't backing down. "But you two? Let me just say I'm disappointed in you both. Now you come quietly with me. I don't want to miss the rest of the Steelers-Titans game."

Boone's expression was inscrutable as they left the bar. He walked quietly, with casual assurance, his boots slapping the hardwood floor.

Anne followed them with a cameraman to the squad car. "Boone! Cissie!"

Boone inhaled and turned to face her. "What is it, Anne?"

"I just want to know if you'd have done anything differently in there." She held out her microphone.

"No," said Boone. "And that's my final word to the audience of *Morning Coffee*." He got in the back of the car.

Anne angled the mike toward Cissie. "How about you, Cissie?"

"Yes," Cissie said instantly. She would have kissed Boone. She would have thanked him for making her feel alive, and . . . and hot.

"Can you tell us a little more?" Anne asked.

Cissie shook her head. "Sorry." No way would she divulge those feelings to the world.

She got in the backseat with Boone. Scotty took off, and thank God, he didn't put on the lights.

Boone's shirt gaped open at the neck, and he slouched low, those massive denim-clad thighs parted wide. The heat at Cissie's collarbone made her suddenly aware of her own subtle gardenia perfume. Every girl part of her jingle-jangled. Their thighs touched, and he didn't move away.

"Scotty should have taped the game," she whispered, hoping to make Boone laugh.

But he didn't. All he did was look at her, his eyes that dark, dark brown. She wanted to look away because he was so quiet, but she couldn't. She looked back. And she vowed that when they got home, she was going to tend to his bruises.

Scotty wouldn't let them call anyone until they got to the station.

"That'll be Nana," Cissie said to Boone. "Not your parents. Not Laurie. Nor any of your friends from school or work. Nana's the one."

"We'll owe her," said Boone.

"I hope she's good and angry." Scotty clicked on a TV set. "I just saw her an hour ago leaving the theater. You two can go sit in the cell until she gets here. It's open. I'll bring her back. I want her to see you suffering in there."

"Scotty?"

"What, Mr. Mayor?"

"Remind me not to give you a Christmas present this year. Or budget for a new police car for the department."

Scotty laughed—not nicely, either—and shook his head. "If you win. I can't believe we have an election coming up, and I have both mayoral candidates in protective custody. What's this world coming to?" He pointed at both of them. "Y'all better be on your best behavior from here on out. The citizens of Kettle Knob deserve candidates who *care*. Not someone who's going to throw the town's reputation to the wolves."

"We did really well today," Cissie said, "until we got to The Log Cabin. Except for me and Boone, Kettle Knob is going to look excellent on national TV. And Boone still might. Anne had a crush on him. But I'm screwed for sure."

Scotty just stared at her.

"Oh, shoot, I don't know *what's* going to happen on that TV program!" She threw her hands in the air and let them fall to her side.

Scotty sat silent as a stone, propped up his feet, and turned away to look at the football game.

"Let's go," Boone told Cissie.

She was glad at least one of the men in the room wasn't treating her like a criminal. Together, they walked around a corner and entered the lone cell at the station. In the tiny space, she was more aware than ever of everything about her partner in crime: his frayed shirt cuffs (it must be one his favorite shirts, which she found endearing); his temples, tanned and smooth; and his perfectly shaped sideburns.

There were two cots, both made up with gray wool blankets. It was cold. Definitely not cozy.

"Here goes." Cissie called Nana and asked for a ride. Nana, good soul that she was, barely asked for an explanation. Vastly relieved, Cissie put her phone away.

Boone said nothing. He had a sort of mysterious vibe about him. He was somewhere else. He hadn't even fought her about who to call to pick them up.

"I thought all cells had windows," she said to pass the time.

"I guess not."

"Apart from the lack of window, this pretty much looks like what I thought a cell would look like. Very boring. I'd want outta here fast if I got locked in."

"That's the idea." He lifted his chin, exposing a tanned, muscular neck. "What's the score?" he called to Scotty.

"I'm not telling," the chief called back.

Misery and irritation were written all over Boone's face.

"Are you going to sit?" she asked.

"Nope." He extended a palm. "Feel free."

There he was being cold and removed. She wished she understood it. She took a peek at her phone. "Nana will be here in ten minutes. She was just getting out of the bath."

"I hate that we had to disrupt her evening." He didn't seem to want to look at her.

"Is something bothering you?"

"You mean, apart from the fact that we got taken into protective custody?"

"Yes."

"That's not enough reason?"

She hitched a shoulder. "I don't know. I think it's kinda fun. In a strange way. I doubt I'll ever forget it." She looked at the cell door. "It's not even locked, though. So it's not like it's a real adventure."

"Damn!" yelled Scotty.

Boone adjusted his stance.

Cissie wished she could get closer to him. "Are you dying to know who just scored? Or maybe intercepted?"

"Yep," he said, then paused. "No, not really." He finally looked at her. But he wasn't happy. That was for sure.

She came up to him. "I'm sorry," she said low. "About tonight." She reached up, curved her palm, let it hover by his nose but didn't touch it—surely, it was sore—then brought her hand back down.

"Don't apologize," he said. "I'm the one who butted in. You were having fun."

"No," she said, "not really." She dared to lift her hand again and brush a lock of hair behind his ear. "The whole time I was there, I was looking to see where you were."

"No, you weren't."

"Yes, I was. I was only pretending to flirt with the fiddler." She put her hands on his chest, stood on tiptoe, and gently pressed her lips against his. Then pulled back. What could she say? She wasn't sure.

He pulled her close. Nudged her mouth with his. Slid his tongue across her lower lip.

She greedily took advantage of the moment, and opened up to him.

God, he tasted good. And he felt like heaven, all warm skin and stubble. Sexy, rhythmic caresses with his thumb across her back made her melt even farther into him.

He pulled back. "We had a talk in the truck," he said low. "We're already breaking our rules."

"Don't blame me," she whispered. "You started it. I was doing really well at The Log Cabin, but then the fight happened, and you told Scotty you wanted to dance with me."

Boone sighed. "Yeah."

"You damn fools!" Scotty yelled as a roar came from the television set. "What kind of call was that?"

Boone cupped both Cissie's sheathed breasts in his palms and kept his eyes on hers. "You're trouble, Miss Rogers."

"No more than you are."

"Are you sure? Jumping on a man's back and blowing out his eardrums with your screaming is pretty crazy." He slid both hands to her backside and inside the back of her skirt and underpants to cup and knead her bottom. She snuggled closer, against that rigid line in his jeans that made her thrill with wanting him.

"That was my Girl Scout training."

"I didn't know they made y'all into ninjas."

"But you nearly broke his jaw."

"No wonder we're in this cell," he said gruffly.

She smiled up at him.

His mouth stayed cold, but his eyes warmed.

They both looked at a cot, then at each other.

Oh, the possibilities!

Which were not possible at all but fun to imagine, so when they pulled back at the same time, there was no weird tension between them. Only a companionable silence. They were cell mates. Cell mates making do. And they had, considering what they had to work with.

They'd grabbed a little fun.

*So there, Scotty!*

Cissie crossed her arms over her chest and sat down. Boone walked up to the cell door and gripped a vertical bar.

Two whole minutes went by. Cissie admired Boone's back, how long and strong it was. She imagined that well-toned back looming above her on a bed—seeing it in a mirror on the ceiling. The very idea was so outrageous and wonderful she couldn't help but squeeze her thighs together in pleasure.

The TV noise blared, and she looked down her blouse, remembered Boone's hands on her blouse cupping her breasts beneath it.

She could have happily sat in the cell daydreaming about all the sexual possibilities between them for hours.

"Hey," she said.

"You don't have to say it," he said without looking back at her. "No more messing around."

Ouch. That hurt. She was actually going to ask him what his favorite song had been at the bar. But he was right. They weren't supposed to mess around.

She sighed. "We'll move out tomorrow. I just need to tell Nana."

He turned to face her, the lines around his mouth etched deep. "That's a good idea."

*Oh.*

Her heart broke right then and there. How could he affect her so?

Another long, lonely few minutes passed.

When Nana finally came, Cissie could tell right away that she should have called Laurie instead.

# CHAPTER TWENTY-SIX

"Let's spring you two jailbirds outta here," Nana said mildly. Yes, she was annoyed to have to drive to the police station at night. However, she would be patient. She remembered how stupid you could get when you were in love and didn't want to admit it.

"I'm so sorry," Cissie said.

"It's all on me." Boone shut the cell door behind them.

The look Scotty threw the two culprits as they passed his desk confirmed what Nana had guessed: *they knew better.*

They filled her in on the details on the car ride home. It all sounded pretty ridiculous.

"Lord, this *Morning Coffee* show is gonna have a field day," she said from the driver's seat.

She hoped they felt like idiots being chauffeured by a little old lady, but it was what it was. Boone was in the backseat. Cissie was up front.

"You were a fool to jump on that man's back," Nana chided her granddaughter.

"I know." Cissie's voice was small. "I-I wasn't really thinking straight."

"That much is clear." Nana's tone was intentionally dry. "What's that outfit you got on? And what happened to your hair? You look ready to rumble."

"Um, thanks?"

Nana refused to say *you're welcome,* even though she secretly approved of the new sexy look. "Boone, it seems to me you were defending yourself. But that man got his back up for a reason. Am I right?"

"Yes," he said. "I could have gone about things differently."

"I'll bet you could have." Nana wasn't letting him off the hook, either. "Any chance you two grown-ass people with responsible positions in our community were liquored up?"

"I know I was," said Cissie.

"Me, too," Boone added.

"Shit," was all Nana said.

But it was enough.

At the house, Cissie was so obviously embarrassed she refused to go to the kitchen and have some of the cocoa Nana offered. "I'm heading up," she said in the foyer. "Good night." She tried to slink up the stairs.

But Nana got one last dig in. "You'd better drink some water and take some headache pills, young lady, before you go to sleep."

"I will," Cissie said softly.

"You're not gonna run away, are you?" Nana asked Boone.

"No, ma'am." He followed her into the kitchen.

He was a good man at heart. Nana knew that very well. She got out some cocoa powder, sugar, and vanilla. "You've got a well-stocked kitchen."

"I live alone, and I like cake."

That simple statement won Nana over like nothing else. "You make cake?"

"Yellow's my favorite. With chocolate frosting. That and a glass of milk."

"Did your mama bake you a lot of cakes growing up?"

"No. Mainly pie."

"Were you a happy boy?"

"Wow. What a question."

"You don't have to answer it."

"I don't mind." He paused. "Overall, I was."

She let that one go. "I like a man who can cook." She poured some milk into a pot on the stove and stirred.

Boone leaned on the counter and watched.

When the milk steamed, she added the other ingredients, stirred some more, then poured the fragrant liquid into two mugs.

"That smells great," he said.

"Got any marshmallows?"

"As a matter of fact, I do. I like cocoa, too. I've just never made the homemade stuff. Now I will."

"It's worth it," she said.

"You want to sit in my study? I'll turn on the fire. It's gas in there. It's always nice to have one room with a quick light up."

"Especially when we lose power during a storm," she said.

They sank into a plush dark-green velvet couch.

"I like your books, dear." Boone's library was so inviting. The whole house was.

"Thanks." He took a sip of cocoa. "This is delicious."

"I'm glad you like it." She refused to make it easy for him by being a chatterbox.

There was a little lull.

"Thank you for getting us tonight," he eventually said, then picked up her hand and kissed the back of it.

What a shock. But a delightful one. She smiled tenderly. "It took a tree going through a roof for us to become friends. But I'm so glad it did. I always thought you were a guy worth getting to know."

When he grinned, the most wonderful crinkles appeared around his eyes. "This supposed disconnect through the generations between the Braddocks and Rogerses is unwarranted."

Said just like a mayor.

"You think so?" Nana said archly. She knew what he was really saying: he wanted Cissie.

"I *know* so," he replied, his desire for her granddaughter written all over his face despite his best efforts to be the cool-headed bachelor. No cool-headed bachelor mayor gets into a fistfight with a redneck over a woman he doesn't desperately want.

"Does that apply to all the Rogerses you know?" she asked.

He stopped short.

Nana laughed. "You're an adorable shade of red right now," she said, and patted his hand. "Just remember this: we can't go back. But we do have the present. Let the Braddocks and Rogerses connect *now*."

He said nothing to that. Why bother? He knew what she meant: he belonged with Cissie.

The fire crackled, and the wind—that steady mountain wind—grew a little wild as it was wont to do as the night grew chill.

"How I love it here." Nana took another sip of her cocoa. "Kettle Knob. Whoever would have guessed that a crazy girl like me would stay tied to a tiny little mountain town? But it's a part of me. I feel my ancestors in that wind. They heard the same whisper. The same howl."

"I know what you mean."

She could tell he really did. They sat quietly again, the gas fire glowing bright.

"Why didn't you go anywhere else?" Nana asked him. "You were a good football player. You had a scholarship, I believe, to NC State."

"I did."

"I seem to remember everyone was stirred up about it when you said no on signing day."

His expression changed subtly. He seemed tense. "I wanted to stay here. Get into the family business."

"Really?" Nana pulled back slightly. "That doesn't seem you at all, real estate development, making the big bucks."

"It doesn't?"

"No." She chuckled. "You're a born leader, obviously, but in another direction, one of service. You mentor. You teach. You protect and inspire."

"I like how you put that."

She could tell he did. He sat up a little higher, which touched her heart. Had his parents not praised him? Apparently not. "It turns out you never did follow in your father's footsteps, did you?"

"I had every intention to," he said, "but I fell into coaching, and not too long after that, politics."

"And a splendid job you've done with both. Kettle Knob's thriving. And the high school's had all winning seasons since you've been coach."

"I work with good people." He was a humble man, which was quite attractive.

Nana smiled. "I like your life, Boone, looking at it from the outside in. There's a lot of love and respect for you in this town."

"I could say the same for you."

She waved a hand. "Oh, people around here think I'm a little eccentric. But you're right, I do believe they're proud of their little theater." She sat for a moment. "I think Cissie's running for mayor because she realizes she's not been reaching anywhere near her full potential. Yes, she participates in church bazaars, helps out at the theater, and runs a lovely little library. But her light has been hidden for too long. And she sees that time's passing. It's time for her to come out of her shell. You spurred her on with this decision to move the library."

"Maybe I did. The truth is, she got me thinking about what I'm doing, too, by running for mayor."

"I'm glad." Nana took his hand and squeezed it. She loved him like a grandson already.

The clock struck one in the morning.

He walked her up to her room, ever the gentleman.

"Don't worry about Cissie," Nana said at her door. "She can take care of herself."

"So I've noticed."

Nana laughed and kissed his cheek. "Good night. I hope your nose feels better in the morning."

When she shut her bedroom door, Boone decided that no way was he letting such a great lady move out because he and Cissie had been immature idiots that night.

The next morning, he found the former Girl Scout in the kitchen sneaking a bagel out of his freezer to toast upstairs.

"Does your nose hurt?" she asked timidly.

"No." It actually did, but he wasn't going to tell her that. Instead, he told her not to bother trying to move out. It wasn't fair to Nana.

"But we need to," Cissie insisted, her hair sticking up all over the place.

"No," he said, "you don't. As energetic as Nana is, she's older now and needs stability. As do you, I might add. I'll keep my distance. I swear it."

He stayed far away on the other side of the kitchen, just to remind her that he was as good as his word.

Cissie's eyes shot all sorts of challenges at him, but

when she shut the freezer door, her shoulders slumped. "You're right about Nana. I'll do as you say, and—and thank you for your hospitality," she added to be polite.

But she couldn't resist casting him one more you're-not-the-boss-of-me look on her way out of the kitchen with her bagel. And maybe—just maybe—that slightly wistful look around her eyes meant that she wished he didn't have to stand so far away.

He wished the same thing. Especially when he watched her go up the stairs in her pj's, obviously braless. He had a hankering to follow her to her room, lift up that shirt, and get down to business.

But then he remembered Nana, hopefully still sleeping hard in her bed. He wasn't going to break the promise he'd just made. So he had a cup of strong coffee and a cold shower instead.

# CHAPTER TWENTY-SEVEN

Cissie did it. She somehow survived living in the same house with Boone without sleeping with him or even flirting with him, and it was likely because he steered clear of her, as she did of him. Not only that, in between working a curtailed schedule at the library, thanks to her friend the substitute librarian, who watched the desk while she was away, she campaigned her heart out for an entire two weeks. Highlights included three separate Q & A events. The first was solo and held by the local Lions Club, which put on a barbecue lunch one Saturday afternoon.

"Bless your heart," she heard over and over—the kiss of death—followed by, "Boone's finally got some competition."

No one really thought she could beat Boone, and no one actually wanted her to, but it made for fine conversation, this mayor's race, and now the whole nation would see it, too! Yes, everyone had heard about the fight at The Log Cabin, but if a man had been so rude that even shy Cissie jumped on his back, then he had it coming!

The second event was held at Starla's diner, which offered a Wednesday breakfast special the following week to anyone who had questions for Cissie. So she talked and ate four waffles, three strips of bacon, and a plate of scrambled eggs over a period of two hours.

It was a lot of fun, although Boone had a table of eight vocal supporters from Campbell. No doubt Janelle was involved in getting them together. They couldn't vote for Kettle Knob's mayor, Cissie reminded them boldly. Even so, they were vociferous in their defense of Boone's record, and one man in a Campbell Country Club golf shirt suggested that Cissie pack up her homemade signs and quit before the race began.

"Those signs are eye-catching for all the wrong reasons," he said at the conclusion of the event, when she was drinking a whole glass of water down to relieve her burning vocal cords.

"How could any reason be wrong?" she answered, panting only slightly when she put the glass down on Starla's counter.

"You don't want people talking about the actual sign." He handed her his card. He was an art director at a gallery in Asheville. "You want them talking about the candidate." He leaned close. "I'll buy those signs from you when you're done with them. Ten dollars each."

"Whatever for?"

"Whoever painted them is *good*."

"Um, we'll talk," she said.

"Don't forget, sugar."

And then Mrs. Hattlebury held a beautiful tea at her house at three o'clock on the Sunday before Election Day. It was a gorgeous afternoon, deep blue skies, a cold crispness to the air, leaves falling on the sidewalk in front of the Hattlebury's old Victorian house with a wrought-iron fence around it covered in ivy. Twenty-five local women came to see both Cissie and Boone, but it was quickly obvious who the favored candidate was.

He really *was* charming. Cissie had brought Mrs. Hattlebury some artisan soaps. He brought her a mixed bouquet of autumn flowers and some lovely locally made chocolates. But the kicker was that he was in a striped forest-green bow tie, starched ivory button-down, dressy tan corduroys, and a smart brown tweed blazer.

A man's man who's taken the time to tie a silk bow tie is a gorgeous sight to behold. The women, including Mrs. Donovan and Laurie, practically swooned.

Everyone partook of tea, delicate chicken salad sandwiches, cucumber sandwiches, and an assortment of sweet things, Cissie's favorites being the lemon drop sugar cookies and salted caramel strawberries rolled in pecans. Boone's mother was there, loudly proclaiming how hard she'd slaved over the mini éclairs everyone knew came from the frozen dessert section at Harris Teeter—not that anyone was a food snob. But it was hard not to giggle, especially when Boone sent Cissie a droll look. On this one issue—his mother and her occasional delusions of grandeur—they were in marked agreement.

Both candidates were given five minutes to make their points. Cissie went first.

Laurie winked at her, their signal that meant *imagine everyone here having sex*, which almost made Cissie laugh. Laurie certainly did. She had to cover her mouth with a napkin and pretend to cough. And then Cissie caught a glimpse of Boone, and the game changed entirely when she imagined him having sex—with her, of course. She had to stir her tea several times to distract herself.

But eventually, she gathered her wits, and in the midst of speaking, finally felt she was making headway in her campaign. Several ladies—who weren't even Friends of the Library—were adamantly against moving it. Another several clapped when she mentioned the need for an indoor pool facility, which could be paid for with a hospitality tax similar to the one already in place in Campbell.

But then Boone spoke. Sure, he hated to see an end to the old library, but Kettle Knob's history would live on as long as the people of the town celebrated it. And that celebration could occur at that strip mall. In fact, the number of people entering that mall every day outnumbered the number of people entering the old library by two hundred fifty to one.

That was a shocking number.

There were gasps all around. Even Mrs. Hattlebury leaned forward and put her hand to her heart when she heard the statistic Boone put out—with proof, damn him. He had the head counts to prove it. While Cissie innocently slept in his guest room, he'd called up a few avid supporters who'd stood outside the strip mall and counted shoppers for three days. He'd recruited another spy to count the number of people entering the library in that same period.

"Imagine," he said, "what kind of reading boom we'll have when you can pick up your book at the same time you get your—"

"Milk and eggs," she mouthed at him silently.

"Milk and eggs," he finished slowly.

She knew she was being mean. But she was tired of that milk-and-eggs story, which the other women gushed over as being so practical.

"Isn't it more practical not to have to drive to pick up a book?" she reminded them. "And practical's not the most important thing anyway. Holding on to something dear *is*."

But they didn't seem to hear her. They kept looking at

Boone. He was eating one of Mrs. Hattlebury's rose, orange, and cardamom mini layer cakes and murmuring, "Mmm, this is delicious."

Cissie knew exactly what all the women were thinking. She was thinking the same thing.

Only Sally and Hank Davis, God bless their loyal hearts, eschewed the milk-and-eggs story along with her. Sally told everyone who'd listen that Hank Davis had decided that the milk was much better at the Exxon station. "Hank Davis has a good palate," Sally assured them. "He got it from watching Rachael Ray."

But then even Sally started watching Boone eat his adorable little cake with a too-small silver fork on a pink-and-white fine bone china plate he could crush with one good squeeze of his hand.

By then, Cissie wanted to crawl under a table. She didn't have a rat's chance in hell of defeating that man.

Still, from the week's campaigning, she learned: 1) how to interrupt excessive talkers without looking as if she were really interrupting them so that she could make her point, 2) how wearing leopard heels and the occasional sequined sweater during the day not only didn't kill her, it made her more confident, and 3) maybe—just maybe—Boone's point about the strip mall version of the library had a ring of validity to it.

Maybe.

But if his had a mere ring, her multiple points about the need for the library to remain in that gorgeous old building smack dab in the center of Kettle Knob sounded like a gong!

Of course, she didn't mention one facet of her argument: the legend. Only the die-hard library goers had heard about it, and if she brought it up, they'd all feel sorry for her because true love hadn't happened to *her*.

At the conclusion of the tea, after everyone had left except Cissie, Mrs. Hattlebury gave her a box of leftover lemon drop cookies and a kindly hug. "You've been a wonderful candidate for mayor," she said. "And I'm not just saying that. You've made everything think in a fresh new way about possibilities for Kettle Knob."

"I hope so." Cissie smiled. "Thanks for today—this was so much fun. I don't think I can beat Boone. But I feel much more . . . dug in."

Her friend sighed happily. "That's what I wanted to hear. Whatever happens in the election"—she was too kind to agree with Cissie about her slim chances—"I hope you'll stay involved." She looked down at Cissie's frilly white blouse that she'd left gaping—Laurie's orders—and the pretty pale pink sweater with tiny crystal sequins, which she wore over a beige-and-pale-pink-plaid skirt. "And keep dressing like this. Sexy and chic look marvelous on you."

"Aw, thanks." Cissie kissed her cheek. "Personal shoppers are the bomb."

Out on the driveway, she inhaled a deep breath. Funny. She hadn't felt the need to go to Paris recently. Or the Cornish moors. Or to Scotland to live in a castle.

"Hey." It was Boone, leaning on his truck, the boring one. But he still looked amazing. He didn't need a cool set of wheels to stand out in a crowd.

"Hi." She felt nervous for some reason.

"You've done great these past couple weeks," he said.

She walked slowly to her car at the curb. "Thanks. You, too. You were a big hit in there."

"I've been hearing nothing but wonderful things about you. I'm telling you, you're a contender. I might not have thought so at first, but I believe so now."

She shrugged. "Thanks. But you have so much momentum behind you. I'll never win."

He paused. "We don't know that for sure. But I'm not going to lie. It'll be an uphill climb. And not because I'm particularly great or anything. It's the Braddock name behind me. My grandfather's legacy. And yeah, maybe having ten years under my belt of doing this job."

"Thank you for not condescending to me."

"I never would. You're the smart one."

She shook her head. "That's just not true anymore. I've been in a rut for a lot of years, I'm coming to realize. And yet I never saw it until recently. It snuck up on me."

He stepped forward. "I think you're terrific," he said. Just like that.

"Boone. You're not supposed to say things like that. They just make me . . . crazy."

He looked up at a tree branch for half a second, then back at her. "In a good way or a bad way?"

She bit her lower lip. And she could swear that box of cookies was trembling in her hand. "In a-a—" She closed her eyes, then opened them. "I don't know. Just . . . crazy. Like, I don't know what to think or even *how* to think anymore. I used to be really good at thinking."

He laughed. "Can I take that box for you?"

She allowed herself a tiny smile. "Only if you don't eat them all. They're my favorite."

He took it. She opened her car door. He handed it back.

"Hey, I've got something for you." He reached into his blazer pocket and pulled out an envelope that said "Ms. Cissie Rogers" on the front in loopy cursive. Tiny hearts dotting the i's.

"What's this?" she murmured as she pulled out a home-made card. And then she smiled. "An invitation from your senior girls to come to powder-puff football practice tonight?"

"Yep. They think it's cool that a woman's running for

mayor. They want you to come check them out, maybe run a few plays with the offense."

"Wow. I'm flabbergasted and touched by this." She looked up at him. "I never did powder-puff in high school. I was too scared. There's tackling, throwing, catching."

All that physical stuff.

"You'll learn fast. Meanwhile"—he grinned—"I can teach you the basics back at the house first."

She laughed nervously.

He pointed to his temple. "We'll talk strategy. On a chalkboard."

"Oh, okay." She was a little disappointed. She wouldn't have minded being tackled by him. "I'm not that great at throwing. Maybe we can play catch, too. And all the rest. Like running."

His eyes gleamed. "Maybe we can."

He knew she was fishing.

She blushed. "So, right now?"

"Sure. Why not? This is our last chance to relax before the big day."

Monday was their final day of campaigning.

"Where are you headed tomorrow?" Cissie asked.

"Breakfast with the senior bowling team. Teaching my PE classes. Then lunch at the Campbell country club. An afternoon visit to the park, just to see who's there. Maybe a visit to the gas station to say hello. Football practice. And tomorrow night, I'm having dinner at Starla's with some teacher friends followed by a cocktail party at my parents' house. What about you?"

"And I thought I was busy." She sighed. "The Friends of the Library are bringing muffins into the library tomorrow morning. I plan to leave at lunch to stop by the hair salon where I got my hair done to say hi to everyone. And after work, I'm hanging out with Laurie and her boys for a while before going to the party Nana's throwing for me at the theater."

"Sounds fun."

"I'm excited."

There was a beat of awkward silence.

"Okay, then." He threw his keys up in the air. "See you at home?"

*Home.* It wasn't really. But it was a great in-between place. "Sure, and—and thanks, Boone."

"For what?"

"For filling in. Giving us a place to stay. Reminding me that we shouldn't rock Nana's boat, even though we surely must be rocking yours. I do appreciate it."

"It's been entirely my pleasure." He grinned, which did nothing to slow the fast beating of her heart.

He walked to his car. "Hey," he called back.

"Yeah?"

"No racing. Scotty can't take anymore high jinx."

She laughed. "I'm the last person to want to race up that mountain."

He was one of the few who knew about her secret old-lady driving style. He was teasing her.

"And one more thing," he added. "Whoever wins this election, don't forget you and Nana can stay as long as you want."

"Wow." She nodded, not sure what to say. There was a lump in her throat, for sure, and for a couple of reasons. "Thanks so much." She lifted her hand in a brief farewell.

He waved back and got in his car. He took off a few seconds later.

But she sat in hers. Leaned her forehead on the steering wheel. Closed her eyes and thought about him. He was a good man. He was also sexy. Sweet. Bossy when he thought he knew best—and charming. Lots of charming.

She was falling in love with him, hard, the guy who'd finally walked over the library threshold—to come see her.

He didn't fit the legend. He was local. Not an out-of-towner. But that didn't matter.

She was enchanted by him anyway.

If she weren't running for mayor herself, she'd vote for him. Like a trillion times. Which made her so angry at herself because she believed in the library, and she couldn't betray her own principles—for a *guy*.

But she wanted to. She wanted *him*.

"You're a mess," she told herself in the rearview mirror, then drove up the steep mountain five miles an hour below the speed limit, her fastest time yet—the sooner to see him again.

# CHAPTER TWENTY-EIGHT

*Hands off* was Boone's mantra that he repeated to himself the rest of that day. Nana was at play practice again, so he and Cissie had the house to themselves.

For two hours, they worked on getting her up to speed on football, first on the couch with a small lap chalkboard, where he taught her basic football rules and a few easy plays. She wore a blue UNC sweatshirt and yoga pants, and she smelled delicious. Her side was warm and soft when they accidentally bumped into each other. Even her elbow nudging his was sensual torture.

Then they went outside and practiced throwing, catching, and dodging imaginary oncoming players. He absolutely refused to tackle her. If he ever got her on the ground, he knew he wouldn't let her up. They used scarves tucked into their pants as flags. When they practiced throwing, he got out two footballs and let her watch him for proper throwing technique.

*Frickin' adorable* were the words that went through his mind about Cissie at the actual powder-puff practice. He had to work really hard not to stare at her butt the entire time. He was surrounded by teenaged girls who looked up to him as a man they could count on to respect women. And he did, but he also couldn't get enough of Cissie's backside.

Cissie laughed almost the entire time—when she wasn't looking very serious as either the quarterback or tight end, the two positions the girls chose for her. She even called them into a huddle and ran one of the two plays he'd taught her, which resulted in a first down.

He was so proud.

And when she looked over at him fleetingly, her face bright, he gave her a thumbs-up. And his heart—

His heart wasn't his own anymore. It was like a fumbled football, heading straight toward Cissie. He needed to chase it down and recover it.

Fast.

After practice, the girls kidnapped her and told him they were taking Cissie to the pizza place and that he could pick her up in an hour and a half.

"Coach!" One girl came running over to his car. "We love her." She was panting from excitement or exertion, he couldn't tell. They'd just finished playing their hearts out. "If I were eighteen, I wouldn't know who to vote for. I hope you don't mind." She ran off before he could answer.

And then another one came up. "Is Miss Rogers your girlfriend? You got in a fight over her at The Log Cabin, right?"

He thought he'd covered the fight this past week at school, where he'd had to address the situation not only with Wendy, the principal, but the kids he taught and coached—per Wendy's instructions. He'd been going to say something anyway because that Monday morning, they'd all eyed him like he was a big celebrity.

But this girl had obviously slipped through the cracks. He gave her the same speech, condensed: "I defended myself against a man who threw a punch at me. Miss

Rogers unfortunately got in the middle, and when it appeared he was getting rough with her, I defended her, too. But no one got seriously hurt, thank goodness. Violence really doesn't pay."

He'd desperately wanted to add "most of the time," but Wendy told him if he did, she'd be pissed.

The girl's face brightened. "I knew you were a hero, Coach Braddock!"

And went running off.

Damn. Teenaged girls loved to state their opinions and go running off before he could say anything back. He was going to tell her that no, Miss Rogers was *not* his girlfriend.

And then he realized how much he'd hate shouting that, so he was glad the young lady seemed to have forgotten the rest of her question.

Ah, well. He watched the convoy of cars leave the parking lot. Cissie was in the silver pickup truck up front. He missed her already.

"You're done for," he said aloud. His chest was heavy with conflicting feelings. Want, misery, desperation, anger, and beneath it all, a simmering happiness that he could not address because it was too big, too able to overwhelm and control him, which couldn't happen because then nothing would be locked away. Nothing. It would rip all his secrets out of their drawers for the world to see.

He went home, putzed around the house all by himself for an hour. It was no fun there anymore, living by himself, he realized.

He checked his watch. Eight o'clock. It wasn't quite time to pick up Cissie at the pizza parlor, but he would anyway. She needed her rest. The Monday before Election Day Tuesday was always exhausting if you were a candidate with an opponent. And then Election Day itself could wipe you out. He remembered his first election against that old guy who'd replaced his grandfather. Boone had been on edge the whole time. He'd run unopposed after that, so he'd never experienced again that sort of nervous agitation that came with knowing you could possibly lose.

Until now, and even now—

No. He was going to win. It saddened him how predictable the outcome was. It seemed so unfair. If people only knew Cissie better. And if she had entered the race sooner, maybe had more campaign signs that actually lasted. He'd seen two of hers melted onto the pavement downtown after a night of rain.

Well. It wasn't the last race of either of their lives. He hoped she'd run against him again.

He showed up at the pizza parlor, and Cissie hugged all the girls and left with him. It was like pulling a pop star away from her adoring fans. She was her quirky, confident librarian self, but she was now also a sassy powder-puff football player and a mayoral candidate who'd run a good campaign on very little notice. It was a captivating mix.

Nana was at the house when they got back, and they watched a thriller together on Netflix. Everyone's adrenaline was running high, so Nana made cocoa afterward, and they had a fun discussion about the reveal of the killer in the movie. It was an ordinary family night—the kind he imagined other people had, the kind he'd like to have more often in his usually quiet house. Everything flowed. Everything was right.

"It's late," Nana said, "and I had a wonderful time. See you kids in the morning." She blew kisses and walked up the stairs.

"You should go to bed, too," Boone said to Cissie. "You need your rest."

"No more than you do. Besides, I'm running out of time to write an acceptance speech."

"Oh, yeah. Gotta have that."

Her brow furrowed. "And a concession one, too, I suppose. Have you come up with yours?"

"Nope." He was terribly tempted to ask if she wanted to write them in his bedroom.

"I guess I'll go upstairs and do mine in my room."

"No desk," he said.

"I can write them in bed, but Dexter will sit on the notebook and rub his face on my pen."

"Cats."

"I'll stay down here. In the kitchen."

Boone couldn't have that. He'd never be able to stay away. "I have a great idea."

"What?"

He went to a cupboard and pulled out a Thermos. "I'm going to make us some hot toddies. We'll bundle up"—the more clothes they had on, the better—"jump in the truck, head to town, and come up with our speeches in the gazebo, which is where we'll be giving them anyway."

"Hey," she said brightly, "that's a great idea."

"Thanks."

"Except that I know what you're doing," she said with a chuckle, "and I'm not going to get naked with you in the gazebo."

He laughed inside. But he kept his expression serious when he put some water in the microwave to heat. "That was a joke."

"It was?"

"Well, no. But it's too cold for gazebo sex. I should have thought of that when I suggested it." He opened a cupboard, pulled out some rum, and poured a friendly amount in the Thermos. "We'll stay busy inventing speeches. And then we'll come back here and sleep the deep, peaceful sleep of two people who have finished their campaign chores."

And kept their hands off each other.

Sometimes he was so smart, he scared himself.

The town square was deserted when they arrived and parked at the curb. Cissie thought the bench with her sign on the back would cheer her, but at midnight, it also looked somehow forlorn. Soon the sign would be gone, her campaign would be over, and so would her hanging out with Boone.

The house fixing was progressing nicely. She and Nana would be able to move back in under a month. It was exciting—but it was also sad.

They grabbed their stuff and headed to the gazebo.

"It'll be fun not having to write," Cissie said. Boone had a dictation app on his phone. "Are you sure it'll work?"

"It might mess up a few words here and there, but overall, it works great. You can go in and fix the typos tomorrow before you print it out. This way you can keep your gloves on and actually say the words out loud, the same way you will when you give the speech."

They decided to have a toddy first.

She sat on a bench, and he poured her a steaming hot drink.

"Mmmm." The sweet-tart combination of honey, lemon, and rum was delicious. "It's so good. Where did you learn to make these?"

"It's an old Braddock recipe. Really old."

"I'll bet they had some before they marched to King's Mountain."

"I'll betcha." He joined her on the bench.

It was cold enough that they squeezed together. Anyone would have. But her pulse thrummed anyway.

"Ahh." He took a sip of his own toddy and grinned at her. "Welcome to Kettle Knob, where you can still drink Revolutionary War–era toddies that your great-great-great-great granddaddy used to make. And not get mugged in the town square if you visit after midnight."

"I might borrow that last line for my speech."

"Wait. I said it first."

She laughed and focused on her mug because Boone looked very cute. She couldn't think about him that way. All day, especially when she'd been playing powder-puff football, she'd been extremely aware of him. "I had a great time with the high school girls."

"I could tell. They really liked you."

"I liked them, too. They look up to you, you know. I think ninety-nine percent of them probably have crushes on you."

"I don't know about that."

"I do."

"Well, I treat them the way I'd want my sister Debbie to be treated."

"Do you ever see her?"

"Every couple months she comes over with her family. She's older, and I love her. But she's almost like a different generation, two years older than my brother." He picked up the Thermos. "How about a little more?"

"Yes, please." It really was good. And it was helping her feel a little less on pins and needles around him. She wanted to kiss him. Badly. But she was also really interested in figuring out who he was. "It must have been hard losing your brother."

"Well, he died when I was a toddler. So, it wasn't. Part of me feels guilty about saying that."

"No, you shouldn't." She found herself reaching out a gloved hand and squeezing his lower arm. But only for a second. "I feel for your parents."

"Yep. It's why I probably give them too many breaks. They've gone through something no one should ever have to. Hey," he said, switching gears, "are you ready to use the app?"

"Sure."

"Should I walk away so you can have privacy?"

"No, that's okay." She felt suddenly wistful. "I wouldn't mind you hearing my acceptance speech, since I probably won't ever get to deliver it."

"Come on, now. You can't say that yet."

"I know I shouldn't." Her spirits perked back up, and she grinned. "I take it back."

"Good," he said, and showed her how to use the app.

She practiced a few times, then began speaking as the victorious mayoral candidate while looking directly at him. It was empowering to role-play being the primary person who could effect change in Kettle Knob. She stopped to consider a phrase. She started up again, then once again paused. Just when she needed him to, he smiled. Or nodded his head emphatically. At one point she wanted to scratch a whole paragraph—it was about how Kettle Knob's past was its bridge to the future, and she thought it sounded way too clichéd—so he helped her delete it.

Eventually, she had a speech that made her happy.

"It's the perfect length," he said, "just enough to keep them wanting more."

"Thanks." She lowered the phone.

He took her elbows, hovered over her. "How about a concession speech?" He was teasing her now.

Slowly, she lifted the phone to her lips. Pressed start. "I concede . . . nothing." She lowered the phone. Kept her eyes on his, which gleamed.

"Is that so?" he asked, moving closer.

She nodded.

"Nothing?" He was a huge fan of twirling a lock of her hair around his finger.

She was captured by his gaze. "That's right," she whispered.

He took the phone out of her hand, put it in his pocket. Pulled her up against his chest. "A mayor has to learn to negotiate. To compromise."

"Only on some things." She felt powerful, focused—confident as a woman—in a way she never had.

"I'd like to try to find out what those things are. Let's have a meeting. Right now." And then he kissed her.

Her senses swam. She didn't want to come up for air. He pulled her to the bench and onto his lap. Their coats were thick shields between them, making the connection of skin on skin that much more exciting.

He stopped and unbuttoned his wool jacket, and she slid her hands in around his shirt.

"Oh, you feel good," she said.

Understatement of the year.

He kept kissing her and unzipped her fleece coat, thrilling her when his hands moved in, caressed her waist and back, then teased her breasts.

Their breath came in clouds.

"How come I'm not cold?" she murmured.

"Me, either."

The darkness of the square enveloped them. There was no sound but their hearts, their breathing, their teenage fumbling with all those clothes.

"It's below freezing, you know," she said when he unbuttoned her shirt and kissed her bare breast with his hot mouth and tongue.

"Not where we are," he murmured.

He was right. There was such heat between them. She

dug her hand like a spade between the front of his shirt and his pants to get to him, and when she made contact, he groaned.

She loved it. He felt silky soft and hard and hot. The juncture between her thighs ached for him.

The houses and businesses around the square were dark.

He pulled back to look at her full-on. "If we do the deed—all the way—I know this is your first time in a long time."

"How can we, in our clothes?" she asked in their cocoon of warmth.

He laughed. "We don't even have to move. But we can always go back to the house."

"I can't wait that long." She smiled. "Besides, I hear sex in a gazebo rocks."

He grinned and kissed her. "We'll make sure it does."

He pulled her black ski pants down to her upper thighs. Her coat covered her bottom.

She helped yank his jeans down just far enough for access. "Do you have something?"

"Always," he said, and pulled a tinfoil packet out of his wallet.

And the rest came naturally. She straddled him, her feet on the bench on either side of his hips. Put her arms around his neck. He held her tight, his hand splayed across her rear, so she wouldn't fall.

And then for the first time in a decade, Cissie Rogers had sex. Inside that warm cave of down and wool, she lowered herself onto Boone—the reality of what he had to offer so much better than any of her fantasies—and rode him hard, with no awkwardness, just utter thrill and abandon, while he teased her with his fingers.

When she slipped over the edge, her moans were low and private, just for him. He suckled one of her breasts and told her things that made her want to start all over again. He sped up. So did she. This time was even more spectacular because she was looking into his eyes when she came harder than before, right when he did, one of his hands on her butt and the other on her breast as he told her she was the most gorgeous thing he'd ever seen.

And then the world came back, and they were sitting on a hard, cold bench in a gazebo in the middle of Kettle Knob, the same gazebo they'd each deliver a speech in two days later.

One would be the victor.

One would be the loser.

But they'd both remember this.

How could they ever forget?

# CHAPTER TWENTY-NINE

Cissie finished work the next day, flush with good feelings about her town and the people in it and heady with the satisfaction that comes from good loving. She couldn't stop thinking about Boone and how much she wanted to be with him—all the time.

She was crazy, madly in love with the mayor.

The worm-in-the-apple sign had come down from behind the desk at the library. In its place was a new sign Sally had made, and it said, "This Library Has My Heart" in that funky writing of hers. She'd drawn lots of hearts on it, and she'd taken it all over town and gotten people to sign their names in the hearts.

Hank Davis hung the sign perfectly straight behind the desk.

"He got real good hanging up your signs everywhere," Sally explained.

"Thank you so much." Cissie hugged her dear friends and felt almost like the library was breathing all around her. It was still alive. She had the feeling it felt appreciated. Surely all her ancestors were smiling down at her because she was doing right by them.

She was on her way to Laurie's house after work when she realized she'd better call her parents before they went to sleep. As it was, it was already eleven o'clock at night in Cambridge, England. She loved the funny overseas ring. Her heart started thumping wildly when they answered. She missed them.

"Mother, Daddy?"

"Hello, darling," her mother said in that Vermont accent, but now it had a slightly British sound to it.

Cissie imagined her father was like Winston Churchill, with a cigar between his teeth, when he said, "Cissie, my love. How goes it?"

"Um, swimmingly," she said with a broad smile.

Would they understand her trying to be elegant? English? Like Elizabeth Bennet?

"That's lovely," said her mother.

"The election is tomorrow," Cissie reminded them.

She'd told them in an email, but they'd yet to talk about it on the phone. They'd written back a short message asking three questions: 1) was her campaign fully funded? 2) by whom? and 3) what was her platform?

All intelligent questions. She only wished . . . Oh, never mind, it was silly to wish that they'd said other things, like *We need to Skype and strategize with you*, or *Maybe we'll take a few days to come back and cheer you on*, or *We'll send you a campaign contribution*.

"Good luck," Daddy said.

"Yes," said Mother. "Are you prepared to be mayor if you win?"

"As prepared as I can be with no experience," Cissie said. "I've learned a lot during the campaign."

"Our quiet little Cissie, on the campaign trail." Her father sounded pleased, which made her happy.

"How's Nana?" Mother asked.

"Boone's house is very comfortable, and she'd holding up well. But I think she's missing home. Every once in a while, I sense a little wistfulness on her part."

"Of course," said Daddy. "That's only natural."

A car whizzed by and honked the horn at Cissie. She waved, having no idea who was inside the vehicle. She was becoming something of a minor celebrity since her campaign started.

"I love you," said Cissie.

"We love you, too," said her father.

Her mother always had trouble getting the words out, but she'd told Cissie once that it was her New England upbringing, and Cissie tried her best to understand.

When she hung up, she felt the old loneliness that made her feel awkward. Gawky. But at Laurie's, she was welcomed with big hugs from Sam and Stephen.

"You two," she said.

They jumped on her together, and she almost fell over.

"Stop it, boys!" their mother said, and clapped her hands at them like they were pets she needed to shoo off.

They ran into the backyard.

Laurie looked more frazzled than usual.

"Everything okay?" Cissie asked her.

"No." Laurie shook her head slowly. "Everything's terrible. I'm sorry. I wish I could hide it. I know tonight's a big night for you. And so is tomorrow." Her voice broke on the last few words.

"Nothing's more important than you being happy." Cissie immediately hugged her. "What happened?"

Laurie sniffled. "Perry—he's been seeing someone. That's why he's been traveling so much."

Cissie sucked in a breath and drew back. "Are you sure?"

Laurie nodded. "He told me himself this afternoon.

He wants a divorce. He's already talking about getting serious with this other person. She's in sales at the company's office in Wilmington. He met her on a work trip."

Cissie grabbed her close again. "I'm so, so sorry. I can't believe this."

"Me, either," squeaked Laurie. "I'm worried about the boys."

"No," said Cissie. "They have a strong mother, and you have a great family and lots of friends to help you. You *will* get through this. But isn't this awfully quick? You just heard about it today. Can you and Perry patch this up? Can't he at least talk about it?"

Laurie shook her head. "I wish I could get the chance. I'm furious with him. And so hurt. I've never felt a pain this bad. And I hate this woman, whoever she is. Perry has a family. Doesn't she care about that?"

"I can't even imagine how upset you are," said Cissie. "I'm so sorry, Laurie. I wish I could help somehow."

"Just being here to listen helps." Laurie's face was pale. "How I feel doesn't matter to Perry anymore. He's already moved on."

The enormity of the situation hit Cissie hard. She paced before the window, where she could look out and see the boys. "Perry's a fool, throwing away the best thing that ever happened to him. I wish he were here right now. I'd tell him. I'd"—she looked at the vase of flowers on the table—"I'd dump those right over his head."

Laurie started to cry again. "*You're* angry? Imagine how *I* feel."

Cissie brought her some tissues, and let her get it all out on her shoulder. She wished she had good answers and then decided that right then, answers didn't matter. Laurie simply needed a good friend.

"Maybe," Laurie said, "just maybe he'll realize later that he's made a mistake. But as of right now, he feels good—if you can believe that—about where he is and what he's doing."

"Where is he?"

"At a hotel in Campbell. We haven't figured out how we'll tell the boys."

The boys!

Cissie's heart ached for them.

They talked for another half hour while Sam and Stephen played outside. And then Laurie insisted that they both get ready for Cissie's party at the theater.

"Are you sure you want to go?" Cissie was wearing an elegant champagne-colored sheath with a surprisingly low back. She put on some Red Rumbler lipstick for even more dramatic flair. "I totally understand if you want to stay home."

"No, I want to go." Laurie shimmied into a pretty green chiffon dress. "If I stop too long to think about what's happening, I cry. But not for the reasons you might think—like hating this other woman and Perry being a selfish jerk."

"What reason, then?"

Laurie sighed. "In my heart, a long time ago, I knew we were having problems. We were on autopilot. We stopped talking and stayed busy. But I didn't have the guts to face what was happening. If I had . . . maybe it wouldn't have come to this."

"Oh, Laurie . . ."

"I know."

"All the more reason you're going to the party," Cissie insisted. "Who's babysitting?"

Laurie's mom couldn't. Mrs. Donovan would be at the theater event, despite admitting that she didn't care about the library moving to the strip mall. Cissie was still her daughter's best friend, and she'd be there to support her.

"My neighbor's coming over," Laurie said. "Mom doesn't know about Perry yet. Only you. I need another day before I can spread the word to the rest of the family."

At the party, Cissie tried hard to put aside Laurie's terrible news. For Nana's sake, she had to try to have fun. Laurie told her the same thing when they went to the theater bathroom to touch up their hair and makeup.

"I was selfish telling you about me right before this started," Laurie said again.

"Stop." Cissie eyed her friend in the mirror sternly. The strips of theatrical lighting surrounding their reflections cast their faces in sharp relief, revealing their heavy hearts. "If you hadn't told me, you wouldn't be here, and you know it. You would have made up some excuse. This is what friends are for—we lean on each other. You being here tonight—after all you've gone through today—is way above and beyond."

"I'll take any praise right now. Are you worried about the election?"

"Yes, but—"

"It's Boone. I can see it in your eyes. Is he causing trouble?"

Cissie sighed. "I think I'm in love with him."

"Oh, God, no," said Laurie.

"Is that so bad? Because if it is, tell me. I need to know."

Laurie shook her head. "You mean apart from the fact that he's going to move the library, which is the opposite of what you want to happen? How about the fact that he hasn't shown any signs of settling down? He's on the football field when he's not in the mayor's office. He'll never be home for breakfast, lunch, or dinner. He dates around. I love the guy. He's a great coach and a damned fine mayor. I thought you two would be cute together, but I don't know anymore. You deserve a man who's going to be there to pay attention to you, to talk to you sometimes about things *you* love. Like books."

Cissie sighed. Books were a huge part of who she was. She read every night in bed, without fail, and sometimes she was up all night with a fantastic book. But when you had a guy who could make you feel the way Boone did, she could see staying up all night with him instead.

Laurie managed a half-hearted smile. "I can tell you're thinking about the sex part. Have you two actually done it?"

"Yes." *In the gazebo*, Cissie thought, and wondered if she should be ashamed that two upstanding citizens like her and Boone had caused a bar scene *and* had sex in a public place.

"I can tell you're afraid to tell me it was amazing because of what's going on with Perry and me. But it's okay." Laurie smiled sadly. "I *want* you to be happy."

That broke Cissie's heart. "Laurie—"

"No. Let's talk about it." Laurie took out her comb and ran it through her hair. "Maybe it means something good will come out of what happened to us. Pay attention to the sex part. If that's good, it goes a long way." She put her comb back in her purse and looked up at Cissie with an earnest expression. "It's not everything, but good sex makes the rest so much easier to navigate. Perry and I quit making time for each other in bed. It was a very bad mistake."

"I can't believe you're thinking of *me* right now," Cissie said.

"Of course, I am. You're my best friend."

They hugged, a long hug that would take them both through the party, which wound up being a wonderful event. Cissie was touched by how beautifully Nana had decorated the large lobby entrance. The food was eclectic—everyone brought different things—and all of it was delicious. And way more partygoers came than she expected—at least fifty, and they were all so supportive.

"This was incredible," she told Nana at the conclusion.

Laurie had gone home with her mother. She seemed in better spirits. Maybe tonight's party had reminded her, too, that she was part of a community.

"I feel so loved." Cissie walked around with Nana and a couple teenage volunteers to pick up napkins and put the glass wine goblets in a big bin for washing.

"That's how I wanted you to feel." Nana smiled, but she looked tired.

Cissie took a napkin out of her hand. "You sit down. I've got this."

"Tell you what. We'll leave the rest up to the volunteers. They're earning service points for the National Honor Society."

"Okay." She took Nana's hand, and they sat down.

"Tomorrow's the big day," said Nana. "I'm so proud of you." Her voice trembled with it.

Cissie leaned her head on her grandmother's shoulder. "You're the one who got me started. Remember the day on the porch?"

"Of course. But that was *you*—you telling me you were in a rut. You saying that something had to change."

"Well, something did," Cissie said. "A tree fell through our roof."

They both chuckled.

"It wasn't the tree," Nana said. "You thought of the sit-in first. But the tree did make us both regroup."

They sat and watched the teens for a few seconds.

Nana took her hand. "I got a text earlier from someone at Boone's party."

"Oh?"

"She said that Boone stayed twenty minutes and left. He told his parents he had something else going on."

"Are you kidding me?"

"No."

"What could be more important right now than his own pre–Election Day party?" Cissie dug through her purse and pulled out her phone on the off chance—the *very* off chance—that he'd tried to contact her, and found a message.

"We've got to go," she told Nana. "He—he texted me. He's at home. He told us to get back as fast as we can. He's lit the fire, made cocktails, and you and I are both invited to our own house preelection party."

"So that's how it is." Nana chuckled. "Honey, he's not getting my vote for mayor, but he wins my vote for Most Adorable Man. I'll have one little drink, but then I'm hitting the hay. Take advantage of that fact."

# CHAPTER THIRTY

This time, after a fun night hanging at home with his two houseguests, Boone took Cissie by the hand and led her to his bedroom. It felt like the most natural thing in the world to do after Nana said goodnight and went upstairs. Cissie belonged with him as she was now, sprawled on his bed, naked, her hair spread on his pillow, her eyes following his as he took off his clothes, slung them over the divan, lit a low lamp, and returned to the bed to join her.

But then his cell phone chirped from his nightstand.

She sat up on her elbow. "It's late."

He checked the screen and immediately tensed. "I can't believe it. It's my parents."

"Great timing." She smiled and kissed his shoulder.

Her enthusiasm for all things sensual—so fresh and honest—turned him on like nothing else. But he also loved that she made an excellent friend in the bargain.

He wrapped his arm around her waist and took the call. "Hey, Dad. Is everything okay?"

Cissie ran her hand down his naked back, her touch soothing yet also a turn-on.

"Your mother and I are fine," his father said. "But we need to come talk to you."

That was weird. "This late?" Boone made a face at Cissie.

Hers registered a budding concern, which was so damned sweet of her. He moved his hand to her thigh to let her know.

"It's imperative," Frank said. "We're leaving now."

He clicked off before Boone could ask more.

"I can't believe it," he said.

"Well, at least they called ahead." Cissie reminded him.

"Yeah. I'm sorry." Boone kissed her, but he was definitely distracted. "This must be punishment for my leaving the party early." He couldn't imagine what else it would be. "They'll be here in ten. You want to stay?"

She sat up. "I think I'll go," she said. "I'd feel funny waiting here. . . ."

"You shouldn't."

She shrugged, leaned forward, and kissed him back. "I'll see you in the morning. It's probably best we both get some sleep. And I can't promise I'll let you sleep if I stay." She slipped out of bed and pulled on her clothes scattered across the floor.

He got up, too, ignored his desire to run his hands over her soft, warm body before she got dressed, and went to his bureau instead. He pulled on a pair of pajama bottoms, donned a T-shirt, and came back to her. She was dressed again and at his reading table and chair.

She looked up at him. "I'm so glad you're reading *To Kill a Mockingbird*. It's one of my favorites. I've read it at least ten times over the years. How far have you gotten, or are you a re-reader, like me?"

Inwardly, he groaned. Maybe that glow on her face came from the book. But he dared to hope it came from him, too. "I'm just starting."

"Oh!" She looked delighted. "You're going to love it."

"Great." He kissed her long and deep. "You'd better go."

When she looked up at him, her eyes were soft. "I wish . . ."

"What?"

"I wish we weren't opposed to each other tomorrow."

"Yeah." He brushed some hair off her face. "Me, too. But politics isn't everything."

"But what I feel politically—that's who I am," she said. "I can't separate. My values, my principles, are all tied up in how I vote."

"Mine, too. But look at James Carville and Mary Matalin. They're together, despite incredibly dissimilar political views. You and I both love Kettle Knob. We just have different ideas about how to nurture what we have here. Sometimes we'll run into snags. But everything's negotiable."

She smiled. "You're right."

Why was he making arguments in support of their being together when he knew—ultimately—that she was going to split when she found out she was shagging the football coach who could barely read?

He watched her go up the stairs. She turned around and blew him a kiss.

When his parents showed up at the door five minutes later, his mother's lips were compressed and his father's bushy eyebrows appeared lower than usual, both ominous signs.

"Good evening, son," his father said in a clipped tone. "I hope those other things you had to do instead of attending your mother's party got done."

"They did." He held the door open. "You know how crazy it gets right before an election. Mom, how'd the rest of the night go?"

His mother launched into a long monologue about all

the gossip she'd heard. "It was a huge success, darling. It's probably good you left—you looked like a man on a mission."

"Oh, I was." Boone felt better than ever about leaving. "Let's head to the study."

"We've seen the *Morning Coffee* tape," Frank said once they were situated with the study door shut. "And they're moving it up to tomorrow morning, instead of Sunday. Eight a.m. sharp—it's going to be a segment on the network's national weekday morning show."

"Are you kidding me?" Boone was . . . Well, he was flabbergasted, to say the least. "Why the full-court press? And how do you know all this?"

His parents exchanged glances.

"Your father has a great deal of influence, as you know," his mother said. "In light of what happened at The Log Cabin, he took it upon himself to contact some of the staff at the show, so we can be ready for whatever comes before the story hits the air."

"I can't believe you did that. Or that they let you see it."

His father shrugged. "Money talks. Your mother and I made sure we took business cards from the TV crew when the show was here."

"The production assistants could always use extra cash," his mother said. "We're only protecting our interests."

"I get it that that's how you work." Boone sat in his grandfather's desk chair, crossed his arms, and stared into the unlit fireplace across the room. "But I don't have to like it. And it was unnecessary. At The Log Cabin, I defended myself, and then I defended Cissie. The show might try to make the situation look worse, but believe me, I'll get my side of the story out there."

"The Log Cabin wasn't the problem," said his dad.

That was a shock. Boone wracked his brain to think what else this so-called problem could be. "What was, then?"

Becky Lee sank gently into a leather armchair. "It's your relationship with Ella Kerrison that has us concerned. And the TV people all aflutter."

*Ella.*

Boone sat forward over his knees. "How would the TV show know about Ella?"

"They have videotape of you going to her house a lot," his father said. "In the mornings. Parking your car in the back."

"It looks like you're having an affair." His mother sounded shocked. And worried.

Boone raked a hand through his hair. "This is ridiculous. How dare they spy on me? And so what if I'm having an affair with Ella?" His parents both drew back a little. "I'm *not*," he assured them. "But she's single, and so am I. Why would a TV program care if we had a romantic relationship?"

"I think it's because they also have footage of you coming out of your shed with Cissie," his mother said. "It's clear you're kissing her. Not to mention she's living with you."

Boone couldn't believe what he was hearing.

"They want to make you look like a two-timer," his dad said. "An untrustworthy guy."

Becky Lee got tears in her eyes. "Do you see now why we didn't want you to live with Cissie? Your reputation is going to be sullied."

A cold hardness formed in Boone's chest. "Who took that film of me and Cissie in the shed?"

Frank shook his head. "Someone in Kettle Knob, I suppose. Someone who wanted to catch you being up to no good."

"Kissing someone—when you're both single—is a sign of poor character?" Boone raised his voice. "That's stupid."

"Maybe you have a stalker," Becky Lee suggested.

"I guess I must," he said. "Why else would someone hide in my woods and take film footage of me in my shed?"

"Is Cissie your girlfriend?" asked his mother.

Boone hated how fearfully she asked the question. "I wish she were, Mom. But I can't say that she is. She's a very nice, smart, *good* woman, and I don't want you and Dad judging her."

"Just what is going on between you two?" asked Frank. "And how about Ella?"

Boone stood. "Frankly, it's no one's business."

"But, son—" his mother began.

Boone held up a hand. "Mom, you and Dad need to back off. I have a right to a private life."

"Well, it's not private anymore!" his dad snapped.

"Then that's even more reason for me to guard whatever's left of it."

There was another long silence. His parents looked absolutely miserable. But that was their fault. "Why are you two asking for answers anyway? When you already know why I must be seeing Ella?"

His mother lifted her shoulders and let them drop. "We don't know why you are, honey."

He shook his head, not really believing her. "You *do*."

"We *don't*," his father reiterated.

Boone prayed for patience. "She's Mrs. Kerrison's daughter."

Why were they still looking at him so blankly? Were they really living that much in their fantasyland? God forbid. Because if so, it made a sham of their relationship, the one he'd been so carefully preserving all these years.

He forced himself to share further. "Ella saw her

mother teach me. Ella would sit with us. You saw her, Mom. You did, too, Dad. When you'd pick me up, we'd be reading a book together. Remember?"

His parents exchanged a pained, shocked look.

"I-I forgot," his mother said.

*On purpose*, Boone wanted to add.

"Are you saying that Ella is teaching you?" his father asked. "She's not a teacher."

"I know that," said Boone. "She's a reader. She's helped me through the piles of papers and emails I get every day from the school and town hall. I've reached a tipping point. The mayor's race has brought that home."

His parents were silent.

"I know you don't like to think about it," Boone said, "but I still have trouble reading."

His mother took out a tissue from her purse and wiped at one of her eyes.

His father's shoulders slumped. He looked anywhere but at Boone.

"It's not the end of the world," he told them, but deep inside, the darkness sat heavy in him. "I don't need or want your pity. I'm coping just fine."

"We don't pity you," said his mother.

"Bullshit. You do."

"Don't swear at your mother," his father said automatically.

"I'm sorry, Mom." *And I'm sorry you got stuck with me instead of Richard.*

Only one thing held him back from saying it. He wanted to spare them the pain of having to look inside themselves and hold that ugly truth up to the light. He was already doing it. And it sucked.

Silence hung heavy in the room.

"I think you need to go," he said quietly. "Tomorrow's a big day."

His mother stood. "All right," she whispered. "Are you going to tell everyone the real reason you're seeing Ella?"

"No. It's no one else's business."

He could see that his mother was faintly relieved, although not entirely. He still looked bad. But one kind of looking bad was better than the other. He knew very well his parents thought it was preferable to look like a horny bachelor with a roving eye than let the public—your constituents, your students, your principal—know you can't read well.

"Good plan," his dad said. "Elections always come up again."

"I still think he'll win by a landslide," said his mother.

"I agree with your mother," said Frank. "You've been an excellent mayor."

"Thanks." Boone just wanted them gone.

He let them see themselves out, swiveled carefully in his grandfather's desk chair, and poured himself some bourbon from Faber Braddock's favorite crystal decanter that he kept inside a cupboard below the bookshelf.

Desperation drink in one hand, he traced the spine of a book on his shelf with the index finger of his other. It was *An Index of Appalachian Poets.* There might even be a Rogers in there somewhere. He searched the contents, turned to page thirty-eight, looked carefully down the row of *R* names, and yes—there it was: "Hiram Rogers, bn. 1889, resident of Kettle Knob, North Carolina, author of poetry anthologies 'Petals Falling,' 'Heroes Tomorrow,' and 'War Song.' "

After the *Morning Coffee* show came out, Cissie would think he was a scumbag. Kissing her, sleeping with her—all the while he was having a so-called affair with Ella.

No doubt the rest of the town, including his football players, would think the same thing.

He topped off his drink. There was no way out of this

mess. He wanted to keep his job at the school, even if it meant he had to do some backpedaling with the players and his other students to win their trust again. He wanted to be able to walk into Starla's diner and order lunch without people assuming he couldn't even read the menu.

He didn't want to wear the scarlet letter *D* for *dyslexia*. It was *his* business.

And if Cissie ever found out . . .

He remembered how excited she was perusing his grandfather's library. Books, words, were her life.

He put the drink down, attached a sticky note to the poetry book: "Enjoy, and please keep. Boone." Then he laid it on the stairs.

She'd have to believe that everything between them had meant nothing more than a good time. That way, they'd have a clean break.

In his room when he looked out the window at the blanket of stars before him, he understood that he was wrong about something. He'd always thought winning was what he did best. There was a drive in him to succeed, to pull it out at the last minute, to change failure to victory.

But now he understood that what he truly excelled at was getting around the thing that had always shut him out. It had started with Mom and Dad pretending he was someone he wasn't. They were still doing it, and it hurt.

It hurt badly enough that he didn't want to give the rest of the world the chance to do the same thing, no matter the consequences to his heart.

He pressed a button on a remote. The window blinds hummed and began to draw together, blocking the panoramic view. Boone's resolve hardened as, one by one, the stars disappeared.

# CHAPTER THIRTY-ONE

On Election Day at 6:30 a.m., Cissie found the poetry book on the stairs. Later on, she realized it was a farewell of sorts. A consolation prize, maybe. But at first, she was excited. A gift from Boone! She could hear him up, moving around his study.

She poked her head in and smiled. "Thanks for the cool book. And good morning."

"You're welcome." He nodded in a perfunctory way and stuffed a bunch of papers into a briefcase. Maybe he just had Election Day nerves.

Cissie ignored the fact that he seemed withdrawn. "Good luck today."

He glanced up. "To you, too."

Their gazes held—which was what she wanted. She'd worn another new outfit, and she was really hoping he'd notice it. It was professional yet feminine and kind of sexy, and she felt very together in it, like the Librarian Who Would Save the Library by Becoming the Mayor— *that* librarian who was going to be called "best" on her tombstone, not once but twice, for her librarian skills.

Her mayor skills were untested as yet, but they were there, she believed, glimmering beneath all her glam.

But his eyes looked bleak, not appreciative or admiring. Or even friendly. She would have taken friendly.

Without looking at her again, he said, "I'll be gone all day, pretty much. We both will."

"Yep." She raised her arm and leaned her elbow against the doorjamb near her ear so that her hand curled over her head in an Audrey Hepburn–ish pose. Could she look any sexier?

She didn't think so.

"Hey," she said super casually, "I'm available for a midnight date. Winner takes all." She didn't know what she meant by that, exactly, but it sounded good.

He didn't say anything, didn't look—but he stopped sifting documents.

"In your room," she added. "Or the hot tub. I'll bring champagne."

Could she give any more qualifications to that offer?

God help him, he looked downright austere as he stared at his papers.

She could tell he wasn't really reading them. He was using them as a prop—so he wouldn't have to talk to her.

"You don't have to worry about me," she said. "If I lose—which might happen—I'll be okay. I even believe the library will survive. It won't be the way I think it would work best," she added in a rush, "but it will survive in a different form, and there's always tomorrow to rethink things."

He finally looked up at her. She was still leaning—like a dork, she now realized—on the doorjamb. "Do you ever quit hoping?" he asked.

Just like that. Dropped into the middle of a perfectly normal one-way conversation.

"No." She pulled her hand down, folded it with her other one. Stayed leaning because she would not admit that her posing was a trifle unnatural. She told herself it came naturally to this new Cissie, that she had to keep putting herself out there and look stupid sometimes. "I can't quit hoping. Ever. About anything."

"Where do you get it?"

"Nana, of course."

"That makes sense. But she's not as . . . sunshiny."

"I know. She has that layer of cosmopolitan that I could never have. She must have gotten that in the sixties."

He went back to his papers.

"You have a lot to be hopeful about," she said. "You'll probably win."

"See?" He stared at her with a perfectly serious face. "You're still thinking that maybe you can." He gave a short laugh. "And guess what? You just might."

The truth was, she understood what he was saying, and she wasn't offended. But she wanted him to wake up from this dark mood he was in. "Of course I think I might win. Why would I run, otherwise? That's like saying you want to ride your bicycle to the store, but you ride it in place instead. I'm not conducting a campaign just to conduct a campaign. It's going somewhere. And even if I lose, I'm not done. Expect to see me at Town Hall."

He shook his head. Clasped the briefcase shut. "I have to go." He walked up to her. Stopped.

Maybe because she refused to move. "You never answered me about tonight." There. She was moving, pumping those bike pedals, *going* somewhere.

He looked at her shoes, beautiful heels bought in Asheville. "I can't make it," he said quietly.

And then he walked by her. He didn't push. He just hoped she would move, and she did. Slowly, like a rusty drawbridge, she moved, and he got by without even having to touch her.

His hard luck.

He walked out the front door, and Cissie went upstairs, picked up the consolation prize of a book, ripped off the sticky note, burned the message from Boone in a candle on the bureau (after having to look for matches for a full minute, which she eventually found in a nightstand drawer), and stuffed the book under the armchair seat cushion, where Dexter had to sit on it. It wasn't fair to Dexter. But he adjusted quite nicely.

And that was that.

Maybe some future guest would find it there.

As for Cissie, she was off to work at the library and campaign when she could for one more day. She had twelve assured votes and trembled with love thinking of those dozen people: Nana, Laurie, Sally, Mrs. Hattlebury (not the colonel—theirs was a house divided), her new hair stylist, the manager at her new favorite clothing store at the outlet mall in Asheville (she lived in Kettle Knob), Starla's dishwasher, and the five members of the Friends of the Library who could vote (one was a Canadian and ineligible).

She really hoped she'd crack a hundred votes so Boone would see he wasn't quite a lock in the town of two thousand constituents. She also hoped he'd see that the woman whose free hot-tub-champagne-and-sex ticket he'd just rejected was someone he'd miss. She wasn't going to hang out with a guy who treated her like a rusty drawbridge he needed to pass—

However much she was in love with him.

The polls opened at 7:00 a.m., and Cissie was there casting her vote, her confusion and heartache about Boone hidden deep away. Today, she was running for mayor. She needed to focus on that. Even so, she couldn't help hoping that she'd see him at the elementary school, where the voting booths were set up in the cafeteria.

All she craved was a smile, some sense that what had happened that morning between them was a mistake.

But they didn't cross paths.

Her heart was heavy when she unlocked the library earlier than usual and started going through old magazines to make up for all the time she'd lose that afternoon. She managed to stay busy—she didn't really want to see anyone; she wished she could hide in the stacks all day—but at 8:00, she got a call from Laurie.

"You're not going to believe this—your Sunday *Morning Coffee* segment is on the network's national weekday morning show instead. They bumped it up! I hit record—I missed getting the first twenty seconds, but that was just Anne Silver introducing the story to the anchors."

*"Why?"*

"Shush, I'm listening!"

Cissie strained to hear. "How is it?"

"Sssh!" said Laurie. "Oh, my God . . . There you are at The Log Cabin, looking like Annette Funicello from one of those old beach movies. You need to do your hair like that again."

"Laurie! Put the phone closer to the TV so I can hear."

"Don't you have a TV down there?"

"But I have to go pull it out of the closet and plug it in!"

"Hurry. That was a preview. They're going to commercial, and they'll run the whole thing when they get back."

Cissie got the TV set up in forty-five seconds. Another twenty seconds went by before it warmed up, then she had to switch channels, and there—

There was Boone, kissing her in the shed. She was leaning on his truck.

"What? Why is that on TV?" she yelled into the phone.

"Um, because it's cute? And romantic?" Laurie said. "You two look so good together."

"But it was private!"

Cissie watched in horror as Anne's voice-over said, "Neither candidate admitted that they were romantically involved, although this video tells a different story." The camera panned across Boone's house. "The two candidates for mayor share this residence, although admittedly, Miss Rogers's own home is uninhabitable at the moment."

Then Cissie was on-screen. "A tree went through the roof. And we needed a place to stay. Boone's got a very nice, big house."

She gasped. "They edited the heck out of that. I sound like such an opportunist! I was trying to say that I was glad we weren't going to get in his way. I told you Anne didn't like me."

"Gosh," said Laurie. "The way they manipulate things, it's . . . it's not right."

"The question is"—Anne was on-screen again—"why stay at the opposing candidate's home at all when you have an entire small town of friends to choose from?"

And then there were brief screenshots of various residents of Kettle Knob chatting at Starla's before the footage returned to Anne in the studio. "Most folks around here," she said, "claim they would have let Miss Rogers and her grandmother live with them, but they also think that the two candidates living together under one roof is a *hoot*—a popular word in North Carolina. Some even hope that Cupid has struck. That scene in the shed suggests he has."

"This is entertaining," said Laurie.

"It's not." Cissie was outraged.

"It is if you're not from Kettle Knob and you just happen to see this on TV," Laurie insisted. "I know you're embarrassed, but you two look so cute together. Whoever is watching this right now is sighing and hoping you'll get married."

"Laurie," Cissie said, "please. Don't talk."

"Okay," Laurie said meekly.

"Boone Braddock," Anne Silver went on, "is a busy football coach, PE teacher, and mayor. He's also apparently involved in a nearly daily activity at this home in Kettle Knob."

A shot of someone's house was shown.

"Where's that?" Cissie asked Laurie.

"I don't know."

And then a shot of Boone's ugly pickup truck pulling into this person's backyard was shown—again and again.

"Every weekday," Anne said, "the mayor comes here, and apparently doesn't want to be seen. He drives his truck to the rear of the home and doesn't come out for at least an hour."

"Why?" Laurie said.

"I don't know," said Cissie.

Then they showed another outdoor shot of Boone at the house, this time with Ella Kerrison, who threw her arms around him in a hug.

"What the hell?" Laurie said. "That's Ella's house?"

Cissie was so stricken and confused, she said nothing.

"Who is this woman?" Anne asked. "And why does Mayor Braddock visit her almost every day? We tried to find out."

There was a shot of Ella at her door. "No comment," she said, her brow furrowed. "Please. Just leave." And then she slammed the door shut.

"I don't understand," Cissie said.

"Me, either," Laurie answered quietly.

"We started with two candidates living in the same house," Anne said. "And when you add a little mystery"—

there was a shot of Ella—"and mayhem"—followed by a shot of Cissie on the stranger's back at The Log Cabin—"we get a small town story with universal appeal."

Anne turned to the news anchors with a charming grin. "Guys, I can't wait to get back to Kettle Knob to see what happens next."

"Me, either," exclaimed the female anchor. "That Mayor Braddock is a real charmer."

"Sounds like he's spreading that charm awfully thin." The male anchor arched his brow.

Anne and her colleagues laughed.

Cissie's heart hurt. Her whole body hurt.

"Later today," Anne continued smoothly, "we'll find out which of these two candidates actually won this election to become Kettle Knob's next mayor."

"Keep us posted," said the male anchor. "Sounds like we need a reality show filmed there."

"Over my dead body," Cissie told Laurie. "Anne Silver doesn't like either of us. She's trying very hard to make Boone look like a two-timing scumbag. I thought she was crazy about him."

"It's a ratings game," Laurie assured her. "It does look like he's having an affair with Ella. But I hope it's not true."

"I don't believe it." Cissie's eyes stung. She so wanted to believe in love. It happened in the books she loved—couldn't it happen to her?

"But why else would he go over there almost every day and stay for an hour?" Laurie was saying. "Did he ever tell you he was going there?"

"No." Cissie sighed. "He never has. We don't cross paths much in the morning."

"Well, he was kissing you in the shed—"

"We did that before Anne Silver even got here." And it was fabulous, at least until she saw it on TV. And then it looked all wrong because that had been a private moment, and tawdry, too, because Boone was also hanging out with Ella.

"I wonder who filmed us in the shed?" Cissie said. "That's so creepy."

"Yeah. Totally creepy." Laurie paused. "I wonder what Boone thinks of this story?"

"Maybe he hasn't seen it."

"Well, if not, someone will tell him about it. That morning news show is on at Starla's every morning. Kettle Knob doesn't take kindly to sneaks. I never thought Perry could be one. But look at him."

Cissie put her hand to her forehead. "This is bad." She'd slept with a guy who was very likely seeing another woman.

"Hang in there," Laurie said. "Maybe Perry and Boone can be put in Kettle Knob's doghouse together."

"Not yet," Cissie said. "I'm going to ask Boone what's going on. I thought—"

"What?"

"I thought he was falling in love with me, too. But this morning—"

"Yes?"

"He basically ignored me."

"Did you by any chance sleep with him last night?" Laurie's voice was wary.

"Almost," Cissie whispered. "And then his parents called. I went back upstairs."

"Hmm. He didn't follow you up to your room later? Most guys would."

"No. He didn't, and it's because we have an election to think about. I specifically told him not to. And then this morning, he barely spoke to me."

"That's weird. I wonder if it was really his parents on the phone."

"I'm sure it was. I heard them come to the door shortly after."

"Still, I think the guilt is getting to him. Sleeping with two women at once."

"Don't be premature," Cissie said, even though she'd thought the exact same thing. "I'll let you know what he says, okay?"

"Great. Meanwhile, happy Election Day."

# CHAPTER THIRTY-TWO

When Boone got Cissie's first text, he was already up to his ears in fallout from the morning show, and it was clear— very clear—that unless the majority of Kettle Knob residents had shown up at voting booths before 8:00 a.m. when the show aired, he was going to win the election only by a hair—

Or not at all.

Hard to believe.

The text showed up when he was eating a takeout country ham biscuit from Starla's at his desk at the mayor's office around nine. He ignored the message, although it hurt to do so.

But Cissie wouldn't let up.

She sent five more texts. And called three times.

Which was why he finally caved and agreed to meet her. *I can spare five minutes,* he texted back using his voice dictation app. *We both have places to be.*

He'd wanted to say he cared about her but had to let her go because he didn't belong with her. Football and politics. Those were his things.

But he couldn't tell her all that. She'd want to make a

go of it, and inevitably, they'd come up against a wall. She'd be disappointed—in him, in their relationship.

No, he had to nip the blossoming feelings between them in the bud.

Even so, his heart leapt when he finally saw her, his stubborn political opponent, looking sexy and pretty in a black brimmed hat and bright purple trench coat, walking toward the theater instead of being where she should be, at the library.

He pressed the little microphone and dictated a message into his cell phone: *Other side of street.*

She got it, crossed over with quick steps.

*Her,* his heart clamored, *that girl.*

He looked behind, to both sides, and in front of the truck. No one appeared to be sitting in any cars watching—none of those network TV people, at least. And if they had some sort of stalker filming them from a nearby house window, he couldn't see one anywhere.

He took his chances, got out, opened the passenger's door, and got Cissie inside. "Great disguise," he said as she climbed in.

Her face was white. "This hat was in the lost and found at the library, and it's Sally's coat."

He liked having her in his truck, he decided, when he returned to the driver's seat. "What's this about?" he asked, knowing full well.

Her eyes were filled with censure. And questions. "Are you sleeping with Ella Kerrison? Dating her in any capacity? And did you ignore me this morning because you're a two-timing sneak?"

"So I guess you saw the TV show."

"Everyone did, and if they didn't, they've heard about it. It's on talk radio in Charlotte and Asheville right now."

"My admin assistant told me. The station managers tried to get me to call in and join the conversation."

"Me, too. And I've had way more visitors than usual at the library. Normally, I'd love that. But no one wanted books. They just wanted to see if I . . . if I was falling apart."

He'd had the opposite happen. There'd been no messages, and only a few people—apart from the local TV station crews—had stopped by to say hello and wish him well at Town Hall. He wondered if he should even bother showing up at his scheduled stops throughout the day.

"I'm sorry this is happening to you." He wished he could take her hand.

Two red spots of color appeared on her cheeks. "You didn't seem to care a jot about me this morning at the house."

"I don't want to hurt you, Cissie." Which was true—truer than anything he'd ever said before.

"So why do you go over to Ella's and hide your truck in her backyard?" She sounded so hurt. And scared.

"I know I look like a real horndog—kissing you one minute, and visiting Ella in secret the next."

"That you do. But I know you. I might not have known you long, but something's off here. I didn't imagine the way things were between us. It was real. Answer me, Boone. What's going on?"

He looked out his window. "You haven't had much experience . . . with relationships."

"So? Experience doesn't necessarily equate to wisdom."

He looked straight at her and willed himself to lie. "In some ways, it does. Not everything lasts."

There was a long, bleak silence he willed himself not to break.

Her eyes filled with tears. "Oh, really?" She threw

open her door. "You're hiding something. And you suck for treating me this way."

One of Cissie's campaign posters—one that Sally had stapled balloons to—came skidding down the sidewalk.

Boone met her gaze. "I understand why you're upset. And I'm sorry."

It hurt like hell when she slammed the door behind her. But that was the way it had to be.

He turned the key in the ignition.

Wished the engine didn't purr like a kitten and start right up.

And took off, wending his way by the gazebo on his way out of town and refusing to look at it.

# CHAPTER THIRTY-THREE

It couldn't have been love, Cissie thought as she picked up her sign with the balloons. She threw it in a public trash can—it took forever to stuff the balloons in—and then began her lonely walk back to the library. Love didn't topple like that, so quickly. Love found solutions. Endured longer than a day or two.

Love didn't lie.

Boone was definitely holding something back that was keeping them apart. She knew him. She knew his soul. Maybe that sounded corny, but it was true. She loved him.

But apparently, he didn't love her.

That was what he was saying, anyway, in so many words.

Yet she couldn't quite believe him. Not yet. She was desperate enough to keep hoping. His eyes had been too flat. Too unlike him.

Without even thinking, she found herself detouring to Ella's. Her house was on the edge of the town proper. It would take a good fifteen minutes to walk there.

As she traveled block after block, passing mainly small brick or clapboard cottages, she had a crazy wish that Boone would catch up with her in his truck, leap out, and lay a reassuring hand on her arm.

"Hey," she could hear his whiskey-and-gravel voice saying. "Everything's going to be fine. *We're* going to be fine."

But he didn't.

Two TV trucks from two different stations drove by, coming from Ella's direction. Cissie pulled her hat brim down lower. Maybe she was walking right into a media circus.

It was a chance she was willing to take.

When she got there, Ella's house looked deserted. Curtains were drawn. No car sat in the driveway. Still, Cissie knocked.

And hoped.

Maybe Ella would know what was wrong with Boone.

But no one came.

She knocked again, but when she was met with silence, she turned to walk away. And as she did, she caught a glimpse of a face behind a curtain. She froze, ran back up to the small porch, and pounded on the door. "I know you're in there! Please answer! It's Cissie, not a reporter. Please, Ella!"

There was another long silence, but then she heard footsteps and her heart lifted. The next second, she grew wary, reminding herself to prepare for utter heartbreak.

The door finally opened. Ella stood there, her mouth thin, her gaze clearly distraught. "What do you want, Cissie? This has been a horrible morning for me, okay? I don't want those nosy reporters coming back."

"I get it." Cissie's throat was tight. "But Ella, I need to ask you something. Is it true that you and Boone are—are having an affair?"

Ella's expression gave nothing away. "I don't want to talk about it. To anyone. I'm sorry."

She started to shut the door, but Cissie held it open. "Please," she said, "for my own peace of mind, I need to know. I won't be angry with you. I promise."

Ella's jaw tightened. "Did he say we were together?"

"In so many words. But not directly. He just refused to deny it."

Ella sighed. "You're asking too much."

"Please," Cissie whispered.

Ella shook her head once, soberly. "I have no right to talk about Boone's private life. And my private life is my business. I'm sorry."

Cissie felt the prick of tears at her eyes. "That's the answer you give reporters. I know we're not close friends, but please, woman to woman, tell me the truth." A crow overhead cawed, such a lonely sound. "Even if it hurts, I want to know."

Ella stared at her a long time. "All right," she said finally. "It's true."

Pain like she'd never known coursed through Cissie's body. "You two"—she could barely get the words out— "are having an affair?"

Ella nodded. Her expression showed no sympathy. It showed nothing—like Boone's.

But maybe that was what two people in love did when there was a third, unwanted party in the mix. They turned cold. Like statues. To protect themselves.

Cissie swallowed. She couldn't believe she was the intruder in this scenario, the one who didn't belong.

She knew she should thank Ella for talking to her. She should. She'd practically forced the woman to confess. But Cissie's manners fled, and she didn't care.

No doubt Ella didn't, either.

"I have to go," Ella said quietly.

This time, when she shut the door, Cissie kept both

hands in her coat pockets. With bowed head, she turned and walked slowly back to the street.

She had no recollection of getting back to the library. But when she found herself there, she ignored Sally's concern.

"Is anyone here?" she asked faintly.

"No," said Sally. "Just me and Hank Davis."

"Can you lock the door?"

"Sure."

"And . . . and do you mind if I stay here alone a little while?"

Sally bit her lower lip and shook her head. "Are you sure?"

"Yes," Cissie whispered.

Hank Davis came up and laid his palm on her ear and cheek.

She tried to smile at him, then said to Sally, "I'll be at Starla's at six for the election results, I promise."

If by some crazy chance she became mayor of Kettle Knob that night, it wouldn't be because the townsfolk were expressing confidence in her and her platform.

If she won tonight, it would be because they were voting against Boone.

Big difference.

"See you then," said Sally, her tone somber.

Cissie pulled Hank Davis's hand off her face and kissed it. "Thank you, honey."

Sally called Hank Davis over to the door. "It's okay to be upset about what happened today," she told Cissie. "Just remember, we love you."

"Love you, too," Cissie eked out over a lump in her throat.

Her two dear friends left, shutting the library door quietly behind them.

As soon as she heard the lock turn, Cissie went straight to her desk, sat behind it, laid her head in the circle of her arms—

And cried all over her stack of manila cards with blue lines.

# CHAPTER THIRTY-FOUR

When Boone lost the election in a real squeaker—Cissie beat him by just enough votes to preclude a runoff—he wasn't surprised. Of course, it meant that all the hard work he'd put in on the town's behalf wasn't rewarded with yet another term in office.

But he hadn't done those things to win an election. He could be proud of what he'd accomplished while he'd held the reins at Town Hall. And he could be happy for Cissie.

But she would have none of it.

She didn't even sound happy for herself.

When she delivered her acceptance speech, it wasn't the one she'd shared with him. It was stilted. Short. Everyone attributed that to her shock that she'd defeated a Braddock, so they gave her a break.

During Boone's concession speech, so many people shook their heads from either regret that he lost or disapproval of his supposed shenanigans that he wanted to laugh about it later with Cissie.

But he couldn't.

When they shook hands in front of the crowd and the cameras, it was the worst moment of his life. Grasping her palm, looking into her eyes, and having to hide his true feelings for her was bad enough. But now, her gaze lacked its usual warmth.

It lacked hope.

She moved out of his house that very same night.

While she was upstairs packing, Laurie—who wasn't the least bit friendly—filled him in on what was happening. Cissie and Nana were going to stay with the Hattleburys for the next two weeks. Laurie was taking Dexter, who meowed plaintively from a cardboard box on his way out.

Cissie's arms were full of clothes. "Bye," she said, not really meeting his eyes. "Thank you very much for letting us stay here."

"You're welcome," he said formally.

She returned the flowers he sent her the day after the election.

He was about to dump them in the trash when he noticed that she hadn't even opened up the small envelope containing his message of congratulations tucked into the blossoms. He picked up the sturdy white rectangle, turned it over, and read on the back: "I'm mayor because they're punishing you, not because they like me.—CR."

That pissed him off. She'd won fair and square. Sure, there was some truth to her statement, but it wasn't the whole truth: Kettle Knob had responded to her fresh approach, her optimism, her devotion to preserving their history and celebrating their town's unique vibe.

But he couldn't tell her that.

She was out of his life—by his choice and hers.

As the days went by and he adjusted to his new reality, he realized that not being mayor was one thing but shrugging off his new less-than-stellar reputation was quite another.

He wasn't going to outright lie to anyone about why

he'd been at Ella's. But the speech he gave to the football players . . . Well, it went over like a load of bricks.

"Ella's a hardworking single mom," he told them, "and we've been friends forever. Friends support each other. I kissed Miss Rogers because I like her, and I had no reason not to. And that's all I'm going to say about my private life. You need to respect my boundaries, and I hope you'll trust me."

But the boys were looking at the guy who'd gotten in a fight at The Log Cabin, who'd been filmed kissing one woman and sneaking into the house of another. They walked away with wary looks in their eyes. Coach might not be playing by his own rules when it came to women and being a gentleman.

Coach might even be a hypocrite.

Boone hated their uncertainty and hurt. But just like the situation with Cissie, there was nothing he could do about it. Nothing he could do, either, about the principal, staff, and faculty members of Kettle Knob Academy—and how they weren't talking to him much. They used to come to him for advice about a lot of things.

That stopped abruptly after the TV show aired.

In the school office, Laurie could barely look at him. He knew about Perry leaving her, so he understood her distance. She was in pain already, and she thought he'd messed with her best friend's heart.

And maybe he had.

He didn't know anymore.

He let it slide.

He let it all slide.

"You can't just sit around home," his mother told him one afternoon a month after the election.

She and Dad had come over and brought lunch. Too bad for them. They didn't know it was Boone's day—his bad day, his one truly bad day of the year.

"I like sitting around home." He poured himself another drink. "I'm not mayor. Why go schmooze with the beautiful people? I don't need their influence anymore to get things done."

Long ago, he'd let his dreams die because he'd thought it was useless to pursue them. There was no way he could keep his secret *and* succeed at college. So why even try?

"It's the Christmas season," his father said. "You look like hell."

His dad had looked like hell on signing day, when Boone hadn't shown up in the school library to sign the scholarship papers and smile for the cameras.

"You should have a party to show everyone you're fine." His mother's eyes were dry now, but on signing day, she'd cried at the dinner table. "You can ask Janelle to help you."

Boone took a swig of bourbon. "That's a great idea. And I'll be sure not to invite any of the Rogers clan."

"You're wise," said his mother. "I'll tell Janelle to give you a call."

"I was being sarcastic, Mom. I don't want a party, and I talk to Nana almost every day." That was a slight exaggeration. He called her a couple times a week to see how she was doing, but they never discussed Cissie. Nana said they were two adults who had to work out their own problems, and if they couldn't, it wasn't meant to be.

Which sucked.

He poured himself another bourbon.

"Be nice to your mother," his father said. "And you've had too much to drink. What are you doing drinking this early in the day anyway?"

Boone had been walking to English class at Kettle Knob Academy on a Tuesday morning when he'd decided not to go to college. Signing day had been three weeks away, but he'd been too afraid to tell anyone about his choice, especially his parents.

He'd let it slide.

The same way he was letting everything slide now.

His parents stayed another half hour, insistent on pretending that nothing was wrong—as usual. But luckily, they had a holiday barbecue to attend at their newest resort, and then a cocktail party that night.

The doorbell rang at five.

It was Ella, and she'd brought him a blackberry pie. "Hey, Boone. I made an extra for you." When she smiled, she looked like sunshine.

He might have said that out loud because she laughed.

"Come on in," he said. "Don't mind me." He still had his glass of bourbon in hand.

She bent her head shyly and walked under his arm.

Ella was a wonderful woman. She understood him. And she would make an excellent hostess at a holiday party at his house. Hell, she even knew blackberry pie was his favorite.

In the kitchen, he threw his bourbon-holding arm around her and didn't spill a drop. "I might have a party. Wanna help me throw it?"

"I-I guess. Are you sure?"

"You don't sound too enthused," he teased her.

She shrugged and grinned. "It's just that people have already been talking. We were on national news together, remember?"

"So? We don't listen to gossip."

"It cost you an election."

He raked his free hand through his hair. "Cissie won because she's smart and upbeat. She has great ideas."

"She's everything you say. But you're smart and upbeat, too. *You* have great ideas."

"I've been faking it a long time. And people are figuring me out."

"You have *not* been faking it. You're a hard worker. You've made a difference." She shot him a dubious look. "But I think I'd better go. You're drunk."

"Sorry." He sighed. "It's been a bad day."

"Why?"

"It has to do with your mother. But I don't wanna make you sad."

"Tell me." She crossed her arms and looked intently at him.

"Today's the day I decided not to go to college fifteen years ago. She'd died the week before. I didn't think I could do it without her."

"*Boone.*" Ella's expression softened. "You could have found a tutor there."

"I know. But it would have meant giving a stranger a chance to judge me, find me lacking, and spread the word. A man can't succeed on those terms."

"Success? What is that, really?" Ella took the bourbon out of his hands. "Can you be successful when you're hiding a secret?"

Boone frowned. "That's too hard a question."

"Because you're drunk." She considered him for a few seconds. "This might be a terrible time to tell you my own secret."

"I'm not *that* drunk. I want to hear it."

She wrapped her arm around his waist and looked up at him. "You were always like a brother. Then that damned TV show put ideas in everyone's heads. Eventually, it occurred to me, too—you're one heckuva man." She pulled back. "Boone, the truth is, I've developed a huge crush on you."

Boone's heart sank. Ella knew him. She accepted him.

She was pretty, sweet, creative, an all-around great person. He *should* have a crush on her.

But . . .

But there was Cissie. He'd never get over her.

"Dang, Ella," he croaked. "I wish—"

"Never mind." She backed away a step, her cheeks flushed. "I can tell you don't see me that way. It's okay. I'm sorry. I'm really sorry—"

Her eyes were shiny.

Damn. He'd messed with the heart of another good woman.

"Ella—"

She took off in the direction of the front door, and he followed.

"Don't be sorry," he said. "I'm flattered. It's not you. Any man would be lucky to be with you."

She shot him a wobbly smile. "But not you. I understand. Really. Although I thought I might have cause to hope. After all, you didn't deny our affair to Cissie. She told me so."

"She did?"

"Yes. She walked to my house on Election Day and asked me."

"Wow." Boone didn't know what to say. Cissie hadn't given up, even after he'd made it clear in that talk in his pickup truck that she should. He could see her now in that funny hat and coat, walking purposefully to Ella's.

"I think," Ella said, "I shouldn't have kept your secret for you. I should have told Cissie I was your reading tutor. Instead, I told her we were having an affair." She shook her head. "I thought I was doing you a favor."

He hated imagining Cissie rapping on Ella's door, asking if they were really involved romantically because she hadn't believed him—

Cissie and her hopes . . .

"I can see it doesn't sit at all well with you," Ella said. "What I told her."

He couldn't deny it. Cissie had believed him. Had *trusted* him.

Guilt assailed him. "I know you were trying to be a good friend to me," he said softly. "I should never have let that happen, you protecting me like that. It was wrong."

"I agree." Ella had never looked so serious. "You would have been better off letting Cissie love you. As you are now"—she gave him a sad, worried once-over—"you're not doing so great, my friend."

"Maybe not," he barely managed to say.

Out of all fifteen bad days he'd had since high school, this one was the worst. Good thing that tomorrow it would be over.

But then he remembered . . . he was having bad days all the time now.

Ella opened the front door. "The truth is, if I can't have you, Boone, I wish at least that Cissie had been able to. Though I'm not sure you deserve her," she added quietly, and left before he could make it up to her.

But how?

How did a guy make up for being an insensitive clod who used an old friend as a crutch in more ways than one?

And how was he ever going to win Cissie back?

He leaned against the door and closed his eyes. He was drunk. But he needed another bourbon so he could stand the pain while he came up with a plan.

His body didn't cooperate, however. He slid down to the floor, and when he woke up at three in the morning with a splitting headache and the wind whistling in his ear from the crack at the bottom of the front door, he knew he had to come up with something else—

Get himself back first.

# CHAPTER THIRTY-FIVE

Cissie-the-mayor and Cissie-the-librarian were still trying to work out their differences.

As mayor, she'd managed to stave off the county: the Kettle Knob library would stay put but with shortened business hours and a total freeze on buying new materials for an unspecified period of time.

But she didn't feel guilty about it. At the strip mall, austerity measures—granted, to a slightly lesser extent—still would have been in place, and they would have had to share their limited resources with the town of Campbell. That wouldn't have been so bad if Janelle didn't tend to steamroll over Kettle Knob when it came to using county resources every chance she got. But she did. And Cissie wasn't going to let her get away with it.

She welcomed the extra time away from the library to look out for Kettle Knob's interests at Town Hall. Her duties there required at least fifteen hours a week. That didn't include the weekend civics lessons with two supportive town council members and Chief Scotty to get her up to speed on the nuts and bolts of running a small community like theirs.

As librarian, she was excited about the new online

campaign she and the Friends of the Library had created to raise funds for building repairs and new reading material. It was slow going, but other people around the nation believed in keeping old libraries active, too. It helped that *Morning Coffee* had raised the profile of Kettle Knob—the town website was getting tons of hits, and she made sure the link to the library fundraiser was prominent there.

"Look at this place," Mrs. Donovan said to Cissie one weekday morning at the library.

Cissie glanced at the chandelier in the main room, its bulbs flickering on and off. "It's not so bad. It gives us atmosphere, right?"

"Wrong." Mrs. Donovan put her books on the desk for checking out. "The roof leaks, too. And the foundation's cracks are bigger than ever. I still think Boone had the right idea."

Cissie smiled patiently. "We're working on raising money. I wish you'd join the Friends of the Library—we could use you."

Mrs. Donovan glowered. "I'm too busy helping Laurie with those boys to be of any use to you or anyone else."

"How is she?" Cissie was worried about her. "Last time I was over there, she was on the phone with Perry. He was getting lawyered up. Since then she's been hard to get a hold of."

Mrs. Donovan's mouth thinned. "He's trying to get partial custody, which makes no sense since he's moving to Wilmington and travels all year. She's scrambling, trying to cover her bases with this new lawyer of hers." She pointed at Cissie's chest. "Be glad you're single, honey. Love hurts. *Bad*."

She stalked out.

*No duh*, Cissie wanted to call after her. *I know all*

*about it.* She stamped cards, filed papers, repaired some bindings, and thought about the man who held her heart hostage.

She was back in her house, which had been made over, much the same way she had been. The porch had doubled in size, and the new windows facing the view were huge. And she was coming out of her shell.

Even so, she still walked around every day with a huge shard of pain in her heart over Boone. She was brooding on the fact that she'd somehow managed not to lay eyes on him for an entire month when the front door opened. She looked up—always hoping.

It wasn't Boone, but she almost fell out of her chair anyway. It was her parents, and they'd brought a stranger with them, a man in his early thirties, she'd guess—a man who looked something like Jude Law, in a stylish European-cut suit and tie.

He stood politely to the side while Cissie and her mother and father had a sweet, teary, and louder-than-was-appropriate-for-a-library reunion.

Some things were more important than library rules, she was willing to admit these days.

The stranger turned out to be Dr. Maxwell Plimpton—*the* Maxwell Plimpton—renowned British poet, at least among scholarly circles, whom her parents had met at Cambridge.

"I've heard so much about you," he told Cissie, and shook her hand warmly.

Wow. A cute guy—from Mr. Darcy territory, no less! And he was interviewing for a two-year position at Appalachian State to become a visiting poet.

Romantic possibilities loomed if he were single—

And he was.

Luckily, the library closed at one o'clock that day. At home over an impromptu afternoon tea that she and Nana prepared, Cissie enjoyed Maxwell's company. He regarded her steadily, rushed swiftly to pull out her chair, and asked her many questions about herself. He even laughed at her jokes.

But her heart was never moved.

She was done for.

Boone was her love.

When the tea things had been put away, Maxwell and Nana went downtown to the theater. A friend of Nana's picked them up because Nana wasn't feeling up to driving, and Maxwell couldn't drive on the right side of the road.

"I want you three to have time together," Nana said to Cissie and her parents.

She was always looking out for Cissie.

"Do you like Max?" her mother said in the kitchen after they'd gone. "He's looking for love. I know it's much too early for anything substantial to develop, but he's already told me he's very charmed by you."

"I like him," Cissie said, wiping down the kitchen counters. "But I'm not interested in him, Mother. He's brilliant, of course." Something she'd always had on her wish list when it came to identifying potential partners.

"Accomplished, too," her father chimed in. He'd come in to sneak another of Nana's delicious homemade scones from the platter Cissie had already wrapped with foil.

"And handsome," her mother added, exchanging an amused glance with her father.

"That's very important," he said with mock smugness.

England had done wonders for bringing out their playful sides.

"Yes," said Cissie, "but I don't feel anything like a . . . a spark."

"Sometimes it takes a while," said Daddy. "You just

met him today. But note where you met him. He came in over the library threshold. And he's from out of town."

Cissie chuckled. "You arranged that, I'm sure."

"No," said Mother. "Max insisted on going there straight from the airport. He told us he wanted to meet you in your natural habitat."

"That's very cool, but the truth is, the legend's a moot point." She paused, wondering how stupid she was to own her feelings. "I've already given my heart away."

There. She'd said it. It was true. For her, there was only Boone, a fact she reluctantly admitted to her parents.

"Well, well," said her father, "falling in love with a Braddock. Who'd ever have seen that coming?"

"You and your Southern drama," Mother said to Daddy. She picked up a dish towel and started to dry. "Cissie, I'm happy for you if you're happy. You know what's best for you."

There was a beat of silence.

"Is something wrong between you two?" her mother asked.

"Apparently, he doesn't love me." Cissie's voice cracked, which was enough for her parents to circle the wagons and hug her.

She told them the long and short of it. "It's been really hard with y'all away. I know I'm thirty-two, but a girl still needs her parents."

"Thank goodness for Nana," her mother said. "She's been such a wonderful grandmother."

"That's Mama for you," Daddy said.

"Let's be honest." Cissie looked back and forth between them. "She's been like my mother and father, too. I love you both"—an awkward second passed—"but . . . you weren't there a lot for me growing up."

Another silence, punctuated only by the sound of the opera music coming from the speakers in the den.

"We know," said her father eventually. "We were so wrapped up in our research. Yet you were the most special project of all."

"If that's true, then why?" Cissie gulped. "Why did you still leave almost everything up to Nana?"

"Academic hubris," said her mother. "We were fools, my dear, and I'm sorry. I really am. We missed so much."

"And then you grew up," her father said. "You went away to college. By the time you came back, we didn't think you needed us anymore."

"You were smart. And dedicated to the library," Mother added. "I was afraid to ask for your time, after the poor job we'd done."

"So we went away again," Daddy said.

"You should have talked to me first." Cissie wiped away another tear. "I did need you. And someday, you'll need me. We should start working toward one another, shouldn't we?"

"That's true," her dad said, but he didn't sound nearly as concerned about it as Cissie wished he did. He sounded almost . . . happy.

Mother laughed. "Your father is bursting to tell you something. He and I are on the same page as you are. We miss you and Nana. We're home for good to lecture at Appalachian State until we retire and write books here in our own home, the way Rogerses have always done. We wanted to tell you in person, not on the phone."

Cissie alternated between wiping her eyes and laughing softly while her parents filled her in on the details.

When Nana and Max came back, Cissie's father shared the wonderful news with her, too, after which Cissie promptly fall into her grandmother's arms and held her close. They clung for a good minute, each one with a wet face from all the happy tears.

"I can't believe we're the cause of all this," Cissie's mother said with a chuckle.

"Dexter's pretending to be unmoved by the spectacle." Max picked the feline up from his comfy perch on a chair.

Everyone left the kitchen but Cissie and Nana.

Nana smoothed Cissie's hair back. "It'll be good to have them home again, won't it?"

Cissie nodded. "Not that they could ever replace you."

"Rule number thirty-one: no one can replace old Nana." The family matriarch smiled. "But it'll be a fine thing to have all of us together. Although someone's missing, I think, to make this happy picture complete." She arched a brow.

"Surely not Max," Cissie whispered. "He's great, but he's not my type."

"No." Nana chuckled. "You know who I mean."

"Boone?" How it hurt to say his name out loud!

"Of course. I know we haven't discussed him much. I've been trying hard not to pry. But I'm guessing you two need to talk."

"I don't see how we can. Both he and Ella said they were having an affair."

"Really? Have you heard any more gossip about this so-called affair? I sure haven't. And do you really believe Boone would have carried on with you both at the same time?"

"No."

"Exactly. That fella was head over heels for you."

Cissie shrugged. She was due to see him the very next night at the football game—for the first time since Election Day. She didn't know what to feel. "He hasn't come around."

"And you haven't gone to see *him*."

"I know. But he doesn't want me to—"

"Oh, really? You saw that in his eyes?"

"No. His eyes were . . . shuttered."

"Which means he's not telling you everything. Maybe you two needed time apart to do some growing up. But don't forget: if you wait for someone to finish growing before you get together, you never will. Life's like a river. You have to jump back in at some point."

"How do you know when to jump back in?"

"Ah." Nana chuckled. "I can't tell you the answer to that. It's different for every person. You have to read the signs all around you. Trust your gut. Then, like that sports ad says, just do it. Either that, or . . ." She hesitated.

"What?"

"Or get in the pickup truck that's waiting outside for you right now. It's a vintage blue one." Nana's eyes twinkled. "Close enough to river color for me."

"Are—are you kidding?" Cissie's heart thumped hard against her ribs.

"No, child. The driver's waiting for you to jump in. And he's awfully handsome."

# CHAPTER THIRTY-SIX

Leaning on the passenger's side of his pickup truck, Boone was nervous when he saw Cissie come out on her new front porch.

But even more, he was excited. He was where he needed to be. Where he wanted to be.

She didn't say a word as she came down the steps, pretty and professional beneath her open coat in a slim navy blue skirt and dark green V-neck sweater, a starched white collar framing her face. He held the truck door open for her, and she slid in.

He wished he knew what she was thinking. "Thanks for coming out," he told her.

"You're—you're welcome." She wouldn't look right at him.

He waited for her to tie her coat and buckle up, and then he took off, hanging a right out of their driveway to head up the mountain. "I wanted to talk with you before the game tomorrow night. Seeing as you'll be speaking and all. We'll be standing just a few feet away from each other. It was bound to happen."

"You're right," she said. "I guess it's a good idea that we . . . break the ice."

They drove along in silence for a few seconds.

"I can't wait to hear your speech," he said.

"I hope you win the game," she said at the same time.

Neither one of them chuckled. Instead, they lapsed back into an uncomfortable silence.

Boone forced himself to remember that time was slipping by and there was no easy way to get through this meet up, especially when he wanted it to be only the first of many they'd continue to have.

"Cissie, I've missed you terribly, and I want to kiss you. I want to do way more than that with you. I want you in my bed. And I want you there the next morning so I can make waffles and bacon for you."

He might as well lay it all out.

She looked pointedly out the passenger's side window. "You shouldn't say things like that." Her voice came out as a whisper.

"But it's true," he said in an easy tone, determined to keep the lines of communication open.

"I don't want to be hurt," she returned quietly.

"I don't want to hurt you." It was the worst feeling he'd ever had, hurting her.

"Ella said you were having an affair."

"It's not true. But I'm not blaming Ella for saying so. I want to explain. Just give me another couple minutes."

They were both silent all the way up the mountain, past his house, to the very top, where he jumped out, unlocked a padlock gate, got back in the car, and drove through.

"What's this?" She was definitely craning her neck to see.

"Close your eyes."

She did. Her mouth curved up a fraction, despite herself. A good sign.

"I'll tell you when you can look." Hell, yes, he was nervous inside. He wouldn't show it, but everything—his happiness, his entire future—depended on the next few minutes.

At their destination, he led her out of the truck, onto a gravel driveway, and then up some flagstones to a simple wooden door.

"Wait," she said. "I think—"

"Sssh," he said back. "No peeking. Keep your eyes closed." He opened the door, and the smell of old cedar came out in a rush.

He took her by the hand. Led her inside.

"Open," he said.

She blinked several times.

They were inside a one-room family cabin with a double bed and a wall with three stacked bunks. That morning, he'd lit the wood stove and set up a small table with white fairy lights all around. It was only four o'clock, but fairy lights were never wrong, and the stove made everything cozy. Two unlit candles, a bottle of champagne, and two glasses sat in the middle of the table. "Mom and Dad never use this place anymore. But I come up here every once in a while."

He hung his coat on a hook by the door.

"I love it." She untied her coat but kept it on.

He pulled out a box of matches, lit the candles, and drew back a chair for her. "Here. Please sit."

Her face registered reluctance.

"Come on," he urged her.

"Okay." She tossed her hat on a couch, then came and sat in the chair, the hem of her coat touching the floor.

He uncorked the champagne. Poured two glasses and handed her one. "There's something I have to tell you here. Anything that matters to me—well, I come to the cabin to think about it." He sat down in the other chair.

"Go ahead." Her voice sounded small, thin.

He tipped his glass to hers. "Cheers."

"Cheers." Her eyes were huge above the rim of the glass when she took a tentative sip.

It was good champagne. He wished he could savor it, but he could take pleasure in nothing until he talked to her.

"Have you ever wondered why I never come to the library?" he began.

She paused. "Yes, actually, I have."

"I'll bet you disapprove that I haven't."

She shook her head. "I can't judge people by whether or not they come to the library."

"Be honest, Cissie. It's a mark against me, isn't it? When you think about guys who are right for you, you don't imagine guys who never come to the library."

She mulled it over, took another sip of champagne. "Okay. That's fair. I do see myself with a scholarly guy. We'd talk a lot about books. It's hard for me to picture myself with a . . . a football coach." She winced. "I don't mean to sound like a snob. And I actually *like* football now. I'm pretty good at it."

"Let's not get carried away." He shot her a mock dubious look that made her chuckle. "At any rate, we're all allowed to have our preferences. It would be ridiculous, otherwise. That would mean everyone's right for everyone, and that's plain dumb." He reached out, laid his hand over her free one. "Here's the thing." He tried to speak. But he couldn't go on.

Not yet.

The deep-seated need to protect himself flared high. He had to let go of that hand, stand, and look away—to the tall pines, the woodpile, the patch of gray cotton sky—to gear himself up.

"Boone?"

He willed himself to turn and look at her. "Reading is a challenge for me."

Her beautiful mouth fell open.

"Being around books," he plowed on before she could speak, "well, it's rough. It reminds me of what I can't do well, what I'm missing out on. It's like I'm in Disney World. And I'm not allowed to go on the rides."

There. It was the hardest thing he'd ever have to say.

She put her fingertips on either side of her lower jaw. "Are you . . . dyslexic?"

"Very much so."

"Are you sure?"

"Yes."

"What's your reading level?" she asked gently but firmly, on librarian ground again.

"Around fourth grade."

"Oh. Okay." She wasn't quite pale. But she was close.

"I had an excellent after-school tutor starting in the sixth grade—Mrs. Kerrison. She stayed with me—and agreed to my parents' demand to keep it all a secret, even from the other teachers—until she died early our senior year."

"Wow." Cissie swallowed more champagne.

"I'm sure some teachers figured something was going on with me, but Mrs. Kerrison made it possible for me to participate at school without a lot of red flags. I don't know how I got through senior year without her, but I did. Apart from you, very few people know. There's my parents and Ella. She's been helping me out with reading lately."

"That's why you were at Ella's?"

"Yes. At that point, I was ready to let you go rather than tell you the truth. I'm sorry. I'm not ashamed of who I am, but I was afraid *you* might be, the way my parents

were when I was a kid—and still are. I couldn't bear
that." He paused. "Ella was only trying to protect me."

Cissie went to him. "I wish I could be mad at you. It's
been horrible not talking."

He put his hands on her shoulders. "That's why I came
today. I had to see you."

"I'm glad you did." Her eyes were curious. Sympathetic.

"I hope you don't feel sorry for me."

"No, I don't." She searched his face. "Your parents
meant well, I'm sure, but they handled this all wrong."

He gave a short laugh. "There's a stigma attached."

She took his hands in hers. Her eyes shimmered with
intense feeling. "Well, there shouldn't be. And I certainly don't care."

"Oh, yeah?" He squeezed back.

"Yeah. You don't have to feel on the outside anymore.
I'm with you. I can help you with reading, too, if you
want."

"I'd love that." He felt free. Wide open. There was
nothing for it but to kiss her—a glorious kiss that filled
the empty place that had been knocking around in him
so long.

Finally, they pulled apart.

She smiled up at him. "I'm happy."

His heart expanded even further. "I am, too."

She burrowed into him. They kissed again, lush
kisses—the cake of their celebration.

"It's cold, but there's a great make-out spot here,"
he said. "Come and see."

Who doesn't want more cake?

He put on his coat and picked up a folded blanket from
the couch. She wrapped up again and took his hand read-
ily. He led her to a small, hidden copse that opened out

onto miles and miles of mountains. The whole town of Kettle Knob lay spread below them. In the distance, they could see the smudge of brown, gray, and black that was Asheville.

He put the blanket out. They settled onto it together, his arm around her, their knees up.

"I want to come here every day," Cissie said, "to see this view in winter, spring, summer, and fall." She leaned on his shoulder. "I feel like one of the heroines in my favorite books. I'm Jane Eyre on the Yorkshire moors. Laura Ingalls on the prairie. Elizabeth Bennet in a garden at Pemberley."

"Pemberley?"

She laughed. "I don't want to overwhelm you, but you're in for a treat. We'll take it slowly, but we can read those books together."

"They sound like chick books."

She laughed. "I don't care what anyone says—those are classics, and you'll love them, too. I haven't even mentioned the heroes. They're wonderful. And I promise we'll get to more modern authors like Dick Frances. Murder, mayhem, mystery, et cetera."

"I can see you're going to throw me headfirst into this reading business."

"Why not?" She lay back on the blanket, and he followed suit. An hour before sunset, the blue sky was deepening to an almost violet color above their heads. "You practically pushed me into that hot tub, remember?"

"Yeah, I do."

They both laughed.

He settled himself over her. Smoothed her hair back with his free hand.

"I can't believe I'm with a librarian," he murmured, "and the sexiest librarian of all time at that."

She smiled. "You're a lucky guy."

"I know. And not just because you'll give me my own custom reading list, either."

"Which is actually a great perk. But you're lucky because I *care* about you. A lot." She looked up at him, her eyes pools of acceptance, desire. He also saw peace, and in their deepest depths, war. This girl was a fighter when she needed to be.

He could tell she was ready to fight for him.

To help him.

To make love with him.

Boone decided then and there that he never wanted to be with anyone else. But he wasn't sure how to tell her that. He should be able to. He really should. He'd revealed a big-ass secret, and she hadn't kicked him to the curb.

If only he'd practiced telling girls about his dyslexia a long time ago.

He wished he could see—really see—what was happening with Cissie, so he could untangle all the emotions coursing through him. He was crazy about her, of course, but what if that feeling was tied into being extremely grateful to her for accepting him for who he was?

Yes, Ella had known, but she'd been almost required to like him because she was her mother's daughter.

Love was a big concept. A huge concept. And an honest romance like this—which he'd never experienced before—was complicated, especially when you were with a girl who daydreamed about the heroes in her favorite books and you were just an average guy.

He'd think about it later. Meanwhile, there were Cissie's breasts, which needed attention. "It's nippy," he said, and unbuttoned her shirt.

She chuckled. "We need to have a name for this kind of fooling around. The outdoor kind with clothes on when it's cold."

She gasped. Maybe because he was teasing her puckered nipple, smoothing it out with the heat of his mouth and tongue.

"How about we call it polar-bear sex?" He caressed her other breast with the flat of his hand. "But you have to take everything off."

"Seriously?"

"Yep."

"Okay," he said. "One, two, three, go!"

They sat up. Ripped their own clothes off.

Hollered.

Laughed.

Lay back down and got each other warm real fast, except the parts of them that weren't. The contrast made the hot spots that much sweeter.

They made out like kids, his erection pressed hard against her belly one minute, then her inner thighs. The kissing, the caressing suddenly wasn't enough.

"I want all of you," Cissie breathed.

He lifted his mouth from the sweet indentation above her collarbone and kissed her deeply.

She clasped her legs around his hips, her shins attempting to cover his freezing cold rear end.

"Cissie," he said against her mouth, then dove into her, deep, filling her, feeling like he was at the center of the earth, its very core, where heat ruled and energy expanded—

And knew he'd arrived home.

# CHAPTER THIRTY-SEVEN

Attending high school football games was the social thing to do in western North Carolina—the place to see and be seen, and this year's final game of the season was extra special.

For four decades the rivalry had stood between Kettle Knob Academy and Black Mountain Prep. They were celebrating the cherished tradition with the usual trophy presentation after the game for the winner and speeches from the coaches, but they also had a dais covered in bunting representing both schools and chairs for both mayors and various VIPs from Buncombe County.

Boone's parents were there, along with a lot of their wealthy business contacts and country club friends, including Janelle. At 5:30, the winter sun had already set, but in the stands the shiny new tubas and trombones the elder Braddocks had bought for the school gleamed in the lights from the field, making Kettle Knob Academy look good.

Boone wanted to be proud of his parents' financial contributions to bettering the town. But he was too embarrassed by the lopsided nature of their donations. They'd never given a dime to the library, for example, which he hadn't noticed until Cissie brought up that point. They'd also never donated to the theater. Sure, they had a right to pick and choose what organizations they wanted to support—and they supported many. But it was painfully obvious that anything involving a Rogers got overlooked.

He was on the sidelines talking to an assistant coach when he saw Cissie out of the corner of his eye, sitting with her family, Laurie, the Hattleburys, and that British guy she'd told him about.

Boone's heart rate kicked up just seeing Cissie's face.

But he had a game to help these boys win, and he needed to focus. Black Mountain had had a very good season. Kettle Knob couldn't afford to slack off in any way. Boone's boys had worked their butts off, and the cheerleaders had gone the extra mile with banners and fun activities to get the school ready to support their football team.

At half-time they were down ten points when the Kettle Knob football players came off the field, looking dazed and distraught while the two school bands showed off, the cheerleaders did complicated routines, and the kids in the stands went crazy with spirit.

"No blame, guys." Boone's tone was firm. "We need to focus on turning this game around. Now huddle up."

He wasn't the popular guy he used to be. Not by a long shot. But all of them did as he asked. A few players wore guilty expressions. Others looked away, anywhere but at him. And then there were the defiant ones who stared right at him, their brows lowered.

"I've got a story to tell you," he said. "And if this story doesn't make you want to go out and kick some major Black Mountain butt in the second half, then nothing will."

A few minutes later, the whistle blew on his last word.

Perfect timing. Almost celestial. Maybe the brother he never knew was looking out for him. Or Grandpa Faber. Or maybe the universe was giving an honest man a lucky break.

But the boys didn't move. No doubt they were in a little bit of shock. But there were grins, too, grins Boone hadn't seen in a long time.

The team captain clapped hard, three times. "Come on, guys. Let's get 'em!"

And then it was like a nuclear bomb went off. The team sprang into action.

Boone paced the sidelines, his throat tight with emotion. These were good boys on the verge of manhood dealing with certain harsh realities of life, like other teams that might be better no matter how well they played, and coaches who'd made mistakes. Yet right before his eyes they were proving that they weren't succumbing to fear or disappointment.

The remaining two quarters were intense. Brutal, in fact. But those boys fought like they never had before. And they won. They came back with a touchdown and two field goals and made sure Black Mountain didn't score, hard as they tried to.

Boone had never been so proud to be a coach. He crossed the field, shook the hand of the other coach, and reveled in Kettle Knob Academy's victory as his players gathered around him on the field.

"We did it for you, Coach!" the team captain said, his words echoed from player to player. There were no defiant glares. No drawn expressions.

Only exhilaration.

Back at the sidelines, a defensive lineman threw a big cooler of Gatorade over Boone's head—just what he needed on that super cold day. But he didn't care.

He was one wet, happy coach when he arrived at the portable stage, which had been pushed out onto the field at the fifty-yard line.

Cissie was already in her chair. "Congratulations, Coach Braddock," she said warmly but with all her professional boundaries in place.

"Why, thank you, Mayor Rogers." He held her gaze maybe a second too long than was warranted between a coach and a mayor at a town event. But he couldn't resist.

The mayors started out by commending both teams. Cissie was engaging and funny as she spoke of the old rivalry, and Boone was totally impressed by her polished yet warm delivery. Then the Black Mountain coach said a few words, after which Boone found himself accepting the winning team's trophy on behalf of the Kettle Knob Knights from Cissie. When their fingers touched, he wanted to stay there—in that moment— their eyes meeting over the trophy, her expression filled with something that made him hope that she was proud of him. He wanted to please her more than anything he'd ever done.

But he still had something to do on the field, another part of his Big Plan.

"I promised my athletes," he said into the mike, "boys who have inspired me with their courage to face the hard things, to share a story with you."

He felt Cissie's supportive presence behind him, but he faced the crowd in the stands, determined to set things right with the rest of Kettle Knob. "The truth is," he said, "I can't read very well. I have dyslexia. Last time I was tested, back in high school, I read at a fourth grade level."

A half beat of silence went by. But teens loved drama, so he wasn't surprised when some benign hoots and hollers erupted from the stands. Maybe even some adults joined in—he didn't know. It didn't matter. He was standing firm in his truth, no matter what.

He told them about Ella being his tutor, and her mother before her. "I thought that if people knew," he said, "I wouldn't belong anymore. But I see now how wrong that thinking was. I put limits on myself. And by hiding my dyslexia, I turned my back on a community that I believe would have supported me if I'd asked for more help."

Hell, he'd nearly turned his back on *love*. . . .

While the crowd clapped wildly for a good ten seconds, everything finally clicked into place. That was what he had with Cissie.

True love.

He wasn't merely grateful to her because she accepted him. Look at all these people . . . accepting him, too!

No. Love was what had given him the courage to confide in her. Love was why he was standing out here in front of hundreds of people baring his soul.

Love had made him a better, braver man.

He needed to get his adorable, exasperating, wonderful librarian out of circulation once and for all.

Impatiently, he waited for the clapping to stop. He told everyone that he wanted to go to college so he could come back to Kettle Knob Academy as a political science teacher. He praised Wendy, the school principal, and the faculty at Appalachian State for all their encouragement and practical support.

"I'll drop in as a volunteer assistant football coach starting this spring," he said, "but with hard work"—he paused, gripped by how huge his commitment would have to be—"hard work that my students have shown me by example that I can handle if I commit myself heart and soul to it, I'll be back full-time someday. Meanwhile, I hope Kettle Knob Academy and Black Mountain students, staff, and faculty will help me pass the word that dyslexia doesn't have to be a barrier between you and your dreams. Thanks for listening. And to the boys on both teams, thanks for giving us a great game tonight."

It was done.

There was a second or two of silence, but like a growing storm, the enthusiastic clapping was joined by foot stomping, beating snare drums, and people shouting, "Go, Coach! We're proud of you!" and "We love you, Coach Braddock!"

"Thanks," he said over and over, hoarsely. "I love y'all, too!"

Both bands were playing the same song now, a recent pop radio hit that got your blood moving.

He'd not linger on regrets. He had a great future to think about. As a matter of fact—

He had to get to Cissie.

And then he saw her out of the corner of his eye, her expression tense as she raced away without trying to speak to him. Not that she could. He was being mobbed by well-wishers, but still—

She hadn't looked happy.

For a second, he had the old, sick feeling in the pit of his stomach: he didn't belong. Cissie had had a chance to think things over and changed her mind about him.

And if she had, it would be his fault—not because of his dyslexia but because he'd held back from her at the cabin. He should have told her he loved her.

Some five minutes later, he broke away from his friends and colleagues. They'd been hammering him with questions, hugging him, advising him, and one even cried on his shoulder (a former Kettle Knob Academy classmate who'd hidden her dyslexia all these years, too).

As he headed to the parking lot, he realized that his

parents hadn't come anywhere near him. But that was their problem.

Cissie hadn't left him a text, but he decided not to text her—not when she'd looked so distraught. His plan was to drive straight to her house instead and speak to her in person.

But a siren sounded in the distance. Then two.

He went on instant alert. Something in his gut told him that whatever the emergency was, Cissie knew about it, too.

Janelle was waiting for him by his truck, dressed to kill in a maroon catsuit with a black necklace—Kettle Knob Academy's school colors.

"Congratulations," she said around a wad of bright pink gum in her mouth. "Great speech."

"Thanks. I gotta go. I want to follow those sirens." He jumped in his truck and turned on the ignition.

She tapped on the window.

Reluctantly, he rolled it down.

"I have to admit," she said, "I'm shocked you can't read."

"You and everyone else." His impatience was building. "And I can read. Just not that well. *Yet.*"

"You haven't been at the country club lately."

"I don't need to anymore," he said. "I'm not the face of Kettle Knob. Cissie Rogers is. Have you asked her to join?"

"No." She tossed her hair artfully over her shoulder. "Out of respect to the Braddocks."

He was mad at himself for getting sucked in, but he couldn't leave that comment unchallenged. "That's an old story that's run out of steam, that Braddocks and Rogerses don't get along. And you trying to stigmatize the Rogers clan is immature, Janelle. I remember the days when you were better than that."

She stood there with her hands on her hips, glowering, then released a big sigh and smiled. "Let's start this conversation over, shall we? I care too much about you *and* your parents—"

"No, you don't. See you later." He was about to drive off, but a sedan pulled into the space opposite him, its front bumper nearly touching his, and blocked his forward path.

Janelle stalked off in her high heels toward her car.

He put the truck into reverse. And that's when he saw a glow of orange and embers floating skyward in the distance behind her.

She whirled back around to face him, her eyebrows high. "Oh, my God. What's burning?"

"I have no idea." His phone buzzed, and when he looked down, there was a message from Scotty: *Library on fire*.

His heart sank. Poor Cissie. So that was where she'd gone. As librarian and mayor, she'd rated first notice from Scotty.

"It's the library." Boone was reluctant to tell Janelle.

She stuck a hand on her hip. "The lease on the space at the shopping center has been taken by a dance studio," she said with some satisfaction. "If Cissie needs an alternative space, I don't know where she's gonna find one."

Boone wasn't surprised by her smug reaction. "Let's think positive, shall we? Maybe it's under control already."

But as he steered the truck out of the parking lot, the orange glow became a tongue of flame rising high into the night sky.

# CHAPTER THIRTY-EIGHT

Cissie hadn't wanted to leave the postgame celebration—as mayor, she needed to be there for the school and town. She'd especially craved being there for Boone. What he was saying was so damned *important*. But when Scotty had texted her, she'd had no choice but to go.

She couldn't believe her beloved library was burning—

And it was all her fault.

"I was worried about the electrical system," she babbled to her friends and family as they gathered as close as they could to the scene. Two fire trucks and a police car blocked their access. "The lights would flicker on and off. I should have done something sooner. Borrowed the money."

Now all the Rogers family documents were up in flames, and Kettle Knob's precious library, with its aging selection of reading materials—and its long, proud history—were no more.

She cried. Everyone cried. It was so sad.

The worst part was when Sally tried to explain to Hank Davis that all his favorite *Where's Waldo?* books could be repurchased. He didn't get it and was inconsolable.

"I hate you, fire!" Sally cried. "Look what you've done to our library. And to Hank Davis. But I'm not gonna throw myself on the ground." She paced a few steps, then pointed at the inferno. "I'm not gonna give you the satisfaction!"

She was wearing a new orange hat and coat. Her Asheville art patron had given her all kinds of art supplies and had already sold her first painting—by "outside artist Sally Morgan"—for fifteen hundred dollars.

"There's nothing we can do about it but go home and collect ourselves," Nana said firmly. "Why don't we all gather at our house? Hank Davis, I have a *Where's Waldo?* book there that I know you'll love."

Maxwell came over and linked his arm through Cissie's. She'd known him a little over twenty-four hours, but he had an offbeat sense of humor she enjoyed. Laurie had, too. They'd talked a lot at the game, which Laurie had explained to him play-by-play. "It's a crying shame," he said now. "I'm so very sorry, Cissie."

"Thanks," she whispered. There were no droll English jokes to be had today.

Laurie hugged her. So did Mrs. Hattlebury. The colonel pulled out his flask and passed it around. Even Cissie's mother had some, and she wasn't a drinker.

Her father put his arm around Cissie's waist. "It had a terrific run," he said quietly. "And it won't be the first long-standing building that has burned down. Why, it happened all the time in the old days. All those candles and open fires."

"But it shouldn't happen now, Daddy."

"We simply have different hazards, honey. We have wires instead of lanterns. And people rebuild. Just like we did with our house, and it's come back better than ever."

"That's true. But there's no money to rebuild."

Her mother came over and slipped her hand around Cissie's waist from the other side. "It's always about money, isn't it?"

Cissie sighed. "I never thought I'd say this, but I wish we'd moved the library to the strip mall."

"It's too late for regrets," Mother said.

Chief Scotty came over. "Mayor Rogers, a word?"

She nodded, her heart sore, and followed him down the sidewalk to his squad car.

Scotty's jowly face was grim. "I'm sorry about this."

"Thanks, Scotty." They'd gotten to be good friends since she'd been elected. He'd forgiven her that wild behavior at The Log Cabin.

"It's a huge loss for Kettle Knob," he said. "But there's something more to think about: We don't know yet that it was a bad wire in the electrical system that started this."

"But what else could it have been? The furnace wasn't on."

"We're calling in someone to see if this was set intentionally."

A jolt of shock made Cissie stand up straighter. "But we don't have people like that in Kettle Knob."

"We might," he said. "We should know more by tomorrow."

"I don't believe it. No one here hates the library."

"I'm wondering if someone hates *you*," Scotty said. "You've been so gung ho about keeping it in town. Someone with a chip on his or her shoulder might want to take the wind out of your sails."

"I still don't believe it." Not even Janelle, whom Cissie had seen at the football game that night, would do such a malicious thing. Campbell's mayor had been dressed to the nines and had pretended not to see when Cissie, her fellow mayor, waved at her.

"Let's wait for some preliminary findings before we start making guesses," said Scotty. "And please keep this information to yourself. We don't want anyone hampering our efforts."

"Of course." Cissie was dying to text Boone, but she was surrounded by so many people trying to make her feel better that she couldn't break away. And no doubt he was still dealing with the reaction to his big revelation at the football field.

He'd find her eventually.

As she walked to her dad's car, she thought how just a short while ago, she'd imagined that moving the library would be the worst thing that could ever happen to her.

But no. Nearly losing Boone had been far worse.

The library—tragic as its burning was—was replaceable.

People were not.

*So this is love*, she thought from the back seat, her hand wrapped around Nana's. Life hadn't become all unicorns and flowers. It was still unpredictable, scary, and hard sometimes. But she also knew more about what mattered.

But did Boone love her back? He hadn't said. She hadn't told him, either, for that matter, and yesterday, on the mountaintop, she wished she had.

She felt a rise of panic as her father drove them up the mountain—but tamped it down. Boone wasn't going to leave town the way her parents always had. She'd get to him soon enough. In fact, she wouldn't let another day go by.

But what about Janelle and all the other women who wanted him? Tonight on the football field, he'd never been more loveable.

He was a real catch, and Cissie couldn't take it for granted that he loved her back. He might *like* her a whole lot—enough to find her so attractive that he'd bedded her on several occasions, much to her extreme delight—but was that love?

Mrs. Hattlebury's and Mrs. Donovan's admonitions came back: *Don't give it away, Cissie.*

She'd done just that.

"Too late," she murmured as they approached the house.

"What was that, dear?" asked Nana.

Cissie leaned close. "Do you believe in the old adage 'Don't give away the milk for free'?"

Nana chuckled. "*No.* When you have a hunk like Boone hovering, who'd want to resist him? You stand tall, darling. He's a lucky man, and I'm sure he knows it."

Cissie decided that he did know it. She'd seen the way he'd looked at her when she'd passed him that trophy. She was going to let go of all her insecurities and trust that he'd come through.

"He's my real-life hero, Nana," she whispered again, a hitch in her voice. "He's brave, and kind. He's smart and sexy, and wonderful, better than any hero on paper—"

"Yes, he is." Nana stuck her arm through hers and squeezed. "You've made a grand choice, my dear."

At the house, the mood was somber, but the good company couldn't help but lift everyone's spirits eventually. Mrs. Hattlebury brought over a couple frozen homemade lasagnas and started heating them. Sally read Hank Davis the *Where's Waldo?* book. Several town council members, some theater people, and various townsfolk, including Starla, came over and commiserated with them.

By suppertime, there were not only two lasagnas but three buckets of chicken, two trays of macaroni and cheese, three pies, and a pineapple upside-down cake. Bad news traveled around Kettle Knob fast.

So did good news.

"It was a great game, and Boone's speech was awesome," could be heard over and over among the crowd still gathering in the den, the kitchen, and at the fire pit outside.

Cissie walked into a group of theater people right as the star of the current play said, "So Ella wasn't his lover, after all. Just his reading tutor."

"That's definitely what he was telling us tonight," a secondary actor said.

"In so many words." A backstage person giggled.

And then everyone seemed to remember Cissie's relationship to the story.

Starla, who wasn't in the play at all, tossed Cissie an apologetic smile. "You're not seeing him anymore, right, hon? I mean, if you ever were. It was just a kiss on the side of a pickup truck. Every Southern woman I know has had one of those."

Cissie reddened. "Right."

"So?" asked the star of the play, not giving up. "What's your status with him?"

It was no one's business. But they were all leaning close to hear, and everyone had been so supportive about the fire. These people were her *friends*. And she'd decided to trust Boone's intentions.

"I really like him," Cissie said quietly, then folded her arms over her chest. "I mean . . . I *love* him."

There was a collective gasp.

"I haven't told him yet, but I plan to. Tonight." She smiled and shrugged. "If you'll excuse me? I need to check on a few things in the kitchen."

"Um, sure," Starla said. "You do what you have to do."

There were a few other awkward remarks as the circle broke open. Cissie forced herself to walk off slowly, her shoulders back.

"Damn," she heard one of the actors say, "Cissie and Boone sure know how to work a moment."

She smiled to herself. If Boone wasn't going to hide, then she wasn't going to, either.

Boone arrived at the library too late to see Cissie. But he had a brief talk with Scotty from his truck.

"Kettle Knob is too nice a town for anyone here to commit arson," Boone said. "You've been watching too many cop shows."

"Maybe," Scotty said. "Maybe not. Where you headed?"

"Cissie's."

"You sure you should?"

"Why not?"

"Lots of people up there right now. They'll be talking about the fire but about you, too."

"I can handle it." Boone's parents had already called. But he hadn't picked up. He wanted to feel good about his decision to speak to the crowd after the football game, and he suspected that they'd bring him down.

The chief shook his head. "I missed your speech, but I heard about it."

"And?"

"I'm pissed you never told me about the reading thing. I thought I was your friend. A *good* friend."

Boone looked him square in the eye. "Sorry. I thought telling you or anyone else would change things."

"That was stupid." Scotty punched Boone's arm.

"I guess so." Boone punched him back.

And that easily, all was right in Man World again.

"So what's going on with you and Cissie?" Scotty asked.

"A lot. And it's all good."

Scotty grinned. "That's the best news I've heard in a while. Linda and I are rooting for you. Can I confess something?"

"Go ahead."

"I was hoping you two would use that jail cell to get close. You know? It was obvious to me you were meant to be."

"You are one kinky son of a bitch."

Scotty laughed, and they shared a lightning fast bro hug above his holster and gun.

Boone's phone rang on the way up the steep mountain road to Cissie's. It was his sister, Debbie's, number in Raleigh. That meant only one thing. His parents had called her, and now she was calling him to tell him he messed up.

This call he picked up. "Hey, Debs."

"I'm not calling to yell at you."

"You're not?"

"No. Mom and Dad called, and they're worried what the fallout could be."

"Well, the fallout on the field was pretty damned awesome. Didn't they notice?"

"Who knows? They tend to care too much what their business cronies think. And they're parents—I think they'll always worry about us."

"Whatever happens will be easier than hiding it anymore. I can handle it."

"That's all I wanted to hear. I'll tell Mom and Dad to step back."

"Thanks."

"And Boone?"

"Yeah?"

"I'm sorry I was never any help to you. Mom and Dad were so into downplaying it, I was reluctant to get involved."

He felt a pain in his chest loosen just a little. "Thanks, Deb."

"There's another reason they may have had a hard time acknowledging what was going on."

"Yeah?"

"I'm almost positive Mom's dyslexic."

Boone's world just turned sideways. Good thing his headlights were picking out every curve in the road. "Are you kidding me?"

"No. Haven't you ever noticed that Dad always orders for her at restaurants?"

"I thought that was them being old-fashioned."

"Have you ever seen her reading a newspaper? Or a magazine? Or a book?"

"No. She's always loved TV. Soap operas. And *The Price Is Right*."

"See? Even our Christmas cards—they get the printed kind so they never have to sign their names. Daddy prints out address labels, too."

"A lot of people do that," he said.

"I know. But there are so many little instances where Mom finds a way to shy away from reading or writing."

"Even if she is dyslexic, would she admit it?"

"I doubt it. Maybe she feels guilty she passed it on. It runs in families, you know."

"I never thought of that. So all that regret I sensed from them . . ." He prepared himself to tell Debbie what was really in his heart. She was his sister. "Maybe," he ventured, "they weren't wishing I was Richard so much as they were just upset that Mom and I—"

It was hard for him to go on.

"Oh, Boone." She sounded so sad for him. "They never wished you were Richard. Ever."

"Yeah, well, it's been easy to think that."

"Believe me, I'm a parent now, and each one of our kids is his or her own special treasure."

ne took the plunge. "I always thought you wanted
tch me with Richard—because you were so up-
out my reading problem."

o," his mother cried. "We never wanted to do

f course not," his father said.

hear them say it out loud—well, it felt good. Really
. Yet he was sad, too. For the first time, thinking
t what his sister had said on the phone, Boone felt
it truly must be like for his parents. Richard should
been in the empty rocking chair on the other side of
k.

I wish you could have had both your boys here
y," Boone said quietly.

His dad nodded. "We do, too."

Yes, indeed," his mother murmured.

here was no competition between Boone and his late
ther. There was only Richard's absence—and their
mories of him. Distant as those recollections were,
y were important. They helped shape who the Brad-
ks were now.

hey sat, looked out at the dark, slumbering moun-
s, some dotted with lights.

I didn't read to you, Boone," said his mother into the
nce, "because I have trouble with it myself."

Do you, Mom?" Boone asked casually, although it
a huge admission on her part.

He shared a look with his father. Frank's gaze told him
read carefully. Boone's mild expression was an at-
pt to reassure his father that he would.

Becky Lee nodded. "I always have wondered if you
your reading problems from me." She kept rocking.
ut he sensed her tension. "I welcome anything you
down to me, Mom. I love you. No one ever said life

---

"That they are, those little rascals." Boone grinned, thinking of his two nephews and two nieces, all under age twelve.

"There's never a thought given to swapping out or wanting do-overs, even when I'm exhausted or one of them is getting on my last nerve. I'm grateful, Boone, that we have them at all. Mom and Dad feel the same way about you."

"Thanks. I wish I'd talked to you a long time ago."

"Guess what—they're headed to your house. Since you didn't answer the phone."

"Dang."

Deb chuckled. "They really need to get a life of their own."

"Tell me about it. I need to take back my keys. They act like it's their house. And I've always given them leeway. I felt bad, you know, that Grandpa skipped over Dad and gave the house to me. Hell, maybe you wanted it, too."

"Dad doesn't need it—with all his properties? And I'm thrilled I didn't get it. Because then I might not have had the gumption to leave Kettle Knob. Do you wish you had?"

"No," he said, and meant it. "I love it here. I'm surprised I'm saying that, after all the regrets I've had. But this is where I belong."

"I'm glad you feel that way. We should talk more often."

"I agree."

Before they hung up, they arranged to see each other in Charlotte for lunch the next week.

A minute later, Boone went straight past the red reflectors that marked the entrance to Cissie's driveway. He'd go back. But he had something to do first. His mother and father were literally opening his front door as he pulled up.

He rolled down his window, fast. "Hey!" he called to them.

They turned around.

He turned off his headlights and jumped out of his truck. "Here I am. Did you need me for something?"

"Yeah," said Frank, standing in a puddle of light cast from a sconce near the door, with his fists curled. "We need you to answer your phone."

Becky Lee, meanwhile, in her upscale clothes and perfect makeup and hair, looked sleek and confident.

But was she really?

Boone walked up on the porch. Sat in a rocker. "I'm sometimes too busy to answer my phone, Dad. Hey, Mom. Why don't you sit down?" He indicated a rocker.

"Well, all right, son." She took a seat somewhat reluctantly.

"You, too, Dad."

"It's cold out here." Frank was a stubborn old coot sometimes.

"You're bundled up from the game," Boone said. "You'll be all right. And we're not going inside."

"Why not?" Frank sat and sighed.

Boone patted his father's knee, just once. "I'll tell you in a minute. Meanwhile, you must want to talk about that speech I gave."

"We sure do." His father glowered.

"Honey, we're worried for you." Becky Lee laced her fingers together.

"You need to stop. Won't that be nice for you, Mom? To be able to relax about me? So far—you saw the reaction on the field—everything's been positive."

She sighed. "I'd like to think it will stay that way and that you can handle your own business."

"Of course I can. Can I ask you About my childhood?"

"Go right ahead." She started rocki

Frank was still sulking, his big arn chest.

"Why didn't you read to me when I

There was a long silence Boone refu

"I was always working," his father mother stayed busy with her volunteering

"Someone read to me," Boone said. "I c it, but I liked it. It was a guy. Somebody wa safe. I remember being happy. If it wasn't it Grandpa Faber?"

His father shook his head, met his moth

"It was Richard," she said in a trembly

"Damn," Boone whispered.

Richard . . . the brother he thought he'd n

While he tried to process that, Frank to hand.

"I can't believe you remember, son." Beck wistfully. "You were barely three when he

"You'd have your thumb in your mouth." short laugh and started rocking. "You'd sit lap while he read you Thomas the Tank En

"I'm glad you have a memory of him t Becky Lee said.

"Me, too," Boone said quietly. He and been brothers. Together. It was a special mo and he could tell his parents enjoyed it, to they smiled at each other and kept rockin

"Mom," Boone said after a little bit, "is t else you want to tell me about those days? handle it. I promise."

They both stopped rocking. Becky Lee certainly. Frank's lower lip jutted out.

was a bed of roses. This is something we can both work on. Together, if you want."

She stopped rocking. "You're a good boy." She smiled gently. "A good man."

That meant a lot to Boone, to hear her say that. He stood, leaned down, and hugged her. "This whole reading thing . . . it's okay."

She clung to him for a minute.

His dad cleared his throat, a sure sign he was feeling emotional, too.

"Hey," Boone said, "I told you we're not going inside. I want to go down the mountain to the Rogerses' house. A lot of people are there right now. It seems the place to be after what happened tonight at the library. Surely you heard about it. Maybe you saw the flames when you left the football field."

"We did," Frank said. "Word spread fast what had happened."

"How tragic." Becky Lee shook her head.

"Wanna come? It would mean a lot to me."

They hesitated.

"Sure," said Frank.

"All right," added Becky Lee.

"I'll be right back." Boone went inside, grabbed the flowers he'd started keeping on his kitchen table to cheer himself up because they reminded him of Cissie, and wrapped a paper napkin around their stems.

They all got in his ugly truck.

At the end of the driveway, he stole a glance at his mom. "Do you really have a thing about the Rogers clan? Janelle likes to say you do."

"No," said his mother with a short laugh.

"That's ridiculous." Frank made a disparaging face.

"The thing is"—Boone steered the truck onto the road

that led to his true love—"y'all donate to everything in Kettle Knob but the theater and the library, and each of those is run by a Rogers. It kind of backs up the old tale about there being a rift."

"We donate to the theater," said his father. "But we do it anonymously. We're on their Gold Patrons list."

"Whoa," Boone said, surprised as he could be. "That's terrific. But does Nana know?"

"I doubt it," said Frank. "Our accountant makes sure no one does."

"Why do you do it that way?" Boone was intrigued by his father's admission.

"It has nothing to do with the Rogers clan." His mother sighed. "It's because the regional theater people in Asheville are always after us. We make a modest donation there. But a much larger one to our own little theater."

"Why don't you ever go to the productions?" Every time Boone asked them to go with him, his parents declined.

Frank tugged on his ear. "I can't hear worth a toot in that place. We really need better acoustics."

"It's freezing in the winter and stuffy in the summer, the few times I've been in," said Becky Lee. "And it's too small. We need a new building."

"Hello?" Boone grinned. "Who can make that happen?"

His father shrugged and sent him an uncharacteristically bashful smile. "I suppose we could."

"Yeah, you could." Boone's tone was teasing. "It would be an in-your-face to the regional theater people, but they'll get over it. Kettle Knob needs some aggressive backers in the cultural department. Maybe if we get that going, we'll attract more businesses, like that German tire company. They're still in the decision phase."

"Always thinking like a mayor," Becky Lee said, but she sounded pleased.

"Now how about the library?" Boone was sure he was pushing them too far. But why not? He had them trapped in his truck. Talking about Richard, and then Mom's reading issues, had softened them. They loved one another. They were family. That much was clear.

And that was all they needed.

His father blew out a breath. "We've shied away from the library. Not because a Rogers runs it."

"No," his mother said, "it's because of you, Boone. And . . . and me."

Poor Mom. Boone could hear it in her voice, how nervous she was to say that. It made him glad he'd spoken up on the football field, if only to give her courage.

"I hope you'll change your mind," he said. "Because I'm going to ask the librarian to marry me. I love her like crazy."

"You do?" Becky Lee's face lit up.

"So much that I'm ready to sell Grandpa Faber's house and land if I have to and use the money to rebuild," he said. "I'll save that little parcel with the cabin. We can be two lovebirds living high up near the clouds with books we borrow from our brand-new big-ass Kettle Knob library."

"Good Lord, don't live in that cabin," his father said. "We'll build a new library if it comes to that."

"Can we name it after Richard?" Becky Lee asked hopefully.

Boone grabbed her hand and squeezed. "I'm sure the town council will strongly consider that possibility."

"Has your librarian even said yes yet?" Frank was teasing him now.

"No." Boone laughed. "But I hope she will. We'll find out in a minute. Either way, you two need to hand over your keys to my place. No more unannounced visits, either. *Call*."

"All right." Becky Lee actually giggled.

Boone hadn't heard her do that in a long time. He looked back at his dad in the rearview mirror. He wore a contented expression, which made Boone happy.

Now for the hard thing.

# CHAPTER THIRTY-NINE

"Grandma burned the library down, Grandma burned the library down!" Stephen and Sam Huffman yelled in unison as they ran into the Rogerses' kitchen.

Cissie looked up from the big pot of cocoa she was stirring—Nana's recipe—and stared at Laurie.

Laurie put a hand on her hip. "Boys! That's not nice!"

"But it's true." Sam puffed up with pride.

"Ask her," said Stephen. "We went to the police station. Chief Scotty gave us Tootsie Pops."

Mrs. Donovan appeared, carrying a giant platter of chocolate chip cookies and smelling like alcohol. "Yes, well . . ." She put the platter on the counter and sighed. "The boys are right. I did burn the place down."

She looked between Cissie and Laurie.

"Well, *shit*, Mother," said Laurie. "We're not talking about burning a pot of oatmeal. We're talking an old, important building filled with books and precious Kettle Knob documents."

"I know." Mrs. Donovan blinked hard. "Cissie, please forgive me. I was so scared, I went home and hid and made cookies. But then I realized I had to come clean, even if it means everyone hates me." She swallowed hard. "Boys, go outside to the fire pit."

They grabbed cookies and ran out of the room. Two big tears rolled down Mrs. Donovan's cheeks. "They should have gone to the game with you, Laurie. They saw me running around like a chicken with my head cut off with all that smoke and fire."

Laurie hugged her. "I'm sorry. Next time I'll take the two tornados with me. But I'm glad I didn't this time. That British professor asked me out."

"He did?" Mrs. Donovan seemed to forget all about the fire.

It was obvious to Cissie that Laurie's mother needed a distraction, at least for a few minutes.

Cissie found herself compartmentalizing, too, as she listened to the romantic tale her best friend told about how Max had taken her aside at the fire and asked her out. And it turned out he was a real English earl!

"I only found out because he answered a phone call on his cell," Laurie said. "He calls it a mobile, Mama." She giggled. "He said, 'This is Lord Marbury.' And after he hung up, he told me his full name is Dr. Maxwell Plimpton, the eighth Lord Marbury. He has a castle in Yorkshire. With a *moat*."

"Oh, my heavens," Mrs. Donovan said, her hand to her cheek.

Cissie didn't even know that about Max! He'd kept it a secret. But then the cocoa started to bubble over, and she remembered she needed to find her phone. Surely, Scotty would have called her with this latest development on the fire.

She found the phone on the table—it was on silent. And yes, Chief Scotty had called, about a million times. The last message said, *Driving Ginger up there. Gave her a couple shots emergency whiskey to calm her down. Save me some of Starla's pie!!!!*

"Okay, enough of me and romance for now," Laurie told her mother. "Tell us how the fire happened."

Cissie cut a huge slab of Starla's pie, hid it in corner for Scotty, and went back to the stove.

Mrs. Donovan sat at the table. "I borrowed the Hattleburys' library key Cissie gave to them for safekeeping to do some archive research for the family genealogy project, and I found a small document detailing my family's role in the King's Mountain takedown. Our ancestor Yorick Steverson joined Silas Braddock's ragtag unit that whooped British ass—or so I thought. But according to a Rogers account, Yorick deserted on the way down. He fell in love with a girl in a small village who'd given them water. So he never joined them." She paused. "I'm so embarrassed on our family's behalf."

"Mom." Laurie tapped her foot. "Get to the point."

Mrs. Donovan sighed. "So I thought I'd burn up that one little paper. I put it in the trash can in the archives room and added just a few pages from my notebook to make sure the flame really got going. I was sure it was done, so I threw another piece of notebook paper over it so no one would see it when I left. I watched and watched, and nothing happened, except that the lights flickered on and off, several times, as you know they often do."

Cissie paused in her stirring.

"Yes, yes?" prompted Laurie.

"And then I picked up the boys in the children's area and left," Ginger said. "Next thing I hear, not an hour later, the library's burned down. There must have been a stray ember in the trash can that a draft whipped up. That archive room is chilly. The window doesn't go quite all the way down. I thought a room like that was supposed to be held to a certain temperature and humidity."

"Maybe so," said Laurie, "but who cares now? You burned everything up!"

"*Laurie,*" Cissie said. "She might not have. It could have been the wiring. Those lights flickering. . . . That wasn't safe, and it had been happening a long time."

The older woman hung her head. "You're just saying that to be nice, Cissie."

"No." Cissie put down her cocoa spoon. "I'm not. And guess what? It doesn't really matter. The library is gone, and we'll probably never know what happened. Okay, maybe Scotty's team will find out eventually, but we need to focus on what comes next."

Mrs. Donovan looked up at her, her eyes hopeful. Laurie's expression lightened, too.

Cissie had had a little while now to get herself together, and she'd already started planning. "We'll recover from this," she told them. "I know it. We already have a website Pay Pal button for donations. We'll tell the world that our library burned down, and maybe we'll raise enough money to build another one."

"Or we can still go in together, Campbell and Kettle Knob," Janelle said from the kitchen door. "I've already figured it out. The strip mall lease isn't available anymore. But I made some calls, and we can get the old barbecue joint by the Exxon. With a few coats of paint, it'll do fine."

Cissie was shocked to see Campbell's mayor standing there with Edwina, who had her notebook out. "Edwina," Cissie said firmly, "you'd better not write about anything you hear at my house tonight. This is Kettle Knob letting off steam. It stays between us."

Then she turned to Janelle. Nothing could surprise her after what had happened to the library. And the truth was, long ago, little Janelle the Girl Scout used to be a sweetheart. "That's so nice of you. We'll think about it."

Janelle lifted a shoulder. "I won the spelling bee in

fifth grade because you messed up on *mileage*, and that gave me a lot of confidence. Plus, you congratulated me when I got my trophy."

"Can you spell *mileage* now?" Edwina said.

"Of course," said Cissie. *"M-i-l-a-g-e."*

"Wrong." Edwina chuckled.

"Spell *vacuum*," Cissie shot back.

Edwina got serious. *"V-a-c-c-u-u-m."*

"Wrong." Cissie smiled. "But I still love you, Edwina. In a journalistic way. You write really well."

"What was the point of that exchange?" asked Mrs. Donovan.

"Nothing." Cissie winked at Janelle. "Just strong women challenging each other."

Edwina tried to slink out of the room.

"Get back here," Cissie ordered her. "Sit down." She got out a bottle of wine and poured a bunch into paper cups. The ladies passed them around.

"I have something to confess," Laurie said.

"Off the record," Cissie reminded Edwina.

"I heard you." Edwina rolled her eyes.

"What is it?" Mrs. Donovan had recovered a little bit of her usual high color.

Laurie looked nervously at Cissie. "When your house was in the process of getting repaired, I took a video of it for the insurance people—remember you asked me to?"

Cissie nodded. "My phone doesn't zoom in on video. Yours does."

"Exactly. So I was bringing the clip up to Boone's house to show you . . . and you were out in the shed, um, kissing, and"—she swallowed hard—"I just happened to catch it on my cell. I thought it was sweet and romantic."

*"Laurie."* Cissie couldn't believe it.

"And then the TV show was here," Laurie gabbled, "and I wanted you two to get together. The whole nation would have been rooting for you. I had no idea they'd have that other video of Boone and Ella. . . ."

Cissie let her forehead fall on the table.

"I know." Laurie rubbed her back. "I am *so* sorry. I was trying to be a matchmaker."

Cissie sat up. "As mayor, I hereby declare you're banned from being a sexy elf on Santa's float in the Christmas parade this year."

"No," said Laurie. "I love doing that!"

"But Perry won't be Santa anymore," said Mrs. Donovan.

There was a brief, awkward silence.

"Thank God," Laurie finally said. "The boys always wondered why Santa looked like he was constipated."

Edwina snorted like a pig at that, which made everyone else laugh, too.

Mrs. Hattlebury, reeking of cigar smoke, wandered in. Cissie suspected she'd already been drinking from the colonel's flask. "Scotty wants his pie," she said. "And we have some interesting visitors."

Cissie grabbed the wedge of Starla's pie she'd set aside, added a fork to the plate, and handed it to her. "Who are the visitors?"

"They're on the porch with Nana." Mrs. Hattlebury was in full Elvis Presley beach-bunny mode. "She won't let them inside until they smoke a cigar with her."

"Who *is* it?" Edwina asked shrilly, her sharp bob swinging.

"I'm not gonna tell." Mrs. Hattlebury disappeared with the pie, weaving just a tad.

"Maybe not having TV news accounts anymore—or old documents—about the goings-on in Kettle Knob is a good thing," Janelle said. "Not everyone's gonna be a hero. Most of us are just *folks*."

"We still have Edwina," said Laurie, and sent the *Bugler* editor the evil eye.

"I *know*," Edwina said. "The reporter in me is off duty tonight. Okay? Gawd!"

But Cissie was thoroughly charmed by what Janelle had said. There was hope for the woman yet. "We *are* just folks," she said, and felt a little teary. Because she knew exactly who her special guests were.

She felt it in her bones.

She walked out on the porch and saw him—Boone sitting in a rocker, his parents doing the same. They were smoking cigars and drinking bourbon with Nana—even Mrs. Braddock, who inhaled shyly on her cigar and then coughed. Mr. Braddock patted her back.

"Good news, baby," said Nana to Cissie. "Our erstwhile ancestors kept separate copies of a lot of the town history at home. Your father reminded me of several secret drawers in the secretary in the library."

"Are you making this up?" Cissie asked her dad. "We have secret drawers?"

"It was standard practice in the old days," her father said, "and ours are packed with historic papers: legit journal entries, a few poems. You weren't supposed to know until I was on my deathbed."

"This is so Southern," said Mother, fanning herself with a cocktail napkin.

The librarian in Cissie was verklempt at the news. "Thank you, erstwhile ancestors," she whispered, hoping they could hear her from their writing desks in the sky.

Nana chuckled. "Tell her what I just found out about you, Boone."

His gorgeous brown eyes met Cissie's. "Thanks to a party my mother swore she couldn't miss, I was born right over the border in Tennessee. Two weeks early."

"So you're not a Kettle Knob native?" Cissie sat on his lap and put her arm around his shoulders.

"No. What's the big deal?"

"Nothin'," she said, the Southern coming out in her strong and sweet. "Nothin' at all. Good speech you gave tonight. And great win, too."

"Thanks. I love you, Mayor Rogers."

"I love you, too, Coach."

"I'm sorry about the library. But we'll fix it together."

"I know we will," she said.

They shared a long kiss, and Cissie didn't even care that everyone was watching. Or that she hated cigars.

"Marry me," Boone whispered huskily. In his hands he held some pink Gerbera daisies—her favorite!—wrapped in a paper towel. "I've already asked your dad's permission."

Her parents sat on the porch railing, eyeing her with such love that tears came to her eyes.

"I'd love to marry you," Cissie whispered back, and took her flowers. They hadn't come to her desk in the library, but someday, there would be a new library, and Boone would bring her Gerbera daisies there. She just knew it.

They kissed again, two ordinary folk among the many in Kettle Knob who messed up, cheered one another on, danced at dive bars, kicked leaves, went whitewater rafting, read good books, and ate casseroles—who played tag football, made love in sheds, cabins, and hot tubs, and slept the sleep of the exhausted because they worked hard and played hard, most of them.

And they were glad to be alive.

Cissie and Boone exchanged a jubilant smile.

"Rule number one," announced Nana, a halo of smoke around her head. *"And they lived happily ever after."*